Sitti Nurbaya

Sitti Nurbaya: A Love Unrealized

First published in Indonesian by Balai Pustaka in 1922
under the title *Sitti Nurbaya: Kasih Tak Sampai.*

English language edition copyright © 2011 The Lontar Foundation
English translation copyright © 2011 George A. Fowler
All rights reserved

Publication of the Modern Library of Indonesia Series, of which this book is one title,
has been made possible by the generous assistance of the Djarum Foundation.
Additional assistance provided by the Ford Foundation.

No part of this publication may be reproduced
or transmitted in any form or by any means
without permission in writing from
The Lontar Foundation
Jl. Danau Laut Tawar No. 53
Jakarta 10210 Indonesia
www.lontar.org

Template design by DesignLab; layout and cover by Cyprianus Jaya Napiun
Cover illustration: *Batavia Gateway* by Carel Lodewejik Dake Jr.;
image courtesy of the OHD Museum of Modern & Contemporary Indonesian Art
Printed in Indonesia by PT Subur Printing

ISBN No. 978-979-8083-79-2

MODERN LIBRARY OF INDONESIA

MARAH RUSLI

Sitti Nurbaya

A Love Unrealized

Translated by George A. Fowler

Jakarta, Indonesia

Contents

Translator's Introduction, *ix*
Sitti Nurbaya: A Love Unrealized

1. Home from School, *1*
2. Sutan Mahmud and His Sister, *9*
3. A Hike to Mount Padang, *21*
4. Putri Rubiah, *51*
5. Samsu's Journey, *61*
6. Datuk Meringgih, *81*
7. Samsulbahri's Letter, *93*
8. Nurbaya's Letter, *113*
9. Return to Padang, *127*
10. Memories of Samsulbahri, *163*
11. Flight to Batavia, *179*
12. A Conversation, *197*
13. Samsu's Fate, *225*
14. Ten Years Later, *239*
15. Rebellion, *257*
16. The Battle, *273*

Glossary, *289*
Acknowledgements, *293*

Translator's Introduction

In 1922, the Netherlands East Indies publishing house, Balai Pustaka, issued the Malay language novel, *Sitti Nurbaya: Kasih tak Sampai* (translated here as *Sitti Nurbaya: A Love Unrealized*). Written by Marah Rusli, a doctor-researcher in the government veterinary service, this novel was instantly popular and is still considered one of the finest works of early modern Indonesian literature. Coincidentally, Balai Pustaka was established the same year (1908) as the brief, violent and futile Tax Rebellion in West Sumatra that forms the climax of the novel. The rebellion itself was but a fleeting disruption in a colonial system whose bright future by then seemed unquestioned, particularly with the military subjugation of Bali that same year and Aceh back in 1904. Indeed, by 1908, direct political and administrative control over the entire Indonesian archipelago from Batavia appeared an unshakeable reality.

The Netherlands East Indies in the nineteenth century and the evolution of education policy

Since the early 1600s, the Dutch had limited their presence in the archipelago to a few trading ports, notably in Java and the Moluccas. Interference in local affairs was generally indirect and only to further commercial interests. A sustained, if fitful, colony building began in 1816, the year the Dutch returned to the East Indies after a brief English interregnum during the Napoleonic Wars. In 1830, in an effort to refinance the Dutch treasury—nearly bankrupt after the secession of Belgium—and that of Batavia following the Java War, the Netherlands East Indies government commenced the

Cultivation System. Beginning in Java and later extending to West Sumatra, the system entailed the compulsory sale of valuable export crops such as coffee to the government at fixed prices. Used in lieu of land taxes and based on corvée labor, this system brought great hardship to native populations, but was phenomenally profitable for the Netherlands: between 19 and 32 percent of state revenues derived from the Cultivation System between the 1830s and 1860s, when it collapsed amid scandals of corruption and oppressive practices in Java that reached all the way to the Netherlands.

Subsequent agrarian reforms allowed private capital to set up vast plantations growing cash crops like sugar, tea and rubber. These enterprises also proved exceedingly profitable and it was said that sugar was the sea on which Holland floated. During the so-called Liberal Policy period after 1870, the entire East Indies was opened up for European private enterprise. However, the call grew louder in both the mother country and in the colony for a "humanized capitalism", particularly in light of reports of the deteriorating lives of Javanese peasants owing to continued exploitation and an exploding population.

In 1899, an article entitled, "The Honor Debt", published in the Netherlands to great acclaim, called upon the home country to make restitution to the people of the Indies for all the fortunes extracted there at little benefit to them. In September 1901, Queen Wilhelmina's annual message from the throne spoke of the "ethical obligation and moral responsibility to the peoples of the East". This marked the beginning of the Ethical Colonial Policy, which envisioned a radically new orientation in the relationship between colonizers and the colonized. Greater autonomy was now given to Batavia to implement far-reaching welfare programs, ambitious infrastructure projects, and even to decentralize political and administrative power.

Home country politicians, scholars and colonial administrators worked to formulate the means by which the relationship between the Netherlands Indies and the home country would be indissolubly bound together. Theories and programs of "unification" of all of Indies society, both native and European, under one legal code—"assimilation" of local cultures by administering the colony with all the institutions of the home country; and "association", by which unforced access to the culture of the home country would be provided—all targeted the growing indigenous elite. This group, it was thought, would sooner or later act in its self-interest to accept a future linked to the Netherlands.

Though not without its detractors, predictably among some Europeans in the Indies itself, the Ethical Policy attracted a great deal of debate, mostly centered on its pace rather than the validity or feasibility of its ultimate aim. Central to these paternalistic visions was the availability of a modern European-style education for native peoples. This would create a modern and progressive Indies leadership elite that would be on increasingly equal social standing with Europeans and identify with home country aspirations and values.

Apart from modest efforts made by the Netherlands East Indies government in Batavia to establish schools for the children of the Javanese aristocracy shortly before the English interregnum, colonial involvement in native education began with the Cultivation System, when specialized knowledge involving crop delivery and storage required at least rudimentary classroom training. Beginning in the 1850s, Batavia established schools for scribes and low-level administrators, teachers' training schools in Sumatra and Java, and the Indies Medical Institute (STOVIA) to train medical corpsmen and sanitary inspectors, the "Doktor Jawa". The Government hoped to recruit local elites for these schools, though these professions had little initial appeal for an aristocracy reluctant for their children to be "employed" and by the colonial power at that.

During the Liberal Period (1870–1899), colonial administrators began to view education as both an integral part of an increasingly complex political economy and a path of enlightenment for the people of the Indies. According to a royal decree issued in 1872, indigenous education was now the responsibility of the Indies government. Accordingly, education was thoroughly reorganized, standardized and expanded under the new Department of Education, Religion and Industry. In 1879, Batavia created the Chiefs' School to train the sons of Javanese regents for low-level positions in the Netherlands East Indies civil service. While the Dutch themselves recognized the overall shortcomings of the government educational system throughout the Liberal Period, demand for European-style education steadily grew among both the old and emerging Indonesian elites for the social and professional advancement it offered during this period of tremendous economic change. During the 1880s, primary education in the larger urban areas was reorganized into First-Class Schools for children of socially prominent families and Second-Class Schools for children of less exalted families. More significantly, foreign schools founded on religious principles were allowed government funding and Indonesian children could attend European primary schools. In 1907, the Government organized village schools throughout the Indies. However physically and pedagogically inadequate such schools invariably were, overall a new era of broad modern education was now beginning in the Indies. After 1910, schools of higher education were set up for girls, particularly the so-called Kartini schools in Java. In addition, Indonesians were entering schools for European children and a small but growing number of them went on to higher study in the Netherlands.

Though Java, with its large population and political importance, remained the dominant policy focus of the Netherlands East Indies government in Batavia, it was in the *Alam Minangkabau* (the World of the Minangkabau People) of the then relatively remote highlands of West Sumatra, that the limited opportunities for education provided by the Dutch were taken up strongly and had a significant effect on Indies society, history and even language.

The Minangkabau of West Sumatra

The *kaba* (stories) and *tambo* (annals) relate the origins of the Minangkabau people, their kings, and the three great highland settlements that constitute the *Alam*. More importantly, they tell of the mythical givers of the systems of unwritten customary beliefs and practices called *adat*. To this day, the *adat* of matrilineality (that is, descent reckoned through the female line) characterizes Minangkabau society.

From stone inscriptions, the first verifiable king, or "raja", of the then largely animistic Minangkabau was the mid-14th century Adityawarman. The export of gold, spices, woven cloth and resins were the basis of the power and prestige of the Minangkabau raja who reigned at Pagaruyung, near today's Bukittinggi. The Minangkabau kingdom as a political and cultural force ended with the destruction of the Pagaruyung court in the early 19th century. However, over the centuries, the descendants of royal viceroys assigned by the Pagaruyung raja to tax trade along the coastal region north and south of Padang formed an hereditary elite whose aristocratic pretentions were stroked by the Dutch in later years.

Traditionally and through the 19th and into the 20th century, villages, called *nagari*, were the basic territorial units of Minangkabau communal and political organization. These communities were independent of outside rule and for the most part self-sufficient in economies based either on wet rice cultivation in the rich volcanic soil of the West Sumatra plateau or dry-crop agriculture in the higher regions. Until 1875, slaves and debt-bondage were an accepted part of Minangkabau society. Slaves were taken from time to time from the pagan, that is, non-Muslim, populations of Sumatra to supplement the labor force of the *nagari*. Bondservants could resume their full rights upon payment of their debts. Manumitted persons and their descendents often constituted a class apart in *nagari* society for decades thereafter.

Social and religious life in the *nagari* was and is guided by *adat*. Historically, *adat* has also guided relations between *nagari*.

Within the *nagari*, the basic political, social and economic unit was the *suku*, matrilineal clan groups descended from a common foremother. A *suku* was comprised of lineage segments often residing in *nagari* neighborhoods called *kampung*. According to *adat*, all inherited immovable property of the *suku*, particularly cultivated land, is a permanent possession of the maternal line and thus can never be sold, only pawned, and then, only under certain *adat*-related circumstances. Such property is ancestral and, as such, inalienable, forming the basis of family wealth, power and prestige. Land acquired or developed by male members of a *suku* belonged to those who worked it. This may be sold or bequeathed as personal property; however, it becomes ancestral land within a few generations and forms part of the matrilineal inheritance.

A husband remains part of his own maternal *suku* and his primary responsibility is to it and not to that of his wife. Night is spent with his wife in her own chamber in the "big house" of her *suku*, but in the daytime the husband returns to his own home base, the house and property of his own maternal clan, where he lives and will be buried. All unmarried males over the age of seven sleep in the local prayer house (*surau*), where they learn the co-existent teachings of *adat* and religion.

Household matters involving a wife, her sisters and their own children are not primarily the responsibility of her husband, but that of the *mamak rumah*, the oldest male member of her family, whether uncle or brother. It is up to the *mamak* to preserve the integrity of the ancestral property and arbitrate over its usage, though, as a male, he has no personal rights over it. A husband, in turn, may become a *mamak* for his own sister's household matters and children.

A man may also serve as *suku* head, or *penghulu*, and, as such, bear the honorific title of *datuk*. The lineage establishing closest proximity to the foremother once held the hereditary right of *penghulu*. Ideally, the wisest repository of *adat* learning and the best ability to teach and lead according to *adat* were the most important criteria in selecting a *penghulu*. The reality of intra-lineage negotiations and rivalries, however, often meant that wealth and power were the final determinants in this process. The *penghulu* was, by consent of the *suku*, its *mamak*-like *adat* leader. *Nagari* government was by a council of *penghulu* and other male lineage heads, in principle an assembly of elected equals. The Nagari Ordinance of 1914 transformed *nagari* autonomy by making civil service merit rather than bloodlines the basis of leadership selection.

Along with its matrilineal system, a defining feature of Minangkabau *adat* has been the tradition of its young men to leave their *nagari* to live for a time in the *rantau*: anywhere in the world outside the boundaries of the *nagari*, which included the next village, the coastal towns, other parts of Sumatra, or Malaya, or even Java and beyond. Going to the *rantau* was a time-honored undertaking to accumulate sufficient personal wealth for marriage upon return to one's village. It was also a kind of rite of passage into maturity, so that the experience accumulated during the often difficult, always lonely, sojourn in the *rantau* would make these men wise and useful members, and perhaps future leaders, of *suku* and *nagari*. Going to the *rantau* has been described as a safety valve for releasing social pressures within the village. But, more positively, the *rantau* was the source of new elements and new perspectives that could, with consensus, be adapted to invigorate village life, in the manner of the *adat* saying: "Adopt what is good from the *rantau* and discard what is bad in the *Alam*".

Islam was surely the greatest of the "new elements" entering the *Alam* from the *rantau* and was probably first propagated in Minangkabau society in the 16th century by traders and Sufi *tareket* (mystical associations) from Aceh, then the dominant political and commercial presence on the West Sumatra coast. The division of Minangkabau royal power into the King of *Alam*, and his subordinates, the King of *Adat* and the King of *Ibadat* ("religious observance") was emblematic of a syncretic acceptance of Islam. At the *nagari* level, mosques and council halls coexisted and the religious officials were placed within the *adat* hierarchy. Historically, Minangkabau society has always sought a balance between *adat* and Islam. The formulation, "*Adat* is based on Syariah and Syariah is based on *adat*", embodied the complementarity of *adat* and religion, at least in the minds of the traditionalists.

This harmonious accommodation between *adat* and eclectic Islam came under serious assault by religious reformists in the early 19th century. Three Minangkabau *hajji*, upon their return from an extended stay in the Arabian Hijaz, then under the power of the Wahhabi movement, launched a violent struggle to purify Minangkabau society of all practices and behavior not in line with Syariah prescriptions as they interpreted them. Major targets of violence were the Sufi *tarekat*, *adat* leaders and the customs of matrilineal inheritance and matrilocal residence. In 1815, most of the Minangkabau royal family was slaughtered and Pagaruyung burned three times before finally being abandoned.

Largely to protect their interests in the coffee trade, the Dutch entered the conflict on the side of the *adat* leaders. Minangkabau society was then torn apart in the shifting alliances of what is now known as the Padri War (1821–1837). Batavia attempted to replicate its arrangements with the Javanese regents by making the surviving raja in effect a salaried business agent. In 1825, realizing that the monarchy could provide little assistance to them, the Dutch restructured local political authority and territorial administration to mesh with their residency system, then newly introduced in West Sumatra. Although the Padri were ultimately crushed by the Dutch forces and their main leaders either killed or exiled, a more orthodox form of Islam had succeeded in establishing itself by expanding religious schools and strengthening the position of religious teachers in the *nagari*. This shift away from the traditional condominium of *adat* and Islam was expressed in the new, consensual reformulation: "*Adat* is based on Syariah and Syariah is based on the Book of God." This would not be the last time that reformism would challenge tradition in Minangkabau West Sumatra, but never again so violently as during the Padri War.

In 1833, *adat* leaders in West Sumatra agreed to the terms of the *Plakaat Panjang* ("Long Declaration") by which Batavia would oversee the affairs of the territory as "Protector of the Minangkabau" and not impose any money tax or interfere with *adat* institutions, notwithstanding Batavia's recent administrative restructuring and political innovations. As skillfully and dramatically depicted in *Sitti Nurbaya*, the 1908 Tax Rebellion was ignited in large part from strong resentment at Batavia's repudiation of the terms of the Long Agreement.

With the end of the Padri War, West Sumatra was now secure for the Cultivation System, which was introduced there in 1847. The impact of colonialism on West Sumatran society was the most intensive in the Indies outside of Java itself during this period. As in Java, opportunities arose for whoever assisted this system. On their part, the Dutch facilitated the emergence of a new kind of Minangkabau elite, one that they could understand and manipulate better than the now-faded monarchy. *Penghulu* were given positions as corvée labor administrators. Other village personages were appointed warehouse masters, crop inspectors etc. New, albeit low-level, positions opened for people literate in the Malay language as the needs of the colonial bureaucracy grew. For this, as in Java, schools were needed.

The initiative for the earliest primary schools in the West Sumatra highlands came in the mid-1840s at the personal initiative of its first Resident, who held progressive views on the uplifting effects of systematic education. Once established, these tuition-free, four-grade schools then became the full responsibility of the local *nagari* councils. Notwithstanding their inadequacy in Dutch pedagogical terms, chronic funding problems and general indifference in Batavia to native education during the Cultivation System, these "*nagari* schools" proliferated in the 1850s and 1860s in response to the opportunities created—and not just in West Sumatra—by a growing and evolving colonial administration.

Minangkabau enthusiasm for employment in foreigner government service may have been predisposed by their outward-looking ethos, which viewed this service as yet another form of *rantau*, with new challenges, new rewards and new social stature. The Dutch certainly saw the Minangkabau as an important Malay-speaking cadre in the colonial administration outside of Java. In 1856, the second teachers' training college in the Indies, and the first outside Java, was opened in Bukittinggi as the *Kweekschool*, with government-subsidized tuition and an ambitious three-year curriculum. As was the case elsewhere in the Indies, recruitment for this school was aimed at children of the local political elite, and many of its graduates went on, not to jobs in the educational field, but to serve as native prosecuting magistrates, the most prestigious jobs in the civil service then open to Indonesians. A period of standardization of education throughout the Indies began in the 1870s and, in the decades that followed, a number of programs were reorganized. STOVIA's "Doktor Jawa" program, hitherto rather denigrated by the traditional elite families, was upgraded for the second time in 1898 to train real doctors, not merely rural vaccinators and the like. It now became prestigious to be a STOVIA graduate. In 1900, the Chiefs' School was closed and reopened as the School for Training Native Officials (OSVIA).

Such developments were well-received by socially and professionally ambitious Minangkabau who, thanks in no little part to their head start in the early educational institutions, were already well entrenched throughout the Dutch administration. In West Sumatra, the *nagari* schools and the Bukittinggi *Kweekschool* (now renamed the Rajas' School) were reorganized at a time when Dutch-style education and not aristocratic patronage was seen as the best means of achieving the ideal of modernity. Demand for education in West Sumatra always outstripped supply and the first decade of the 20th century saw the establishment of private "people's" schools and wider education for girls. By 1910, it is estimated these institutions totaled half of their counterparts in Java, with its far greater population.

Development of the Malay language

Throughout the second half of the 19th century, as Netherland East Indies rule grew in geography and complexity, there was much debate over the language to be used by the colonial administrators in its dealings with native rulers and subjects. In fact, Malay (or dialects of Malay, as the language had considerable regional variants) had served as a trade lingua franca throughout the archipelago and much of coastal Southeast Asia for a period long predating the arrival of the Dutch and became the medium of communication de facto between colonizer and colonized in political, administrative and business matters. Ironically, Malay had long been used by proselytizers of Christianity much as it had been by their earlier Muslim counterparts.

Batavia officially adopted Malay for instruction in elementary schools outside Java. Thus it was requisite for the modernization of the Indies that the Malay used in the educational system be standardized in morphology, spelling and vocabulary. Formulating a standardized spelling was especially important as a tool for converting Malay from the *jawi* Arabic script system to Latin letters. This was both for wider accessibility and to weaken the putative link of Malay with Islam, given the potential for "disruptive" influences of modernist Islamic Reformism, then gathering strength in the Middle East, on Muslim Indonesians.

Ultimately, the Malay used in the former Riau-Johor Sultanate—considered by some Dutch scholars to be the Malay "heartland"—was chosen as the purest and most real dialect of that language. Although this choice was opposed on the grounds that it was not well understood or particularly relevant to life in many other parts of the Indies, it was argued that as a direct descendant of the court of the once powerful kingdom of Malacca, with its administrative and literary language, rich in Arabic and Persian terminology, this Malay was the best equipped to encourage self-reliance and maturity among native peoples. Dutch scholars and administrators hoped that promotion of Riau-Johor Malay, or "High Malay", in the educational system would eventually eliminate the widespread use of various demotic, and to some degree, almost-pidgin "low" or "market" variants of the language. A wordlist of about 10,000 entries in standardized spelling was completed in 1901 in Batavia and circularized as the officially prescribed terms for the native school system where Malay was the medium of instruction.

Riau-Johor Malay is linguistically very close to the Minangkabau language and the Raja's School in Bukittinggi and the large number of educators in the colonial civil service who graduated from it were influential in this effort to standardize and optimize modern Malay. As a result, this officially-sanctioned "High Malay" was infused with Minangkabau linguistic elements. But certainly the most formative influence on the shaping of the modern Malay, soon to be termed "Indonesian", language in the Netherlands East Indies was the government-sponsored publishing house, Balai Pustaka.

Balai Pustaka publishing house

After the beginning of the 20th century, concomitant to the rapid growth of a Europeanized, indigenous professional elite, demand increased tremendously for European-style education, whether in government or private schools (including missionary schools, where all levels of indigenous society were accepted). Under these circumstances, Batavia determined a need for suitable local language reading materials more appropriate for a growing (though still small) portion of the population being exposed to modern education. Development of Malay as a modern, "serious" language was an important policy objective to counter the raucous, and occasionally politically subversive, Low Malay "wild literature" of the popular press. In 1908, the Committee for Indies School and Popular Literature was formed to advise on appropriate literature and to commission and publish grammars, school texts, traditional tales and modern fiction in the major regional languages as well as Dutch. In addition, Western fiction was to be translated into Malay. In 1917, the Commission was renamed Balai Pustaka ("The Hall of Literature") and over the next decade it established public libraries and even motorized lending-bookstalls for remote areas throughout the Indies. It is estimated these travelling libraries lent out 2.5 million books annually. Though it aimed at cultivating a taste for serious literature, the publishing house also sought to stimulate enthusiasm for lighter and more general reading, and so published vastly popular Malay magazines of a practical or entertaining nature.

Balai Pustaka had strict publishing criteria: no writing critical of Dutch rule, partial to a particular religion or portraying heterodox moral standards in anything but an unequivocally negative light would be accepted. Furthermore, writings had to be of a didactic nature. In regard to its Malay literary output, Balai Pustaka's editorial policies have been criticized for imposing a rigid uniformity of style, which among other things denied a real place in this early modern literature to the demotic language. As a result, a certain artificiality and stiltedness infuses the texts, particularly the dialogue. To some degree, this reflected the ideas about proper High Malay of the predominantly Minangkabau writers themselves or their counterparts on the Balai Pustaka editorial staff. Nonetheless, it was through Balai Pustaka's willingness to publish writers like Merari Siregar, Marah Rusli, Mohammed Yamin, Sutan Takdir Alisyahbana and Achdiat Karamihardja, to name but a few, that early modern Indonesian literature of a high quality was born. Its earliest genre was, not surprisingly in view of the origin of the writers, focused on issues specifically relevant to West Sumatran society and culture. Later in the 1920s, Balai Pustaka began to publish more complex works by non-Minangkabau authors that transcended regional interest themes.

Sitti Nurbaya: A Love Unrealized was only the second novel published by Balai Pustaka and surely its most popular. Since 1922, this story portraying the clash between traditionalism and modernism in Minangkabau society has been reprinted at least twenty-two times and for decades was required reading in Indonesian high schools. The author, Marah Rusli, was born in Padang, West Sumatra, on August 7, 1889, the only child of a civil service district head in West Sumatra. His father's title, Sultan Pangeran, indicated descent from the old Pagaruyung monarchy. Marah Rusli's mother also claimed aristocratic lineage, but from Java. Cross-ethnic marriages in those days and for many decades to come were discouraged because of the difficulties arising from differences in *adat* of the various ethnic groups in the Indies. Marah Rusli was educated at a Dutch medium school in Padang and thereafter at the influential Raja's School in Bukittinggi. Upon graduation in 1910, he entered the Veterinary School and commenced his lifelong career in government veterinary service. In 1911, Marah Rusli married a titled girl from Bogor, West Java, Nyai Raden Ratna Kecana Wati. Although this marriage was against his parents' wishes, it proved to be a happy and lasting one that produced three children.

During his long and interesting veterinary career, Marah Rusli had postings in Sumbawa and throughout Java. In 1926, he co-authored the first report on *Lepora bubalorum*, a form of leprosy in water buffalo, an exotic disease found only in Indonesia. It is, of course, for *Sitti Nurbaya: A Love*

Unrealized that Marah Rusli is most remembered. Written in Batavia in 1921, at a low point in his professional life, the novel skillfully incorporated within the contemporary European novelistic structure Malay-Minangkabau *syair* and *pantun* verse forms, *adat* proverbs and Islamic sermon-like exhortations brimming with Quranic and *hadith* references, to launch, in an idiom his readers could never mistake, a fierce attack on the stagnation of *adat*-bound Minangkabau society, religious fanaticism and, in particular, its repression of the innate talents and genius of women.

Sitti Nurbaya: A Love Unrealized envisions the confident future of the East Indies, embodied in a new generation of Indonesian youth well-grounded in the culture of the Indies as well as educated in the *rantau* of modernity and thus superbly equipped to bring the Good into Indies society and lead it in discarding the Bad. It suggests a society where European and native Indies-born would together walk the road of progress in friendship and trust. And yet, the story concludes on a note of troubling ambiguity on the feasibility of any deep union between the people of the colony and the Netherlands. This deeply romantic and socially explosive novel certainly complied with Balai Pustaka's policy on didacticism for it raised provocative issues still being debated in today's Indonesia, as many of the early Balai Pustaka novels still do. Marah Rusli, who died in Bandung in 1968, wrote two other works of fiction, but neither of these was considered an equal to *Sitti Nurbaya: A Love Unrealized*.

Poetic forms in *Sitti Nurbaya*

Sitti Nurbaya makes abundantly clear the abiding love of poetry in Minangkabau society. Two verse forms profusely displayed in the novel are the *pantun* and *syair*. Pantun are Malay-Minangkabau quatrains dating back at least to the 15th century. Structurally, they usually follow an ABAB rhyming pattern and consist of two equal parts which, upon first glance, appear unrelated, but in fact usually are, though in highly allusive and metaphorical ways. The first part of a *pantun* is known as "shadowing", while its "intention" is embodied in the second part. More so than other types of verse, the symbol-laden *pantun* formed an integral part of traditional Malay-Minangkabau social life, conveying proverbs of conventional wisdom, oblique messages of love, longing (as well as cynical disillusionment), diplomacy, biting satire and historical evocation. Skill in reciting *pantun*, and especially their *ex tempore* composition, precisely appropriate to a given situation, was a paramount sign of intelligence and cultivation.

Similarly dated in the Malay-Minangkabau world, the *syair* verse form is probably of Arab or Persian origin. While both *syair* and *pantun* consist of quatrains, the *syair* is a single unit in an elaborate exposition of some story or moral advice, whereas a *pantun* is complete with a single four-line verse. The rhyming pattern of the *syair* is TTTT, BBBB, QQQQ etc., in no particular alphabetical order. While a *pantun* may be wry, emotional, and cryptic, and indeed cover a wide range of moods and purposes, the *syair* is comparatively direct and clear in its function of elaborating its particular theme or story. Moreover, the characteristic "shadowing-and-intention" structure of the *pantun* has no counterpart in the *syair*, where each line is an integral part of the verse. Finally, *pantun* generally are recited; *syair* are to be sung. This translation generally observes the rhyme pattern of the *pantun*. On the other hand, little attempt was made to recreate uniform rhyme in translating the *syair* in Chapter Seven and Chapter Ten, generally using blank verse instead to emphasize the feelings of desperation and longing poured out by the two lovers as they used this poetry.

Rich in description, dense with ironic foreboding and the inexorable workings of fate, *Sitti Nurbaya: A Love Unrealized* is indeed Samsu and Nurbaya's sad love story. Within it resound strong echoes of the classic twelfth-century Persian verse epic *Leyla and Majnun*, a tale of love, melancholy and madness. But we may also sense one man's tantalizing and provocative vision of what Indies society might become, indeed *could* become, if only Indies genius, embodied in youth emancipated from stifling traditions, could fuse with European genius in mutual respect and admiration. This too, of course, would prove a melancholy dream never to be realized and one, perhaps, which never could have been realized.

In terms of its social impact in the Indies, *Sitti Nurbaya* may be compared to *Max Havelaar* in the Netherlands of the 1860s and *Uncle Tom's Cabin* in the ante-bellum United States. However, while these two once-controversial works now languish largely unread, *Sitti Nurbaya*, both the story and its eponymous persona, continue to touch something very deep in Indonesia, not just in its Minangkabau West Sumatran setting. A well-received miniseries was televised nationally in 1990. Pop songs are still being composed and sung about Sitti Nurbaya. If you cross the Arau River, then climb Mount Padang just outside the city of the same name, you will find the real graves of the fictional Sitti Nurbaya and her beloved Samsulbahri. The issues of injustice and indignities suffered by women that this novel raised and which clashed so sharply with Minangkabau *adat* traditional law, continue to be debated to this day in West Sumatra. In the end, this is not only a compelling story of thwarted love and an eloquent broadside against the then-prevailing traditionalist attitudes in West Sumatra (and by extension the entire Indies). It is, above all, a work of extraordinary linguistic beauty.

Sources

Abdullah, Taufik. "Some Notes on the Kaba Tjindua Mato: an Example of Minangkabau Trade Literature." In *Indonesia*, Vol. 9 (April 1970).

Abdullah, Taufik. *Schools and Politics: Kaum Muda Movement in West Sumatra (1927–1933)*. Ithaca: Modern Indonesia Project, Cornell University, 1971.

Drakard, Jane. *A Kingdom of Words: Language and Power in Sumatra*. Oxford: Oxford University Press, 1999.

Graves, Elizabeth E. *Minangkabau Response to Dutch Colonial Rule in the Nineteenth Century*. Ithaca: Cornell Modern Indonesia Project. Monograph Series pub. no. 60, 1984.

Hadler, Jeffrey. *Muslims and Matriarchs*. Ithaca and London: Cornell University Press, 2008.

Kahn, Joel S. *Constituting the Minangkabau: Peasants, Culture and Modernity in Colonial Indonesia*. Oxford: Berg Publishers, 1993.

Kahn, Joel S. *Minangkabau Social Formations*. Cambridge: Cambridge University Press, 1980.

Mitchell, Istutiah Gunawan. "Socio-Cultural Environment and Mental Disturbance: Three Minangkabau Case Histories." In *Indonesia*, Vol. 7 (April 1969).

Sneddon, James. *The Indonesian Language: Its History and Role in Modern Society*. University of New South Wales Press, 2003.

Teeuw, A.A. "The Impact of Balai Pustaka on Modern Indonesian Literature" in *Bulletin of the School of Oriental and African Studies*, University of London, Vol. 35, No. 1 (1972), pp. 111–127.

Van Niel, Robert. *Emergence of Modern Indonesian Elite.* The Hague: W. van Hoeve Publishers Ltd., 1970. Ch.1: East India Society 1900.

1

Home from School

Around one in the afternoon, in front of the Dutch school in Padang's Ambacang Market district, a young man and woman stood in the shade of a dense almond tree. All around them, the ground steamed and heat poured from the sky. The young man, who was about eighteen years-old, wore a white, high-collared, lapel-less jacket of Western cut and short, black breeches fastened with buttons. His black shoes were high, like boots, and topped by silk stockings, also black, that clasped his calves with elastic hose bands. A straw hat covered his head; the kind Dutch men usually wore. In his right hand, he held several books and a map of the earth. In his left, a ruler he slapped now and then against his leg.

From afar, the young man might have been mistaken for a Dutchman on his way home from school. But, up close, with his tawny skin and ink-black hair and eyes, it was clear he was no European. Below his generous forehead were thick, black eyebrows, an aquiline nose and a refined mouth. He was of medium build, neither fat nor thin, but solid. His open and calm expression reflected the straightforward and willful character of a person not easily crossed. From the look of his clothing and his school, it was obvious he was the son of someone well-to-do, while his courtly bearing confirmed his high birth.

The young man's companion was a girl of some fifteen years. She, too, wore Western clothes. Her dress was of fine, sheer *batiste* and had a guava-pink flower pattern. Her shoes were brown, as were her stockings. In her right hand she carried a writing slate and a box of slate markers, pencils and pens. In her left was a light-yellow, silk parasol decorated with a green border and flowers. Her luxuriant, dark plaits were tied with silk thread and dressed with black ribbons.

How comely she was, standing there like "someone who, rarely leaving her home, yearns for something not easy to attain", or so the saying goes.

Her cheeks were as round as two mango halves and their slight ruddiness, reflecting her dress and parasol, was made more intense by the heat of the sun. When she laughed, her cheeks dimpled, sweetening her face, an effect heightened by the presence of a small beauty mark. Her gaze was calm and soft, like someone who had just awoken. Her nose was prominent, but finely shaped, like a jasmine blossom; her lips, as red and delicate as pomegranate seeds; while her teeth were as straight and even as two rows of ivory. Her chin was like the finely carved figurehead that graces a ship's prow. On each ear, a small polished diamond radiated the light of morning dew, as did the diamonds studding the bracelets on her lower arms. On her left ring finger, she wore a ring fitted with a pearl. And around her long and slender neck, hung a ruby-encrusted pendant in the shape of an Ambon mint leaf. When she drank water, it was as if a shade passed down her throat. Her voice was low and gentle, like a bamboo wind-chime, and aroused such tender sorrow in all who heard it that they dropped whatever was at hand. She had an ample chest and a slender waist. Her legs were quite shapely and when she walked she moved with a gentle sway.

Yes, whoever gazed at her could not help but be fixed by a kind of mysterious captivation. From her bearing, complexion and adornments it was clear she was native to the region; the child, perhaps, of a rich man or someone of high position. Everyone supposed that someday, when she came of age, she would become the very flower of Padang, with a fragrance so pervasive even the butterflies and bees would be driven half-mad with love.

The young man glanced down the road leading to Kampung Jawa's marketplace. "Why is Ali so late today?" he asked. "Has he forgotten us?"

"He's usually here before one," the girl remarked. "Look! The clock on the telephone office shows almost one-thirty."

"Let's hope he didn't doze off," the young man replied, seemingly irritated. "Last night he asked my father if he could go see the circus. If that's why he's late, I'm definitely going to complain to Father."

"Oh, don't, Sam! Have some pity on the poor fellow. It's not like he just started working for your father. He's been with him for years and in all that time he's done nothing wrong. How would *we* feel if *we* were that old and still got scolded? Something must have delayed him. Let's hope he didn't have an accident on his way here. The poor old man!" she said. "Let's just walk back home slowly and maybe we'll meet him halfway there." She opened her parasol, exiting the schoolhouse yard.

"All right," he grumbled, as he began to follow his friend. "But I'd rather take a buggy than walk because now I'm really tired and it's so hot. Look at your face: as red as an apple under all this sun!"

"I know it's hot, but never mind that. I've got a parasol, so let's both use it. And my face isn't just red from the heat: it got that way in school."

"How come? Scolded by the teacher, perhaps?" the young man asked as he looked at his friend.

"No, it wasn't that, Sam. It was only... oh, there's Ali now!"

A moment later, a small buggy pulled up beside the pair. The horse, drenched in sweat, looked as if it had been driven for quite a while. The coachman was about forty-five, but appeared quite sturdy for his age. And from his expression, he was clearly a frank and kind-hearted man, even if no longer young.

Sam approached the cart angrily. "Why are you so late?" he shouted at the driver. "It's one-thirty! We've been standing here for a half-hour, like a pair of chicks left behind by their mother!"

"Please don't be angry with me," the driver pleaded. "I didn't mean to be late. I had the cart rigged up and ready to go by twelve-thirty, but then your father told me to fetch Datuk Meringgih. There was something he wanted to discuss with him. So I went to his store—he's usually at his store around this time—but he wasn't there. So I had to go all the way to his house in Ranah to look for him. That's why I'm late," he concluded, breathless.

"Hm..." Sam growled. "Come on, Nur, climb up, so we can go home. My stomach's rumbling."

No sooner had they climbed aboard the buggy than the horse took off towards Kampung Java Dalam, nimbly bearing its load toward the home of the young man on board.

In the cart, Sam pursued his earlier query.

"Nur, you haven't told me why your face is red."

"Oh, that's right. It's because Mrs van der Stier gave me a calculation to do," Nur told him, "about the way the short hand and the long hand travel on a clock. I tried to figure it out two or three times, until my head was spinning, but I just couldn't get it. How do you solve a problem like that?"

"What was the question?" Sam asked.

"It went like this. At 12 o'clock, the little hand and the big hand come together. At what time do the two hands come together again?

"Oh, it's almost the same as the problem I explained to you before," Sam told her, "the one about a man traveling on foot and on horseback. What you need to know in this particular kind of calculation is the distance the hands must travel to come back to 12 on the clock, supposing the circles were cut and made into a straight line. So, what is it?"

Nur sat silently thinking.

"Here, lend me your writing slate," he said, taking the slate and drawing a long line on its surface.

A moment later, Nur answered, "Sixty minutes."

"Correct. Sixty minutes or sixty meters or sixty road markers: all of these are just names. We can treat as equal the sixty minutes it takes for the hand to come back around to 12 and the sixty kilometers between two villages—say, for example, between P and M. Now, which is faster, the big hand or the little one?" asked Sam.

"The big hand, of course."

"So, let's call the big hand 'A.' He goes on horseback from P to M. And we'll call the little hand, 'B.' He walks there instead. Now, how fast do the two hands go?"

"The big hand goes sixty minutes per hour and the little hand goes five minutes per hour."

"What's the difference between how far the two hands go in one hour?"

"Fifty-five minutes."

"So, have them both set off together! A from P to M, and B from P to M," said Sam.

"Oh, yes, right, right!" said Nur. "Now I understand."

If you know the trick, it's really easy, isn't it?"

"Yes. Thank you, Sam!" the girl exclaimed, raising her head. "Look, we've come home without even knowing it."

At that moment, the buggy came to a halt in front of a whitewashed, wooden house whose roof was tiled in the Dutch manner. The girl got down from the cart and started to go inside.

"Hold on a minute, Nur," Sam called out. "I almost forgot. I told Arifin and Bakhtiar I'd go with them to Mount Padang tomorrow to look for India plums. Since it's a Sunday, would you like to come along?"

"Oh, sure," Nur replied joyfully. "But, I have to ask permission from my father first. If I can go, I'll send word later this afternoon."

"Fine. But if you join us, you have to bring something to eat. Arifin is bringing fruit juice and I'm bringing bread. I'm going to borrow Hendrik's air rifle, if I can, to do some hunting in case there are birds.

"Oh, that sounds like fun! I'll go with you if I get permission and I'll think about what to bring."

"Fine. Goodbye, Nur!"

"Goodbye, Sam!"

After their parting, the buggy pulled into the very next yard, where Sam could see a carriage parked in front of his house. His father was on the veranda, talking to a guest.

Sam's real name was Samsulbahri and he was the son of Sutan Mahmud Syah—the *penghulu*, or district head, of Padang—a man of high office and birth. Sam was in his seventh year at the Dutch School in Ambacang Market. On account of his intelligence, his teacher had submitted a request to the Government that he be allowed to continue his studies in Batavia, at the School Tot Opleiding Van Inlandsche Artsen, more commonly known as STOVIA, the so-called "Java Doctors' School", one of the few post-secondary educational institutions open to indigenous people of the Indies.

Samsulbahri was not just bright, but also courteous, refined in speech and manners, straightforward and trustworthy. And though he looked both gracious and graceful, if need be, he would not have been afraid to test his mettle against anyone, especially when defending the weak. In such matters, he never took birth or position into account and was, for that reason, very well-respected by friends. Barring any unusual circumstances, he would depart for Java in three months to pursue his studies.

His friend "Nur" was actually Sitti Nurbaya, the child of Baginda Sulaiman, a rich merchant from Padang who owned several large shops and estates, as well as ships that plied his trade across the sea. Nur was flawless, it may be said, for she was as lovely in appearance as she was courteous, neat, generous and circumspect in the observation of customary forms and practices.

As she was the child of a rich man, and so astute and clever, she was liked, and even loved, by her friends. Unlike her neighbor, the district head, her father was not of high birth. Nevertheless, Sutan and Nur's fathers were more than just companions: they were like "brothers of the same womb". They visited each other's homes almost every day and always treated each other to a meal if it was to be had. And neither did anything without first consulting his friend.

As a result, Samsulbahri and Nurbaya never saw any real difference between them and felt as though they shared the same parents, particularly since each was an only child. From the time they were little until the day our story begins, the two had never spent a day apart. You might even say that they "ate from the same plate and slept on the same pillow".

What would happen to them when the time came for Sam to leave his home? We shall have to wait and see.

The person on the veranda to whom Sam's father spoke also numbered among the district head's friends and was frequently seen taking meals at the house. From his face and his hair, which had gone white with sprinklings of grey, it was clear he was no youth. Be that as it may, his body was perfectly fit: strong and healthy, in fact, for he was a rich man.

His name was Datuk Meringgih and he, too, was a merchant, famed even in distant lands for his wealth, which was unmatched among Padang's Malay traders. He owned nearly all the large shops and houses in Gedang Market, as well as most of the land in Padang: vast rice fields and plantations. Nearly every vessel that berthed at Muara belonged to him. Shipload after shipload of copra he sent to Europe, while his warehouses took in all the rattan and resin from Painan and Terusan to the south.

European, Chinese, Arab, Indian: there wasn't a single rich or highly-placed person of foreign or local persuasion who wasn't on close terms with him. And Datuk Meringgih cultivated such contacts, especially those in high positions. Did he have some purpose in doing so? Or was it out of kindness? We shall have to wait and see.

Although prodigiously wealthy, Datuk Meringgih was not of high birth. In fact, rumor had it that, in his youth, he had been very poor. How he came to be so rich, no one really knew, except, of course, him. Aside from his wealth, one thing above all marked him: he was extraordinarily stingy. In his heart, he knew he could kill over a single cent. If he had to spend, he would turn the decision over and over in his mind, as if faced with an impossible parting, all the while asking himself, "Do I give this money away or not?" There was only one area of life in which he did not act the miser: women. No one could count how many times he had divorced and married and his children could be found in nearly every village. The old man could not even look at an attractive woman without proposing. Even though he had to spend a thousand rupiah each time, it didn't matter, as long as he got what he wanted. Most of the women who fell into his hands did so for the money; apart from that, there was nothing else to recommend him. Pleasing to the eye he was not, well advanced in years as he was. His house and clothes were dirty, he was coarse and rude, of low birth, and lacking in position and skills, other than in business. Nevertheless, with the power of money, high became low; the hard, now soft; and the distant, near. Such is the power of money. The world revolves around it and, in the end, everything takes its shape.

"Hey, it must be one o'clock!" said Sutan Mahmud, when he noticed his son had returned from school.

"It's one-thirty," replied Datuk Meringgih, looking at the big watch he kept linked by twists of ribbon to the upper pocket of his shirt.

"So, Datuk, will you loan me the three thousand rupiah?" asked Sutan Mahmud.

"Certainly," his friend firmly replied.

"But what shall I provide as collateral?"

"Nothing. I trust you, on account of how long I've known you. If it were anyone else, I would, of course, ask for security of some kind."

"I can't allow you to do that," said Sutan Mahmud. "I'm very grateful for your trust, Datuk, but debt has to be clearly marked. If I were to leave this world, tomorrow or the day after, before the debt was paid, what would happen? I will send a contract pledging my house and lands, in the amount of 3,000 rupiah."

"As you wish. Now, with your permission, I'll take my leave, as I'm sure you must want to eat."

"Won't you join me?"

"I don't want to inconvenience you. Perhaps another time," Datuk Meringgih answered, rising from his chair.

The two men shook hands and then Datuk Meringgih walked down the steps of the house and into his carriage. A moment later, he was gone from Sutan Mahmud's view.

Sutan Mahmud took a deep breath, as though having slipped out of danger. Re-entering the house, he thought, "If I hadn't been able to borrow from him I would have been forced to sell our ancestral rice fields. This *is* good luck! I won't have to ask Baginda Sulaiman for help. I would be ashamed if he refused my payment."

Once inside the house, Sutan saw Samsulbahri coming out of his room. He had changed from his school uniform and was wearing a white Chinese tunic and gingham trousers.

With his father staring at him, Samsu approached and said, "With your permission, I would like to go to Mount Padang tomorrow."

"With whom?"

"With Arifin and Bakhtiar and maybe Nurbaya."

"With Nurbaya?" Sutan Mahmud mused. "All right, but make sure you take good care of yourself and Nurbaya. Don't get into trouble along the way and don't do anything unpleasant."

"Yes, Father."

A moment later, father and son sat down to eat, joined by Samsu's mother, who had been waiting for them for some time.

2

Sutan Mahmud and His Sister

At twilight on the same day, Sutan Mahmud's buggy entered the yard of a brick house in Kampung Alang Lawas.

Seated in his cart, leaning on a hardwood cane, the district head looked quite heroic, especially his headband, which had the look of a crown with its "descending boar" style. His white jacket was embossed with "W" buttons and gold-braided cuffs, very much like an officer's uniform. Between his jacket and white trousers, a *sarong* of black Buginese silk was fastened around his waist, reaching almost to his knees. On his feet were black, polished leather shoes.

As for the district head's face, he and his son, Samsulbahri, were as alike in looks as an areca nut split in two. Sutan Mahmud was the most respected of Padang's eight district heads because of his high birth, his elegant appearance and good manners. Towards subordinates he was, as they say, "compassionate and merciful", besides being fair and straightforward in his dealings.

As the buggy came to a halt in front of the house, the Penghulu stepped down and ascended a set of stairs. It was clearly a rich person's home, with its classical appearance, large grounds and black wooden fence. In the yard stood many trees and flowers in full fruit and bloom.

A half-moon path led up to the doors, whose white, iron grilles lay open. It was an old building, quite tall, with large carved pillars, wooden walls and floors and palm thatch above a tiled roof. Black latticework skirted the bottom portion of the house on all sides, covering the front veranda, too, where an engraved tin lamp hung. Under the lamp a round marble table stood on carved legs, surrounded by four old-fashioned rocking chairs. Where the middle portion of the veranda jutted out slightly, two flanking sets of stairs joined. Inside, several pictures of the Turkish Sultan and his viziers hung on the whitewashed walls.

Sutan Mahmud knew his way around the house and walked straight to its rear veranda, where a girl of about fifteen was seated on a pandanus mat, sewing with a lamp by her side.

Seeing her, he stopped and asked, "Where did your mother go, Rukiah?"

Startled by his words, the young woman looked up suddenly. When she saw that it was the district head standing before her, she put down her sewing and rose, saying, "She is praying, Uncle."

She was about to go see if her mother had finished, when Sutan Mahmud interrupted her. "It's all right," he said. "Don't bother her! I can wait a bit." He then sat in a chair beside a small marble dining table.

Just then he heard a woman's voice from inside the room the girl had been about to enter.

"Who is it, Rukiah?"

"It's Uncle, the district head," the girl replied.

"Oh, wait a minute! I'm done and am just getting dressed."

While he waited, Sutan Mahmud turned to his niece. "What are you sewing?" he asked.

"A lace shirt," she replied, gathering up her cloth.

"Let me see!" her uncle exclaimed, prompting Rukiah to display the work in progress.

"That's really fine work you've done," Sutan Mahmud said. "Who's it for?"

At the question, Rukiah fell silent, lowering her head and replying shyly, "For whoever likes it."

"A lot of people would like it, that's for sure. Me, for example. I would very much like to wear a lace shirt like this," he teased.

"If you like it, you can have it, but I think it would be too small for you."

"I think so, too, Rukiah. Only a young person could wear this, someone about your age, and just as slender; not an old, stout man like me."

Blushing, Rukiah again bowed her head shyly. Just then, from the other room, came a woman who looked to be about forty-five, wearing a long *kebaya* blouse made from black *céla* fabric and Buginese cloth. She was nearly identical to Sutan Mahmud, though thinner than him. So, too, the expression on her face was rather different than his and suggested something unpleasant lurking beneath the surface: a spiteful and cruel disposition.

Noticing her brother sitting in the chair, the woman exclaimed, "Oh, it's you! How delightful to see you again! It's been so long since your last visit, I almost thought you'd forgotten us."

"Not at all! You of all people should know what it's like to work for the government! It never ends: the labor levies, the patrols, the road works, police investigations, this and that."

"Yes, of course. But... Rukiah, go boil some water for your uncle here. Are there any cakes left in the cupboard?"

"Yes, there are," replied the girl.

"There's no need for all that. I just had some tea at home, Rukiah," interrupted Sutan Mahmud.

"What? You're no longer willing to eat here? Don't you trust your sister anymore?" the woman asked, with a glint of anger in her eye.

"What are you saying? You think I'm suspicious of you? Who else can I trust, if not you?" her brother calmly asked, though the smile was beginning to fade from his lips.

"Rukiah, go and boil some water, but don't make the coffee too strong!" said the woman.

With that, the young girl hastened to carry out her mother's command.

"Don't be angry about what I'm saying. To tell you the truth, it seems like you visit us less and less these days. Before, you used to come almost every day to eat here and sometimes even to sleep. Whatever you needed, you only had to ask and I'd go get it myself. You considered this house your very own. But now, not only do you not sleep here and watch over us, you don't even drop by once a week.

"If I give you something to eat, you don't want it, as if you were afraid and didn't trust this house and the people in it. But, as you know, this is where both you and I were born. And it was here, too, that our parents lived for more than eighty years and where they returned to the mercy of God. How you could have it in you to be like that, I just can't imagine," said Putri Rubiah, as she wiped away the tears that began to trickle down her cheeks.

At the sight of his sister weeping, the anger which had begun to grow inside Sutan Mahmud suddenly ceased.

"Don't be offended. I had nothing of the sort in mind. It's just that, as you know, there is a new High District Officer and he issues harsh orders. So a person has to be very careful in doing his job to avoid gaining a bad reputation. Not one of our ancestors who worked for the East Indies government ever earned a bad name for themselves. For them the Company had only praise, always. I'd feel so ashamed and remorseful if that good name suffered because of me.

"I suppose you'd still forget about us, even if you weren't the district head," said Putri Rubiah. "Since you got married and had a child, you've thought of nothing else but your family and your own household."

"How could it be otherwise? Who else would be there to look after my wife and child?" he asked, stunned by his sister's comments.

"You see! It's just as I thought. You have strayed from our ways. Never mind your wife, because she lives in your house, but your child? What about that uncle of his, your wife's older brother? Isn't your child his nephew? Doesn't he have the obligation to take care of your son, according to our ways? Or have you also forgotten our ancestral laws?"

"You're right, but Marhum doesn't make much and he has lots of other responsibilities to worry about. So, I would be ashamed to put Samsu in his care," replied Sutan Mahmud.

"Yes, but when your niece becomes your responsibility, though to no purpose, you're not ashamed," his sister shot back.

"What do you mean 'to no purpose'?"

"Wouldn't you call it 'to no purpose'? Not visited, nor paid any attention to? Whether she has any clothes or not, whether she's hungry or in trouble, whether she's sick or dead? You put your own child in the Dutch school. Whatever he wants, you do it for him. He has enough to eat and wear. If he wants to go somewhere, your horse cart is made ready for him. Soon you'll be sending him to Batavia to continue his studies. And from there perhaps even to Holland, since the education at Batavia won't be adequate for him. If there were a school for making kings, I'm sure that's where you'd put your son, because he can't become just anybody. No, he's got to become a person of high office. Doesn't all that take a lot of money? For *your* child there's always money, but for *mine* there's never any."

"It's not my fault that Rukiah doesn't go to school: it's yours!" Sutan Mahmud said, now angered. "How many times have I asked you to send the child to school? But you're the one who doesn't like it, because you think it's not good for a girl to be adept at reading and writing, because it makes them disobedient. Now you blame me. Besides, it's not for nothing that I'm sending Samsu to school: as I see it, a father is obligated to improve and advance his child."

"That's not *your* obligation, it's the obligation of your wife's older brother," replied Putri Rubiah, her voice reaching a new pitch of severity. "Luckily, my daughter is not too much of a burden to you. But, even if she were a boy, it's not clear you would hand her over to a school, because girls who go to school are base-born and poor, unable to get anything to eat if they don't have skills. My daughter is of high birth and doesn't need to work in order to eat. Even if she were stupid, there are still a lot of rich and well-born men who would appreciate her lineage. That's not the case with your child. He will never be a noble because his mother was just a commoner. If it weren't for his skills, he wouldn't even be marriageable...." her voice broke, as if suddenly unable to contain her regret.

"To this day, I still can't understand what you were thinking when you married that woman," she continued. "What did you see in her? Was it just her good looks? What's the use of a good-looking wife if she has no background to speak of? A Dutch soldier looks good too, but who would want to give them proposal money?"

"So, in your opinion, a woman has to be high-born before she can be given in marriage," her brother snorted back. "I was of a different mind and was willing to marry anyone at all, so long as I liked her and she liked me. I gave no thought to lineage or appearance or wealth."

"Your habits and behavior have truly changed. A little longer and you'll convert to Christianity and become a Nazarene," said Putri Rubiah defiantly.

Her brother said nothing and simply shrugged his shoulders, turning away from her.

"I have no idea what love potion your wife gave you so that you'd never leave her. It's as if you were bound hand and foot by her. All the district heads in Padang have two or three, even four, wives. You alone have just that one woman and haven't replaced her or added new wives. Isn't an important man supposed to have lots of wives? Isn't it good for a man of high birth to keep changing his wives to maximize his lineage? Isn't it degrading if he only has one wife? When commoners with no ranking and no lineage have as many as four wives, why is it you don't follow suit?"

"The way I see it, only animals take on many mates, not humans," replied Sutan Mahmud, his face now reddened with growing rage. "If a woman can't have two or three husbands, then certainly it shouldn't be required that a man have many wives!"

"Just listen to you! Are such thoughts even proper? Every male of good stock who occupies a high position would be ashamed to have only one wife, but you'd be ashamed to have many. Your thinking really *has* changed, hasn't it? Have you forgotten that you are a person of good birth and high position? It's so embarrassing to think my brother isn't eligible among Padang's ladies, even though he has a high position and comes from a good line," Putri Rubiah exclaimed. "Isn't that a shame? Of course, you wouldn't have enough for household expenses if you relied on just your salary. Look at your younger brother! Even though he has no salary, he's never short of money. He never comes here without bringing something for me and his niece.

"My poor child!" she sighed. "She's known nothing but misfortune. Her uncle pays her no mind and no suitor can be found for her. Children twelve or thirteen years-old—fourteen at the oldest—have been given away in marriage, but my child, who's almost going grey, is still a maiden. If her father were alive, he would surely never have allowed anything like this to happen, even if he had to pawn his own head. And why should this be my destiny, when I'm no ordinary woman? Even though I have a brother who holds a high position, I'm like someone adrift in foreign lands with no family to turn to. Ignored and never visited, I'm not even given money for my household and clothing! From whom else shall I seek help if not from you, Mahmud?" she cried, her heart now broken.

Once again, at the sight of her tears, his anger subsided just as it had begun to reach its peak.

"There, there, don't cry anymore. My purpose in coming here was to talk to you about Rukiah."

"What's the use of speaking about it any more? It would just make me sadder. If you have no money, do you really suppose she would want to talk to you? Never mind, let my child become an old maid. I'm not the only one who will be ashamed, but, above all, you. Because people are going to say, 'A district head unable to find a husband for his own niece!'"

"How much proposal money is he asking for?" Sutan Mahmud inquired, ignoring his sister's comments.

"I've said it several times now: 300 guilders."

"Would he settle for less than that, say, 200 or 250?"

"If she were to be married to a fishmonger, naturally not even a cent would be necessary. But, as you surely know, my child may not and would not want me to marry her to just anybody. What would happen to our descendants?

"All right, what else does he want?" her brother proceeded patiently.

"A gold watch and chain, a diamond ring, a new set of clothing with several meters of Buginese *sarong* cloth and Javanese batik, and a buggy with horse," she shot back in rapid succession.

"My God! Where am I going to get all that?" he exclaimed.

"Have I not said, if you are not up to meeting his requests, let's not discuss the matter any further. What's the use of making me sad? I don't like any of the other men."

"All right, then. What else can I do? Agree to his proposal price!" Sutan Mahmud groaned. "The matter of the buggy is easy. If there isn't another one available, you can have mine."

"Really?" Putri Rubiah asked, her eyes coming back to life at the sound of her brother's words.

"Really," Sutan Mahmud replied curtly.

"Where will you get the money?"

"From Datuk Meringgih," he answered.

"How much?"

"Three thousand guilders."

"Oh, that would certainly be enough, because, as you yourself know, when Rukiah greets her husband, her dowry must be adequate. Naturally, the bedstead will have three layers of mosquito netting, of silk, at least. And the round ceremonial pillow, the high one, must also be of silk, and everything embroidered with Macao thread. Furniture rental for seven days and seven nights, with the cost of the procession and the bridal litter.... Well, all of that will not be cheap."

At that moment, Rukiah entered the room with a tray on which was placed a cup of coffee and some cakes that she brought directly to her uncle, placing them on the table beside him. She then returned to her room. She seemed to understand that her elders were discussing a matter she was not permitted to hear, as they stopped talking when she entered the room. Nevertheless, she heard her name mentioned. "Perhaps they're discussing my marriage," she caught herself thinking, only to wave away such thoughts, telling herself, "It's not proper for a maiden to think about such things."

"So when do you intend to hold this celebration, sister?" asked Sutan Mahmud, waiting for Rukiah to leave the room and lifting to his lips the cup of coffee he had been served.

"I want it to be done as quickly as possible," replied Putri Rubiah, "but, as you know, this sort of thing can't be done in a rush. As I see it, I'll need three months, since I have to prepare for everything in advance. We haven't got Rukiah's clothes yet and even the clothes for receiving Sutan Mansyur, who is to be her husband, are still not adequate. The dowry bedstead and the round pillows haven't been prepared yet, nor have the cakes been made. And, naturally, all our family members and close friends, both near and far, must be notified in advance."

"For those who live far away, I can write letters, but just let Hamza tell those that are nearby," Sutan Mahmud interjected.

Before he even had the chance to finish his coffee, he and his sister were startled by the distant sound of a *ketuk-ketuk*, a large wooden cylinder used as an alarm. Usually, it meant that someone had gone amok and was causing a disturbance. Sutan Mahmud shot up in his chair, listening intently to the sound that had begun to ring out ever louder and more urgently. A moment later came a response from the alarm at the watchman's house nearby.

"Someone's gone amok!" exclaimed Sutan Mahmud, bolting from his chair.

"You're right," said Putri Rubiah in a shaky voice, "but you don't have to go out."

"I must," her brother replied, "it could be in my area." At that moment, Rukiah came out of her room, went straight for her uncle and, taking his hand in hers, said in a trembling voice and with a face gone white with fear, "Uncle, don't go! I'm so afraid of him getting into the house."

"Maybe it's in Kampung Java or in Olo, not in this village," replied Sutan Mahmud, to dispel his niece's fear.

"Don't go! We have no man to protect us. Lasa's sick and Hamza's away," Putri Rubiah cried out.

Sutan Mahmud stood for a second, unsure of what to do: should he go and tend to his official duties or abandon them to guard his sister and niece?

"Where did Hamza go?" he asked, after a brief silence.

"Who knows?" his sister replied, "Let's hope he's not the one in danger."

Just then came the sound of somebody quickly climbing the steps to the house. The two women grew petrified and took cover behind Sutan Mahmud.

"Who is it?" Putri Rubiah turned to her brother.

"Ali perhaps, to tell us what this is all about," he replied.

"Is that you, Ali?" he asked.

There was no response.

All of a sudden, a young man entered the room and stood before them. Except for the difference in age, he looked almost exactly like Sutan Mahmud. He wore a white lace shirt, a sarong in the Palembang style, black slippers, and a black silk hat slightly tilted on his head. His lips were red, as if he had just been chewing betel-leaf. From his shirt pocket hung the chain of a gold watch shaped like a dragon. The buttons on his shirt were also made of gold while a diamond ring glinted on his finger. From his face and the delicate appearance of his body, it was clear he was of good birth and well-off, someone who from childhood had never known suffering or hardship. For that reason, all he cared about was having a good time. As to what would happen in the future or to things that had occurred in the past, he never gave a thought. If he had a hundred guilders, he would squander it or gamble it away on the very day he made it. When without money, he would sell or pawn everything he owned, and for this reason, led a very precarious life, feeling the pauper one minute, and the prince the next. Nevertheless, because he was "clever at living", as the Malay saying goes, he seemed never to lack for anything.

"Hah! It's lucky that you've come, Hamza! If you hadn't, I don't know what I would have done just now. But where are you coming from?" enquired Sutan Mahmud.

"From the village square. On the way over, I heard the alarm go off at the end of the road. That's why I came running."

"Have they found the person who went amok?" asked Sutan Mahmud.

"Who knows? Even the watchmen don't know," replied Sutan Hamzah.

"All right, then, stay here. I have to go and look into this."

"Mahmud, don't! Let them kill each other out there. What do you care?" Putri Rubiah exclaimed.

"I can't do that. A headman has to know what's going on in a case like this, especially if the attack has occurred in a village under my control," Sutan Mahmud replied.

"Do you love your position more than your life?" his sister shot back.

"Don't worry! There's no reason to think I'm going to die out there."

"If someone has gone amok in your area and you're not there, it will certainly harm your reputation," interjected Hamza.

As she began to sense she could not hold her brother back, Putri Rubiah finally blurted, "So be it, but be careful and protect yourself! Office and position can be sought, but life cannot be lengthened. And take Father's *kris* with you. It will bring good luck."

"All right," her brother replied, "where is it?"

"Hold on!" shouted Rubiah, rushing to her room.

A moment later, she came out holding an old dagger wrapped in white cloth, which she handed to Sutan Mahmud.

"Hamzah, close the door and stay here! Guard the house well!" Mahmud yelled.

He then left, leaping down the stairs and into his buggy.

3

A Hike to Mount Padang

The following morning, Samsulbahri awoke with a start as the large clock in his room rung out five times. He rose to see whether sunlight had yet begun to enter the house through the many cracks in the walls. Perhaps he had overslept, he worried. Though he checked here and there, listening very closely for the sound of voices, the only thing he could make out was the gleam of the lamp shining in his room. Everything was as still and silent as the grave. Nobody stirred from their bed; the only disturbance, the distant crowing of roosters calling out from all sides, a crowd cheering an exultant welcome to the dawn.

To the east, a train's reedy whistle sounded from time to time at the Padang station, as if sending a reminder to those who wanted to board for an early departure. While to the west came the sound of breaking waves like morning thunder announcing the day's rain ahead. Listening intently, Samsu began to worry his plans to visit Mount Padang would be ruined. From a little prayer house nearby, the muezzin reminded those who wished to perform their devotion to God the Most Holy and the Most High that the time for the dawn prayer had arrived.

As Samsu knew it was only five o'clock in the morning, he lay down again on his mattress, not intending to go back to sleep, but just to lie there a bit, waiting for the day to begin. He was restless and his thoughts were teased by the prospect of a good time to be had on the mountain with his friends. He rolled from side to side, as if pricked by a bed of thorns. Finally, when he could no longer stand it, he rose from his bed and very softly opened the door to his room, anxious his father, who was still sleeping, might awaken.

Outside, he saw the day was already quite clear and bright, not from the rays of the sun, but because of the glow of the moon, which had nearly sunk in the west. Stars shimmered and twinkled in the sky, like dew in the midst of a broad field, gleaming through clefts in the grass. Venus, the Eastern Star, whose light was beginning to fade, was enveloped in the glow of dawn now breaking in the east. Magpies were beginning to twitter in the trees, diving to the ground to snatch up careless slugs and crickets not yet hidden in their lairs. Other birds began leaving their nests in search of prey, hopping from branch to branch on trees that looked refreshed from the morning's covering of dew. Others chirped and called, as if joyous in greeting the arrival of the sunlight that gives life to all the creatures of the earth, while some fed their young with sustenance obtained that very morning; an uproar of cheeping and chittering could be heard from the trees' many nests. Little bats flitted here and there, swiftly and energetically, in search of dark places, as if afraid the daylight would crush them in mid-flight. Hens started out from their roosts, at the head of lines of tiny chicks, calling out and gathering those who wandered off or were left behind, afraid their little darlings might lose their way on the still-dark roads. Roosters rushed here and there in search of the hens, only to stop, raise their heads and crow with great skill, like generals mobilizing their troops on the field of battle. People, in pairs or alone, now came hurrying along the main roads, as if hot on the trail of something or other. From carts pulled by water buffalo or cows, or pushed by men, bells sounded, announcing the day's beginning. And indeed, over in the east, the first glow of sunlight began to appear, illuminating everything it touched.

Samsu went to the coachman's room and knocked on the door. "Wake up, Ali! It's daylight already."

A moment later, the door opened and Ali stuck his head out while rubbing his eyes.

"What time is it?" the coachman asked.

"Almost six o'clock."

Hearing this, the coachman dressed and left his room, entering the stable to clean the buggy, harness and the horse's stall, while Samsu went to wash at the well. When he returned to the house, Samsu saw that his father had already risen and was sitting in his chair on the rear veranda.

"You got up very early this morning," said his father.

"So we wouldn't get too hot while on the road," his son answered.

"So, you *are* going?"

"Yes, Father."

"And Nurbaya's going, too?"

"She said she would last night."

"Take good care of my friend's child!"

"Yes, Father."

"Good," said Sutan Mahmud, rising from his chair and entering the backyard.

At about a quarter past six that morning, Samsulbahri and Nurbaya were in the buggy, with Ali at the reins. They were out of the yard and headed in the direction of Muara.

Once underway, Ali, looking straight ahead, asked Samsu, "Straight on to Muara, young sir?"

"No, Ali. First, we're going to Arifin's house, on Church Street."

Receiving his instructions, the coachman headed the buggy in the right direction.

"I nearly overslept, Sam," Nurbaya said, "Last night, I couldn't sleep at all I was so scared by the sound of the alarm."

"I was scared, too. I didn't fall asleep until two in the morning, when my father came home. But I woke up at five."

"Where was the attack?" asked Nurbaya.

"I don't know," replied Samsu. "Alarms were sounding all over the place, for a long time, too."

Without their noticing it, as they chatted on and on, the buggy had stopped in front of the house of Head Prosecutor Sutan Pamuncak, in Kampung Sebelah. Two young men, about the same age as Samsu, stood in front. When they saw the buggy come to a halt, they ran up and cried out, "Hey! Nurbaya's coming too!" at the sight of the young woman seated next to Sam. "All right! The more the merrier."

"What's the matter, Tiar? I'm not allowed to come along just because I'm a woman?" Nurbaya asked with a smile.

"Come on, of course you can," the young man smiled back. "I didn't say that because I disliked seeing you, but because I was happy about it."

"What a lie! He was worried he wouldn't get enough of the cakes we're bringing," broke in Arifin.

"All right, then. If you really are glad to have me along, you won't be afraid to climb a rose-apple tree for me," Nurbaya cajoled Bakhtiar.

"Later, you'll be able to see for yourself who's better at climbing: a monkey or me," Bakhtiar replied proudly.

"When it comes to getting something to eat, of course, Tiar is better," teased Arifin.

As they went on in this way, the two young men climbed aboard Samsu's buggy and the little group set off for Muara.

Arifin's, whose full name was Zainularifin, was the son of Head Prosecutor Pamuncak, while Muhammad Bakhtiar was the son of the headmaster of the Native School, Second Class, in Belakang Tangsi. Both were schoolmates of Samsulbahri and would accompany him in three months to Batavia to continue their studies: Arifin to the Native Doctors Training School and Bakhtiar to the Overseers School, also known as the Queen Wilhelmina School of the Trades.

"I thought I was going to be late," said Arifin, taking a seat next to Samsu.

"Even if you *were* late, I would have waited for you because that was our agreement," answered Samsu.

"Why would you have been late?" Nurbaya asked.

"Because I'm the type of person who likes to sleep. Plus, last night I couldn't get to sleep right away," Arifin replied.

"Why? Was there a get-together at your house last night?" Samsu inquired.

"There sure was. A really major get-together. I was still awake at midnight," said Arifin, closing his mouth to stifle a yawn.

"You see how nice Arifin is, Sam? There's a get-together at his house and we're not even invited," Nurbaya said in an accusing tone.

"Oh, come on now. You mean you really didn't get an invitation?" exclaimed Arifin.

"Really, I didn't," Nurbaya replied.

"If that's the case, then the invitation didn't reach you."

"Why not?" Bakhtiar interjected, sensing something was amiss.

"Because the invitation was sent via the alarm."

"By the alarm?" asked Nurbaya, amazed.

"It's a new method, inviting people using an alarm."

While Samsu smiled at Arifin's joke, Nurbaya failed to register the sarcasm.

"Didn't you hear the alarms last night?" Arifin finally asked her.

"Yes, I did, but I thought it was because someone was running amok," she said.

"Yeah, that was the one! Isn't it the case that every time someone goes amok, there's a big get-together at my house? Because the attacker, the victims, runners, witnesses, the heads and elders of the village and so on, and even some of the onlookers, everyone gathers at my house to congratulate us," Arifin said, smiling.

"Ah, so that's what you meant. I thought you really did have a dinner party," Nurbaya replied, somewhat embarrassed, as it was only just now beginning to dawn on her that she was being had by her friend.

"There was no dinner, but there *was* a get-together," the boy said with a laugh.

"You're quite the joker. You could've been a court jester," Nurbaya said, laughing back.

"Who went amok and where did it happen?" asked Samsu.

"I don't know who it was, but he looked like a criminal when I saw him."

"You *saw* the man?" Bakhtiar interjected.

"Of course, he was brought to my house before being put in jail."

"So tell us what set him off and what happened."

"Oh, since you're all asking me about it, you must want to know, right? Well, because we're almost at Muara, I'm going to hold off until later, when telling you will cure us of our fatigue from the climb," Arifin said.

"See how stingy Arifin is," replied Bakhtiar, to get back at his friend. "He doesn't invite us when there's something going on at his house and now he won't tell us what happened. He's raising the price of his goods because he knows a lot of people are looking to buy."

"Are *you* really that brave? In fact, I didn't invite you on purpose because I knew you'd prefer to go where there are cakes rather than blood," retorted Arifin.

Bakhtiar could only listen, irritated, to his companion's sarcasm.

"The way I see it, Arifin had better become a merchant instead of a doctor because that's how merchants act. Whenever he sees that people like his merchandise, he hordes it and raises the price," Samsu blurted out, regretting instantly that he went on in this way, as Nurbaya might have found it annoying. From the corner of his eye he glanced at her sitting beside him, but it seemed she had not heard his rebuke, engrossed as she was in looking at several fishing vessels that had just entered the mouth of the Arau River.

By now, the four had arrived near a watchman's house in Muara. Behind the house, on the shore where the Arau emptied into the sea, a few cart horses were being washed by their coachman. Nearby was a pier that jutted out over the riverbank, where small steamships destined for Terusan were docked as well as several long fishing vessels, just in from the sea with their haul hooked the previous night. Before the pier stood a house where fishermen sold their catch. To the west soared Mount Padang, its peak like a dragon's head surfacing from the sea, while a low range formed the creature's neck: the spot where enthusiasts climbed. Further along to the south, the mountain gained height as the dragon grew in size before veering to the east, accompanied along the way by the Arau at its base.

On the south side of the pier, a customs office had been built to process the vessels that entered the river as well as for those moored at Pulau Pisang, where the harbor of Padang once stood before being moved further down to Bayur Bay. At the edge of the Arau, which separates Mount Padang from the town of the same name, several large vessels and small steamships were moored in a row, all along the stone-revetted riverbank. A railroad track ran parallel, as did the main road for hauling goods to Padang. To the north was a line of warehouses serving shops all the way to Kampung Cina and the town's main market.

It was a beautiful part of Padang that drew many who liked to stroll about in the late afternoon, breathing in the good air as the sun was about to set, for the harbor was well-situated and provided many fine views.

At the end of Ramadan, the month of fasting, and for two or three days after that, the road in this area was almost impassable on foot owing to the many buggies that raced each other with their tops down, testing the speed of their horses.

Heading north along the road, one reaches Padang's coast, which for about a mile is covered by a flower park. Along its length, there are benches in the shade of leafy almond trees, while in the middle of the park stands a pretty gazebo, round in shape, built on a mound, like a bower in a palace. It should come as no surprise that the park appealed to the Europeans living in Padang, not only for its fine grounds, but because of the beautiful view it offered of the sun setting.

For those who have never been there, the flower park is an utterly silent place. It was there, on a bench in a bower in the park's very center, in the sheltering shade of a tree, that a young man sat, lost in thought and gazing to the west toward the vast pool that extended the length of the park. Its waves broke at his feet, sprinkling the flowers with spray. Farther to the west, in the middle of the pond, several islands stretched in a row, as if enclosing the pool. Behind them was a kind of round bezoar, a glowing golden ball that radiated its glittering light on the surface of the water, which, mirror-like, refracted the beams that fell into the park, sending them back out among the flowers and trees.

Slowly the bezoar descended, as if pulled by an invisible spirit, until finally it sank into the pool, whose far end collided with the sky, creating images that seemed to rise from the liquid surface: a fighting dragon, a horse in full gallop, a ship under way, an island floating on water.

Those who are plagued by troubling thoughts should stay away from the pond in such moments, for as far distant as the horizon is from the side of the pool, so too will their thoughts and memories be some day. For lovers, however, its waters, glowing in the moonlight, seem to have been specially created for them.

Unfortunately, at the southern end of the park there is a prison, while at the northern end, a courthouse. Both elicit a kind of awe and melancholy when one recalls how many have been sentenced there, some of whom, perhaps, were innocent.

Let us return now and follow our four friends, whom we last saw in the buggy, for if we pause too long in the park, we won't be able to keep up with their journey.

"That's not the way it is," Arifin said, replying to a comment from Samsu. "There are several reasons why I don't want to tell you about this very important matter. First, so that you can learn to restrain yourselves, because that's a trait that is truly beneficial to the human race. The patient person, the one who can control his heart's desires, rarely goes astray in whatever undertaking. Remember the story of the woman and her cat and the one about the chicken that laid a golden egg!"

"How do those stories go?" Nurbaya asked.

"You don't know them, Nur? I'll tell you later," Samsu replied.

"Secondly..." said Arifin, continuing his exposition.

"Hey! We've arrived," Bakhtiar cried out, just as the buggy came to a halt near a warehouse.

"Right," replied Samsu. "We'd better get down."

They all jumped out of the cart, each carrying their provisions, and went to the bank of the river in search of a sampan to take them across.

"What time will you be returning?" asked Ali.

"Oh, right," said Samsu, looking back. "Just come for us at twelve o'clock."

"Very well," the coachman replied, turning the horse cart around and heading home.

When the little group reached the bank of the Arau, several sampans approached, calling out for hire.

"Take this sampan!" "This one's good. It don't pitch." "Here, one *duit* per person," called out the boatmen.

"We'd better wait for that big one coming now. It won't rock," Nurbaya explained.

"Exactly," replied Samsu.

A moment later the craft arrived at the river's edge. The four climbed aboard and were paddled across.

"Secondly," Arifin said once inside the sampan, carrying on with what he had been saying, "if we want something badly and quickly achieve our heart's desire, it can make us sick.

"Third, the feeling of elation from getting our wish right away doesn't last long, for we quickly become disgusted with the thing we so badly desired. For example, let's suppose Bakhtiar really loves cakes; in just a manner of speaking, Bakhtiar. Don't get mad," Arifin said, pretending to be earnest, but actually laughing to himself, as he intended to have some fun at his friend's expense.

"Even though you said I like cakes, I'm not angry," said Bakhtiar, "because it's true."

"Yeah, that's the reason I'm using this metaphor, to be accurate," his friend replied. "If, for example, for one year Bakhtiar is kept away from the cakes he so craves, certainly his desire to eat cakes cannot be said to be great."

"I'd sell my own head to buy cakes," retorted Bakhtiar.

"But if you didn't have a head, how could you eat the cakes?" Arifin said in jest, sparking laughter from his friends.

"Of course, my answer wasn't exactly correct," the butt of the joke chimed in, laughing now too.

"After a year away from his cakes, suddenly Bakhtiar is brought to Mevrouw Jansen's cake shop and is told, 'You may eat whatever you like!'" the young man went on.

"That's something I certainly wouldn't have to be told twice to do," his friend replied, nearly drooling at the very thought of cakes. "I'd immediately pounce on the tarts, the steamed white cakes, the sponge cakes and the spicy layer cakes: so delicious and delectable."

"Would you eat many or a few?" Arifin asked.

"I'd eat to my heart's desire, until I couldn't eat any more."

"Well, there you have it! Because you ate too much, you could get sick, or find cakes disgusting and have no wish to eat them any more. That wouldn't be so good, would it?"

"Yeah, true," Sam offered.

"Did you say 'disgusted'? Me, disgusted with cakes? I reckon to the end of my days I still won't have lost my appetite for cakes," answered Bakhtiar.

"I don't understand someone whose end has come and who'd still have an appetite for cakes," Arifin replied.

"Bakhtiar, Bakhtiar!" Nurbaya interrupted, shaking her head. "You'd better become a cake-maker, like Mevrouw Jansen, so your belly will always be full."

"My shop would fail within a week, for sure, because I'd eat all the cakes in it. I'd run off anyone who wanted to buy them from me, so that nobody got them but me."

At that, the group erupted into laughter.

"Fourth," said Arifin, "there is physical ruination. Bear in mind that if a horse that is too hot and thus excessively thirsty, or a person who has gone for four or five days without a thing to drink, is suddenly given too much to drink, this can bring the end to one's allotted span.

"And fifth, the most important of all and what I almost forgot to mention: don't get too tired from climbing later, just because you have been fascinated by my very interesting story."

"Sixth," cut in Bakhtiar, "since we have now arrived at the other side, we have to pay for renting the man's sampan," he said, taking out four coins from his pocket, which he gave to the boatman, before jumping onto the shore. His three companions followed suit.

"I see some sugar cane in that stall over there. Let's buy some! We'll definitely get thirsty along the way," said Samsu.

"I brought two bottles of fruit squash," replied Bakhtiar.

"It might be enough... but if not, where are we going to find water later on?" Sam asked.

And so, the group bought some sugar cane and began their climb.

Approximately 322 meters high, Mount Padang forms the northern end of a low mountain range that extends to the south of the town of the same name. The coast leading to Padang is precipitous in a number of spots and sparsely inhabited. The mountain begins at the Bukit Barisan range, which runs down the middle of Sumatra between its northwestern and southeastern ends. In fact, it is an offshoot of that range, which stretches to the west, right up to the Padang's shoreline.

The Dutch named Mount Padang, *Apenberg*—Monkey Mountain—because at its summit there live many tame monkeys that have for years amused the mountain's climbers. Visitors to the peak who call them over with offers of a banana soon find themselves surrounded by the creatures, approaching by the dozens and fighting for the chance for some food. The larger of the monkeys would even boldly snatch snacks from a climber's hand. Despite this, no one was brave enough to rid the area of the animals because the townspeople of Padang believed them to be a kind of numinous creature, best left undisturbed. If a monkey were murdered, the killer would surely die as well, they thought. And, if one of them were captured, its captor would be unable to find his way home. Likewise, some believed the creatures to be reincarnations of those who had died and were buried on the mountain, only to return in simian form.

To be sure, the mountain had many graves, while at its peak climbers could enter a cave with a shrine and make their vows to God. Once a year, right before Ramadan, and again on Idul Fitri, the mountain would become crowded with men and women visiting the graves of their loved ones, praying for their souls.

Though Mount Padang was, in many ways, a sad and mournful place, nevertheless the vistas from its peak were beautiful enough to make of it a joyous place. At the top, a tall flagpole could be seen set into the earth, with a flag fluttering in the wind nearly every Sunday. Near the flagpole a circular belvedere of lathwork had been fabricated, complete with benches and a table where climbers could relax. For cooling off after the climb, a swing had been erected. And all of it maintained and kept clean by convicts and enjoyed by the visitors who came to the mountain to relax or to exercise.

As Nurbaya and her friends reached the mid-point of the mountain, the climb became steep and she looked for a large rock on which to sit, calling out, "Wouldn't it be nice if there were a vehicle we could take right to the top?"

"What? We haven't even gone halfway up and you're already tired," Arifin said, unfastening the buttons of his shirt to let out the hot air radiating from his skin.

"If my bones were as big as yours, I wouldn't be saying this," Nurbaya replied.

"Ha! I suppose the time has come for me to give the reason for the gathering at my house last night, since I see you all crying from exhaustion," began Arifin.

"Yeah! Yeah!" Bakhtiar shouted. "Begin!"

"All right then, listen and pay close attention!" Arifin ordered, launching into his tale. "When the alarm sounded, I was with my parents on the rear veranda, about to eat. We were very startled because the sound was coming from the watchman's house, which is not very far from where we live. My father jumped up from his chair and shouted to the servant, 'Saban, get them to hitch up the buggy.' Then he went to his room to change his clothes. A moment later, he came out again and, buttoning his shirt, shouted, "All ready, Saban?"

"'All ready, sir,' answered the servant.

"My father went down the stairs, yelling at my mother, 'Go inside and shut the door!'

"My mom, looking very frightened, was unable to say anything at all, only 'Be careful', when she saw my father going down.

"Don't worry," he said, leaping into the buggy.

"So we stayed with Baki, since the stable boy wasn't at home. With the alarms going off more and more loudly, we all became very scared. My mother then ordered the doors and windows shut and we went into the living room. Because we were so terrified, we forgot how hungry we were."

"Yeah, that's right," said Samsu. "It was the same with us at our place: only the three of us and the servant. My father was away beginning at five o'clock in the afternoon. Just think, if anything had happened, how could we have held out? Luckily, Nurbaya's father came over and told us not to be afraid, because the person who had gone amok was a way off. Also, that if anything happened, he would come over immediately."

"That's what worried me," Arifin continued, "because, naturally, people who hold the positions our fathers do will have more enemies than friends.

Although I tried to get rid of my fear by saying this and that to my mother, or by reading a book, those horrible thoughts just wouldn't go away, especially since we could hear the clamor on the main street every once and a while.

"As time went on, the sound of the alarm grew stronger, as if to say that one more person had been stabbed. For two hours we remained in fear. It was only at about eleven o'clock that the sounds of the alarm grew quieter. Not long after that, they stopped altogether so that all the earlier uproar became a deep silence. It was only then that my fear pretty much went away, for I knew the rampaging person had finally been caught. But my father had not yet returned. My eyes began to grow heavy and without knowing it, I fell asleep on the chair. I think my mother couldn't shut her eyes because she was worried about my father, that something had happened to him."

"Police work sure is dangerous," Samsu said, "yet people often see *us* as the enemy!"

"But if we're good to the people of the district," Bakhtiar offered, "you wouldn't think we'd be seen as the enemy."

"For sure they'd like us better than people who are wicked. Even so, we're still hated," Samsu replied.

"But there's a way not to be hated: don't arrest and punish the guilty, but grant them their every wish, since, no matter how serious or light their crime, they certainly don't want to be punished. And if punishment is carried out anyway, they'll harbor a grudge in their hearts, especially if those who are punished are of high birth or rich and the ones punishing them are just commoners."

"If that were so, we wouldn't be what you call civil servants, but rather people who don't keep their oaths and promises, who cheat the Government, people who have a paid sinecure or 'steal their salaries'. If the Government found out about our behavior, we'd be sacked from our jobs, for sure," Arifin retorted.

"And what's more, how could we satisfy everyone?" he went on. "You can't meet the wishes of even two opposing parties. For example, a person who's not devout and learned in religion wouldn't want a prayer house built next to his home, because of the noise, he would say. But the person next door to *him*, who *is* fervently religious, would want one built there, so as to make his religious practice more convenient. How could you satisfy two such opposing wishes?"

"You certainly couldn't," replied Samsu. "Of course, for a civil servant, such issues remind us of the old saying, 'Damned if you do, damned if you don't'. It's as if not doing something would please your father but offend your mother. Would you choose to act or not?"

"For me, maybe I'd just avoid the situation all together," Bakhtiar offered.

"So, it looks like you love your father more than your mother," Nurbaya spoke up.

"That's not true, Nur. When it comes to that, I certainly love my mother more than my father, because she likes to give me a box of cakes every now and then, while he only likes to give me a box on the ear. And for me, eating cakes is a lot nicer than being boxed. But if my father were to die, my mother would not be able to make a living like him. True, she could remarry, but you really don't think my stepfather could love me like my real father, do you? So what'd happen to me after that? Could I even continue my studies?"

"All right, but if your father re-married after your mother died, what then?" Nurbaya asked.

"It wouldn't matter, because my father would still be here and could help me," Bakhtiar replied.

"If your stepmother loved you... But, if she hated you, as often happens in our neighborhood, she would surely bait your father, until even he would hate you. So, then what? You've lost your real mother and your father hates you. But if your mother were still alive, even if she were unable to help you or if she even remarried, her love for you would still be there. She could not be moved against you. Isn't there a saying, that, 'The love of a father towards his child is as long as the punting pole, which ends somewhere, but the love of a mother towards her child is as long as an unbroken road.'"

"Yes, that's true," answered Bakhtiar, looking worried, as though all of this could come to pass. "The very best thing would be if I never come across a situation like that and have my mother and father live until I get a job that can provide me with a livelihood."

"In fact, people who become Government employees have to be able to work like machines and do everything as best as they can," interjected Sam, as if trying to blot out Bakhtiar's unpleasant idea. "That means no looking to each other for help, no taking pity on anyone, no bias towards others, and no being tempted by money or presents and other such things."

"Are there such people?" Arifin wondered aloud.

"Scarcely one in a hundred, probably," said Samsu, "because it's very difficult to be that way."

"If that's true, then why are there so many people who want to work for the police? There're even some who do so without pay, even though they have to have the right clothes for work. Only after several years do they get a subsidy of five or ten guilders and then have to wait several more before being promoted to the position of clerk. Finally, when they're old enough, they get to be called police 'minister' or 'deputy prosecutor'," Arifin said.

"There are a lot of reasons for this. There are some who work seriously because they want to make a living and have no other motives. That's a good thing. But there are others who look at rank only because, as they see it, when they become civil servants, they have risen in position and are respected and feared by others. They can do as they please to the people of their village. But, I think people like that are neither admired nor respected. If they were, they wouldn't feel the need to act that way, nor would they strive so hard and spend all their money trying to gain position and glory, especially since, in this matter it's not the person but rather the position that is honored and exalted. That is, the honor and exaltation only last as long as the position. As soon as it ends, no one pays them any mind. The best thing would be if honor and glory didn't arise from power, but from a pure heart: the result of your own goodness.

"Then again, there are people who seek position from evil motives because they know great power comes with such a position. And in that way, they quickly and easily obtain everything they want. However, only those with crooked hearts think this way. Those who understand will certainly know their power is no greater than that of villagers, that their position is actually lower than those who don't make a wage. For *those* people are free and can do as they please. *They* don't need to follow orders, because they don't work for pay. If they do something wrong, it's not the civil servants that punish them, but the law. A civil servant is merely someone who gets paid by the government to exercise a certain authority, and those who do no wrong can't be punished by him in any honest way. Fortunately, not all civil servants are like that. Many function in their jobs with good intent. Honestly, there is much good that they can do as a result of this power.

"Well, I for one am not looking for honor, power or position," Bakhtiar suddenly interjected. "As long as I can make enough money, I'm not particular about what work I do. Call me a coolie, but give me enough pay."

"So that you don't run short of cakes, right? Even if they called you the 'cake thief', it wouldn't be a big deal," Arifin laughed, harassing his friend.

"What else are you looking for in this world, other than comfort and pleasure? Are you studying now to have problems later?" Bakhtiar retorted.

"Of course not," interrupted Samsu, hoping to calm his two friends, who looked as if they might square off against each other. "But where did we leave off in your story, Arifin? Please continue!"

"Right, but we'd better keep moving, because if we stay here, we won't make it to the top, even before Judgment Day. I'll carry on with my story as we go along."

And so, the four began to climb once again. After ascending a bit, Arifin recommenced his tale. "I hadn't been asleep for long when I awoke with a start, for I heard someone say, 'Keep your mouth shut or I'll knock you silly!'

"My whole body was trembling, because I thought it was the man who had gone amok, having seized my servant so he could have his way with us and, especially because, just before that, I heard the voice of someone mounting the steps of our house, knocking on the door and demanding it be opened. I was so scared, I didn't know what to do. I wanted to find a weapon to defend my mother and myself, but I couldn't. My feet felt so heavy they seemed nailed to the floor. When I tried to cry out for help, no voice would come because I felt like someone was choking me. Luckily, my mother bravely asked, 'Who's there?'"

"'Me,' came the answer from outside.

"Even though the voice sounded like my father's, my mother was still suspicious, so she asked again, 'Who's 'Me'?'

"'The Chief,' answered my father's runner.

"Only then was it clear that my father was outside, and only after my mother replied, 'Open the door, Arifin,' was I able to get up from my chair and go open the door. But I didn't let go of the crossbar so I could use it to hit whoever entered, if it wasn't my father. But, it was, in fact, my father. When he saw that I was still awake, he asked, 'Hey, not yet asleep?'

"'Not yet,' I replied, 'I was too scared to sleep.'

"'You should be a commander,' my dad said, smiling then ordering the lamps in his office be lit.

"After dinner, he began an investigation into the attack. It was then I saw the man."

"What did he look like?" Nurbaya asked.

"Ah, just like any ordinary person. One nose, two eyes."

"Yes, of course. But that's not what I meant. Did he look like a criminal or did he look like a person who was nice? Was he old or was he young? Was he from here or from another village?"

"I think he was a gambler, but still young. His hands were shackled and his shirt was torn and bloody. His face was pale, his body was trembling and his eyes moved back and forth wildly, as if he were still enraged."

"Yeow! I'd be scared if I saw someone like that," exclaimed Nurbaya, shuddering, for all her fine hairs were standing on end.

"Of course! Even I was afraid of getting close to him... afraid in case his insanity returned and enabled him to break his shackles."

"Yes, but without a knife, how could he break out?" Bakhtiar ridiculed Arifin.

"With his hands and teeth, just like you go insane with your cakes," Arifin shot back with a laugh.

"Where was he from and what started him off in the first place?" Nurbaya pursued her query, as if to extinguish the dispute between Bakhtiar and Arifin.

"Apparently, he comes from Kampung Sawahan. The cause of the quarrel was gambling. He lost quite a bit and went berserk," Arifin responded, ignoring Bakhtiar, who now frowned.

"How many people did he injure?" asked Samsu.

"Two. One of them died after being stabbed in the chest. The other was badly wounded in the head and was taken to the hospital."

"Poor fellow!" Nurbaya said.

"Why'd it take so long to catch him?" Samsu repeated.

"Because at first he ran off and hid, and when he was about to be captured, he fought back. But with so many people chasing him, he was overpowered in the end," Arifin replied. "After being questioned, the man was taken straight to jail."

"What do you think will be the outcome of the case?" Nurbaya asked.

"As I see it, the man will be punished with a ten-year exile from the village," Arifin answered.

"Hurray!" Bakhtiar cheered all of a sudden. "We're there."

And as it happened, the small group had nearly reached the summit of Mount Padang without realizing it, for the flagpole and the rest house were now in view. Once inside the house, Nurbaya threw herself down on a bench and sighed, "We're finally here!"

"As long as there is patience, confidence and reliance on God, an eternal purpose will surely be attained," Bakhtiar said slowly in reply, speaking with the voice of the pious and learned.

"But if we hadn't made the effort ourselves, then what?" Arifin asked, still giving Bakhtiar a hard time. "Could Teacher have gotten here without walking first? Could this pious and learned Teacher recite the Quran if he hadn't closely studied it first? And could he have become a drummer boy, because his stomach had been first filled, not with cakes, but with just patience, confidence and reliance on God?"

"There's no sense in talking to you. I'd better just go over there," Bakhtiar said grumpily, leaving the rest house and approaching the swing outside.

"Yes, go on and have a chat with the trees!" Arifin shot back. "What you say won't be refuted, because they aren't that good at answering. So, you can talk to your heart's content, all by yourself, like a person who... umm...," he trailed off, seeking out his own place.

Just then, Samsulbahri, who was still standing and looking eastward, turned his head slowly to the north and finally towards the west. His thoughts seemed very distant from his companions, far beyond the high mountains and across the deep ocean. It was as if some voice were whispering in his ear,

"Samsulbahri, gaze out and consider this land of your birth carefully, the place where your birthing blood was spilled, for soon you will be departing and leaving all this behind. You will be going far into the world of people not your own, and your journey will not be for one day or two, but for months and even years. And who knows, perhaps you will not be able to return home, for the fate of every creature on this earth is in the hands of God and their lives are as if hanging by a single strand of silk, one so delicate and fragile that occasionally the winds which stir up even soft zephyrs can break that suspending cord."

Whether he was moved by such thoughts, or merely impassioned by the beautiful view from the peak of the mountain, could not be read from his downcast eyes and gloomy expression, which seemed to possess an odd mixture of grief and joy.

The view from the top of Mount Padang was, indeed, very fine because from there one could see clearly where the shore and sea met. It appeared as a white line stretching from the foot of Mount Padang along a twisting, winding road to the north, sometimes veering out into the water, so that in a number of places lovely bays were formed to the right and left of capes.

In several spots, the coastline appeared to move and shift instantaneously, as the surf broke and white foam was hurled to the shore. Fishermen with their nets looked like ants moving here and there. How excellent seemed the bond between land and water, two substances that comprise the world, yet are so different in color, character and circumstance.

To the west and north appeared a vast and flat plain, nearly blue, across which in several places crouched, as it were, a row of small islands from north to south. It was like a very great lake, walled in by the white sky to the west. According to geologists, these islands had once been connected to Sumatra, in eons past, but because of the collapse of the ocean floor, the bridge between them sunk, leaving behind only a few islands.

To the east was the mainland, green and fully blanketed with coconut trees stretching into the distance like a vast plantation, as well as casuarina and almond trees soaring above the crush of palms, yearning to catch the wind and sunlight. Here and there, red and white roofs peered through gaps in the foliage. Near the foot of Mount Padang, houses and streets were laid out in straight rows that ran parallel to the Arau River.

Farther east, this large plantation was fenced in by mountains that stretched the length of the island of Sumatra, while to the north, tall peaks broke from the ridge, anointed by a white cloud: the summit of Mount Merapi in Padang Panjang, whose billowing smoke occasionally appeared when the weather was clear.

Every creature inhabiting this eastern land received its sustenance and pleasure, while only danger and death awaited in the watery west. Likewise, if the two sides were to trade places, they would quickly come to an end in their new homes. For his part, man had staked a foothold to the east, but would sink to the depths in the unforgiving west.

After brooding this way for a while, Samsulbahri suddenly gave a start, as if awoken from a dream, for he felt someone taking hold of his shoulder from behind, then heard Nurbaya's voice. "What are you looking at, Sam?"

"Ah, nothing in particular, Nur," he said, composing himself. "The view from here is truly wonderful. Look at those palm trees. They stretch out nearly without end and nothing in between. And that mountain range there, so mysteriously green in the east! And see that strand along the Pariaman, Tiku and Air Bangis villages that forms a clear line all the way to the north?"

"Yes, it really is very beautiful," she answered. "But there's not much to see on the ocean. Where are Pulau Pandan and Pulau Angsa Dua?"

"That one, way off, is Pulau Pandan and the one on this side of it is Pulau Angsa Dua," he replied, pointing to two islands lined up in a row.

"So, what the *pantun* says is true," Nurbaya remarked and then recited:

> *Pandan Island lies far out at sea*
> *its sight by Angsa Dua Isle conceals*

"Indeed. But how does the rest of the poem go?" she wondered.

"Ah, surely you know it, don't you? Don't pretend you don't," Samsu teased her. "Actually, it's an old *pantun* and it goes like this:

> *Pandan Island lies far out at sea*
> *its sight by Angsa Dua Isle conceals*
> *However broken the body may be*
> *Kindness is always the balm that heals.*

"But nowadays, young people have changed it to:

Pandan Island lies far out at sea
its sight by Angsa Dua Isle there conceals
However broken the body may be,
the light in your eyes my memory seals.

"Sure, it can go like that also. Whatever the need, just compose a *pantun*," Nurbaya said.

In contrast to her comment, the poem actually made her think of something important, only she did not reveal what it was. Turning her gaze away and back to the land, she said, "That high mountain there, what's it called?"

"Mount Merapi, I think," Samsu replied.

"The Mount Merapi that's near Padang Panjang?"

"Yes, between Bukit Tinggi and Padang Panjang. And do you know the *pantun* that's linked to Padang Panjang?"

"No," Nurbaya replied, her heart quickening its beat.

"It goes like this," Samsu said:

Padang Panjang is ringed by hills
Upon which hills, teak forests grow.
Love and affection are no mere frills,
from mouth to heart, love does flow.

Nurbaya suddenly blushed and had to bow her head and stare at the ground to conceal her face. If she had not heard Bakhtiar's call for help, her heart's secret might have been revealed, the secret that caused her cheeks to redden this way.

When Samsu heard his friend crying out, he ran without thinking towards the sound of the voice, frightened by what might have happened. Reaching Bakhtiar, he saw that his friend was being attacked by several rather large monkeys, who tried to grab the bananas he held in his hand.

Samsu picked up a length of wood and began beating the creatures, but was unable to drive them off, there were so many. In the end, he was forced to leave the bananas behind and, leading Bakhtiar out of the ring of long-tailed bandits, took him to the rest house. Along the way, they met Nurbaya, who had been following from behind, intending to help. A moment later, Arifin emerged from the bushes and ran towards them holding a bag in his hand. When he reached them, he called out, flustered and rushed, "Who was that calling? What's happening?"

When Samsu told him about Bakhtiar and the monkeys, Arifin roared with laughter and held his stomach, trying unsuccessfully to contain his glee. He even forgot how tired he was from running, he laughed so hard. But Bakhtiar paid no heed to Arifin's gibes, particularly as he had not yet fully recovered from his ordeal.

"Naturally, I supposed that our generalissimo here would have been braver in coming to blows with food than with monkeys. He rightly deserves to have his chest decorated with a star of monkeywood bark in honor of his incomparable valor," Arifin said, between laughs.

Though their hearts were still beating and their empathy stirred after seeing what had happened to their friend, Samsu and Nurbaya were unable to keep from laughing at Arifin's words. To hide his amusement, Samsu asked Bakhtiar, with feigned interest, how he came to be attacked by the monkeys. Bakhtiar said he had brought a bunch of bananas to give to the creatures. Suddenly, a crowd began to form on all sides, grabbing the fruit right out of his hands. Bakhtiar's blows seemed to have no effect, as some of the beasts even climbed on his shoulders and head. Finally, when the swarm had become too large and enraged, Bakhtiar cried out for help, as the bandits gnashed their teeth, bit at him and grunted.

"It was all because of your stinginess. You were afraid you wouldn't get any bananas. You thought you could just sit there by yourself, eating bananas in their presence, like the king of the monkeys, surrounded by all his ministers, commanders and servants, with only the scraps thrown to your people. Who'd have wanted that? When you finished, there wouldn't have been anything left, not even the peels. Naturally, your subjects weren't happy seeing you eating all by yourself. They wanted to join in the fun, because they were hungry, too. You should have said, 'My beloved young brothers! Please eat with your long-lost older brother,'" said Arifin, seemingly earnest. Nobody responded, while Samsu and Nurbaya looked the other way, to hide their laughter.

As Bakhtiar made no reply, Arifin spoke again, "Something's still not clear to me. Why didn't you just eat all the bananas? When they all were gone and in your stomach, what else could the monkeys have snatched? You're modest in front of monkeys, but not so in front of humans."

"Lucky I didn't eat those bananas," replied Bakhtiar, still shaken from the event, "if I had, they might have torn my stomach open."

"Yes, but wouldn't that have lightened the load in you and maybe cured your gluttony?" Arifin asked, seeing that Bakhtiar hadn't gotten angry yet.

"Don't be annoyed, Bakhtiar. If I had been nearby just then, I certainly wouldn't have helped you. Not because I wouldn't have felt sorry for you, but because the beautiful love I show you would be lost so quickly."

"That's just like you, pulling people's legs," replied Bakhtiar, "but, if something like this happened to you, maybe you'd be more scared than I was. You might be howling in tears. Just hearing your father's voice last night, you went stiff with fear."

"I wouldn't be howling in tears," Arifin retorted sarcastically, "but would just offer submission, asking forgiveness from the monkeys. I would raise the white flag, the sign of surrender, bow low, and give myself up in the hope of gaining their mercy. Let the king step down and become the prisoner. No matter, just so long as I weren't torn apart by monkeys."

"Oh, enough of this! Let's go to the rest house now. I'm hungry," said Samsu, striking off towards the house.

When they arrived, Arifin looked around. "Since I didn't get to see your war with the monkeys, show us your war with food! Here, I've brought a bag of rose apples. How many dozen can you vanquish with those sharp teeth of yours?" he asked, holding up the bag and laughing.

"Don't eat them plain! Let me toss them with some sugar, pepper and salt so they'll taste nicer," said Nurbaya.

"But not before eating bread," Samsu replied. "If not, we'll get stomach aches later on. Let's eat the fruit when it gets hotter outside. It'll taste better then."

"Bakhtiar's stomach won't get upset, even if he ate stones, 'cause he's used to beating down all kinds of food, even poisonous stuff," Arifin carried on, apparently unsatisfied with the torment he had already put his friend through. The mockery went unanswered by Bakhtiar, as his mouth was just then filled with bread.

When they finished eating, Bakhtiar announced his intention to shoot some birds, and went off with the rifle Samsu had brought. Samsu, for his part, worried about letting his friend go off on his own and told Arifin to accompany him. With that, Samsu and Nurbaya were left alone in the house: Nurbaya, because she wanted to make a spicy rose apple salad, and Sam, to watch over her.

After Nurbaya mixed the fruit with the sugar, salt and pepper in a large bowl, she covered it and shook its contents, tiring after a while so that Sam had to take over. They worked this way in turns until the fruit softened and Nurbaya was able to try it.

"That's enough, Sam. Too soft and it won't be nice. Try it!"

"You're right, it tastes good, but we should wait for Bakhtiar and Arifin."

"Of course! If not, Bakhtiar might think we've eaten some of his share."

They grew silent for a moment, until Nurbaya suddenly said, "I just remembered that promise of yours to tell me about the woman and her cat and the one about the hen that laid the golden egg. How do those stories go?"

"You've really never heard them?"

"Really, I haven't."

"Both are short tales that present in parable form the old adage, 'Every time there's something to be done or said, think first and weigh it in your mind carefully. When saying something, think first, before you make a mistake, because a mistake can bring unending regret. Regret beforehand and there's a gain. Regret later and it's no use.'

"The first story goes like this: There was once a woman who had a cat and a newborn she was still breast-feeding. One day, intending to go out, she left the child on top of its bed and told the cat to watch over it. When she returned, she saw the cat sitting in front of the house, its mouth smeared with blood. Her heart beating wildly, she dashed over to the child. She was too late: the baby was dead and covered with blood. She assumed the cat had killed her child and, without so much as a thought, gave vent to her rage and beat the animal to death. But when she lifted her child's body, she saw beneath it a snake, a very poisonous snake, which had been bitten to death by the cat. It looked as if the cat had defended the child from the serpent and then waited in front of the house, as if wanting to tell its mistress what happened.

"Right then and there, this woman was overwhelmed with the most bitter regret, since not only was her child dead, but her most loyal and beloved cat was gone as well."

"It's only natural that a mistake like that would lead to unending regret," Nurbaya said thoughtfully, her expression clouded by sadness.

"The story of the hen that laid golden eggs is even more of a parable, this time for those who are greedy and covetous," Sam went on. "It goes like this: There was a farmer who had several hens in his coop. One day, one of the hens laid a golden egg. I'm sure you can imagine, Nur, just how overjoyed he was. Because he was greedy, he wanted to get rich quickly and so he slaughtered the hen, thinking he could get all the golden eggs in the hen's stomach at once. But what to say? The hen's stomach was just like any other ordinary hen's and had not a single golden egg. If the farmer had waited patiently, on the second day, perhaps the hen would have laid another golden egg. Instead, his hen was dead, as were his hopes."

"A greedy person has to be punished like that," Nurbaya replied. "If he hadn't killed his hen, he might have received a golden egg each day."

"Maybe, but, Nur, since we got here we haven't moved from this spot. Don't you want to have some fun on the swing there?"

"Sure," replied Nur, "as long as it's you who swings me."

"Of course, who else? Arif and Tiar aren't here. I'll swing you for as long as you like," Samsu replied. They left the house and walked over to the swing, which was fastened to two tall, sturdy wooden poles.

"Don't push the swing too hard, Sam!" said Nurbaya, taking her seat.

"However you like."

After swinging for a while, Nurbaya suddenly shouted, "There's a steamship out at sea! You can see it from here."

Samsu immediately stopped the swing and they both looked for high ground from which to see the ship.

Now on a rock, the two could make out the ship, which must have just left Bayur Bay harbor, heading gently to the north, with its thick, black smoke billowing in the same direction.

"Where's it going, Sam?" Nurbaya inquired.

"To Aceh and Sabang, for sure. Maybe to Sibolga, too."

"Then on to where?"

"Back here and then on to Batavia. Its job is to go back and forth, carrying passengers and cargo from south to north."

"Maybe you'll be going to Batavia on that ship later on."

Hearing her words, Samsu's expression changed. His mood darkened and he was lost in thought for some time, saying nothing.

Nurbaya, surprised to see her companion affected like this, turned to Sam and asked, "Why are you so quiet all of a sudden, Sam? Do you feel ill?"

"No, Nur. It's only that you just mentioned the name of the place I'll be going to in three months."

"I suppose you're very happy and proud to be going to Batavia."

"Of course, Nur, of course! Because I'll get to see the capital of the Indies, the biggest and best town in the country. And there, also, I'll get the kind of education it takes to become a man of science. But... my heart feels heavy at the thought of leaving Padang, the land where I was born, where my birthing blood was shed, my native place. Because this is where my father and mother, my family and all of my friends are. I don't know who I'll be with there or what kind of people they'll be. Up to now, I've become used to my parents' protection, but there I'll be on my own."

"Of course, Sam. It's not easy being separated from everyone you know. But you won't feel awkward for too long. Every new beginning is difficult. After you've arrived in Batavia, all your difficulties will disappear and you'll be delighted by all the wonderful sights and sounds. Maybe you'll find a new mother and father to watch over you and new acquaintances, so that you'll gradually forget us," Nurbaya teased, smiling at Samsu.

"If you don't stop missing us, just comfort yourself with thoughts like these: 'I am here in Batavia only for a while, to pursue studies which will give me intelligence, position and a big salary. Therefore, my mind isn't going to be distracted by other things. After I have achieved my goals, I will return home immediately and be reunited with those I love."

"Think of the *pantun*:

> In the meadow there is a spring,
> surely you may use it to bathe in.
> If many years my life doth bring,
> Then surely, too, we will meet again.

"Mountain and valley shall never meet, but humans, as long as there is life in their bodies, surely will. Even 'the fish in the sea and the tamarind on the land meet in the sauce pan,'" said Nurbaya playfully, assuming her friend only feigned having a heavy heart about his voyage to Batavia.

"Maybe you think I'm just pretending," exclaimed Sam, "but, it's true, I'm *very* worried about leaving behind...."

At this point, he stopped, as if he were not brave enough to say the name of the person he worried about.

"Leaving behind who, Sam?" asked Nurbaya. "Is there someone here you're stuck on?"

"Leaving you, Nur," Sam blurted out.

"Me?" Nurbaya said, stunned.

"Yes, you."

Nurbaya tried to comprehend what she was hearing, then bowed her head low so as not to show the color rushing to her face.

"Don't misunderstand me, Nur! Listen to why I'm worried about leaving you. For several days now, I've been tormented by an unpleasant thought," Samsu said.

"Where does your thought come?" she asked, feigning a smile to blot out the change in her face that so mirrored the feelings in her heart.

"How could I not worry?" Samsu replied. "Last Friday night, I had a dream. I seemed to be climbing this same mountain. Reaching the summit, I suddenly felt I was in the big, bustling city of Batavia, in the middle of which was a lofty tower. An old man said to me, 'Hey, Samsu, if you want to get what you're after, climb up this tower."

"As I was about to climb the tower, I suddenly saw you following me, all alone. I waited for you, so we could climb together. Suddenly, there was Datuk Meringgih, pulling you back down and running off with you pressed up against him. In a rage, I pulled you from his grasp, and he and I fought. But he was stronger than I was and hurled me to the foot of the mountain. And because you wouldn't give in to him, you too were thrown headlong below. We fell, rolling and tumbling to the foot of the mountain and into a great hole from which we could not escape. At that moment, I woke up, startled and covered in sweat. I couldn't sleep for the rest of the night, and from that moment on, this dream hasn't left my thoughts."

"Ah! That's why I sometimes saw you off by yourself, brooding," Nurbaya exclaimed. "Don't put too much store in your dream, because dreams play tricks on us and don't always come true. They often lie and don't bear interpreting. Instead, let's get up and stretch forth our hands to God the Almighty, begging Him to keep us in His care in all things," she said, to comfort Samsu. However, her words did not match the worry in her heart, as Samsu's dream seemed to her very strange.

At that moment, Bakhtiar and Arifin came hurrying back from their hunt, like prey running from a beast in pursuit.

"What'd you get?" asked Nurbaya.

"*Sssshh*, quiet! Don't make a sound!" exclaimed Bakhtiar, hiding his rifle.

"Bakhtiar shot someone," Arifin said in a near whisper.

"Shot someone?" Samsu exclaimed, startled.

"Yeah, but I'll tell you about it later. Let's get home fast!"

"What about the food?" Nurbaya asked.

"We'll eat it quickly and then go back immediately," replied Arifin.

As they spoke, Bakhtiar hid the rifle in the grass, then came over to eat with them. Although he was famished, he couldn't bring himself to eat, so great was his fear. His face had gone pale and his hands trembled.

When they finished eating, Bakhtiar wrapped the rifle in the leaf of a banana plant so it would not be seen from a distance. The group then quickly descended the mountain.

Arriving at the spot where they first began, they stopped at a small shop to rest. It was there, a little while later, that they saw two soldiers coming down the mountain. One of them walked with a limp, clutching his left thigh.

The moment Bakhtiar and Arifin saw the soldiers, they hid themselves inside the shop. Within minutes, the two men were standing at the threshold, poised to enter.

"Does your leg still hurt?" the soldier asked his wounded friend. "We can rest here a minute."

"No need. We better get back right away, so we won't be late reporting to base," replied the man who had been shot.

"Who do you think shot you?"

"Kids, for sure, and if I catch them, I'll wring their necks."

They moved off, entering a sampan to cross the Arau River.

Only when the two soldiers reached the other side did Bakhtiar and Arifin dare to come out. "That's the one I just shot," Bakhtiar said.

"How did he get hit? Tell us!" exclaimed Nurbaya, whose face had gone quite pale.

"I was about to shoot some bulbuls in the bushes and I didn't see him, since he was standing behind a tree. When I fired, all of a sudden I heard someone yell, 'Ow! What the...? Help!' It was obvious I had hit one of those soldiers. I immediately ran off and hid."

"Really, just about everything happens to you, Bakhtiar! I haven't even gotten over my fright from you being attacked by the monkeys and now you go and shoot someone. If you'd gotten caught by them just now, then what?" exclaimed Nurbaya, shaking her head.

"I didn't do it on purpose, Nur. I thought his leg was a dark tree limb, because his body was hidden behind the tree. Who can be sure from a distance? But where was he was hit, Nur, when they passed by?" asked Bakhtiar.

"On the back of his left thigh," she replied. "It looked like he was bleeding and in pain: he kept holding on to his leg."

"Let's get home, because it's already one-thirty in the afternoon. Ali will be there for sure and my stomach's growling," said Samsu.

With that, they each drank a glass of fruit squash, crossed the river, and returned to their homes.

4

Putri Rubiah

On Sunday afternoon, while Samsu and his companions were out hiking on Mount Padang, Putri Rubiah took to sewing on the rear verandah of her house, seated on a woven grass mat. Her younger brother, Sutan Hamzah, sat nearby rolling a *nipah* leaf cigarette.

"What do you think of your brother Mahmud, Hamzah?" Putri Rubiah asked without looking up from her work.

"I think he acts very differently now."

"That's what I think, too. He comes here less and less often and pays less and less attention to Rukiah and me or the other members of the family. It's as if he's afraid of coming here. He says it's because he has so much work to do and worries his performance won't garner a high mark. Do you think that's true?"

"Hah, what a lie! Isn't he a district head here? Why aren't the heads of other districts like him?" asked Sutan Hamzah.

"I often think that, too. Naturally, I like his position and it must be maintained properly so our family name doesn't become blemished. But traditional behavior and thinking shouldn't be changed for that reason. Just think! Rukiah and I are his dependants, but he doesn't care about us, he never socializes with us, never comes by to see how we're doing, let alone provide for us. In short, he places no importance on us at all. The only ones he looks after, cares for, and attends to, are his wife and child. If something were to happen, if we were in danger, 'though said once, may Allah avert this a thousand times!', what then? One of us would probably die," she said, with a trace of sadness in her voice.

"Word has it he is going to send his child to Batavia, to the Java Doctors' School," she continued. "He treats the one who is *not* his dependent as if he were, while ignoring the one who is. If the mother's older brother can't provide for the child, as is our custom, so be it. Help the child out of pity then. But you must never forget your obligations. In fact, that must be thought of before all else."

"Young Samsu is going to Batavia?" Sutan Hamzah asked, astonished.

"Yes, in three months. And from there, who knows where else? Maybe to Holland. What he wants to make of that child, I have no idea."

"A general, most likely," Sutan Hamzah said in jest.

"Doesn't all that eat up a lot of money? That's probably why he rarely gives me any when I ask. He just says he doesn't have any. What does he spend that big salary on? Naturally, it should all go to his wife and child. Why does he have to improve his child so much? The Dutch school here is more than adequate. How many people are there who can attain high positions without knowing Dutch, anyway? Our own father, what was he good at? He almost couldn't write. So how did he manage to hold the position of Chief Minister of State? Who among the district heads here in Padang speaks good Dutch? Not one of them. Doesn't it all depend on a person's destiny and fortune? If fortune favors you, even if you're not good at anything, you'll certainly still obtain a position. But if your lot in life is bad, even with skills reaching to the sky, into the cesspit you'll fall just the same."

"The way I see it, that child is not destined for good things. All the efforts of our brother, Mahmud, will be in vain. Just keep in mind the saying, 'When the charcoal runs out, the iron is ruined,'" replied Sutan Hamzah, drawing on the cigarette he had made.

"What do you mean by that?"

"There's a mark on him. He will die a bloody death as our enemy."

Putri Rubiah sat quietly pondering her younger brother's words for a while, then said, "I wish the Dutch school here were good enough for him. After that, put him in an office as a clerk or whatever. Even if there's no money in it, it won't matter at first. Later on, of course, he'll rise in rank and then command a large salary, as long as he's lucky. Don't we have a saying for this? 'Misfortune cannot be avoided; good luck cannot be snatched'. After choosing a course of action, devote yourself to it! But this fellow doesn't do that, because he wants to develop his child to the utmost. He's practically meddled with our ancestors' possessions."

"Our ancestors' possessions?" Sutan Hamzah exclaimed, looking up. "I'll have to see whether he'll be so bold as to liquidate them. Though I don't hold rank, I'm not afraid to oppose him."

"That's what worries me, day and night, to the point that I often can't sleep. I'm afraid he might really do such a thing and make us all quarrel, brother against sister. Not only would that sort of thing be bad in itself, but I'd feel ashamed if others found out. It wouldn't be proper for people as well-born as we are to act like that," she said with a sigh.

"But if it can't be avoided, what can we do? Don't be afraid! I'll be the first to come out against this when the time comes," Sutan Hamzah said fiercely. "Of course, he's always without money and beset with difficulties like that. That's because he's stupid and crazy. Why does he make a dependant of someone who doesn't need to be, someone who is, moreover, sent all over to study? That's what people call 'shouldering stones, for want of a load'. Who'd want to do that nowadays? Just him. He supposes people will praise him for it. He doesn't realize he's being mocked and ridiculed behind his back.

"And why won't he accept marriage proposals from other families or take on more than one wife? Isn't it all because of money? Each time he got married, he'd receive two or three hundred rupiah in proposal money, so why would he even need a salary anymore? If all the money gets spent, marry again. What's the problem with having lots of wives and children? After all, an aristocrat need not look after and provide for his wife's children. That is someone else's responsibility. What's the use of a high birth and position if they don't get you anything?

"Look at me! Even without a position I never go hungry and my pockets are never empty! When I go to one of my wives' houses, there's always delicious and refined food available, and clean clothes as well. If I go for a walk, my pockets are filled with cigarettes and anything else I might need. If I feel like taking a buggy some afternoon, one of my parents-in-law prepares one. Every pleasure is arranged and no desire is prohibited. What more could I wish for? Wouldn't a man be stupid to dislike such customs and traditions?"

"Of course, you're my true and genuine brother, someone who understands custom and tradition and defends our ancestral inheritance. You appreciate how exalted our noble birth is and you perform your obligations toward your sister and niece," said Putri Rubiah, heaping praise on her younger brother.

"What burdens do I have?" exclaimed Sutan Hamza. "Even if I had dozens of wives and hundreds of children, no payments need come out of my pockets, for my wives all have parents and uncles. And the same goes for my children. None of these are my responsibility. If my parents-in-law are unable or unwilling to keep on supporting me, I'll just divorce their child and marry another woman, a woman of means. By getting two or three hundred guilders in proposal money, my pockets are kept full. Not like our older brother, Mahmud. Let's not even talk about his prospects for *getting* money, he loses and wastes even what he has. Why did he throw away his good birth and position? He has enough problems with just one wife and child. What would happen if he had as many as me? God forbid he die of exhaustion under such conflicting conditions. Because I, though younger than him, have already had ten wives and eighteen children.

"In spite of all that, I never feel inconvenienced or short of money, and don't go borrowing here and there. And isn't it better, the more children one has? There would be more offspring and more persons of high birth here in Padang. Even in the Quran, having four wives at a time is permitted. Why doesn't he observe that if he's a true Muslim? They say he's resourceful and clever because he's been to school and has a high position, but his own cleverness makes life difficult for him. Wouldn't it be better to be stupid like me? I never have problems and never make trouble for other people.

"He sends his child to this school and that to study this and that subject, but in the end, what will the child become? A king? Impossible. Though his position be the highest of the high, as long as he receives a salary, he'll always have a superior. He won't be able to do as he pleases. He'll have to obey whatever order comes from above. Day or night, in sickness or comfort, the work will go on. There's no saying, 'No'. If he's disinclined to work he's sure to be sacked or receive a bad reputation. But me? Free as a bird, subject to no limitations or orders, doing as I please, 'a sovereign at heart and a noble in his own eyes', as they say. Even if I slept the whole day or just sat around chatting with friends, enjoying life day in and day out, or going where I pleased, there'd be no one to stop me. So, is it the case that a man with knowledge and learning and high position is more content than someone who is stupid and of low rank? Here's your example, right here. No need to go looking for one. Just compare me and our older brother Mahmud.

"Of course, his child Samsu has to be educated in various places to pursue knowledge, otherwise there'd be no way for him to make something of himself. A person like him has to sweat and slave away if he's not rich, because he's not fully well-born. But to my thinking, even if that child does not become somebody, so what? He's not our dependent. The person who should be ashamed is his mother's older brother, his *mamak*. For that reason, I've always wondered why his *mamak* doesn't take on the responsibility of educating him. Furthermore, whose fault is it that our brother, Mahmud, ended up having that child? Who told him to marry that common woman? Were there not enough good ladies here in Padang? What's the use of focusing on good looks, if there's no breeding behind them? Imagine! If he had married a lady of the aristocracy, his child's social status wouldn't have been degraded: he would have remained a noble. Instead, the boy's a half-breed."

"That's what I find amazing. I can't image what he's thinking right now. Aren't these our ancestors' customs and traditions?" Putri Rubiah asked. "Why wouldn't he follow them? I'm ashamed to have such a brother. If you didn't know better, you'd say my brother is unpopular with women because of some defect. When I told him he'd gone astray in his thinking, he replied, 'Only animals take on more than one mate.' Just imagine! Was that a fitting reply to be uttered in my presence?"

"That was his answer?" asked Sutan Hamzah, his face beginning to flush.

"Yes, it was."

"So, all the men here in Padang are animals, because they all have many wives! He's the only one with just one wife. If that's what he says, then he really has gone crazy and his brain has slipped to one side. Perhaps he's consumed some potion someone had prepared for him without knowing it. He's forgotten who he is and where lies the true path," replied Sutan Hamzah, shaking his head.

"We're of the same mind on this. My feeling is that there's more going on here than meets the eye,'" Putri Rubiah said while glancing at her brother.

"I now know why he hates seeing us. He even criticizes my daily work," Sutan Hamzah replied.

"What work?" his sister asked.

"According to him, it's not proper for the high-born to gamble and play with fighting cocks. But isn't that what princes and wealthy merchants do? Only those without money and breeding receive wages and fear starving to death. But surely he can't mean I'm one of them."

"Of course not," she replied. "A person of high birth doesn't have to work for a living. Rather, seeking pleasure and enjoyment is his work."

"Let's talk about what we should do with Mahmud. How best, in your view, to make him return to normal? Because, after all, he's still our brother and we can't simply repudiate him. Everyone knows that. If anything happens to him, we'd be implicated and our good name would be smeared. If we make trouble for him, it'll only come back to haunt us."

"If he has been affected by some sorcery we're the ones who will have to treat him. That's our obligation as his family. We can't be hostile to him, as this would surely make his illness all the more serious, because he wouldn't find help from any other quarter. If he were to have an accident—let's hope that never happens—but if, for example, he departs this world or becomes sick, his wife won't be the one to suffer, we will. That's the truth, and this district head of ours won't even consider it. Now, what do you think?" Putri Rubiah inquired.

"We should look for a sorcerer, skilled in the use of herbs and potions, to treat and cure him," her brother replied.

"Do you know of such a person?"

"Yes, I do. His house is close by. They call him the Champ."

"Is it possible he's home now? Have Abu go and look for him. Perhaps he's at home. Let's tell him to come here right away so we can get this done quickly."

"Abu!" shouted Sutan Hamzah.

When the servant came, Sutan Hamzah spoke to him softly so as not to be overheard.

"Abu, go get the Champ. If he's home, ask him to come here quickly. There's something we want to discuss with him. If anyone else is there, wait until they've left so that no one knows you're summoning him."

"Yes, sir," Abu replied, before leaving.

"When he comes, you should tell him to cast a spell to see whether our district head really has been affected by someone's sorcery. If he has been, have the Champ free him from whatever's been done to him. Then you should tell the sorcerer to make Mahmud hate his wife," Putri Rubiah said very quietly.

"Of course," her brother replied. "What's the use of a woman like that? Only good for her looks. She has no property and is of low birth. In my opinion, a woman like that is useless. I'm sure she's cast a spell over Mahmud. If not, he would never have submitted to her and arranged for even more education for his child. Surely, she's the one who constantly stirs up his hatred of us. She's afraid Mahmud will marry again and she'll be of no more use. That wicked woman really is merciless. Not only has she subjugated her husband, but he doesn't even think the way he used to," Sutan Hamzah said, once again shaking his head in disbelief. "Have you discussed Rukiah with him?"

"I have."

"What was his reply?"

"He said, 'All right'."

"How much must he pay?"

"According to him, three thousand guilders."

"That's sufficient, just so long as the arrangements aren't too extravagant. I'll be responsible for everything involved in the procession. But where is he going to get that amount from? Not from pawning or selling our ancestral possessions, I hope."

"No," Putri Rubiah replied. "He's pledged his house and land in Kampung Java Dalam to Datuk Meringgih."

"Let him do what he likes with his house. Rukiah wouldn't get it anyway, since it's said to be registered in his wife's name. Just think! Is that right?

That property he acquired with his own labor should be registered in his wife's name, so his niece can't get to it? Ah well, so be it. It doesn't matter! When he dies, all of that can be seized anyway, because everyone knows it belonged to him."

They hadn't been talking for long when Abu returned with the sorcerer. Sutan Hamzah invited him to enter the middle room. After closing the front and back doors, he sat next to the man and offered him some cigarettes before saying, "I invited you here, Champ, my brother, because there's something important I'd like to request. However, before I reveal what's in my heart, I ask that you not mention what I'm about to say to anyone."

"Of course not. How could I be so bold?" the sorcerer replied. "I fear the district head."

"That's what I was hoping, especially as this matter concerns the district head himself, my older brother," Sutan Hamzah said.

"Which matter is that?"

"Aren't you surprised at my older brother's behavior, behavior that differs so starkly from that of other district heads? Particularly, his not wanting to accept marriage proposals and his lack of desire to marry again, together with his disregard for his niece and sister, who is my older sister."

"To tell you the truth, the others and I have long been puzzled by that. While other district heads have four wives, this gentleman has only one. It's unbecoming for such an important person," replied the sorcerer.

"You see, if the Champ and others think this way, just imagine how his niece and his own brother and sister, of the same womb, feel. He's the only one who doesn't sense that he's done something wrong, For that reason, we suspect my elder brother has been struck by someone's sorcery, leading him to change his ways. If it's true, naturally I can't just stand by and let that happen."

"I completely agree, he must be helped."

"In that case, I hope that you are willing to think the matter over."

"All right," replied the Champ. "I'll need some incense and a burner for it, along with a large bowl of fresh water and seven yellow betel leaves."

"I shall bring them," Putri Rubiah interjected, rising to find the items. She returned a moment later.

After the Champ had burned the incense, he recited several mantras, before wafting smoke over the bowl three times using different leaves, which he then placed into the bowl, reciting all the while. Taking the leaves back out one by one, he examined them closely and said, "It's true what you suspected, sir. The change in the gentleman's behavior is indeed due to someone else's actions. Because of the strength of that sorcerer's spell, the gentleman is no longer free to do as he wishes but must abide by the will of whoever did this."

"What did I say? Wasn't I right?" Putri Rubiah exclaimed. "Who did this?"

"It's someone the district head knows. A person of the house and apparently very close to him," the Champ said.

"A woman or a man?"

"A woman."

"If so, it *has* to be his wife, for there's no other woman in his house."

"I was thinking the same thing," offered Sutan Hamzah.

"Now, what can we do to free him from these bonds?" Putri Rubiah asked.

"There's no other way than to treat him with amulets and potions," the Champ replied.

"Yes, but he also has to hate his wife, so that he divorces her. That's a fitting requital for a woman like her!" she exclaimed.

"Leave the matter to me. I will certainly assist with this to the best of my ability. I have only one request: is there a shirt or coat of the district head's that I can borrow or a sarong he's worn?" the sorcerer asked.

"I think so. Let me see," replied Putri Rubiah as she rushed off to find the clothing. A moment later, she returned with a *Balanipah* sarong and said, "Here! He left this a while ago. I suppose he forgot to take it back with him."

"May I take it? It will be useful when working on her."

"You may! Take it with you!"

"Also, I'll need some hair from the district head's esteemed wife. One strand is enough. If a hating spell doesn't work, I'll work straightway on an infatuation charm, for it seems the resistance of her protection spell is quite strong. May I work on her until she goes mad?" the Champ asked.

"That would be even better," replied Sutan Hamzah, "It doesn't even matter if she dies. There's no need to take care of a woman like that. Once she goes mad or dies, my brother will surely be willing to marry again."

"In the matter of the hair, I'll go by his house a little later for it," Putri Rubiah explained.

She then brought out cakes and coffee for the sorcerer. After eating, the Champ was given the sum of one *ringgit* for his trouble, after which he excused himself and went home.

5

Samsu's Journey

"Ali, it's nearly dark. I think we'd better start lighting the lamps," Samsu said to the coachman as they stood in his parents' house. At the time, Samsu was dressed as if he had to go somewhere important.

"Yes, sir," Ali replied, before going in search of matches.

"Have Amat come help you," Samsu called after him.

A little while later, the coachman came with Amat and lit the lamps on the front veranda.

"All the lamps have to be lit, Ali," Samsu said. "Throughout half the house and on the back veranda. And you, Amat, take the flower pots down below and set up those tables and chairs. That's where the dancing will be, and there can't be anything in the way."

The two servants did what they were told and, once finished with the rear verandah, were instructed to set up two long dining tables in the middle room. Samsu explained that enough chairs had to be brought in and the tables covered with white linen cloths decorated with flowers.

While they were thus occupied, Nurbaya arrived, exquisitely attired and carrying two wreaths made from various types of flowers, all well-matched in color. "Not finished yet, Sam?" she asked.

When he heard these words, Sam looked around, and catching sight of Nur, was for a moment rendered speechless. His face, at first a portrait of high spirits, suddenly clouded over with sadness. If Nurbaya had not quickly spoken, her arrival might have brought tears to his eyes.

"Are you not feeling well, Sam?" she asked.

Only then, as if startled, did Samsu pull himself together and, steadying himself, reply, "You look so pretty today, Nur, I lost track of myself for an instant."

"I dressed this way on purpose, because I won't see you again tomorrow afternoon," she replied with a smile.

Far from consoling him, these words only seemed to deepen Samsu's feeling of gloom and melancholy. "That's true," he said tersely, before looking down.

Nurbaya went to him and, taking hold of his shoulder, said, "Come, Sam! We have to have a good time tonight. If you, the host, are all grief and sorrow, what'll happen with the guests when they arrive?"

"You're right, Nur, but I can't help it. I've been feeling down since yesterday, no matter how much I try to talk myself out of it. The closer I get to tomorrow, the more miserable I feel. In a little while, I'll explain what I'm feeling right now."

Just then, Bakhtiar entered the middle room, took off his Panama hat and bowed so low his head came almost to his knees. "Greetings, you ladies and gentlemen, all!" he exclaimed.

"How many ladies and gentlemen are here, Bakhtiar?" Nurbaya asked.

"There are one hundred and *one* ladies and one hundred and *one* gentlemen," Bakhtiar replied, emphasizing the word "one".

"H... e... e... e... y, you've arrived early! How very diligent of you," Samsu said to his friend.

"Done intentionally, master of thy servant. This early arrival is to make sure that everything is in order and ready for the arrival of all the gentlemen and lady guests invited here for a good time," Bakhtiar said, affecting his speech and bowing low again.

"Liar!" shouted Arifin, who had been standing behind Bakhtiar. "Mr Bakhtiar first wants to see whether or not lots of food has been prepared. If there's not enough, he'll just go back home, afraid his stomach won't get its fill. He said so in the buggy just now."

"Of course, you can't keep a secret, Arifin. I told you clearly not to let anyone at all know of my real intentions. And now you've revealed my secret to the first people you meet and later on you'll tell everyone for sure.

I feel ashamed, especially in front of Ms Nurbaya, to be seen coming here only for the cakes," Bakhtiar said, feigning anger and embarrassment.

"There's no need for you to weep, Bakhtiar, just because you're ashamed," Nurbaya joined in. "That secret of yours is a secret no longer. I've known this for a long time already. If you don't think there's enough food, even for ten Bakhtiars, come, I'll take you to the back, just for a quick look. But you have to promise and swear you'll restrain your craving and not touch the food," Nurbaya joked, approaching Bakhtiar.

Bakhtiar scratched his head and thought, "It's true: I'm really too interested in seeing everything I'll be tasting later on, but can I stop myself from taking some now?"

"As if I couldn't hold my cravings in check!" he replied loudly to Nurbaya, though it was obvious from looking at him he would not be able to keep to his word. He then took off his hat, raised his hand high and, standing at attention, swore, "In the name of all the cakes I love, especially spiced layer cakes, yellow cakes, tarts, steamed white-flour cakes, *srikaya* cakes, and cream puffs and such, I swear in front of three witnesses that I will not disturb the food in back. If I do not keep this promise, let my stomach and the stomachs of the next seven generations after me forever be filled with them."

"Good!" Nurbaya responded, smiling. "That's a strong oath, but it doesn't imply anything bad for you. Guilty or not, your stomach will be filled with cakes. No matter! I'll take you there!" And holding Bakhtiar's hand, she made to go to the kitchen with him.

"Don't believe it!" yelled Arifin. "I could see it in his eyes: he's not going to abide by his oath. I know another way, a much better way, and that's to tie his hands behind his back."

"You're really too much, Arifin!" Bakhtiar exclaimed, pretending to grumble. "As if I'd be so foolish as to violate an oath like that! Naturally, I'd be afraid of sinning against all those tasty cakes."

"I don't believe it," Arifin repeated, coming forward to tie Bakhtiar's hands behind him with a handkerchief. That accomplished, Bakhtiar was led away by Nurbaya.

"Ali," Nurbaya went on as she led Bakhtiar, "put these floral arrangements in the vases and place them on the dining table."

"Very good, Miss," Ali replied.

In the back of the house, Nurbaya showed Bakhtiar the food and cakes and drink that had been prepared and set on several tables, each with its distinct color and smell.

"I bought all of that at the Jansen's store and arranged it. Is it enough for you?" asked Nurbaya.

Seeing the delicious spread, a seemingly irresistible desire arose within Bakhtiar to taste it all. Had his hands not been tied, he undoubtedly would have forgone his oath, no matter its strength, and fallen on the cakes. But what could he do now? Nothing with his hands, surely, so he just walked along, moving from table to table, consoling himself with the thought, "How nicely they made this cake! I wonder what it would taste like? And this one, it smells so delicious," he said of one cake in particular, stopping to sniff the air around it.

Driven on by his cravings—and before he could even think of his oath—he sunk his teeth into the cake, pulling off a chunk that left a gaping hole. Icing now covered his nose and lips, indeed his whole face.

When Nurbaya saw what happened, she pulled Bakhtiar back, saying, "Have you gone crazy, Bakhtiar?" only to burst out laughing when she saw his face smeared with icing. Samsu and Arifin, standing at the ready outside, rushed to the back at the sound of her laughter.

Once they got there, Nurbaya explained why Bakhtiar's face had the look of a mask. The two young men roared with laughter. Arifin held on to his stomach, the sight of his friend standing there with the look of a court jester just too much to bear. Only Bakhtiar remained silent, either too ashamed or too remorseful to say anything. But that did not stop him from licking the cake off his face and swallowing.

After they all had had enough of laughing at Bakhtiar, Arifin said, "This is a major crime. First of all, he didn't abide by his oath and, second, he stole using his mouth. Even very dangerous thieves only steal using their hands. Because Bakhtiar's skill will provide a bad example to other criminals, he must be punished with a punishment equal to his crime. Let's be his judges! What's a good punishment for him?"

"I know a good punishment," said Nurbaya. "He can't have any cake later on, because he has already eaten his portion."

"No, not that!" replied Samsu. "That would be too hard on him. I'd be afraid he'd go wild if he saw all his friends eating delicious things when he could not."

"Plus, who could guarantee he'd undergo his punishment obediently, unless they were to bind him hand and foot?" put in Arifin.

"I have a better idea, but don't reveal it yet, otherwise he'll know our secret. You'll see in a bit!

"Are you willing to accept my punishment?" Arifin asked.

"All right, just so long as I can have some cake later, too," Bakhtiar replied, pretending to cry, all the while licking at the icing that clung to his mouth.

"Good! Just be patient!" Arifin said.

Not long afterwards, they heard several guests arriving on the front veranda. Samsu and Nurbaya went out to greet their classmates from the Dutch school, inviting them to sit and then laughing and chatting in an animated scene. As the group moved inside, members of the orchestra gathered together to play a marching tune.

While they were having such fun, Arifin brought Bakhtiar into their midst. At first everyone was stunned, for they had no idea what this spectacle before them was all about. But once Arifin told them the story of Bakhtiar's stealing the cake with his mouth, tumultuous laughter shook the crowd in a seemingly unstoppable fit. Only then did Arifin release Bakhtiar from the knots binding his hands. No sooner was Bakhtiar released than he took the icing that remained clumped to his mouth and flung it straight into Arifin's face. He then ran off to wash his own face, followed by Arifin, who had everyone doubled-up in laughter all over again.

A moment later, the band struck up and a waltz commenced. The young schoolmates partnered off and began to dance, including Samsu, who led Nurbaya by the hand to the dance floor. After twirling with Samsu, Nurbaya took turns with Arifin and Bakhtiar, both of whom kept the jokes flowing even while moving about. By turns standing and dancing and sitting and chatting, all the while bursting with laughter or telling jokes, the group passed the evening in delight.

In the meantime, tasty cakes were being served to the guests, along with coffee, tea, chocolate, fruit squash and lemonade.

Bakhtiar, pretending to be a houseboy, helped serve the food and drink, but only after stuffing as many cakes as he could fit in his shirt and trouser pockets, which, by now, were fairly bulging. Without his knowing it, Arifin had hung a broad piece of paper from the end of his shirt that read, "Here I am, The Cake Monster". The students' laughter at Bakhtiar was all the more uproarious as he had no idea what was tickling them so.

When he discovered what Arifin had done, Bakhtiar began plotting his revenge. An idea came to him and he rushed off to the kitchen to ask for some flea peppers, very hot, for he knew how much Arifin disliked them. He sprinkled a few pepper seeds between slices of a layer cake, covered them neatly and placed the cake on a plate. He then brought it to Arifin and, with enough politeness to dispel any suspicion on the other's part, said, "If the master of thy servant would be so willing, kindly partake of this sweetmeat!" Everyone smiled at Bakhtiar's words.

Without giving it a moment's notice, Arifin plunged on the cake. After just two or three bites, he let out a sudden shriek as the fire from the seeds began to spread across his tongue. The cake in his gaping mouth fell suddenly to the floor. With spittle and tears flowing down his face, it was all he could do to beg for water to cool his burning throat.

The guests, in an uproar from not knowing what had caused all the commotion, soon convulsed with laughter upon learning Bakhtiar had tricked Arifin into eating the peppers.

As the clock struck nine, the group proceeded to the middle room and sat down to dinner. The soup and wine were served first. One of Samsu's companions rose and, holding a glass of wine, offered a toast. He began by congratulating Samsu, Arifin and Bakhtiar, in the name of everyone present, for having finished their studies at the Dutch school and continuing on at the Java Doctors' and Overseers' schools. He hoped with all his heart they would advance in their studies, so they might one day attain a high position and enjoy the pleasures of the days to come.

For as long as they had all known the three comrades now about to leave, he went on to say, there had never been a quarrel with any of them. There was only friendship and affection instead. For that reason, he was convinced the three of them would make new friends and acquaintances right away in

Batavia. So they would not easily forget their friends and acquaintances in Padang, he presented each with a group picture of the students and teachers of the school in Pasar Ambacang. Finally, he wished them a safe and peaceful journey and long and healthy lives, praying they would one day return to Padang in the positions they now hoped for. At that, everyone cheered, "Hip, hip, hurrah!" three times, and the music started up in response.

Samsu rose to respond. First, he expressed his thanks to all his companions for their presence there that evening and for the mementos the three of them had been given. He promised to hold the photo very dear and to always think of the friends and acquaintances he would be leaving behind in Padang, who had helped so much and were a source of great pleasure to him. He hoped they would all complete their studies quickly so they could continue their education at a higher level and promised to send souvenirs after he arrived in Batavia. Then he bade them a peaceful stay in Padang, success in their studies, and a long life. At the end of his speech, he cheered three times.

Then they dined. First, the soup and then croquettes, after that, potatoes, salad and cakes, and all of it topped off with fruit and coffee. Throughout dinner, Arifin and Bakhtiar never let up with their jokes and foolishness, causing many diners to cough hard from swallowing the wrong way. After dinner, the guests strolled about the front yard in the moonlight, as that evening there was a full moon. They danced some more and laughed until midnight, when the group finally began to disperse and go home. Those who were staying behind in Padang wished a safe and peaceful journey to those who were leaving and vice versa.

As Nurbaya was getting ready to leave, Samsu approached her and said, "Let me take you home. It's very late and it's not good for a woman to walk by herself in the dark."

Nurbaya agreed and the two of them walked slowly toward her house. At that time, the moonlight shone as bright as day. The stars were like bezoars glittering in the heavens or fireflies swarming in the dark. Clouds moved in a solemn procession, one after the other, from west to east.

"The moon is so bright," Samsu said as they walked along. "It only adds to my sorrow and the heaviness of my thoughts, making it harder for me to leave Padang. In fact, since yesterday it hasn't made me feel any better to think of seeing distant places and pursuing higher studies. The closer I get to departure, the more broken inside I feel."

"What's troubling you? Everything has been prepared. All you have to do now is leave. When you get there, you'll study. And after you've finished your studies, you'll surely be given a high position and a good salary. All we'll be able to do is stare and admire you from afar. Being away from your mother and father and from all of us will, of course, be hard on you, at first. But, I think you'll adjust quickly to the new situation. And after you've gotten used to it, it won't feel like such a difficult separation. Chin up! Don't think too much about it."

"Sure, sure, but there's one thought which troubles me, one that always crosses my mind, and which I'm unable to forget, day or night."

"And what thought is that? Is there someone or something that's caught your heart so much you can't leave?" Nurbaya asked, looking Samsu straight in the eye.

"It's not that, Nur. The time we were on our way up Mount Padang, I told you about my dream. From then on, those troubling thoughts won't leave me alone. For several nights now, I haven't been able to sleep well. I keep recalling that dream. It's like danger is spying on us and following us wherever we go, waiting for the moment we separate to pounce. That's what lies so heavily in my heart and what makes me so anxious and worried. If I forget the promise I made to Father to go, there's no question I'd prefer to stay and watch over you."

While talking and walking this way, they arrived at Nurbaya's home and sat side by side on a bench under a shady tree in her garden.

"As I've said before," Nurbaya said somewhat forcefully, "don't trust these dreams too much, because dreams don't always mean something. What harm could come to us? I mean, we haven't committed any sin or any crime against anyone. If we're truly ill-fated, what more is there to say? Because all that is decreed by God the Almighty. Whether we like it or not, if that's our fate, it can't be changed. Who can change what's written on the tablet of fate?

"So, take good care of yourself and let's ask the Lord of the Universe to protect and keep us in all things. If you torment yourself with such thoughts, you won't get ahead in your studies later on, that's for sure. And *that* would be a pity!

"When you become a doctor, how proud your father and mother will be to see their son and his friends attain high positions. If you still find it hard to leave Padang just ask to work here instead so you'll always be close to those you love."

"You have no idea how I feel right now. That's probably why you're making this sound so simple. I guess I think about this differently than you do, so you don't see what I see," Samsu replied.

"So, what *are* you thinking?" Nurbaya asked, looking into Samsu's eyes.

"Nurbaya, tomorrow I'm leaving Padang for a place full of strangers and who knows whether I'll come back or not, so, I think I should open my heart to you. Nur, I want you to know that I'm in love with you. I've kept this feeling hidden within me for a long time. I'm only revealing it now because I feel you ought to know before we part. Who knows, maybe I'll never be able to return and we'll never be together again. But if I don't tell you my secret now, I know it will become an eternal thorn in my flesh.

"At first, I felt the love that two friends feel for each other. But over time, and without my realizing it, those feelings turned into a real and true love. Maybe you think it's not right for me to do this, but what else is there for me to say? We've known each other since we were little, not just for a day or two, but eating from the same plate, sleeping on the same mat, more so than a real brother and sister. How could my heart not be bound to you? We've never been apart for even a moment and now, all of a sudden, I have to leave you without knowing when I'll return. How could my heart not be completely shattered? How can I leave you?"

'It's like the *pantun* says," he continued,

> *Even with the moon full and radiant,*
> *leaves on the ironwood are not clear.*
> *Do not speak of a long estrangement,*
> *when a day apart is like a year.*

"Since we can't change our destiny, I want to know how you feel about me. Or am I alone in this yearning?" Samsu asked, taking hold of Nurbaya's hand.

Rendered speechless by Samsu's words, Nurbaya bowed her head and said nothing for a time, as if afraid she might reveal what she kept hidden inside her. Samsu approached her and, bringing his face close to hers, asked very softly, "Would you be willing to be my wife, when I hold a doctor's position?"

"How could I not be willing!" Nurbaya softly replied, as if afraid to say the words out loud.

Samsu gently kissed the back of her hand.

Nurbaya did not resist.

"Naturally, I supposed," he said in a gentle voice, "that you didn't hate me, and even loved me."

"Listen to this *pantun*!" Samsu said.

> *They say it is better to fold than to roll,*
> *cloth of simple design made on a loom.*
> *The young couple seem to be of one soul,*
> *as if the progeny of a single womb.*

"True," replied Nurbaya, responding with a *pantun* of her own:

> *Sail the ship from Medan to Banda Isle,*
> *And then on to Bintuhan but don't tarry.*
> *Three months with Mother is but a while,*
> *it is in the hands of God if we shall marry.*

Samsu answered her with another:

> *A Chinese boy sits to pen a text,*
> *his desk being nothing but a stone.*
> *Both in his world and in the next,*
> *as one the couple will be known.*

"So now you know. Shouldn't I be worried about leaving you? If you were in real danger here, how would I feel then? Shattered. I can't say it.

When I'm near you, I can't even think about that. I don't think about living or dying, so long as I'm with you."

> Following harvest time in the village,
> betel nuts are placed on a silver plate.
> If my body they should crush or pillage,
> I care not as long as you are my fate.

"Of course," Nurbaya said, "I agree."

> On Penang Island dried leaves rustle,
> as each male bird constructs a nest.
> Even apart there's no reason to tussle,
> for it is certain our love will never rest.
>
> If in the meadow there is a spring,
> surely you may use it to bathe in.
> If more years my life doth bring,
> then surely, too, we will meet again.
>
> Whether in the forest or open field,
> frangipani flowers will always be blue.
> Against my longing, there is no shield,
> but never doubt that my love is true.
>
> Deep into the jungle people from Kinanti go,
> with flaming banana-stalks held above.
> If the love in your heart you cannot show,
> send it to thy beloved on the wings of a dove.

"That's very true, Nurbaya! Now it's your turn, compose some of your own! We can joke and banter tonight, but tomorrow I'll be gone," Samsu said, kissing the back of his beloved's delicate hand several more times before beginning another poem:

> On the island are mangos lush on the tree,
> shake a branch and on the ground they lie.
> This night we shall spend in light colloquy,
> but come the morning, I must say goodbye.

To which Nurbaya replied:

Sailing off to the island for various provisions,
the ship's skipper eats food from home.
So sweet the farewells of the girl left in indecision,
so sad the goodbyes of the lad who must roam.

At the side of the road, ferns grow high,
from tilled ground, turmeric does surge.
When in longing, gaze up at the sky,
there, in the moon, our love will merge.

After the two of them were quiet for a time, Samsu improvised some lines again:

To sail from Java is the ship's goal,
then to set anchor in Inderagiri bay.
In leaving you behind, I leave my soul,
yet in the morn I must make my way.

Nurbaya then responded:

In Pauh the air resounds with tympani,
in the square a dance where all take part.
Wherever I go, no matter how far I may be,
if not in my eyes, you'll be there in my heart.

"One more," she then exclaimed:

Near Banten, Krakatoa volcano blew its top,
the island falling into the sea, as if in a breath.
Our love for each other won't change, full stop!
If parted in life, we shall be together in death.

And Samsu came back with:

When Friday comes and it's time to pray,
the pilgrims put on their Arabian dress.
Even were it the time for Judgment Day,
let not our hearts a change of love confess.

"One more," he cried:

> *In Perak are Tamil scribes who write,*
> *to go to Tapak, the sea you must cross.*
> *Ivory will turn black and crows white,*
> *before my love for you will ever be lost.*

The clock in the watchman's house struck one in the morning. Only then did the entranced pair return to their senses.

"Sam!" exclaimed Nurbaya. "It's one in the morning. My father might ask where I've been. Let's part for now and meet again tomorrow. I'm sure you have a lot to do before you leave and you mustn't forget anything. Go to bed so you won't be too tired. You'll probably have to get up early tomorrow."

"Nur! As long as I'm with you, I never feel tired. I'd like it even if we stayed up till the morning. I'd really like that. I can't describe how I feel right now. And I can't tell you how happy I am. Only God knows better. I've dreamed for so long of us being together like this. And only now has it come true, as the *pantun* from the stage shows says:

> *The sun moves west in a sky so blue,*
> *soon the cattle must come home.*
> *It was so very long I looked for you,*
> *why, oh why, did I ever start to roam?*

"Even though my joy and pleasure won't last long, it doesn't matter. Now I know you also love me. I can leave Padang and go abroad without suspicion or misgivings!" Samsu exclaimed, embracing Nurbaya.

"Tonight has been so important for me and my future. I have found my love, the one I was made for and longed for, day and night. So long as there is life in my body, I'll never forget this night. Now I can be hopeful about what lies ahead. Up there are my witnesses, Nur," Samsu said, pointing at the moon and stars.

"I shall never love another woman, just you. No other shall be my wife, only you. You are my hope, you are the bezoar that brings me ease and calm. When you're not with me, other women are forbidden to me," he said. Approaching Nurbaya, he once again kissed her.

"I feel the same way, Sam," Nurbaya said. "As God is my witness, you're the only man on this earth that I love. You are my husband in the world to come."

"You ought to go in now, before somebody discovers our secret," Sam replied, leading his beloved by the hand to the steps of her house. After locking her fingers in his, Nurbaya opened the door and went inside, while Samsu started for his home.

Not far from Padang, and to the town's south, is a harbor known as Teluk Bayur, a port famous even in distant lands. Poised between Java, Hindustan and Arabia on the one hand and the European continent, on the other, large ships destined for, or returning from, Europe often made their way to it. It was also a good point for taking in coal from Ombilin. Moreover, the harbor was very expertly constructed. It stretches from the west to the east, and then turns to the north, hidden behind a promontory and a sandy island, protected from the large waves which are especially fearsome during the western monsoon. For this reason, the sea inside this bay is very calm and does not give any difficulty at all to boats anchoring there. And since the coastline is very steep, with all the mountains fencing in the harbor on the northern, eastern and southern sides, the depth of the water there is very great, so that large vessels can enter and easily come alongside the several piers that jut out into the water.

To the north and west of the harbor and behind these piers are several warehouses that see a heavy traffic of goods both in and out while nearby a railway and the main road connect the harbor with Padang. Not far from the train station a large coal dump sits on high ground. An elevated steel railway bridge juts out over the bay, from which coal can be easily dumped into ships tied up and waiting below, all of it adding to the fame of the harbor as a place to take in coal.

Ships of every size and origin moored in the harbor. Some were headed south, some north to China and Japan via Penang and Singapore, while still others went straight on to Bombay, Calcutta, Egypt and Europe. Flags from as far away as Britain and Germany were flown above some of the vessels. And the day after his goodbye party, at which his friends reveled in his honor, one of the ships docked in the harbor was to take Samsu and his companions on to Batavia.

As the ship was to depart at noon and it was now already ten o'clock, passengers and workers moved frenetically in and out, stirring up an indescribable din. Some took on coal, some off-loaded goods or broke open cargo, while others ran up and down the gangway as if they had left things behind.

On the ship itself, seamen were busy with their tasks and the ship's mates were noisily shouting orders. Deck-class passengers went in search of good resting spots for the long voyage, all the while organizing the things they brought. Some of those in first and second class sat and chatted at mess tables, while others stood on the quarter deck, taking in the tumultuous scene. Nor were vendors in short supply, offering fruits and other goods as they walked up and down the ship's deck calling out prices.

The pier was filled with hundreds of men and women, both locals and foreigners, sailing together or there to see off family members or friends. Some sat and talked, some walked up and down, as if bored with waiting, while others simply stood around, sheltered from the heat by their parasols.

Over by the side of a warehouse, an old lady sat talking with her child, who would soon be traveling. She spoke of the need to be vigilant, both on the voyage and when in strange lands. An old fellow sat on a rock, deep in conversation with his brother, who was about to leave his native home and sail off to make a living among foreigners. More than a few had come just to look, laughing uproariously as they asked their companions when *they* would be sailing, too.

Samsulbahri was in a second-class cabin, along with his parents, relatives and friends.

"You haven't forgotten anything, have you, Sam?" Sutan Mahmud asked.

"No, Father."

"Where's your trunk?"

"Everything's right here."

"And your spending money, have you put it in your trunk?"

"It's here with me."

"Remember who you are when you're there, Samsu!" said his mother. "Know how to behave: 'Wash upstream and speak from below.' Don't just think of things as they are here. And don't think of yourself as the child of a person of position, because you're going to have to stand alone, far away from all of us. If anything happens, quickly write to your Father!" When she was done speaking, Sitti Maryam wiped away the tears that streamed down her cheeks.

"Study hard and don't play around in the wrong places and at the wrong times," his father added. "Don't mix with people who may not be so good and don't be a spendthrift, so that the money sent to you each month will be enough."

While listening to his parents speak, Nurbaya stood next to Samsu, leaning on the edge of his bunk. Even though she seemed unconcerned with what was being said, her every thought was of Samsu and she never took her eyes off her beloved. At that very moment, it dawned on her just how hard this parting would be. Earlier, when she stood at the edge of the sea that would soon separate her from her love, confronting the sadness of separation had not seemed such a great challenge. But seeing the ship that would bear her heart away, she now knew how deeply it would wound her. That the light from his eyes would disappear from her, and not just for a day or two, nor even for a week, made her heart beat fiercely in her chest. Just how many years it would be before she saw Samsu's face again, she had no way of telling. And when she recalled his terrible dream, her sadness and fear grew even stronger. And so she kept her gaze fixed on Samsu, filling her heart with the sight of the schoolmate she loved.

At that moment, several well-wishers entered the cabin bearing mangoes, citrus and pineapples. "This is for the young man, to ward off seasickness during the voyage. We pray that Allah will grant him a safe trip and return."

"Thank you," Samsu replied, accepting the gifts. "I, too, hope that Allah will watch over and care for my younger and elder brothers who are staying here."

After shaking hands, they all left, until finally only Samsu and Nurbaya were left. Samsu took Nurbaya's hands in his and looked deeply into her eyes. His own brimmed with tears. He stood silent for a while, his chest suddenly tight and his mouth locked shut. Finally, he found his voice, though only haltingly.

"Nurbaya, please be careful. If anything happens, write to me quickly. If my strength or means cannot help you, there is always advice or wisdom to be offered from afar. My parents... just think of them as your own. Visit them often, even though I won't be there. Whatever difficulties you may have, tell them, because they love you as much they love me.

"If something happens in my parents' house, let me know right away, especially if it concerns my mother. She seems to be taking my departure very hard. I beg of you, don't forget the promise and vows we made last night, because we've been married in spirit since then. You were happy to become my wife, as I was to become your husband. It's only in a worldly sense that we haven't yet been joined. Send me a letter every time a ship leaves from here and tell me everything that goes on, so I don't feel so sad and alone.

"When I get to Batavia, I'll send back whatever I can buy you. For now, I can only give you this as a memento. Please accept this locket. There's a picture of me inside. If you miss me, let it remind you of me."

Nurbaya took the locket from Samsu and brought it to her lips, while tears flowed from her cheeks.

"Oh, thank you, Sam!" she said, "I promise to wear it all my life. The only thing I can give you as a keepsake is this ring. I hope you will wear it!" Nurbaya removed the pearl ring from her finger and gave it to Samsu. "And you, too, if you ever find yourself thinking of me, take this ring as a symbol of my love and keep it safe, because for me it's the cord that binds us from this world to the next. I'll have a portrait of me done right away, which I'll send to you later.

"I also wish you peace and safety on your journey. May God watch over you in your travels to foreign lands and on your return. May you attain everything you strive for, so that when you come back, your name won't be just Samsu, but 'Doctor Samsu'.

"Always take good care of yourself when you're on your own, far from family and friends. In all matters, you alone will be the one to decide what's best. And don't be tempted by what's not good for you, because Batavia is a big city and there are many unsuitable distractions there."

The ship's whistle sounded its first call, reminding the crew and passengers to prepare for departure. Samsu came out of the cabin with Nurbaya and descended to the pier. There, he shook hands with those who had come to see him off, asking their forgiveness and pardon for all his sins and wrongs, both material and spiritual, which could weigh him down in this world and the next.

His friends and family cried, the tears streaming down their faces, for they would miss Samsu's good manners and ways. He could not hold back tears either, though he had steeled himself against crying. He kissed his father's hand, embraced his mother and kissed her cheek.

Finally, he went over to Nurbaya and held her hand, as if unwilling to ever let it go. He felt suffocated, holding back the sorrow that welled up in him. He couldn't say anything at all, except, "May your stay here be a peaceful one, Nur! I hope we can be together again soon." With that, he quickly went back on board.

Nurbaya could say nothing more than, "A peaceful and safe journey, Sam... all the way to Batavia!"

Once aboard, Samsu stood at the edge of the ship's deck, his chin resting on the steel railing. The second whistle blew, and then the third, the lines were cast off and the anchor weighed.

The ship's propellers began to turn, slowly at first, then gathering more and more speed As the vessel pulled away from the dock the many who stood at the rail waved their handkerchiefs in farewell and were answered by a chorus of fluttering waves from the dock. Among the latter, some shouted, "Don't forget!" while others called out, "Come back soon". From the ship, the voyagers shouted back, "Yes! All right!"

As he waved his blue handkerchief, Samsu never took his eyes off Nurbaya , who signaled back with a pink cloth of her own.

The ship drew farther and farther away from the jetty, its course growing more rapid until, finally, Samsu could no longer make out the figures standing on the dock. He went back down to his cabin to sleep beneath the sheets, for the land he had left was no longer in view. He flung himself on his bed and pressed a pillow to his chest to contain the pain constricting his heart. His head was spinning, like a man plagued with hallucinations.

Back on the dock, Nurbaya could no longer distinguish her beloved from the others she saw on board; she slowly made her way to the end of a cape to follow the vessel with her eyes. It seemed to her the world was growing more and more silent around her. All the shouting and yelling of those working at the harbor, and the many sounds of equipment smashing open cargo, the raising and moving of loads, while still noisy, grew more and more distant in her ears. The scores of workers rushing back and forth to the harbor warehouses now appeared tiny. Finally, she sat down on a rock, propping her chin in her hands while gazing at the ship leaving the estuary behind, her beloved onboard.

Only when the ship's cannon sounded its farewell to the harbor of Teluk Bayur was it clear to Nurbaya that the ship was now headed west. And at that point, she thought about what it would be like, later on, when she was alone at home. Who would she talk to and make jokes with on the way to school and back? When something important happened, whom would she tell? To whom would she reveal her innermost secrets? Who would she address her questions to and discuss difficult subjects with? And who would help her with tough calculations assigned at school?

Such were Nurbaya's thoughts as she sat on the rock, gazing out at the ship now almost gone from view.

Not long after, the vessel moved behind Sikabau Hill and disappeared. Only its smoke could be seen hanging in the air over the ocean. Just then, Nurbaya's senses failed her, as if the ground beneath her planted feet were slipping away and her body now hung in the space between heaven and earth. If her father, who was standing nearby, had not gently taken hold of her shoulder, she would have collapsed to the ground. Fortunately, Baginda Sulaiman quickly came to his child's aid and, lifting her up, led her slowly home.

6

Datuk Meringgih

In Padang's Kampung Ranah, a wooden house with a zinc roof sat in the midst of a large plantation, far from the main roads and hidden beneath leafy trees. Everything in it was worn and disorderly, including the dirty, mismatched furniture that was haphazardly arranged throughout.

On the front veranda hung an old, rusty lamp. Lit only when there were guests—which was rare—its kerosene sometimes lasted for weeks. Below it was a round table, very old by the look of it, surrounded by four wooden rocking chairs whose color had faded along with their paint. In the middle room stood a single serving cabinet nearly half a century in age, judging by its appearance.

A small marble table, its surface now yellowed and pitted, had been placed next to the wall and squeezed between two wooden chairs with goatskin seats. On the floor stretched an old rattan mat. At night, this middle room was brightened by a single wall lamp that was lit between six-thirty and ten. On the back veranda the only decoration was a cloth sofa whose patterns had been worn away.

This was the home of Datuk Meringgih, the most famous of Padang's wealthy merchants. He was called "datuk" not because he was a traditional headman, but simply because people called him that. Though he said the house was merely a place to park buggies and carriages and horses in reality it was his home. For here he lived, while one of his shops, which he said was his actual home, was only used for greeting and receiving his associates and acquaintances. Was Datuk Meringgih ashamed to claim the house in Ranah as his true residence? Perhaps we shall discover the answer to such a question later on. But on this particular day, Datuk Meringgih sat on the back porch of his home in Ranah on that very same sofa.

Before discussing his wealth, we should first give some sense of his physical appearance and build, bringing to light as well his character and behavior, so that we may know him well and not forget him when we meet him again, later in the story.

The "datuk" was tall and thin, with the bowed back of a prawn, a sunken chest and crooked legs. His head was large and nearly hairless while his face was narrow. What little hair did remain, ringing his head, was as white as ginned cotton. His mustache and beard were long and wispy and hung from his chin and lip in curls. He had small but sharp eyes, a hooked nose, and a large mouth filled with black and filthy teeth that protruded like a squirrel's. His ears were as large as an elephant's and framed a wrinkled face covered with smallpox scars. He was more than fifty years old.

From such a description, we can see that Datuk Meringgih was no longer young or attractive, but rather a decrepit and repulsive fellow. Let us now turn to his habits and behavior, and judge whether these were in keeping with his appearance.

He was a mean-spirited, grasping and greedy person, without compassion and mercy, and by nature rough and brutal. As long as he could get money, or his way, nothing else concerned him whatsoever. He feared nothing and he had no use for feelings of mutual respect. "Stand aside, and be safe. Stand in the way, and be broken," he'd say.

If he was forced to spend, he would agonize for hours whether it was not possible to get what he wanted without paying at all. He would choke himself, bind his belly and beat down his appetites, all to avoid spending a cent. If he ate rice, it was only with pepper sauce or the dried fish he saved for days. In his view a simple meal was better than a kitchen from which smoke furled every day. Food is merely eaten and its savor is in the swallowing, he thought. After that it just becomes waste.

That his home was like a goat pen and his clothing like a coolie's rags did not bother him, so long as he did not spend his money on such trifles. "What's on the outside is cleaned and cleaned again, while filth lies without limit within one's own belly," he would say.

He turned a deaf ear to the abuse, contempt and calumny levied against him, and closed his eyes to every sight that gave delight, as long as his money was kept safe. Indeed, Datuk Meringgih knew no better pleasure than to gaze at his strongbox while counting coins and rubbing his bills.

He would shake his money box just to hear the sound it made, turning it over and over in his hand to feel its heft. At the very sight and sound of jingling, gleaming silver and gold his eyes would light up and his spirit would stir and become animated. He would shut his ears and, with his mouth agape, his hands trembling and his body swelling, he would take the coins, one by one, examining the imprint on their serrated edges and delighting in their images and wording, which to him, were more beautiful than the paintings done by famous artists. Indeed, the clinking of coins was more musical to him than a song played by a master musician. In this way, he could amuse himself for hours on end—or even days—and in doing so forget the world and his worries. Sometimes, he even took his money to bed in order to ensure pleasant dreams.

His hopes, thoughts and desires, day and night, morning and evening, were of nothing more than adding to his already great store of possessions, without interruption and without limit. He wanted all the wealth of the world to fall, not into the hands of others, but into his own. And even that didn't quite satisfy him. He would only know abundance when the precious things of his life could be piled in heaps around him. He feared sickness and death because he could not bear parting with the goods of this world. Parents, children and wives, relatives, acquaintances, good friends, confidants: they could not stand in the way of what he wanted. Besides, to him, money was all of these things, plus his lover and God. "Live with money and die with money," were the words he lived by.

To get what he wanted, no ruthless or malicious act, no matter how despicable and base, was beyond him. Nor had he had any sense of fear, horror, pity or sorrow. Not for him were the common concerns of mutual regard, mutual respect, and mutual admiration. Whoever was noble, he degraded. Whoever was rich, he impoverished. Whoever held rank, he deposed. He placed underlings on the throne and brought unclean dogs to the summit of the beloved and beautiful Mount Merapi. "Stand aside and be safe. Stand in the way and be broken." Whatever the case, he must have his money.

That was Datuk Meringgih, the wealthiest and most famous merchant in Padang, who wanted to become even richer simply because he desired it.

Hey, Datuk Meringgih! Where's the profit in such wealth to you and your fellow man? Born from the stomach of your mother, you brought nothing with you. When the time comes for you to leave this fleeting world—for you cannot avoid death—even were your possessions as numerous as those of King Karun, you will bring nothing with you to your eternal home, save a piece of white cloth sufficient to cover your body.

For as long as you still live, you exhaust yourself amassing goods, but you never get tired of doing this. How much trouble and sickness have you experienced, how much pain and suffering have you suffered, how many the mockeries and oaths you have endured, how many curses and abuses of the tongue have you heard? But later when you return to the mercy of God, your possessions will be left behind and doled out among the living. Worldly goods return to the world and only those of the hereafter can you bring to help you on your journey to the eternal country and the eternal life.

As long as you live, you snatch goods from others' grasp, but when you are dead, such goods will surely fall back into the hands of those from which you took. That is what is meant by: "What goes around comes around." Nothing lasts forever, save the exchanging and shifting of things. The moon revolves around the sun, and the sun itself rotates through the universe. What is there that is fixed? Nothing, save God, Who is One.

Your wealth, God's bounty, is of no use to you, your fellow man, or the creatures of this world and brings instead only sorrow and suffering to all.

It is true that greed is mankind's way—though not to the same degree in each person—for, as long as life is born of the womb, if a finger's length is had, a hand's span is wanted, and if a hand's span is had, the span of one's outstretched arms is wanted, and if that is had, still more is wanted, without end, as long as there is life inside the body. And though man's nature has brought him to the plain of progress, take care, for the road to be taken there is forked: one way points toward virtue and the other toward sin. If you follow the former, your works will prosper, for they will profit you and your fellow man. But take the road of sin and there is nothing you will do that will not bring danger and disaster to your fellow man and to you yourself.

If you use your possessions in defense, to achieve a happy life, to have enough food and drink, a nice home and clothes to wear, or consume them to satisfy your rightful appetites, that is well and good. For mankind should endeavor to find happiness and progress in all things, so long as the boundaries of virtue are not transgressed.

But your works would profit you more if they were used for the good of your fellow man and to pay homage to your God, so as to repair what is broken, resolve what is confused, help those in distress, comfort those in need, and thus reduce the pain and suffering of this world. For let it be known by you, that this world has in it more of those in distress than are happy, more who are low than exalted, more in want than in plenty, more who are poor than are rich, more weak than strong, and more unlucky than blessed. If not from you and other rich men like you, from who should such as these obtain help?

Think! Riches and poverty, nobility and baseness, distress and happiness, yes, all of these, indeed come from God, Who is One. If it is His wish, in the blink of an eye, those riches can turn to poverty, nobility to baseness, joy to sorrow, the low made high, the poor made rich, the base exalted, and weeping turned into laughter.

Therefore, do not be arrogant and haughty on account of your wealth, exaltation, comfort or joy. Rather realize that such things are but loans that may be taken back at any time by the one who owns them.

And you, too, who feel poverty and the meanness of life, who are forever weighed down by danger and suffering and sorrow, do not despair, but be patient and rely on your God, and pray for His help and bounty. After the rain, the sun will certainly come.

You, who are fortunate, do not scorn the unlucky, and you who are unlucky, envy not the fortunate. Rather, love one another always, and help each other in all things, for those whose luck is good need those whose luck is not, just as the unlucky need the blessed. If there were none who were unfortunate, certainly there would be none with good fortune. And if there were none who had good luck, there would be none whose luck is bad.

When you use your possessions—you, Datuk Meringgih!—for good, nothing but good will come to you, more so than the joy and happiness provided by the sounds and bright reflections of your precious treasure. For a deed—even a thought, bad or good—never disappears as does the rain falling on sand, but lives on forever and will rise again in you or your fellow man.

And when someday the time comes for you to leave this world and you look behind you to the road you have traveled, surely feelings of prosperity and tranquility will follow, for I know that your life has not been empty, like a rice plant without fruit, but rather one which has brought much of service to your fellow man...

Although people disliked Datuk Meringgih because of his malevolence and greed, his vast wealth meant he was feared and held in awe. This was especially true for those who found themselves in financial straits. For he was the one to go to for a loan, though he sometimes charged nearly half the principal amount in interest. When payment was due and the borrower was late, Datuk Meringgih showed no mercy, hauling the defaulter to court and seizing his collateral.

Where did Datuk Meringgih get all his money? The secret to his success was "the play of tongues and the fruit of thoughts" around Padang. Frequently discussed, often guessed at, unknown for certain. Nor did anyone know who the real Datuk Meringgih was and where he came from.

Some twenty years before, he had been known in Padang as a dried fish vendor at the Kampung Jawa market. All of a sudden he bought a small plot and from then on his wealth grew so rapidly that by the time he was over forty, he owned several large shops and warehouses filled with goods, was renting out dozens of houses and had gained title to nearly all the land in Padang. His coconut plantations and padi fields were vast and nearly every vessel at Muara carrying trade was his. The entire town marveled at such wealth yet no one could say how the Datuk amassed it so quickly, for the only thing that was heard or seen of the man was his miserliness and greed.

All sorts of stories floated around about the source of his wealth. Some said he won a hundred thousand guilders in the lottery; others, that he found buried treasure. Those of strong faith believed he had met the Prophet Khidir on the night of the twenty-seventh day of the Fasting Month. The superstitious held that he consorted with a *djini*. And those who hated the datuk said he imported black-market opium. Datuk Meringgih alone knew the real story.

Let us return to the man himself, to learn what he was thinking as he sat alone on the sofa of his back veranda.

Datuk Meringgih had not been sitting long before day turned to night, the darkness around him becoming deeper, particularly near his house. At that time of day, most of the creatures that walked the earth or took to the sky had already entered their lairs. Only the bats skittered here and there in search of prey. Flying foxes flew high and to the south, one after the other, in search of ripe fruit. Owls began hooting from the hollows of trees, and polecats awoke from their slumber, scanning this way and that for signs of danger lurking outside their dens. A snake slithered between stones in search of frogs and other small creatures.

Over in the west, black, rain-laden clouds drifted in from the sea. The clear sky suddenly became dark as pitch, until not a single thing could be seen, not even the stars overhead, which were now covered as if by a black curtain. The night was still, not a breeze moving, a sure sign a tempest was gathering. All was deserted and quiet on the main roads, like a village subdued by mythical beasts. From time to time a person would pass by, walking quickly as if fearful of a downpour. No lamps were seen in any house, for the windows had all been shut. Yet, as dark as it was, Datuk Meringgih did not give the order to have the back veranda lighted. Was even this due to his stinginess, or was there another reason? We shall soon see.

A flash of lightning brightened the pitch-black world, followed by a crack of thunder that seemed to cleave the earth in two. A dense rain began to fall like water pouring straight from the heavens and not long afterwards, the gusts of a typhoon brought down several large trees.

Though it was like Judgment Day outside, Datuk Meringgih did not venture from his house, as if nature's chaos were not his concern, but rather his very wish. He sat placidly on his sofa pondering an important matter.

Out of the darkness, someone suddenly coughed three times. Only then did Datuk Meringgih awake to his surroundings, peering right and left to see who was nearby. He coughed two times in reply. At that, a shadowy figure began to move in the dark, a man dressed completely in black. He came out of the darkness and up the stairs, entering a room on the back veranda at Datuk Meringgih's beckoning. The datuk immediately shut the door behind them.

Inside, the light of a single oil lamp revealed a mattress, a trunk and a *pandanus* mat, on which the two men now sat.

The man's head was covered in a soft black cloth whose ends were knotted on his forehead. He wore black Acehnese trousers and a black shirt with long sleeves in the Chinese style. Over his shoulder was slung a black Bugis sarong.

"You didn't get wet, did you, Number Five?" Datuk Meringgih quietly asked his guest.

"No, Boss. I was just about here when it started to rain."

"What's the news of our work at Hulu Limau Manis?"

"It didn't turn out so well."

"Not well? And why not?" Datuk Meringgih asked, looking straight at Number Five. The man could see that the Datuk was angry.

"Our pupils didn't follow the rules."

"Who was their teacher at that time?"

"Si Patah"

"Why weren't you teaching there yourself? Didn't I order you to do so?"

"At the time, I had to teach at Bukit Putus. There were some newly arrived goods from the Javalands, which were of very great value."

"Si Patah isn't yet up to teaching pupils about large targets. He also lacks patience. That's where his teaching goes wrong. Where is he now?"

"In jail."

"In jail?" asked Datuk Meringgih, again raising his head. "Where?"

"The one at Lubuk Bagulung, along with two pupils."

"A wage that suits him fine. But has he been interrogated about this matter?"

"He has, and it looks like he held fast to his oath, because he didn't mention my name."

"Start from the beginning and tell me why things turned out as they did."

"When I found out that I couldn't go to Hulu Limau Manis," said Number Five, "I told an old pupil, Si Patah, to go there, and I also told him the rules you had passed along to us. At first, he seemed to obey them, for everything fell into his hands. But he didn't store these gains in the stipulated place, but instead, on that very day, sent them here. He stuffed them into several sacks and had them carried by a wagoner, who left for here that very night. Then I think the wagoner stopped for a while at Lubuk Bagulung, where he was picked up by the police. When the wagoner told them who he had received the goods from, Si Patah was arrested that same day, along with two of his pupils."

"All right, but come up with an escape plan before sentencing is passed, and once they're out, tell Si Patah to go to Terusan or to Painan and lay low for a while gathering rattan. And have his two pupils go to Bukit Tumpukan Tulang, and study hard there," Datuk Meringgih said.

"All right, Boss."

"About the goods you were looking into at Bukit Putus, what was that all about? I wasn't aware of it."

"To tell you the truth, Boss, I hadn't told you about that yet, because since then I haven't had the chance to come here."

"But why didn't you consult with me earlier on?"

"I didn't have the chance. In fact, that night I was supposed to go to Hulu Limau Manis, to assist Si Patah, as you, sir, said to. But just when I got to Bukit Putus, one of the pupils brought news that goods from Java were arriving by boat that very day. Valuable goods. Since I couldn't get back here to inform you, because I was worried the shipment would be immediately taken elsewhere, I went after it myself, because it seemed easy to do."

"And did you get it?"

"Yes, and now it's planted in the ground, near Red Lands."

"Approximate value?"

"Approximately six or seven hundred guilders. It's all gold and diamonds. That's what I wanted to talk about, because the two pupils who went with me now want their share."

"I'll give each of them fifty later on."

"If possible, they're asking for a hundred each."

"Be serious! A hundred? When the value of the goods is still uncertain and they aren't thinking of their monthly wages? All right, I'll give each seventy-five and a hundred and fifty to you if it's true that its value is six or seven hundred. Now let's have less chatter. Bring the goods here first! When I have appraised it, each one of you will get your share right away. And bring our goldsmith here so he can break out the gold from the other items. Then give our diamonds to the gold peddlers, and tell them to sell it all in the other villages."

"Yes, sir," Number Five replied happily, while his owl-like eyes gleamed with the thought of the money he would soon receive. Of those three hundred guilders, at least two hundred would surely be his, so that for several days he would again be able to smoke opium and gamble to his heart's content.

"There's one other thing to report. Our minter died the other night," Number Five said.

"Died? What happened?"

"A stomach ailment."

"Who'll replace him?"

"That's what I wanted to ask. Who will it be?"

"Hasn't his friend, Baso, been able to work on his own?"

"He has. The way I see it, Baso would be a good replacement for the dead man, but then who would replace *him*?"

"Find someone among our people you can trust!"

"All right."

"Only, for now, don't make too much silver. We've got to do more gold coins, because people quickly recognize silver ones."

"All right. Also, wouldn't it be a good idea to change locations? I've recently found a cave in the mountains near the old spot. It looks good, and is hidden on the coast."

"Good! Later we'll both go and take a closer look at it together."

"What about the matter of the Bombay man's shop?" Number Five asked, apparently eager to get to work, thinking as he was about the two hundred guilders he stood to gain.

"Later. I first want to think up a good trick. Right now there's something else I want to tell you."

"What is it, Boss?"

"It makes me very unhappy to see Sulaiman Baginda's business growing larger by the day. It's gotten to the point that he dares to compete with me. He has to be brought down."

"But how do we do that? He's got so much stuff, it couldn't be carried off in one or two days. And he wouldn't feel it if only a part of it were taken," Number Five replied.

"I am not telling you to steal his goods. How much could you make off with, anyway? I'm not stupid. I have a better idea. His warehouses and shops must be burned to the ground. The vessels that bring his goods from Painan must be sunk, the people who work there persuaded not to work with him any longer, and all his coconut palms at Ujung Karang poisoned so they'll rot and not bear fruit," Datuk Meringgih said, furiously pounding his fist into his palm with each new detail of the plan.

"Tomorrow you'll begin working at Ujung Karang. Tell the pupils there to sprinkle poison on all the coconut palms so they'll die. Then go to Terusan and Painan and talk everyone there into leaving their jobs and joining us. Also, get the shipmen to scuttle all his vessels and everything in them. When you're done, go to Padang Darat and elsewhere, and convince all the shops that buy from him to cease working with him. That way, I can buy from him cheap. Let me lose a bit, so long as Baginda Sulaiman falls. When that's done, set about burning down his shops and warehouses."

Upon hearing his orders, Number Five had to stop and gather his wits for a moment, for he had never done anything like this before and now realized it would not be without its costs and troubles.

Seeing the man grow silent in this way, Datuk Meringgih felt compelled to say, "I know this won't be easy and great care must be taken in doing it to prevent anyone else from finding out. But it will bring tens of thousands of guilders in profit to us. And I know you can get this done. So I'm not concerned with the cost. It doesn't matter if I lose thousands, so long as I get my way. I don't like having a merchant here in Padang bold enough to compete with me. Only his complete ruin will make me happy. Use as much money as you want and my people, too, if you have to."

Listening to his master's words, Number Five's reservations and fear vanished. He happily answered, "Good, sir. I'd even be willing to kill someone from my own village, so long as it was you who ordered it."

In saying so, his thoughts soared to the thousands of guilders he would soon receive.

"But remember!" Datuk Meringgih said suddenly, "if my objectives are not met, you needn't keep coming here."

Number Five's heart began to beat faster, for failure meant he would be dismissed. And where would he be able to find another boss like Datuk Meringgih? True, the man was awfully stingy, but if his mind was set on a particular task, he could overlook anything. So Number Five made up his mind to carry out his duty, regardless of what happened to him.

While he thought this over, Datuk Meringgih went back into his house, re-emerging a moment later. "Here's a hundred for your expenses in the meantime," he said. "When this is finished, just ask me or my people who handle money for more. Later I will send a letter to them all."

"Thanks! But what about my work here?"

"Hand it over to Number Four and tell him to come here, so I can tell him what he has to do."

Shortly thereafter, Number Five left the Datuk's house and disappeared into the night.

7

Samsulbahri's Letter

It had been three months since Samsulbahri had left behind his home for Batavia. For three months Nurbaya had been separated from him, neither seeing his face nor hearing his voice, unable even to tease her sweetheart. Since that time, her thoughts had not strayed from him, not even for a moment. And though her heart's desire had disappeared from view, she still saw him in her mind's eye, his voice ringing out loud and clear, his life and actions welling up all the more vividly.

At first, Nurbaya thought it would be easy to find consolation once her sadness passed, but a week later, she succumbed to a kind of fever. Though she recovered physically, inwardly her suffering became more and more acute and, with it, the feeling of helplessness and separation. The more she tried to forget her sadness, the more it resurfaced. The more she sought to console herself, the heavier her burden weighed; the more she distanced herself from it, the closer it pressed upon her. Only then did she truly realize how valuable her friend and beloved was, for it was in such moments she felt the true weight of their separation, just as in the words of the *pantun*:

> *Chinese boys with shadows play,*
> *Indian boys play on beds of coal.*
> *If in the day you are on my mind,*
> *at night I dream of you in my soul.*
>
> *As fireflies fill the air, flitting here and there*
> *A dove's chick falls from nest to ground,*
> *Landing on a bed of flowers,*
> *Breathing its last in frangipani blooms.*

> *By day I find no pleasure,*
> *At night I cannot sleep,*
> *My thoughts are tangled, my heart unsure,*
> *In dwelling on my darling Samsu.*

When tormented in this way, she tried to comfort herself with the thought that Samsu would be coming back before long, and surely she would be able to see him again. He had gone in pursuit of knowledge, which could later bring him happiness and glory, when he was finally a doctor.

"Oh, how happy I'll be then, when I become my darling Samsu's wife. Naturally, I *should* marry him: he is my destined match. When he passes his exams, I'll become a doctor's wife. Later, if my child or I become ill, there'll be no need to call for any other physician, since my own husband will know how to cure us.

"There, I have said it: 'my child'. How happy I'd be to have a child with a husband like him. Surely the child will also be well-mannered, just like his father. And he'll take after him in looks, too, and they'll be just like the two halves of a split areca nut. Ah! How funny that little Samsu will be then, fooling around all the time, just like his father, and when he grows up, he'll become a doctor, too, I'm sure.

"If the child's a girl, let her look like me. When she gets older, I will teach her everything a girl needs to know. I'll make her into a woman who will be of use to her future husband. Someone he can take with him here and there, someone who will be by his side in times of joy and sorrow, so that my son-in-law can someday know the same joy and happiness I will bring Samsu."

Such were Nurbaya's musings that Saturday evening, as she sat on the front veranda of her house, gazing at the bench in front of the garden, the very bench on which she used to sit and tease her sweetheart.

"Oh, but that seems so far away now," she said to herself, "still seven years to go. Will I be able to wait that long? Why not?" she replied to her own question. "Remember the words of the *pantun*:

> *The road leading to Payakumbuh is straight,*
> *but to go to Kinbali, it's there you divaricate.*
> *If the love we have between us does not abate,*
> *we can wait until all the oceans evaporate.*

"Yes, I'm worried just the same. He might be tempted by other women. Batavia is a big city, and every manner of temptation is there. Superb and elegant ladies are surely not few in number, and they say that many Sundanese women are very pretty. I'd better ask that we be married quickly, to bind him to me."

A moment later, Nurbaya changed her mind, thinking instead, "Oh, such thoughts are not nice. Since he's still in school, his studies might be disturbed. 'That which is pursued will not get caught, while that which is contained trickles away.' Don't be so impetuous, and pay attention to *this* pantun!

Amat completes the rite, no time to waste,
reciting the Koran as dawn becomes day,
Better to arrive safely, no need for haste,
even if chased, a mountain won't run away.

"As if he would go back on his promise... Impossible! I shouldn't be thinking like that. I'm still too young. Later, when he becomes a doctor and I'm twenty-two, then we should get married.

"And it's true, it's not good to marry too young. Look at Alia who was married off by her parents when she was thirteen years-old. She couldn't grow anymore and five of the children she had died. The sixth one, the one that lived, seems to have something wrong with it. It's weak, like it has no strength. When the child was two years old, it still couldn't walk and seemed to have trouble speaking. My little Samsu can't be like that. He has to be healthy and have a sturdy body, so he'll be flawless.

"So, I shouldn't marry too young. It wouldn't be good for me physically or for my offspring. How could a seed not fully formed when planted grow into a fruitful tree? Of course it can't. But most parents here in Padang don't think of that. Just so long as luck comes their way, they say they're happy and give no thought to their children and grandchildren and future descendents.

"If everyone were to marry young, certainly in the end our people would diminish in number and deteriorate in health, size, intelligence and other ways until we became an enfeebled race. Usually, old-fashioned people don't take this into consideration, or even think about such things. For them it's a disgrace if their daughters marry when they're old, as if they had no appeal. So they marry them off young, sometimes when they're eleven years-old. And when they're twelve, these young girls give birth. But Western people, who tend not to marry so young... just look at their bodies: big, strong, and healthy."

As she was lost in thought this way, Nurbaya was startled by a voice that suddenly called out, "Mail!" She turned and saw a postman standing on the steps of her house, holding a letter. She immediately rose, took the letter in hand and, reading the address on it, saw it was from Samsu. The letter must have come by ship that same day.

Nurbaya's face shone with joy, the smile that pursed her lips and sunk dimples in her cheeks only accentuating the sweetness of her expression. She cheered up immediately, for two weeks had already passed without any news from Samsu. Her heart beating, she went straight to her room and opened the letter. It looked to be quite long and filled with quatrains. In it, Samsu said the following:

Batavia 10 August 1896

'Tis now, at one hour before midnight,
That I pick up my pen to write.
The night is awash with moonlight,
And like glittering sapphires, the stars.

The sky is clear and all is bright,
The city shines and all is light.
Breezes blow in from here and there,
As waves break on the reef.

Clouds move by, as if in turns,
Passing swiftly, without end,
Following a steady course southward,
Where at the mountains, they cease.

The air is calm, the night is clear,
A singular silence envelops all,
Bulbuls chirping in the ebony tree,
Give cheer to this traveler's aching heart.

Here thunder roars, there it rumbles,
The owl on its perch calls for the moon,
A heart once joyful now turns sad,
As thoughts return to the Malay homeland.

The wind holds a steady rhythm,
This melancholy heart grows sore,
Pain bites at both heart and soul,
As if pierced by a bamboo dagger.

When the breeze dies in calm,
It is you, so far away, that I recall,
Tears well and then spilling, fall,
The Indian Sea, I am tempted to crawl.

When I think, when I bring the memories back,
My spirit flies and my strength soars,
My body's trembling is too much to bear
My head once cool now boils all the more.

How could it not be this way?
Hearing the cocks crow, here and there,
I think that my love, my precious jewel,
Will soon be coming to visit.

I imagine my dearest flying to me,
Bringing balm for my lovelorn heart,
A heart once sad now feels a joy,
A soul once steady now trembles.

My every sadness finds solace,
From the sight of my sweet, golden beloved,
Coming to me who's long been waiting,
With a yearning so painful, it feels like death.

Come in, dear one, my fine-wrought gold,
Come in and heal this lovelorn lad,
One whose ailment the body infests,
Like a mold covering a wooden plank.

Enter, sweet one, please do come in,
Come and heal this heart's wound,
If you wait too long in treating me,
Death is for certain to be my fate.

When awake, my gaiety fades,
I am but a stranger, adrift in Java,
Feeling crushed in body and soul,
As if to be thwarted is my fate.

I can see in my mind a person's shape,
One who lives far away, beyond the sea,
My heart mourns, unbearably alone,
Like a bead separated from its thread.

With head bowed and swollen lids,
Tears stream downward from my eyes,
Weakness courses through my limbs,
With yearning for you, my precious jewel.

Thinking of you, my golden one,
I groan with an endless misery,
Longing envelops my heart's depth,
As if wrenching from me my very soul.

I recall now, those days now past,
All that happened three months ago,
The laughter and the constant cheer,
When being with you, my gentle dear.

But now I find myself alone,
Far from my village, far from home,
Pining away, day after day,
With no other thought on my mind.

But what can we do, what can we say,
If by God our fate has been predestined,
That for a time, I must pine and yearn,
As I wait to be with my sweetheart again.

When it is far into the night,
And I am asleep on my bed,
I dream of you, my sapphire jewel,
Coming and healing the despondency I feel.

You come to me, all by yourself,
And lie down beside me, at my left,
I embrace you, my opal, my jewel,
And kiss both of your cheeks.

Not too long after this happens,
After this solitary form appears,
I am suddenly startled awake,
My longing bears feelings even more sad.

My bolster, it seems, had deceived me,
And I exclaimed "Oh God in Heaven!"
Such is my fate, Allah's will it seems,
That my ailing body feels weaker still.

Indeed, what more is there to say?
It is but fate and miserable fortune.
Both morning and night, my heart is anxious,
In bearing a longing that breaks my bones.

But even with a fate as such,
It is not fitting I despair too much,
My life by the One God has been prefigured,
To have to wait for my love a certain time.

Far into the night and now, approaching light,
Even with my eyes closed, I can see you there,
And in imagining you there before me,
My heart beats with strong palpitation.

Outside the cocks begin to crow,
In the west, the east, and in the south,
My longing for you, jewel of my heart,
Is something that I could never feign.

I think of Mother, of Father,
And relatives and kin of all kind,
Friends and companions, rich and poor,
All rise in me, not to be forgotten.

Such is my fate in this foreign land,
Where one's survival is not certain,
Where pain is sharp and almost unbearable,
As if stepping on a thorn in a bed of coral.

With evening come and day is gone,
I pace back and forth within my room,
Not knowing what I am looking for,
Not knowing what I am hoping to find.

I take a sheet of paper on which to write,
Hoping to forget my aching body,
And the miserable fortune that is my own,
As I prepare a letter bound for West Sumatra.

With ink and a pen between my fingers,
I write in the early hours of morning,
I send you this letter to take my place,
And so to be with you at your side.

Oh, my darling, so delicate and refined,
I send you my love, my greetings unfurled
This letter of mine shall act as a keel,
And carry me to the lap of my golden girl.

I would win the hand of my dearest,
A young woman of charm, an opal is she,
In Padang, her name is known to all,
Though she sits alone in her home's hall.

If I were a spirit or some kind of sprite,
I would fly to you very quickly in time.
I'd cross the sea, skimming the waves,
To make my way to the love I call mine.

A crown would be fitting for your head,
You, with your ivory skin of such allure,
You make me pine, you stir my desire,
I am like a man intoxicated by mushrooms.

In following the love in my heart,
Passion has become disposition's master,
And although I'm living, I feel like dying,
It is now I know the reason for this all.

Love's passion may no longer be denied,
God alone knows what hearts do hide,
In this pain I feel, is my love for thee,
And any challenge means nothing to me.

Throughout the day and into the night,
I think of you only, my golden girl,
You are forever there within my heart,
Forever there in dreams and desire.

My sweet, Nurbaya, you are my soul,
My ivory one, my measured gold,
You lighten me of all my gloom.
May we be together until our doom.

I surrender myself to you, beloved one,
With truth and sincerity in my heart,
There is no other hope, I have but one,
To breath my last in the lap of my loved one.

My darling Nurbaya, my shining ruby,
Long have I been by love enflamed,
The only desire I hold in my heart,
With my darling, my lovely hibiscus.

I wish only to fill my heart's desire,
To be with you, my precious treasure,
I pray for the help of the gods in heaven,
That you I might one day call my own.

Do the golden gods feel no remorse,
To see this humble traveler,
A man who cannot eat and cannot sleep,
Because of longing for his youthful darling.

Longing for my darling and her bright features,
Day and night, worry consumes me,
My love eternally blossoms in my heart,
I am a boat adrift being rocked by waves.

Every day for me is one of grief,
When remembering my precious jewel,
My pain I can no longer describe,
A boil with no head that grows and grows.

I cannot describe for you,
The passionate longing I must endure,
You are the one I most desire,
With a longing that never ebbs.

Alone, I feel my heart is broken,
I hunt for your face everywhere I go,
From the time I arrived, up until now,
I have felt unable to do any work at all.

I think of nothing other than you,
Day upon day I spend in pining,
I have no other desire than this:
To be with you, my opal, jewel.

Oh, Sitti Nurbaya, my beloved,
Please read now this letter from me,
My skills in writing, having so faded,
I enclose my love in this poem for thee

As Nurbaya read this poem, tears streamed down her face, for she saw in it her own lot in life. She wiped her face and began to read the text of the letter.

My darling Nurbaya! That is the weight I bear from our separation. It's not just your image traced in my mind's eye, but also those of Mother and Father, my friends and classmates, all of whom I left behind in Padang, and whom I'll never forget. Before, my parents spoiled me, and I had everything provided and arranged for. But now, I must do everything myself. I have to wash, fold, and put away my own clothes. I have to clean my room and make my bed, too. Even my shoes... There's no one else to polish them. My life isn't free and easy, now that I live at school. I sleep in a dormitory with my friends, just like soldiers in a barracks. I was the only one who got their own room because there wasn't enough space for me to sleep with the others.

At ten o'clock at night it's lights out. We can't talk to each other after that or keep working. We have to get up at six in the morning and, after eating, classes from eight o'clock on. They don't teach the way they did at our school in Padang, because everything is up to the student himself. If you want to be smart, you have to be diligent. If not, well, you know best. At one o'clock, classes end, though sometimes we go back in the afternoons, too.

Actually, these rules are good, since this way we get to learn how to live on our own. When we're grown up, it's certainly going to be like that. Surely we can't always depend on our parents, can we?

Nonetheless, it was hard for me, unaccustomed as I was to living like that. But over time, that feeling went away. Right now, I'm getting a bit used to the rules, and things don't seem as tough as they did in the beginning.

Perhaps you don't know about this yet, but in nearly every high school there's a tradition called in Dutch, ontgroening, *or "initiation". It has its good points, of course, for by getting everybody to have fun together it aims to teach the incoming students the customs and traditions here: how to be polite, how to show proper etiquette when with colleagues or outsiders, and how to be brave in standing up for the truth.*

If you consider initiation just a game, it doesn't seem so important. But sometimes it's done roughly, and something bad happens to the student involved. Rough games like these, in my view, shouldn't be continued. For example, I've heard that at a middle school there's a game called "passing through the Strait of Gibraltar".

Surely you remember from geography that Gibraltar is a narrow strait between Spain and the African continent. Twenty or so students from the higher classes would form a narrow passage like that, lined up in two rows. All the new students have to go through this strait, one by one, while those from the higher classes punch and kick them as they pass, so that they're knocked about from right to left, left to right until they finally make it through the strait of torture. Then the initiates are lifted up and dunked in a pool of water.

What's the good of such rough play, especially since it can be dangerous? Plus, I think in this way the students become vengeful and hostile to one another. For example, a Sundanese student who doesn't much like the Javanese students, or who was bullied by them upon arrival, has built up a grudge in his heart and is determined to take his revenge on the Javanese one day. So, the camaraderie between these two peoples, which you might expect because they socialize together in school, could weaken and in the end be severed altogether.

Fortunately, we don't have such rough games at our school and all the initiation arrangements here are really just for fun or for some useful purpose. For example, the newcomers have to sing, dance, or perform self-defense exercises in front of the higher classes, each in the style of the regions they come from.

As I said in my earlier letters, because the students who enter this school come from various regions such as Padang, the Bataklands, Deli, Palembang, Batavia, the Sundalands, Java, Madura, Ambon, Manado, and others, all kinds of songs are heard, and sung in various languages. And a variety of dances and self-defense movements are performed, too. The people of Manado have a terrific dance called cakalele. *This is none other than the fighting movements made by people going to war, accompanied by much yelling and shouting.*

Other than the games I've mentioned, there are tests of strength, like a tug-of-war, foot races, and high jumping. It was particularly funny when I had to go to a shop to buy a cent's worth of oil carrying a bottle nearly as big as me: it's really amusing to see a student walking back shouldering a bottle that big with so little in it.

Others might be told to chase a wild chicken let loose in the schoolyard. Two students have to catch it. Oh, what a pitiful sight to see the two of them exhausting themselves running around after it. But, fortunately for everyone, after being caught, the chicken is cut up and fried in one way or another.

And then there are those who have to dress elegantly in the blackest and thickest clothes possible. As you know, Nur, Batavia is very hot, so the students really felt the heat wearing all that clothing. After getting dressed up like that, they have to walk along the main road, and greet and tip their hats to everyone they meet, no matter what race or group. As I've mentioned, Batavia is very lively and bustling. There are always hundreds of people endlessly walking up and down the main roads. Greeting them, by itself nothing very strenuous, can within half an hour become very exhausting because of the number of the people you meet.

And the people being greeted behave in different ways. Those who already know about the game just smile. But those who don't sometimes get angry because they think they're being made fun of. Then there are some who pay no attention whatsoever, and others who laugh at the students. Still others are confused and don't understand what's happening. So they return the greetings with even greater courtesy, since to them it's not a game, but rather somebody they don't know paying them respect and honor. Children on the main streets think the students are off their heads, and play jokes and bother them. There are all kinds of people, and they are the ones, not the students, whom the upperclassmen watch.

What's not so funny is being made to swallow quinine, which is quite bitter, or smell something rotten, or eat a bunch of bananas within sight of a carcass. One student who is very easily nauseated was told to do that. Not only the bananas, but everything in his stomach came up. So pitiful!

None of this is particularly funny, but there are lessons here, nonetheless. Doctors have to be able to stand rotten smells and bitter tastes, and they can't be afraid or go all shuddery at the sight of a dead body. After all, that's what you're there to learn. After everything else, you have to sleep in a morgue. But, first, I should tell you Arifin's and my part in these games, since you'll probably want to know. Arifin had to demonstrate fighting moves, participate in a tug-of-war, buy oil in a big bottle, catch a chicken, and eat a banana near a corpse. How happy Bakhtiar was to see him chasing the chicken around like a dog! But I reckon that no matter what Bakhtiar's stomach is like, he couldn't have finished off that many bananas in a place like that.

Here Nurbaya had to smile, remembering Bakhtiar.

I had to sing, dance, take quinine, and sleep in a morgue. The morgue is where they keep dead bodies. In the room, hanging on a pole, is a human skeleton used for teaching. One night, around eight-thirty, I was told to go there with a jittery student. He wasn't just disgusted easily but was a total coward to boot. Though I wasn't sure what would happen, I wasn't afraid, because I knew it was just a game. We sat at a table across from each other; me, facing the skeleton, him, with his back to it. We thought we just had to stay in the room for a short while. To pass the time, we chatted about the little things in our lives. I got him to tell me about his village and I told him things about Padang.

While we were busy chatting away, all of a sudden I saw the skeleton raise its hand, as if beckoning to me, with its eyes appearing to light up. Though I'm no coward and was sure those bones couldn't move on their own that way, my heart started beating nonetheless. But I didn't show my friend my surprise, so as not to scare him. I just pretended to be absorbed in what he was saying and, from time to time, looked at the skeleton.

It raised its hand again, higher this time, and moved its fingers, as if calling out. That did startle me and because of that my friend looked behind him. When he saw the skeleton's hand moving and its eyes all aglow, he shrieked at the top of his lungs and jumped over the table, grabbing onto me and knocking over the chair and table in the process. I was thrown back by his sudden and tight embrace and we both toppled over backwards. I was almost choking, but he wouldn't let go of my neck. It was only with some difficulty that I pried loose his hands.

After I broke free of him, he fell to the floor, unconscious. His face was pale, and he was trembling and covered in sweat. Seeing that, I didn't know what to do.

So, I ran out of the room and called for help. Just then, I saw two upper-class students, coming from who knows where, and they asked why I was shouting. After I told them what had happened, they helped me carry the student and dealt with him until he had regained consciousness. Even so, he still couldn't speak and seemed to be in shock. Later, the two upper classmen tried to calm us down. They said it was impossible for the bones of a dead person to move, and that everything we had just seen was the product of our own fear. One of them then brought me over to the skeleton and had me take hold of its bones. And it was true: they couldn't move.

It wasn't until the next day that I discovered why the skeleton moved. A wire had been attached to its hand, to pull it back and forth from outside. The blazing eyes were due to some chemical agent that glows in the dark. Even though it was just a game intended to rid us of our fear and show us that ghosts and devils were the products of fear, the terrified student was sick with a fever for three days. Such were the tests at the Java Doctors' School.

Ah, right, I almost forget to tell you about Bakhtiar. He looks a bit thin these days. Maybe it's because the work of sawing and planing wood has been too hard on him. That was his daily chore in the beginning. And what he eats apparently doesn't appeal to him. I often meet up with him in the evening. For him and

Arifin, this initial period seems to have been difficult. But it doesn't matter because such beginnings are always tough and challenging. When they get used to it later on, their difficulties and troubles will disappear. They often think of you, their parents, and their close friends in Padang, and ask me to convey their regards whenever I write to you.

So that's all for now, my dear Nurbaya! Very soon you'll receive more news from me. If nothing else comes up, this Sunday Arifin, Bakhtiar and I will take a walk in Bogor and have a look at the town, the palace, and the Botanical Gardens there. If that trip works out, I'll certainly tell you all about the things I see.

Please give my humble and reverent respects to both your parents and mine and respectful greetings to all our friends and schoolmates. And accept this embrace and kiss from your beloved, who is far away.

    Samsulbahri

PS: I received the letter you sent last Friday and was saddened to hear you're still distressed about our separation. Just be patient, steady your heart, and resign yourself to the will of God the Almighty. May all our difficulties quickly vanish and all our intentions and desires be speedily fulfilled by Him. I'm sending Father some salak, sawo, and citrus, in care of one our people who's returning to Padang. I have set aside a portion for you in the package. Please accept this gift. I selected and bought these fruits myself. There are some other things I can't send this time.

Nurbaya kissed the letter and held it to her beating heart for a moment, then placed it in her closet with the others her beloved had sent.

Just then, Ali the coachman arrived, bearing a sack of fruit from Sutan Mahmud's house. Nurbaya felt an indescribable joy at seeing the gift and opened it immediately. The fruit inside was still fresh, none having rotted. She ate some and shared the rest with her family, explaining they came from her beloved. Unfortunately, her father was not at home just then, for he had gone to Padang Panjang to attend to some business matters. (It appeared the shops that used to buy his goods were no longer inclined to order from his stores.)

After Nurbaya finished with the fruit, she lay on her bed until late in the evening, thinking about her life and love. Finally, she took Samsulbahri's letters from the closet and re-read them, page by page, until she fell asleep.

Around two in the morning, she woke with a start. From every quarter came the terrifying sound of drums signaling a house had caught fire. She leapt out of bed and threw her window open to see where the noise was coming from. The sky to the southwest was burning red, indicating a blaze in the distance. At that very moment, she saw Sutan Mahmud rushing off in his buggy, heading in the direction of the flames.

To find the fire, let us leave Sitti Nurbaya at home and follow the District Head Sutan Mahmud. Arriving at Kampung Jawa market, Mahmud asked the watchmen where the fire was. "At the main market!" they shouted back and with that, he ordered the whip laid to his horse. Along the way, residents could be seen emerging from their homes, startled by the drumming. The closer Sutan Mahmud got to the market, the larger the crowd on the main road became. Some walked along at a measured pace, others ran toward the fire. Some were shouting, others crying, afraid it was their house or a relative's that was burning. Even the water pump had been brought out and was now being hauled to the blaze.

Eventually, the district head could go no further in his buggy, as there were just too many people on the road, blocking vehicles from going forward. And so he got down from the cart and proceeded on foot, accompanied by the watchmen. Reaching the scene of the fire, he saw that the stores of Baginda Sulaiman, Nurbaya's father, were ablaze. One of them had been razed, while flames from another continued to pour out. As there was no water to fill the pump, the third could not be saved. In fact, nothing could be salvaged from any of the buildings due to the voracity of the blaze and its terrible heat. No one dared to get too close, not even the police, who merely stood guard at a distance, to prevent any accidents. Embers from the fire played in the wind, lighting up the night. From time to time, small explosions sent sparks hurtling into the sky while the sound of wood splitting was like a shot from a bamboo cannon. Bats darted frantically through the air, trapped by the rising heat and flames.

An hour later, all three of Baginda Sulaiman's stores had burned to the ground, the entirety of their contents lost. Only ash and building fragments remained. A man's livelihood, the work of years, built slowly and painstakingly: snuffed out in an hour. Just then, a gale blew in, followed by heavy rain that extinguished the fire instantly.

Too late! If only the downpour had come an hour earlier, maybe one of the shops would have been saved. But it didn't happen that way. Instead, God seemed willing to spare nearby stores, while singling out Baginda Sulaiman's for destruction.

When the wind and rain did come, the crowd that had gathered round the conflagration scattered in all directions, taking cover in their homes or with neighbors nearby. Only the merchants remained, busily restoring the goods they had frantically removed from their stores. Eventually, Sutan Mahmud sought his buggy and set off for home, feeling both saddened and astonished.

"Amazing!" he said to himself as he made his way. "Why did that fire work its ruin so quickly, and why didn't the second store catch fire after the first? Could the fire really have leapt from the first store to the third, right over the one in between? And why did the two stores at either end catch fire almost at the same moment, as if they had been set ablaze on purpose, and not accidentally? Who on earth would do such a thing? Baginda Sulaiman has no enemies," he thought.

"And furthermore," he went on in his mind, "why did the rain come just when the three stores had been completely burned down? Why not earlier? Why and for what purpose did all of this happen?" Such were the thoughts of Sutan Mahmud as he rode in his little horse cart, for he could not fathom this strange event. A little while later, he arrived at his home.

8

Nurbaya's Letter

The sun sets and the stars appear only to slip away again as soon as dawn breaks. Daylight fades and becomes night, only to vanish again with the emergence of day. A day is lost and then replaced. A month ends, yet remains linked to the next. The seasons turn and the years change, but time pays no attention, instead marching on and on, ceaseless, from day to day, year to year, century to century. And whence comes time and where does it go? Does it have a beginning? An end? *Wallahualam*: Allah alone knows the truth.

At the Java Doctors' School in Batavia, there hadn't been many changes for nearly a year. The academic work kept intensifying, as the fasting month of Ramadan was not far off and the school would soon be closed, giving the students a break from their studies.

Samsulbahri and his friend Arifin had made a good deal of progress in their own school work. From the exams held that year it was obvious they had not been left behind by their classmates. So, too, the difficulties and misery they suffered when they first arrived in Batavia had by now vanished, leaving them accustomed to their new lives. Nonetheless, Samsulbahri's thoughts and his longing for Nurbaya showed little sign of diminishing, growing instead stronger with each passing day, such that love's penalty was sometimes nearly too much for him to bear. In the past few days, he had been feeling both anxious and sad, without knowing why. He feared some sort of danger had befallen his beloved and the more he thought of her, the stronger he felt he had to be with Nurbaya.

"It's surprising," he said to himself one day, sitting alone on a rock in the schoolyard, deep in thought. "That earlier dream has returned. I was glad to stop thinking about the damned thing. But why has it all of a sudden returned to haunt me? Maybe because my thoughts have reached Padang ahead of me, since it won't be long before the fasting begins and I'll be able to see my beloved again"

While lost in thought this way, Arifin came along with a letter addressed to Samsu, which he handed over. Seeing that it was from Nurbaya, Samsu rose and went to his room to read it. His heart beat wildly and just before opening the letter he had the eerie sensation that he would receive bad news, especially as he could see some water stains on the envelope.

"Did the letter get wet in the rain or the sea?" he wondered.

Just as he was about to tear open the envelope, a photograph of Nurbaya that hung on the wall fell to the floor, smashing both the frame and glass. The picture itself was damaged and a shard pierced the breast of his beloved, right in the heart. Samsu picked up the picture and slowly plucked out the piece of glass. But no matter how hard he tried to smooth it over, a tear marred the photo at Nurbaya's chest.

"That's strange. What does this mean? What news am I about to hear?"

After tidying up the bits of broken glass, he opened the letter with trembling hands and a throbbing heart. He saw now that the piece of paper on which Nurbaya had written was covered with water stains while much of the handwriting was hard to make out, as if written by someone whose thoughts were disturbed and confused. The letter said the following:

Padang, 13 March 1897

Samsulbahri, My Beloved!

Although I know this ill-starred letter that I have written with flowing tears and a heart full of sadness and pain, worse than if salt was poured into the wound in my heart, and with dim and confused thoughts, comes bearing very sorrowful news for you, and may perhaps bring to an end your hopes, which you nurture day and night, and although I feel my heart breaking to think of the sorrow and grief which will strike you when you hear this disastrous news, I have nonetheless steeled myself to write this letter, out of a concern that you might suppose my heart has really turned from you.

Perhaps, too, this news will anger you, Sam, and make you suspicious and lose faith in me. You won't want to bother with me anymore and you'll throw me away, like garbage onto the trash heap, because you see me as someone who breaks her word and cannot be trusted.

Therefore, let me swear to you right now, and then perhaps you might trust me again. I swear by Allah and the prophets my heart has not changed towards you and I have had no thought of hurting you and crushing your hopes. May God the Almighty be my witness, if I am untrue in this let me be tormented and tortured from this world to the everlasting one. I would prefer to die a thousand times and have the earth for my pillow than to live on in shame like this. And were I not afraid and were I not thinking of you, I would surely kill myself, so as not to endure this suffering any longer.

Now what is there for me to say? This is how it seems my fate has been shaped. However much I try to fend it off, such effort would surely be in vain, because human fortune and fate are fixed in the mother's womb.

Haven't I said so with a proverb? Bad luck cannot be averted, good luck cannot be snatched? Wasn't it a year ago that you knew my fate, because you had a dream about it? Now it seems the time has come for me to fulfill my promise to the Lord of all Mankind. I cannot avoid it any longer. Oh, no! My dreams for the future and my memories have all been in vain, all my hopes have vanished, the rope I was clinging to has been cut and....

At this point, Samsu was unable to read any further, for the paper was covered in what appeared to be tear stains, so that it swelled in places and what was written was hard to read. And so Samsu passed over the illegible parts and continued with the following words:

... *So that you can know the causes of this disaster, I am writing you this letter. That way, you can measure how much I've been to blame in this matter.*

As I have told you, Father's stores all burned down. That was the beginning of my suffering, and from there started my torment. From what I heard from Father at the investigation afterwards, there were signs the fire was intentionally started, for traces of kerosene and the stubs of torches were found close by. Even so, Sam, up to now there has been no explanation as to who carried out this wicked act.

The suspicion grows daily in Father's heart that the fire was an act of treachery because, of the three stores, the two at the ends caught fire first. Both went up in flames at nearly the same time. If someone hadn't set them ablaze, how could the fire have leapt from the first store to the third, passing over the one in the middle? And even if fire could leap like that, certainly the first store would have had to catch fire first before the flames could leap to the third. But, as I said, the two stores on the ends went up in flames before the one in the middle.

Because this fire was started by someone and because it moved so quickly, not a thing could be saved, because by the time people realized there was a fire, the two stores had almost burned to the ground. And with the heat of the blaze, nobody dared go near. That was also why not a single thread was saved. Everything was destroyed, consumed by the flames. Because the three stores had not been insured, my Father lost about fifty thousand rupiah that night.

Another thing that surprised Father was that the store watchmen were apparently sleeping so soundly that they were burned to death. Only the watchman of the middle store escaped unharmed. Had he not been rescued, he too would surely have died for by the time the flames began consuming the middle store, he was still asleep and had to be dragged out by the soldiers. Once outside, he looked like a drunken man, unaware of who or where he was.

As I've told you, that night Father was not at home. He had gone to Padang Panjang to take care of a matter with some shops with whom he does business. They apparently intended to renege on their payables and were unwilling to take any more of Father's goods. I've wondered about that. Could it be that all this was the work of the same person? If so, what was his purpose, and who is this hidden enemy?

When Father returned the following day—he had received the cable sent to him by your father—I told him about the disaster and my suspicion concerning that man in your dream. But Father wouldn't hear what I had to say, because he strongly trusts that person, it seems.

'He didn't do this wicked thing,' my Father said, 'it was just fate. Even so, don't trouble yourself about it!' he added, 'because I still have my coconut plantations and the forest produce which I'll receive this month, plus five boats: enough for me to begin business as before. With the help of Allah, all that has been lost will be regained'.

Father, in his patience, seemed to fully surrender his fate to God the Almighty and to request His bounty. That's what amazed me, for it will become clear that God has left us behind and no longer helps us, even though I have no idea what sin we have committed or what our fault has been. We have been struck and struck again by suffering and misfortune, as if a curse has been laid upon our heads. Two days after that, Father's crewmen, who normally bring trading goods back and forth from Terusan and Painan, reported that his five vessels had all capsized, struck by a tempest that blew in the same night of the fire. Not one piece of cargo could be saved, and all the crewmen would surely have drowned had they not been picked up by other boats.

I can't even describe how Father felt hearing this news, except to say that Allah also knows. Father's expression remained steady and unchanging, and it seemed as though he had surrendered and resigned himself to Allah's will. But I knew that, deep inside, his heart must have been utterly shattered, like a piece of glass hitting stone. Since that day we have been living very frugally.

A while later, Father borrowed money from Datuk Meringgih, about ten thousand, on the basis of some kind of agreement I wasn't aware of, perhaps to repay another debt or to be used to build the business that had crashed. But for three months he continued to fail, until the money had been used up. The merchants in Terusan and Painan ran from Father, taking their money with them, and even the shops that had done business with him in Padang Darat reneged on what they owed him.

One last hope remained for my Father, and that was his coconut plantation at Ujung Karang. But that hope was dashed as well, for we had to fall into the mud, beyond all help. The Fiend which had brought this disaster and danger upon us was apparently still not satisfied. Aside from making all our possessions vanish into thin air, it wanted to rip our spirits out, and if our misfortune doesn't end, that hellish intent will surely be achieved soon.

The coconut trees on which Father had placed his hopes would not produce anymore and their fruit, old and new alike, had gone bad and fallen to the ground. Even their trunks had died.

How could disaster come one after the other like this, I kept wondering. I wracked my brain trying to recall what Father had done wrong to bring such punishment upon him. I don't think he's done anything so terrible or made such a mistake as to deserve torture like this.

But what else can be said? If we're out of luck, all of these could be the reasons. For me, luck is like the proverb says: 'You thought it would be hot until evening; in fact, it rained at noon'. That is where God's greatness is clear, and can be an example for the wealthy. If He so requires it, your possessions, however many these may be, can disappear within the blink of an eye.

At this point, the tears that Samsu had been holding back began to flow. This is what I had been so afraid of, he thought. What will happen to my beloved? Wiping his eyes, he went back to reading the letter.

> After three months had passed, Datuk Meringgih asked for his money back, saying he now needed it. But Father had no more money. No matter the terms on which Father asked for a postponement, Datuk would not allow it.
>
> Only then did Father realize Datuk Meringgih's feelings toward him. Only then did he sense that Datuk Meringgih was not his friend, but his enemy, the greatest enemy possible. Father now began to believe all the suspicions I had expressed to him. But what could we do, Sam? The pledge had gone to China, been lost and gone forever. There was nothing we could do. Who knows, maybe it was Datuk Meringgih himself who had created all those disasters, causing Father to fall the way he did. Afterwards he purposely lent Father money, so that he would fall again, this time into his hands. If that is the case, truly Datuk Meringgih is the worst kind of criminal, someone who takes advantage of his friends, someone who would cheat his own family.
>
> Only after Father begged him repeatedly was he allowed one more week to pay, but with the agreement that if the debt were not paid after that, Father's house and possessions would be seized and he himself would be thrown into jail. Only if I were given to him, that cruel monster, could father repay the amount whenever he had the funds to do so.

As he read of this infamy, Samsu's face turned deep red. His eyes seemed to blaze, the veins of his temples swelled, and his whole body trembled. He clenched his fists around the letter, as if about to attack Datuk Meringgih, whom he imagined standing in front of him.

"You damned villain!" the words gushed from Samsu's mouth. "Old dog without a single shred of decency! At your age and with the way you look! So you want to marry Nurbaya? Marrying a ghost would be more like it for you!"

After calming himself, he went back to reading what Nurbaya had written, for he had to find out what happened to his beloved.

> That week, Father went here and there looking for money, but his credit was no longer good, as he had fallen onto hard times. Even his close friends, whom he helped in better times, have abandoned him. That seems to be the way of the world, as Batavians aptly put it with their sly remark: 'You've got money? Then from love I'm dying. You don't? Then from you I'm flying.' Yes, friends to laugh with are many, but those to cry with? You'll have a hard time finding them. <u>Money seems to be the thing that people honor, fear, respect and love. Money is the boon companion, the mother and father, the sibling and cousin. Whoever is without money is an orphan, deserted by all, alone in the world.</u>
>
> If that's true, this world is so deceitful and mankind so wicked! Is there really no one in this world who doesn't admire money? Is respect given because respect is really due? Does fear arise because something is fearsome? Are love and affection expressed because these are truly felt? I used to believe there were people who didn't worship money, honest people among the inhabitants of Padang; but after this string of disasters I'm beginning to doubt it, or believe less so than I did.
>
> Now let me go on with my account, so this letter won't be too long.
>
> That coconut plantation at Ujung Karang, Father's last possession, proved difficult to sell, for all the trees were dead.

Samsu broke off reading and shook his head, as if to stem his rage.

> For that reason, the night before Father was to meet his obligation to Datuk Meringgih, he came to me and asked what I thought of the matter. The next day, the Datuk was to come hear our decision.
>
> There was nothing I could say. Since Father's stores had burnt down, I hadn't been able to cheer myself up. I often cried at night, thinking of my wretched fate. Your dream was always in my mind's eye, too. After Datuk Meringgih insisted on payment, I couldn't sleep at all, but wept and cried my heart out every night.

Often I became stiff with fear, as if I could see Datuk Meringgih coming to have his way with me. I have lost so much weight that I'm little more than bones wrapped in skin. If you could see me now, you wouldn't recognize me, I'm sure. It's because of the sorrow and distress, the fear and anxiety.

'I realize, Nur, that you dislike Datuk Meringgih,' Father said to me that night. 'First of all, he's old. Second, he's not goodlooking. And third, because he's vicious. He's not the right match for you. And I also know how you feel about Samsu, and how he feels about you. And I myself dream of nothing else, and hope day and night that I will see you married to Samsu some day, for you're meant for each other.

'I also believe Samsu's father is very saddened to see what's happened to me and really wants to help, but he can't, he can only be moved by it and keep his distance. And I believe that he, Sutan Mahmud, would not try to thwart our dreams, and instead would join with us to accomplish your perfect match. Really, I know all this, but I have to ask your views as well, so that this doesn't become a cause for regret later on, for you yourself are the only one capable of making this decision. If you're willing to become Datuk Meringgih's wife, I will be saved, and won't go to jail, and of course our house and lands will not be sold. But if you're not willing, for sure I—and everything we have—will fall into his hands.'

When I heard those words, I couldn't restrain my sadness any longer. My heart shattered, and I began weeping and sobbing on Father's chest, until his shirt and sarong were soaked with tears. I couldn't speak a single word, my chest felt broken and my throat locked shut.

Seeing me like that, Father began to cry as well. He kissed me on the head and said, 'Nurbaya, I have no intention whatsoever of forcing you. If you're not willing to, then we'll leave it at that. It doesn't matter. Let the possessions we still have be lost, or let me go to jail, as long as I don't add to your misery and sorrow. I don't think I'll end up in prison. Maybe he can still be talked out of it.

I would rather die than force you to marry someone you dislike. And if it wasn't for you or my fear of God, I certainly would have left this world long ago. But you're the one who keeps me from doing that. How would you fare later on, if I were no longer here? Who would take care of you?'

Then Father really began to cry. *'Truth to tell, our things would be of no use to me, if you were no longer here. What would I look after? No one else depends on me. Your mother has long since departed this world. It was the thought of you that spurred me on to do business, to make big profits, so that later you wouldn't have difficulties in life. I desired and pursued and pleaded with the Lord of the Universe for nothing more than your happiness, your peace and security when the time came for me to go on home. Now, you don't like that man: over and done with! I have carried out my responsibility so that you would have no cause to blame me later. Let us now await with trust and resignation all that God requires of us!'*

Hearing Father's words of persuasion, I finally found my voice and asked, *'If all my possessions are sold, along with the house and land, would that be enough to pay off the debt? I would rather be poor than become Datuk Meringgih's wife.'*

'The land is not selling well. No one wants to buy it and the value of your belongings together with this house wouldn't amount to more than six or seven thousand rupiah. Where would we find the rest with those interest rates? So be it. Don't give any more thought to the matter. Cheer up, and we'll await what's to come.'

All night long, I couldn't close my eyes, not for an instant. I couldn't even cry. It was as if my tears had dried up. And yet, even though my eyes were open, I couldn't think of anything, my brain was simply too exhausted. So, all night I lay with my eyes open, thinking crazy thoughts. I seemed to be somewhere between consciousness and sleep, between living and dying. Terrible visions and feelings tormented me. This is probably what people call dreaming while awake.

Only after dawn broke in the east and the roosters began crowing back and forth, did I realize a new day had begun. I went out and rinsed my head, which still felt hot, like a glowing iron. Then I bathed. After that, I could more or less think straight. But when I remembered my situation, my insides seemed to shrivel, my heart pounded, and my joints and bones quaked, for in a little while either my own punishment or that of Father's would be meted out. If I escaped being pounced on by that ravaging beast, it only meant that Father would be tortured by him instead.

Not much later, Datuk Meringgih arrived, along with two Dutchmen. After climbing the steps to my house and without so much as taking a seat he said to Father, 'Well?'

'I am unable to repay the debt,' Father replied, 'and I cannot give my daughter to you.'

When Datuk Meringgih heard these words, he stamped his foot in anger and said, 'If that's so, then bear the consequences!' He then handed the matter over to the Dutch officials who had come with him. One of them, approaching Father, said, 'Regrettably, I am enjoined to take you to prison, sir, at the behest of Datuk Meringgih.'

And I am enjoined to confiscate your house, sir, and all your belongings,' said the other official.

Father could say nothing in reply, only, 'Carry out your duties, gentlemen!'

When I saw Father about to be taken to prison, as if he were some kind of criminal, my eyes went black and the thoughts vanished from my head. Without realizing what I was doing, I ran out onto the veranda and shouted, 'Don't take my father! I will marry Datuk Meringgih instead!'

When he heard that, Datuk Meringgih smiled like a tiger ready to pounce on its prey and his pleasure, passion, and animal lust were so clearly reflected in his eyes that I was forced to close my own.

Father said nothing but came over to embrace me and asked, 'Do you mean what you say?' I nodded mechanically, for I could no longer utter a single sound.

Because she wishes to help me, my child is giving herself to you, to satisfy your lusts and desires, which are those of an animal,' Father said to Datuk Meringgih. 'Now I see that my downfall was entirely your doing, with your rotten heart and envy. You couldn't stand seeing someone else with property and wealth to match yours. By pretending to be my dear friend, you tricked me into going along with your base desires. But, no matter, Datuk Meringgih! God is not blind. In the end, you will surely be punished for this treachery.' Father then led me by the hand back into the house. In that moment, Samsu, I became Datuk Meringgih's wife...."

Here, the letter could no longer be made out, for the paper was everywhere stained with tears.

When he finished reading what had happened to Nurbaya, Samsu placed his head on the table and wept bitterly for his beloved's fate and his own wretched destiny. The ideals and dreams he had cultivated for so long had, at that very moment, vanished forever, like a stone falling into a deep pool, or rain falling on sand, gone without a trace! The hope that had for so long formed part of his heart's flesh and blood had suddenly been cleaved by Datuk Meringgih, with a severance that could never be re-joined.

"This is what has become of the memories I have longed for all this time. Here is the fruit of the petitions and prayers I have sent to heaven day and night, to God the Almighty. How awful!" Such were Samsulbahri's tears, alone in his room.

After crying inconsolably for a time, he suddenly stood up, gnashing his teeth and clenching his fists. His face now pale and his eyes burning with the strain of checked anger, he grabbed Nurbaya's picture, held it before his face and vowed, "By Allah and his Apostle, for as long as there is breath in me, I will avenge this evil deed. My heart will not be satisfied until I have my vengeance. Oh Allah, Oh my God! Grant my request and do not take my life before I have attained this goal."

After making his vow, Samsu bowed for several seconds, as if trying to restrain his sorrow and anger. Then he returned to his chair without uttering another word. Regaining his senses, he continued reading Nurbaya's letter with damp, reddened eyes.

Perhaps you can't imagine, Samsu, just how crushed I now feel. First, because I have gone back on my promise to you and brought your hopes to an end. Second, because I'm being forced to marry Datuk Meringgih: an old devil I hate. There's nothing about him I respect. Though wealthy, in form he is just like a dog-demon and as for his lineage, Allah knows, he was originally a peddler of dried fish. His character is worse than an animal's and he is rough and cruel. Furthermore, he was the one who took Father's wealth and ruined his good name. He is our greatest enemy, the executioner who will take my life from me. It is to such a man that I must now give myself. With him, I must live side by side. Just think of it, Samsu!

There is no one in this world who suffers as I do!

You might not believe what I've told you, and may even suspect I've made it all up to trick you. But Allah the Most Holy and the Most High is my witness, Sam, and He also is the One who knows how I feel when I must surrender myself.

Though things are this way, I can't let myself be discouraged if you don't believe me, because I have, in fact, gone back on my promise and have not kept my word. I'm a woman who has destroyed the hopes of her beloved. That, I cannot deny. Is there another path I can take in this disaster?

Since I cannot endure such a burden, I've thought of killing myself. That is a punishment befitting my sin. I would rather die a thousand times, with my head resting on the earth, than live in shame like this. But when I think of taking poison, that seems wrong as well.

So, I'm writing you this letter so that you know the entire story, from beginning to end, and all the reasons I have gone back on my word. When you read this, you might think to punish me, which I will gladly accept with all my heart. If you cannot forgive me, I will know that, in this world, there is no more hope. For that reason, I am begging you to reply to this letter right away.

As I see it, part of your dream has already occurred, with only the fall into the chasm still left. If it comes to that, my final moments on earth will have arrived. So my downfall at Datuk Meringgih's hands couldn't have been postponed any longer. It was my fate and destiny. And so, it would be better for me to end my life quickly, rather than endure this for too long.

One thing will console me later on, if it comes to that; the end of your dream, when we fall into the chasm together. Perhaps there we can finally be together, even if we are separated in this life. In the hereafter, we will be united forever.

I have to end this letter now, my love. Some day, if there's life left in my body, I will continue telling you this tale of calamity, so long as you're willing to read about this wretched fate of mine. Maybe I'll no longer call you my beloved, but 'brother'. Maybe you'll still be fond of such a notion and will return the embrace and kiss of your sister, who has suffered so much.

Nurbaya

When he finished reading the letter, Samsu could only throw himself face-down on his bed, and sob the whole night through.

9

Return to Padang

One day, a little more than a year after Samsulbahri and Nurbaya had gone hiking on Mount Padang with their friends, hundreds of men and women, children and adults, young and old alike could be seen gathered around the mountain's graves and under its trees, some absorbed in reciting prayers on behalf of the departed, others cleaning their elders' final resting places. Here and there, someone wept for a child taken from this world or placed a small bouquet of flowers on the grave of a much-beloved sibling or cousin. Some simply sat around and chatted, having come merely to take a look or to be part of the general hustle and bustle. All along the road to the mountain, people came and went, stopping at some point to catch their breath, filling the lower reaches and lending the whole scene the air of a vast market.

Down by the Arau River, dozens of sampans ferried passengers back and forth, while along the main highway, buggies lined up, waiting for fares. Holy mendicants known as *fakir* and the ordinary poor, together with religious scholars and those who had undertaken the pilgrimage to Mecca, all came to pray. Some could be heard chanting God's greatness, while others recited the Confession of Faith.

Why all this commotion on Mount Padang? It was the last day before the fasting month of Ramadan would begin. Before commencing this worthy month, the inhabitants of Padang visit the graves of family members who have gone home to the Mercy of Allah, praying for their souls and asking for blessings, that those who have died, and those still living, might be protected by Him.

As it is the final day before the fasting period begins, Muslims are allowed to eat all day long, satisfying their appetites to the fullest with all manner of delicious foods. For that reason, the people of Padang call it "the day for eating".

That evening, the moon, radiating its light from the west, was like a paper cut-out hung low over the ocean while the drums beating within all the prayer houses and mosques signaled the start of the fasting period the very next day.

On the fourth day of that month, a ship from Batavia entered Teluk Bayur harbor, bearing several students returning home to West Sumatra to visit their parents and friends, as during Ramadan the schools for native students were closed.

Among that group were Samsulbahri and his friends, Arifin and Bakhtiar. When their vessel drew up to the pier, the three of them went ashore and hurried off home, longing to see their parents. Only Samsulbahri seemed indifferent, for the woman he loved and had left behind was no longer his; only his mother and father would be there to greet him. His return was sure to arouse thoughts and memories of an earlier time.

When Samsu arrived at his house, he shook his father's hand and embraced his mother before heading to his room to change his clothes. Re-emerging a short time later, he sat with his parents and recounted his experience of studying and living in Batavia, describing as well the return voyage to Padang. Though he spoke of such things, his heart and mind seemed to wander off, to who knows where. His mother, Sitti Maryam, noticed this and grieved for him, thinking of her poor child's luck. Yet, Samsu's face showed no sign of the turmoil he must have felt.

"Such a pity," he sighed, overwhelmed with sadness at the sight of his parents' home and the thought of Nurbaya, and all the memories now brought to mind. He nearly regretted having come home.

"I saw a convict throw himself overboard like someone who had lost all hope," he said.

"Where was that?" his mother asked, startled by such awful news and afraid her child might do the same.

"In the sea near Tanjung Cina, the night before last. When the waves grew especially big, he leapt from the deck and was lost without a trace."

"Oh, Allah, Lord, how pitiful!" exclaimed his mother in horror.

"It seemed he had given up from despair and preferred to die at sea rather than bear suffering, disgrace, and shame. It's not surprising: I often saw him brooding and sometimes crying by the side of the ship. Many times, he didn't even want to eat."

"Perhaps he wanted to escape," said Sutan Mahmud.

"I don't think so. At that point, the ship was in the middle of the ocean, with no land in sight. There was no way he could have reached the shore. Besides, his hands were in fetters. How could he have swum?"

"That's so sad! How will his wife and children feel, and his relatives, when they hear the news?" his mother asked.

"Maybe he was all alone in this world, or had committed some great crime," his father replied.

"The wrongs done by mankind, Allah alone knows them," his wife said in response.

"They say he had been convicted of murder, and was banished to Sawah Lunto for fifteen years," Samsu added.

"Well, there you are! If he wasn't guilty, would he have been given such a heavy sentence?" rejoined Sutan Mahmud.

"Even though he was sentenced, that doesn't mean his guilt was beyond question. A sentence, though just, is still made in this world. And his judge was a human being, capable of error and weakness, like all of us," Sitti Maryam interjected.

"Fine, but the judge was not stupid. He was skilled in the law, learned and highly educated. Furthermore, sentence isn't passed by one judge alone, but jointly. How could they all be wrong, too?"

"Even so, we still can't be sure he was guilty, for a man's inner life cannot be known to other men."

Samsulbahri did not wish to become embroiled in this debate, particularly as his thoughts remained elsewhere.

"What do you mean?" he heard his father ask. "Do you really think the judge would punish someone for no good reason? Surely, he would have been sentenced only once the case had been sufficiently clarified, with testimony from all the witnesses."

"It's the witnesses who often distract the judge from getting at the truth. Now, don't get angry at what I have to say. Just listen to these examples. A rich person, or one in a high position, wants to destroy a poor man. With his money and rank, it would be easy for him to arrange a few false witnesses. If the judge listens only to those witnesses, then surely our poor man, who is guilty of nothing, will be convicted. A second example. A person passing through a deserted area is murdered by a villain, who intends to rob him of his possessions. A righteous, innocent person then arrives at the scene. When he sees the man lying there, abandoned on the high road, he examines him in case he might still be saved. While he is examining him, he gets some blood on his clothes. Then, four others arrive and see our righteous friend near the corpse with his blood-stained clothes. Wouldn't he be indicted for committing that evil deed? Surely all the witnesses would be able to claim in front of the judge that they saw with their own eyes the righteous fellow near the corpse with blood on his clothes. The witnesses would be telling the truth, not lying. Couldn't this be called sufficient evidence? That is, four or five witnesses speaking the truth, together with the bloody clothing? Therefore, the judge convicts our innocent man. But is it true he was guilty of murder?"

Because he heard the truth in what his wife said, Sutan Mahmud arose from his chair and went to sit on the front veranda, bested as he had been in this exchange and ashamed to admit his faulty reasoning.

Only after Sutan Mahmud left did Sitti Maryam notice her child gazing wistfully at Nurbaya's house. Though she knew full well what was going on in his mind, she asked, "Samsu, what are you thinking about?"

"Ah, nothing, Mother," the young man replied, "My thoughts haven't shaken free from what I was just telling you. It seems that despair can be very dangerous."

Sitti Maryam's heart beat faster at her son's reply, for she was worried Samsu might be in despair as well. She tested his feelings by asking, "Did you know that Nurbaya married Datuk Meringgih? I told your father to inform you, but whether he did so or not, I don't know."

In fact, Sitti Maryam had forbidden her husband to write a letter to Samsu about the matter, for she was afraid Samsu would be very upset.

"Yes," replied Samsu tersely, unable to bear the news yet again.

"Perhaps you don't much like the idea of this marriage, for, really, it wasn't proper that your friend should sit on the marriage dais with Datuk Meringgih. But what more can be said? All of that was God's absolute predestination and cannot be undone. But go to her house! Her dear father has been ill for several days now. You'll hear that what happened was the best way to free them from calamity," she said to soothe her son.

"What is wrong with Uncle Baginda Sulaiman?"

"He has a fever and a headache."

"All right, I'll go over there immediately," Samsu replied, and went to his room to change again. Soon after, Ali came to take the fruit brought from Batavia.

"Give a plate to your master out front and another for Baginda Sulaiman," Sitti Maryam told the coachman. "Maybe he has an appetite for fruit. It's been several days since he's eaten."

"Very good," the coachman replied.

A little while later, accompanied by Ali, Samsu went to the home of Baginda Sulaiman.

Inside his neighbor's yard, Samsu saw the bench where he and Nurbaya had sat the night before he left for Batavia one year ago. His heart began to race and he recalled all he had done and said that night, the promise he had made to her. Had he not been ashamed to do so in front of Ali, he would have wept at the thought of it all.

"Will Nurbaya be here?" he wondered. And if she were there, how would he greet the beloved who had left him?

Entering, he found the house empty and so went quietly into Baginda Sulaiman's room. There, he found Nurbaya's father lying on his bed under a flannel sheet. Samsu was shocked and saddened to see how much the merchant had changed. The person lying there hardly seemed like his adoptive uncle.

The sick man's hair had begun to turn white and his pale face and thin body would, from time to time, summon but a small movement, as if utterly worn out.

"Is that you, Nurbaya? Come over here!" Baginda Sulaiman said.

"I'm not Nurbaya," Samsu replied through trembling lips that held back his grief. "It's Samsulbahri, just in from Batavia. When I heard that you were sick, I came right over."

Hearing these words, the old man's eyes widened as he tried to get a better look at the young man standing before him.

"Samsulbahri?" he asked weakly.

"Yes, Uncle."

"Come closer, Samsu!"

Samsu approached with the souvenirs he had brought from Java. "Here's some fruit I brought from Batavia in case you find it in you to eat."

"What kind of fruit? I haven't been able to eat for several days now."

"There are *sawo*, mangoes, snakefruits, pineapple, as well as grapes and apples. Perhaps they might revive your appetite."

"Give me one of those *sawo*. Pick out a soft one!"

Samsu selected a ripe *sawo*, wiped it clean, and handed it to Nurbaya's father, who ate it slowly. His appetite seemed to return somewhat, whether because of the fruit or because it had been Samsu who brought it, Allah alone knows. In any case, he ate several of them.

While Baginda Sulaiman ate, Samsu fixed his eyes on the man's face, gratified that his gifts had been able to revive his appetite.

"This is very nice fruit you've brought, Sam. I feel refreshed now," Baginda Sulaiman said. "I'm very grateful to you, for I can see your feelings for me haven't been changed by the calamity that's befallen me. I thought you were Nurbaya just now because I had called for her. But I'm all the more pleased knowing you are here. It seems God has granted my prayer, for I've prayed a long time for this meeting. I have wished very much to see you again, for there's something I want to ask of you."

"What is it? Tell me! If it's within my strength to give it or do it, I will," Samsu replied.

"I don't think I'll be on this earth very much longer. I have seen omens and signs that I'll soon be returning to the mercy of Allah."

"Don't think like that! Think of Nurbaya!" exclaimed Samsu, his eyes brimming with tears.

"That is what thwarts me and disturbs my thoughts. When I'm no longer in this world, Nurbaya will become an orphan, motherless and fatherless, bereft of family or relatives. What will happen to her once I die? Will she be alone in the world? Who will be there to help her during hard times? Who will guide her and teach her to avoid mistakes? As you know, in age she is still as green as the growing corn and just as innocent. She hasn't learned how to live by herself. She doesn't yet realize the wickedness of the world. She hasn't yet felt real pain and suffering.

"Although in this world we can obtain pleasure, joy, wealth and glory, nevertheless the world contains various forms of hardship, suffering, poverty and degradation. They are hidden everywhere, peering out at their victims at any time, ready to pounce on whatever comes near.

"So, too, is this world full of pitfalls and temptations, enslavement, cruelty, deceit, envy and dispute, arrogance and snobbery, spite and betrayal. If we're not careful and can't avoid such wicked traps, we'll fall right into them and our lives will be destroyed. We can meet such danger at any time and in any place, whether on land, at sea, in the air, under the earth, in our homes, along the road, in the forest, or in the midst of open fields. We're never safe from these perils. While we sit, while we walk and sleep, eat and drink, speak, look, listen, or smell, we can find ourselves faced with them. Truly, Samsu, it isn't easy to live in this world. Life is a razor-thin bridge to heaven, finer even than a split hair.

"It's not easy to cross this bridge. Most people fall off and plunge into the fires of hell blazing beneath. Only those who are careful in what they do, those with perfect thoughts, who are pure of heart and straightforward, patient and trusting in God's will, are the ones who often reach the other side safely. That is the difficulty, if we are to live righteously in this world, and how much more so for someone who's all alone. I felt this myself, Samsu, when I was still young. That's why, for most people, the world is the most hellish of hells, the ceaseless joining of thousands and thousands of strands of pleasure and supernatural power. 'Broken, they grow back; lost, they are replaced', from beginning to end. What is rather fortunate is that our luck keeps changing, sometimes touching bottom, sometimes reaching the top. Like a spinning wheel it turns. There are only a few people who can attain heaven on this earth....

"Give me a few more grapes... I feel weak from talking on and on like this."

Samsu quickly handed the grapes to Nurbaya's father. After he had eaten a few of them, he continued with what he had been saying. "Because I myself have known and experienced all this, I grow more and more worried about leaving Nurbaya behind. While for men life is very difficult, it is especially so for women, who are weak in character and who are viewed by our people as being of lower stature compared to men. And for most Muslims women have almost no worth, but are instead the same as household slaves. What will be her fate later on? My heart becomes confused when I think about it. Nonetheless, what should I say? For the time of one's death, fortune and affinity cannot be fixed.

"Since there's no one else on this earth except you, my second child—and you *are* a brother to Nurbaya—I beseech you from the depths of my heart to please help and assist your sister in every way possible. She will be an orphan. Don't forsake or cast her aside, but, please, look after her as would a mother and father. Don't be vengeful and offended because she has become Datuk Meringgih's wife! You know full well, Samsu, her marriage was neither to her liking, nor to mine, but was fully foreordained by the One God, and cannot be undone. Although she and I would have preferred to die rather than go through with it, what authority do we have to dispute the will of God? It wasn't Nurbaya's fault, nor mine, nor anybody's that such a thing happened, but rather Nurbaya's destiny."

Baginda Sulaiman paused for a moment, as if waiting for a reply from Samsu. But since the young man remained silent, he repeated his question. "Are you willing to grant my request?"

"How could I not be willing? Please don't worry. No matter what, Nurbaya will always be my younger sister, in this world and in the next. She could never be cast aside or wiped from my heart. I promise before God and His apostles, for as long as I live, I shall not forsake Nurbaya."

At that, Baginda Sulaiman took Samsu's hand in both of his, and placing it on his chest, closed his eyes for a short time, saying with a voice now at ease, "Thank you."

Just then, Nurbaya entered the room.

In fact, she had arrived at the house some time ago, called there by her father, but when she heard Samsulbahri's voice coming from her father's room, she did not know what to do. She wanted to go in and see her father, but felt shame and fear at the thought of seeing Samsu. In her sudden state of confusion, she could only stand frozen outside the room, with her heart pounding in her chest.

Only after hearing Samsu's promise to her father did her confusion vanish, replaced by great happiness, for she now realized that her brother and beloved had not changed toward her. And so, she gathered her courage and entered the room to greet them.

When Samsu finally saw Nurbaya's face, his mouth dropped in astonishment, though no words could come. In his heart, joy vied with grief: joy, because he was, at long last, seeing his beloved; grief, because he then remembered his hopes had been shattered. Nurbaya's physical appearance had altered drastically since the two had parted. Her body, once elegant and graceful, had become thin. Her face, formerly ivory in hue, and even slightly ruddy when exposed to the sun, was now pale. Her eyes, once so clear, were now faded and encircled by dark, deep lines while her cheeks appeared sunken and her hair tangled, as if she no longer cared for it. All of this bespoke the deepest of grief and pain. Samsu felt great sadness, seeing his beloved in such a state and could not bring himself to utter a word.

When her eyes fell on her beloved, Nurbaya feigned surprise and exclaimed in apparent joy, "Sam, you're here! How are you? When did you arrive?" She then came toward him and took hold of his hand.

"Just now, by boat," Samsu said, shaking Nurbaya's hand. "When I got home, I heard that Uncle was ill. That's why I came right over. How are things with you?"

"As you see, not everything speaks of happiness. But I will tell you more about it later."

She then drew near her father and said, "How are you, Father? How do you feel? And what's happened, that you should be call me here?"

"Come close to me and sit. There's something important I wish to tell you," her father replied.

Once Nurbaya had taken a seat next to him, Baginda Sulaiman began to speak.

"Nurbaya, my child! The truth is I've been ill for a long time. I've never told you, but instead endured it the best I could, lest my condition add to your grief. I'm old now. My journey through this world will reach no new heights. Instead, it will descend to my eternal place, where I shall be at rest forever. From nothingness I was created. Once small, I grew big, and after growing up, I grew old. Having grown old, I'm going back to the place of my beginning. That is the journey of all that live in this world. There is no deviation from this, nor can it be changed. Everything that lives will die in the end and the appearance of all things that exist will continue changing.

"Although such things usually pass unnoticed because people are absorbed in their own joys and sorrows, and because for most people thoughts like that bring horror and fear, death being something mysterious, none of that is going to change this natural journey. Truth be told, thinking about death is terrifying, but we really mustn't banish such thoughts, but instead fully understand that death is going to come at some point anyway. Thus, we shouldn't imagine we're going to live forever and be together with the things of this earth for eternity. In this way, when the time comes for us to leave this world and part from everything we loved and cherished, we won't be too shocked or lose our minds. For that is what frequently leads those astray who go on this journey, and damages the bodies and minds of those who stay, for all are filled with regret and longing, as well as being exceedingly saddened and distressed.

"I know very well that parting from those things that have so captivated me won't be easy. Especially if this is to be a final separation, after which we are never to meet again, as some people see it. But let's not forget, all of this is as it must be. Whether we like it or not, whether we are joyful or full of remorse, fearful or courageous, resigned or resisting, when that allotted hour comes, it cannot be avoided any longer, but must be accepted with submission and sincerity. What power do we humble and weak humans have? None. The haughty and arrogant have power, and there are those who exalt themselves because of their intelligence, wealth, high birth or position. But how much power do they really have, compared with this natural power? Much like a drop of water compared to the oceans of this world. Perhaps not even that much.

"As for intelligence and skill, I admit that much has been discovered by science, but probably only a millionth of what actually exists. Maybe you don't believe this. So, let me ask you a simple question: which came first, the chicken or the egg? Ask those who are clever. Who can explain this?

"As for great wealth and birth of high degree, I won't say anything more about those. You yourself have seen and heard many examples of both. No matter their wealth or title, such people can disappear in the blink of an eye, if it be the will of God. Being high-born shouldn't be a cause for conceit, for birth is high only because man made it so. So, too, is lowness man-made. If no one did such raising and lowering, certainly everyone would be equal. And who is it doing the raising and lowering? Only man. And does not all mankind stem from the Prophet, Adam and Eve? And how can some be high, some low, some different from others, when our origins are all the same? It's not that I wish to treat all mankind the same. No. There are indeed differences, though not from noble birth, but in one's status in society. These are not the same. Nonetheless, even social ranking comes from God. What is the use of being conceited about something that has been given? And even things beyond this, things a person has obtained himself, like knowledge from science or skills, are nothing to be haughty about, for anyone can obtain them, as long as it's one's destiny to receive such gifts.

"Yes, Nur, were I not so exhausted, I certainly would unravel all this for you, as there is much more you need to know. However, so that this won't go on too long, I'll return to my original point."

After pausing for a bit, Baginda Sulaiman began again, speaking slowly. "Wouldn't it be better not to be too moved by emotion? Rather, we should strengthen our patience and trust in the One God with an attitude of submission, praying that those who go on and those who stay are both under His care. I'm telling you this, for my illness seems to get worse with each new day. Who knows, it could be that I will leave you tomorrow or the day after that."

Hearing these words, Nurbaya shrieked, then began sobbing and fell upon her father, kissing his brow and crying out "Father, no! Stay here with me. If you have to go, take me with you. Don't leave me all alone in this world. Who will help me? Where will I go to seek counsel and make requests? If I were sick, who would care for me? If I were in distress, who would comfort me? Your child would be orphaned, alone and lonely in this world, with no mother, no father, nor brothers or sisters. Oh Allah, what would happen to me then, when my father is no more?"

She collapsed and wept bitterly on her father's chest.

"Don't cry, Nur!" Baginda Sulaiman tried to soothe her. "Nothing is certain. I hope and pray day and night that we can be together for a long time to come. I'm telling you these things so that you'll bear it in mind and not be too shocked when the time comes. For no matter what, that time will surely come. If not now, then soon. One cannot live forever. Life is in Allah's hands. If He so wills it, at any time it will surely fly away in the blink of an eye. As long as I'm capable of speaking, it is my obligation to remind you, so that this does not become a cause for remorse later on.

"Of course, it saddens me to think of my situation now. If I pass on at this time, I have nothing to leave to you except my love and prayers, for my possessions have been exhausted. But do not worry or despair! Entrust your fate to the Lord of the Universe. It is He who will look after you. It is He who will aid and cherish you, and much better than I can. And it's not just mankind He cares for, but even the worm in its rocky hole receives from Him the sustenance of life. Therefore do not lose your senses, but day and night beseech the Almighty to protect you in all that you do. And do not forget Samsu either! Even if he is not your real brother, he is a better brother to you than if he were my own son. He has promised me he will be loyal to you in this world and in the next."

"Is that true?" Nurbaya asked, taking Sam's hands in hers while looking straight into his eyes. "I cannot tell you how it makes me feel to hear my father's words. So, is it true, you haven't changed towards me?"

"It's true, Nur," Samsu replied. "Why would I change towards you? I cannot feel anger about your present situation, for none of it is your fault, but rather a sign from God. I should double and re-double my love and concern for you through all the danger you face, because you will need my help and protection. Never doubt me in this! Whatever happens, you will always be my younger sister. I cannot and will not abandon you. The rope connecting me to you has been knotted fast and cannot be undone. Your flesh has become my flesh, your blood my blood. Who can separate us?"

"I'm so grateful to you, Samsu! Allah alone knows how happy I feel to hear your words, and He will also reward you for your goodness!"

As she said this, Nurbaya could not hold back the tears that began streaming from her eyes and onto the mat below, like beads from a string that has suddenly been severed.

"When I'm no longer here," Baginda Sulaiman began again, "be even more careful in protecting yourself. Be prudent and wise in taking care of your body. 'Speak upwards, and wash downstream', as the saying goes. For, really, how you speak demonstrates character. This is particularly true since all those who are good prefer attractive and amiable character and breeding, and soft and gentle speech to coarse behavior and unseemly words. We achieve our aims and receive aid more easily with good behavior than with force and compulsion. If you want to be esteemed, humble yourself, for esteem and humility come not from ourselves, but from others.

"And what is wrong with being humble? We do not lose position and noble birth from humble action and speech. 'The snake does not die when it squeezes into the creepers', as our proverb has it. Humble speech and a sweet disposition can never be wrong, and frequently even carry us to higher places. The opposite—big-sounding words and an arrogant personality—breeds hatred. If you go to other villages, you must 'scoop water from the well of others and break their branches'. This means we mustn't apply our own rules. Instead, we must use and apply the customs and habits of those people, from that village, so that we'll be liked and soon win companions who are good and willing to aid us in all our difficulties. Don't make friends only when times are good, for this rarely proves advantageous, and often ends up making us sad. Friends in bad times, they are the ones to cultivate. False friends, those who look for favors among relatives and friends and who deceive the same, who feign friendship because they wish to bring ruin upon us, with them you must be truly cautious, for they appear too intimate with their sweet and ingratiating ways. For that reason, don't forget the proverb, 'Even the sweetest fruit can bear maggots'.

"The old must be respected, the young cherished, while peers should honor and esteem each other. Even if the old seem beneath us in knowledge, wealth, position, breeding, or other such attainments, remember they ate salt before we did and have tasted more of life, both the good and the bad. Remember, too, 'Much experience comes in a long life, and much is seen on a long journey'. Therefore, it must be that they possess the knowledge and perspective and responsibility that we ourselves do not yet have or have not yet experienced. That is the reason such people are to be respected.

"The young must be cherished, for they are our younger brothers and sisters whose strength and knowledge is less than ours. It is not proper to use our advantages to mistreat them. So, too, all creatures, especially the weak and the wretched, must be loved with compassion. Do not hurt them, for they are all Allah's servants, just as we are. We must be loving towards our fellow man, and amiable and helpful with each other in our work, our pleasures and our sorrows. In particular, we must aid those who suffer or are in trouble. And the grand and the rich need not be excluded here, for the poor can help with their strength and advice, just as the rich can help with money. Don't be haughty and conceited, particularly as we now have nothing to be conceited about. We have no money and very little social standing. Even if we did have possessions, lineage, and high position, these are nothing to be arrogant about, for, as I've said, all such things are lent to us and have value only in this world. When the owner at some point asks for them back, they must be returned.

"Do not take pleasure in cruel and wicked acts, but love only benevolence instead. The proverb says, 'A just king is revered, an unjust king opposed'. If kings are treated this way, how much more so it should be with us. Even your thoughts must be clean and pure. Avoid harboring the wrong intentions for yourself or towards others, for all such deeds and thoughts do not disappear, for 'whatever has a beginning also has an end'. Evil actions and thoughts cannot but rebound to you or your fellow man. So, too, the opposite is true: all good deeds and thoughts cannot but bring goodness to you or others. Although on occasion the results of an action or intention appear to be different from what was intended, do not be doubtful, for nothing can go wrong. If not now, then certainly later, goodness and evil repay in kind. What is good cannot give rise to evil and so, too, the opposite.

"If your request is not granted and your purpose yet to be achieved, if you experience some difficulty or are in peril, don't be quick to despair or regret your luck, or become angry with God, for of course all such things are gifts from God, who is a just God and merciful towards his servants. At no time does He wish to bring ruin to them. For that reason, all that He has bestowed on his servants, even though seemingly evil for those who do not understand, is really and truly good. If you carefully reflect and pay attention, it will become clear to you that everything that has befallen you which seems evil contains some good as well. Learning that brings true cultivation. Because of those predicaments and sufferings, your understanding and knowledge of the secrets of our universe and life in this world will grow. Comfort and pleasure rarely provide lessons, and even frequently cause men to forget themselves and their God, making them haughty and arrogant.

"To explain how calamity is but a lesson, listen to this example. A child did not yet know of the danger of fire. How might this have been explained to it, so that it would understand how great the danger was and keep away from it? It is very difficult, isn't it? Almost impossible, for the danger could not be demonstrated, or conveyed accurately to a child who had not yet experienced it. One day, when it was playing with fire, the child's hand got burned, as had been fated by Allah. Only then did it realize the danger of fire. Those who did not know, or who did not wish to think very deeply, said the child had received God's punishment. But really the child had received a gift, that is, an understanding and lesson it could not have gained without this experience. Because of this mishap, the child's understanding grew and it was able to keep away from the danger represented by fire, which might be many times greater than what it had experienced. Is this not a bounty? And so, too, are all the other difficulties and misfortunes. There will always be these, and they have some good in them, too. If you reflect on all the dangers that beset you, you will surely be farthest from worry and regret, as well as from the various ailments which spring from them.

"Mournful thoughts, sadness and anxiety do not bring any good, but in fact evil. Instead, it is patience and trust in God, along with pure thoughts, that increase the body's health. Has it not been said, 'Patience is the key to the door of heaven'? Is not patience the sign of deep understanding, a firm faith, in other words, a noble quality? Patience is what often provides the road to earthly heaven as well as the heaven of the hereafter, while impatience, scandal-mongering, maligning, envy, treachery, greed and covertness, and all qualities like them, frequently guide us to hell. If you can be patient and restrain your heart from all sadness, anxiety and anger, you can surely withstand those appetites which aren't good. Such qualities are to be resisted with all your might and banished from your heart.

"Great wealth, high position and glorious lineage do not always bring happiness, for most of mankind is greedy, and does not accept what has been bestowed by God. Instead, they want their fortune to continue increasing. And even when they are able to fulfill all their wishes and aims, they are not only unsatisfied, but their greed and covetness even grow, as they continue to forget themselves and their God, absorbed as they are in satisfying their insatiable lusts. If they are unable to achieve all their goals, they rue their luck and repine to Allah. Such a person will never obtain happiness and tranquility.

"Therefore, accept all that God has bestowed upon you with patience. If you wish to increase what you have, you may, but you must ask this of Him, and take a righteous path in doing so. If your request is not granted right away, be patient and it might come later, for that which is necessary will surely be obtained in the end, so long as you ask for it with faith and sincerity. As I have said, God is All-Merciful.

"Sometimes, a low-born person, poor and weak, exceeds in happiness someone who is rich, grand or of high position. For example, a child who lives hidden away in the forest or mountains, far from worldly beauty, pleasures, riches and intelligence, is often happier than a city-dweller cloaked in grandeur and magnificence, because what the forest child requires of life does not amount to much, so that it has almost no wants and its appetite is meager. Desire and appetite, those are the greatest seducers."

After pausing for a moment to eat some more fruit, Baginda Sulaiman continued counseling his daughter. "Do not suppose that progress in the world always brings advantages for mankind. It doesn't. An easy example is the fact that old people lived longer and were healthier in prior times than today. Their lives were not perfect and what they had to live on was far less than what people have today. Sometimes their clothes were merely a piece of cloth made from tree bark, their food uncooked, unseasoned and unspiced, and their homes, a tree trunk or a rocky cave.

"And not only did they surpass today's population in age and health, but their knowledge was exceedingly deep as well. For example, the knowledge of rice farming, which originated with the Hindus of old, has not been improved upon to the present day. In terms of their power, the temples that the Hindus built have yet to be reproduced by today's clever engineers. The Egyptian's science of wrapping the corpses of kings to preserve them for thousands of years remains unknown even today. Right up to the present, there are still traces of those ancient men, even if they don't live as they once did.

"Just think of the mountain folk, who in our villages live a secluded and sheltered life, far from the city, in lonely places! Aren't they healthier and stronger than city dwellers? Don't they think and feel better and purer, too? And their food? Rice with sour tamarind and vegetables that haven't been cooked with much sophistication. Nonetheless, they are as strong as elephants. They pay no mind at all to the rain or the heat, things which even seem to add to their wellbeing. Their clothes are merely a cut of cloth and the rain gets into their homes, but rarely do they fall sick.

"As for the man of progress who lives in the city, he uses all sorts of ideas and medicines to keep from getting ill. His house has to be good, he follows the science of his doctor, his clothing is mostly from fine cloth, he is very particular about what he eats, there always must be enough, and it cannot be dirty. In my view, such a life poisons people, shortens their years and weakens their body.

"I myself have often experienced the virtues of people who are said to be half-savage. They tend to be friendly and helpful, to feel compassion for one another, to be straightforward, reliable, loyal, respectful, orderly, quiet, dignified and just. Such attributes have been forgotten by most city dwellers. It's a pity. As time goes by, they become fewer and fewer, replaced by the resourceful, the smart and the civilized. But the truth is, the cleverer such men are, the more malicious and violent they become. They have traded the qualities of their noble ancestors for spitefulness, treachery, greed, seclusion, unwillingness to help others or to be affable and compassionate, arrogance, haughtiness, stinginess, conceit, unreliability, disloyalty, cruelty, and all the rest. Ah, what will finally become of this world, when progress, so loved by society nowadays, has brought mankind to such a pass?

"Furthermore, you must know, progress is a tool which can be directed to a benign or an evil end. If, in the future, it is directed to the benign, its results will be benign as well. If it is directed to an evil end, then surely evil will come of it. People today seem to want to show off the progress their ship has made on the way to the island of evil, so this will not perfect humanity, but instead annihilate everything that lives.

"What is the use of guns, if not to end life? What good are cannons, if not to blast the world? And why is this so? Only so man, who claims to be more clever and civilized than his forbearers, whom he terms uncouth, has in truth become more malicious and violent.

"The more advanced mankind becomes, the more good and evil grow. The science and knowledge of doctors, a result of such progress, can be used to heal the sick, but can also be used to kill the living. Since those who live without any religious belief are naturally all too easily tempted by evil rather than led by good, progress becomes a kind of venom that poisons the world. That's why it isn't good to hand over the weapon of progress to such people. Isn't an educated criminal far more dangerous than an ignorant one? When a stupid person wants to steal, he waits first until the owner is gone or asleep. If the owner is there, or still awake, the thief is unable to achieve his end. But an educated criminal will use his knowledge, which is sometimes highly dangerous, to attain his goals. Therefore, all knowledge which falls to those who do not harbor good intentions will become venomous weapons. Before pursuing knowledge, the heart must first be cleansed. How great the benefit if the science of a pure heart were taught in schools."

Here Baginda Sulaiman stopped and asked for an apple. After taking a bite, he began again. "If you are fortunate in life, use your surplus to help the poor or those in distress. Use your intelligence to show and teach those who do not yet understand. And use your position to bring your fellow man to the place of your own wellbeing. If you do this, you cannot but be kept safe and protected in this world and in the next. And when the time comes for you to leave this world, surely there will be nothing more to block your journey and obstruct your return home, filled with sincere feelings. For you will know that for as long as you have lived, you have done no wrong, that your heart is pure and devoted to goodness.

"There is something else I would like to tell you, and that is our proverb, 'Thought is the light of the heart'. That is a very true saying, in both the physical and spiritual sense. In anything that you have to do or say, take pains first to think it through. Don't be in a hurry, like a frog that leaps before it looks. Often, it leaps the wrong way and brings disaster upon itself. If you are ruined, this will bring endless regret. But what will be the use of such regret? Neither words that have left the mouth, nor something that has already happened can be taken back. 'Regret in advance, and there's a gain.

Regret later, what's the use?' people say. The troubles that beset us because of our errors have simply to be borne.

"Therefore, act slowly and prudently. Remember, 'the mountain won't run, even if chased'. Think through the advantages and disadvantages, the profit and loss, and when this has been weighted back and forth, and the course of action is clearly a good one, act! Allah willing, your path will be safe. Also, do not be inclined to lend your ears to incitements and backbiting or to bad counsel. Put good counsel into your heart and use it all your life. If you are too inclined to listen to what others say, your thoughts will become confused and will often bring regret when you're wrong, as it is told in the story of the farmer and his donkey."

"How does that story go?" Nurbaya asked.

"Samsu surely knows it. Let him tell it, so I can pause for a moment and recover from all my talking."

"What's the story, Samsu?"

"It goes like this," he began. "Isn't a donkey a conveyance of man? But because the owner of a donkey liked to listen to what other people said, without thinking very deeply about their words, he became the conveyance of his donkey."

"Amazing," replied Nurbaya.

"Of course. Because that's what happens if we are too inclined to listen to other people. For not everyone is nice to us, and even if they mean well, evil things can happen anyway, for human affairs are different for each person. What's good for one may be bad for another. If we follow without thinking beforehand, we will tumble into a pit.

"The story of the donkey goes like this. A farmer once owned a donkey. One day, he went with his child to buy some things at the market, riding his donkey while his child walked beside them. They had only been walking for a short time when they met a woman on the road. When she saw them, she cried out, 'This old man isn't thinking! He lets his little child walk, though he isn't strong enough to do so, while he sits happily on a donkey.'

"The farmer overheard her words and placed his child on the donkey while he walked alongside.

"They then came across a scholar who, seeing the situation, shook his head and said, 'This child has no character. Is it right that he makes his father go on foot while he sits in ease and comfort on this beast?'

"Our farmer thought these words over as well then said, 'All right then, let's both ride on the donkey.'

"The two of them rode on for a bit and met an official who, seeing the farmer and his child riding on the donkey, exclaimed angrily, 'This boy and his father aren't using their brains at all, nor do they have any compassion! Is it right that such a small animal should be ridden by two people? If you don't get down from it, I will take you to court for abusing an animal.'

"So the farmer and his child got down from the donkey and walked on either side of it. A moment later, they met up with a good friend of theirs, who said, 'How stupid you both are! What's the use of having a donkey if it can't be ridden, and you two walking alongside it with such difficulty?'

"Upon hearing that, the father and his son were at loss for words.

"'If I ride the donkey, it's wrong. If you ride the donkey, it's wrong. If we both ride, it's wrong, and if it's not ridden, that's not right either. So what's right?' lamented our farmer. He threw his little hat to the ground and sat down on a rock, for he hadn't the courage to go on. 'If that's the way it is, let's carry the donkey on a pole! Maybe that will be right, since there's no other way left,' he said to his son as he searched for a length of wood. Then they fastened the donkey by its four hooves and shouldered the pole while proceeding to the market. Everyone who laid eyes upon them was dumbstruck. One person even cried out, 'In all my life I have never seen a donkey borne by men. Is that farmer crazy?' They all laughed uproariously and ridiculed the farmer and his son.

"'Even this is wrong,' the farmer said. In his confusion, he let the donkey fall to the ground."

"What a great story!" said Nurbaya.

"Let's end here, Nur! In the next day or so, we can talk again. Right now, I want to sleep. I'm very tired. When will you be going back?" asked Baginda Sulaiman.

"I have requested the Datuk's permission to stay two or three days," replied Nurbaya.

"Good."

Once Nurbaya drew the covers over her father, he went right to sleep. With that, Samsu excused himself and was about to return home.

"As I mentioned, later I will tell you what's happened to me, Sam," Nurbaya said, as Samsu was about to leave the room.

"Fine," he replied, before returning to his parent's home.

The next night, around nine o'clock, Nurbaya was sitting on the front veranda of her house. As the moon, a small comb-like crescent, had just gone down, the night was brightened only by the stars sparkling in the blue sky. In the yard and on the veranda all was dark, as no lamps had been lit except one on the main road whose rays penetrated here and there a few dark places. Sitting on the porch in all that darkness, Nurbaya seemed uneasy, looking over at Samsu's house from time to time, as if waiting for something to come out of it.

She had not been sitting long when a shadowy form came walking out of Sutan Mahmud's yard and headed toward her house. Seeing the shadow, Nurbaya rose and walked softly to her father's room. She came back out soon after and walked down the steps towards the bench under the tree, continually peering all around her, as if fearful someone might see what she was doing. Reaching the bench, she sat down and waited. A moment later, she heard someone say softly, "Is that you, Nur?"

"Yes, it's me," she said.

"No one will spy on us or hear what we're saying?" came the reply.

"I don't think so," Nurbaya said, once again looking about her. But there was nothing to be seen or heard. "Sit beside me here."

The man sat down and asked, "How is your father?"

"He seems a little better. He's beginning to eat again. But he's still too weak and the doctor said earlier that he can't move around a lot or be startled. Won't it be wonderful when you become a doctor, Samsu! Surely you'll be able to treat him yourself."

"Yes, Nur, but that's still far off. I have to study for six more years. And even then it's not certain. Who knows if it'll work out or not: six years is a long time. Lots of things could happen over such a long period."

"Why wouldn't it work out?" Nurbaya asked.

"How could it work out with temptations like this? What I've had to bear over this past year Allah alone knows. Several times I felt as if I had reached the limit of my ability to resist such enticements. Several times I thought I would lose the war against my desires and fall into the hands of Satan and his devils. Only with the help of Allah was I able to sail over such mine-laden seas and reach landfall. Before the wound in my heart from our parting had healed, your father's downfall happened. I hadn't finished wondering about *that* when your letter arrived and, with it, the news that crushed my heart and severed all my hopes.

"Although I can ease the pain of those first two events, this final disaster cut the rope I was hanging from, cast down the pillar I was leaning against, and snapped the branch I was standing on. When that happened, a sentence was handed down against me and my hopes for all that would sustain my future life disappeared. I became sick and couldn't study for several days. I don't know how I advanced to the second year. I thought I'd surely remain in my first year, as my studies were a mess."

"I knew you wouldn't be happy to hear such news. But what was I to do?" Nurbaya pleaded. "I had to write that letter. I was afraid you would blame me if I didn't tell you what happened. What would I do if even you turned from me?"

"As far as my feelings are concerned, don't harbor any suspicions or doubts. Didn't I say that to you before, and didn't I make that promise to your father just now? How could I go back on my word?"

"Is it really true, that your feelings for me haven't changed, Sam? Has your heart really stayed pure and unspoiled, as it was before all this happened? And can you truly forgive me for the wrong I've committed? Or were you just saying that in front of my father, trying to make me feel good with such promises? Tell me the absolute truth, so I know what to do," Nurbaya exclaimed, taking Samsu's hand and looking straight into his eyes.

"Nurbaya, why don't you trust me? Have I ever lied to you? How could I be that offended by what happened to you? It wasn't something you yourself wanted, but something you were forced into. Don't doubt me anymore. Look at the heavens above. With those thousands of stars scattered across the sky as my witness, I am telling you the truth."

"Don't be angry with me, Sam, if it seems like I don't believe you. That's not how I feel. It's just that my mind has become confused ever since this peril, and my thoughts have become jumbled. I'm often tormented by the evil intention of killing myself just to be quickly freed from this torture. But when I think of you and Father, that wish recedes, and I'm afraid of the sorrow you both would feel if I did that."

"Nur, don't think that way! Be more patient and trust in Allah! Think of your father's teachings! You're still young. You will live a long life and have much to hope for. Don't despair!" Samsu cried out, trying to calm Nurbaya.

"All that is true, Sam. But what strength do I have to endure such suffering? I don't have the words to express how I feel. It's like my heart has been set adrift from its moorings, like I've vanished from the place I'm standing, and hang suspended between heaven and earth, between life and death.

"And why would it not be so? Just think of it! I have to live with a person, someone I not only dislike, but who has severed all the hope I nurtured day and night, who has separated me from my beloved, tyrannized my father and brought him down, causing him such suffering. He is my father's greatest enemy, and mine, too, and in the end he will be my executioner. What's more, a person who is in no way my equal in age, intelligence, character, talent or behavior. He's never even loved me, only desires me, for he just wants to satisfy his base appetites. When he's satisfied, I'll surely be thrown away, like garbage thrown into the sewer. Or he might just kill me.

"How can I tell my heart to be patient, how can I make my thoughts happy, and how can I live on pleasant terms with a person like that? With each passing day, the more tangled my thoughts become, the more my grief and sorrow grow. As does my hatred whenever I see him. I can see nothing good in this world, and feel no pleasure, not even when eating. I can hardly sleep. And when I wake up, I become even more confused. A home, food and drink, clothing and amusement, in short, everything he owns or that comes from him, are of no comfort to me, but only bring anger, sadness and grief. How can I live with someone like that?

"At night, I want the day to come quickly, and during the day, I long for the night. Let this year become a day, and this month become an hour.

I don't know what I'll do and I can't find consolation anywhere. An hour feels like a month, and a day, like a year. This is hell on earth, a true hell." With that, Nurbaya broke off speaking and finally wiped away the tears that had begun to flow without her realizing it. Samsu could say nothing, as he was too saddened to hear of his beloved's fate.

"So, I beg you, Sam," she continued, "if someday you have a daughter, no matter what happens, don't force her to marry a man she doesn't like. I myself now know the pain and disgust of living with such a person. I'm no longer surprised when a woman, whose fate is similar to mine, does bad things, simply out of despair. For me, never mind, it's all because I had to help Father. But don't compel a woman who isn't as unfortunate as I am to go along with the wishes of her mother and father and relatives concerning her marriage, with no thought given to the child's wishes, preferences, age, intelligence, character and conduct. Because no one else will bear the trouble if it turns out badly, except the one who marries. The parents and family will merely look on from afar. Shouldn't they ask her opinion of the marriage? Doesn't the girl have thoughts and feelings and views, just like any other woman?

"Even if the parents understand and know their child, it is the child who knows herself best. Many mothers and fathers suppose they know what is best for their daughter. As they see it, she has to obey them in every way. A mother and father like that don't appreciate their child's worth. And if they themselves don't appreciate their child, they shouldn't expect her parents-in-law, or anyone else, to be concerned with her, either. And they shouldn't become upset if a man considers this woman far beneath the soles of his feet, for she'll never be able to compete with a man if she doesn't yet know her own worth.

"If, in time, the child and her in-laws do get along with each other, the marriage will last forever. If not, the couple will divorce, after her parents have spent who knows how many thousands of rupiah, perhaps even selling off or pawning their possessions, down to the last piece, to marry off their daughter. Isn't it a pity that so much money should be thrown away for nothing?

"When it comes to their child's marriage, I think the parents' first responsibility is to think of her age. If she's married off too young, it will surely damage her body and her offspring. Here in the Indies, girls should not be married off until they are twenty; unlike me, forced to marry at a mere sixteen. The older, the better."

"Yes, but the way women see it here, it's something of a disgrace if they don't marry young, as if they were goods that could no longer be sold," Samsu interjected.

"They think that way because of bad customs. If it's clear that a tradition is wrong, why isn't it just done away with? Instead it's simply followed blindly. Look at Western people! Sometimes they don't marry until after the age of thirty and nobody holds them in contempt for it. And really, when a woman is thirty-five—or forty, even—she still looks young, and her body's still firm and strong. When she gives birth at that age, the child will be perfectly formed, and will become a healthy person, both in body and mind. It will be a big baby and live a long life. But women here, sometimes by the time they're thirty, they already have grandchildren. That's the reason they and their children have defects, and in the end the race itself will degenerate, since all are the descendents of young women who had not yet come of age.

"Secondly, the parents should ask their daughter if she has the intention of getting married. And if she doesn't yet, they shouldn't force her, so this doesn't become a source of conflict later. There are women who don't want to tie themselves with the bonds of marriage just yet because, for example, they enjoy being independent, like children, or because they have some special purpose that stands in the way of their getting married.

"Third, she should be asked whether or not she likes the match they've arranged for her. Best of all, of course, would be if she herself searched for the perfect match. It's not that I would wish to have the women of our race liberated like those in the West, who socialize with men day and night. No, because Western ways are not good for our people. But two people who are being given in marriage should get to know each other first. If you worry about a certain danger, guard the girl closely. Don't let her spend too much time with the one to whom she is engaged, but just enough to learn about each other. And if the parents don't like it or are afraid the girl will go astray in looking for her true match, then they should go ahead and select someone they think is good. But after that, they have to ask their child if she likes their choice. Best of all would be to introduce the two so that they get to know each before being married."

"The old folks say that love will come anyway, later, after marriage," Samsu said with a smile.

"Not always," Nurbaya replied, "How could I love someone like Datuk Meringgih? What is there to attract me? We don't have a single thing in common.

"Fourth, their ages must match. The man may be a little older, that's normal. If both are the same age, that's good, too. It's not a problem if the woman is a bit older, as long as there's not too great a difference between them. Of course, a fifty-year-old man with a sixteen-year-old girl would not be a good fit, and a granny of fifty with a man of twenty certainly wouldn't be harmonious. That's what becomes a thorn in the flesh, always felt by the younger ones. For that reason, they are often unfaithful, turning towards someone else of the same age. And the old person is sometimes unhappy, too: embarrassed in front of others because the difference in age becomes the talk of the whole village.

"Besides, elders differ from the young in their thinking, wishes, likes, behavior, character, customs and intelligence. For example, elders prefer not to walk too much, for they're not up to it anymore. But for young people, walking's exactly what they want to do, for they can't stand to always be at home. And young people, for example, like hard things to eat, but old folks can't eat such things, though they might like to, for their teeth have fallen out. Old people are usually cynical, but the young go about in high spirits, playing around and telling jokes. Character and habit frequently change as age advances. I still appreciate all the fine things and pleasures, but Datuk Meringgih is, heart and soul, fixed only on money and business. What's the use of that to me, if I can't use it to fulfill my desires? All this must be borne in mind by parents who want to marry off their daughters, for it's exceedingly difficult to bring together characteristics and behavior so different from one another.

"They must be equal in intelligence, too, so as to be able to discuss everything. If one person is smart and the other stupid, sometimes the smart one becomes haughty and the stupid one becomes melancholy. If the man comes from a high lineage, and the woman is just a commoner, he will look down on his wife, and if the man is rich, but his wife poor, it becomes easy to ignore the wife.

"In looks, they shouldn't be like night and day, for that too can cause trouble. Finally, the size and height of their bodies should be kept in mind. Would it be nice to see a huge elephant and a tiny mouse united in marriage? Remember, the two of them must become one, a good bonding of two bodies.

"As you can see, it's not easy to find two people who can be matched as a pair. That's why marriage is so important. It's not good to make it too simple, as our people do. The married couple will only be happy and well off if the man and woman can agree on things. If so, a household can become like heaven on earth, bringing pleasure, happiness, love and affection forever. And when children come, that happiness and pleasure grow all the more. But, if not, the home becomes the pit of hell, where disputes, clashes, hatred, anger, sorrow, troubles, and sometimes disaster and danger arise, ending in divorce.

"Especially for the man, who has to work himself to the bone to make ends meet," Samsu put in. "He values happiness in the home, for when he returns from work all fatigued and exhausted, and finds solace in his home, it's as if his exhaustion has been cured with medication, and the next day he joyfully carries on with his heavy load. In that way, he doesn't feel the weight of his job, stays healthy, and lives a long life. When it's not like that, his life becomes a torment. When, exhausted by his work, he comes home; complication and confusion are what his little family serves him. It isn't surprising if such a man can't stand to be at home, as if afraid of his fixed abode. So he runs out, seeking consolation elsewhere. That's what makes such men wicked and harsh and likely to go astray."

"Of course, a woman's tasks aren't easy," Nurbaya replied. "She has to know how to interest and comfort her husband, and not just with a pretty face, but with her kind deeds, her orderliness, and her industry."

"It's like that for the man, too," said Sam. "He must be good at leading his family, so they feel comfortable staying at home and carrying out their responsibilities with joy and happiness. All that can bring comfort to the heart, for when a woman can't endure being at home, calamity ensues, as there's nowhere else that can bring her pleasure.

"To be honest, our people don't pay much attention to such things," Samsu added, after a brief pause. "That's probably the reason there are so many divorces in our land, leading men and women to marry several times."

"Not only that, but as long as Islamic law only permits a man to initiate divorce, and to take several wives, it will be difficult to change this," said Nurbaya.

"You're right, that's not fair, either," Samsu replied.

"If women could divorce, and I weren't bound by Father, I certainly wouldn't go on with this match. But what can I do? I'm bound hand and foot. Don't you pity me, Sam? Have you no idea how to free me from these bonds? Then listen to these *pantun* about my fate:

One goes not to the field to sein for fish,
though in a paddy fish sometimes nest.
In my constant troubles I find no relish,
I simply must bear them in my breast

Two cords hanging from the sill,
dangle over a large wooden chest.
Do what you do, do what you will,
Pain still wracks this lonely breast.

Though betel nuts are ready on the plate,
their cutters were dulled on a whetstone.
Is it possible for you to not pity the fate
of this orphan child all alone?

The bay is fine, the river bed not riven,
along the delta there extends a beach.
To take bad with the good is a given,
But suffering fills me, beyond all reach.

Unsheathe your dagger, put it away,
atop it then affix a banana flower.
A heart's desire might want its say,
but if the cord is cut there is no power.

"Nur, be patient! It's not that I don't feel for you. It's just that right now we can't do anything: your bonds are tied too tight. But I promise you, I will devise a plan. For now, let's just pray that Allah frees you quickly... Shh, quiet!" Sam suddenly whispered. "What's that noise behind the fence?" He searched for the source of the sound, but could see nothing.

"Maybe it was a frog or some small animal looking for something to eat," Nurbaya replied before continuing with what she had been saying. "Who would have supposed, Sam, when we sat on this bench a year ago, filled with great hope, that things would turn out the way they have? It's like the *pantun* says:

Sail from Perak to Persia's land,
and then return to one's home bay.
Hope not for good luck beforehand,
even the bird in hand, can go astray.

The Pagai people search for clams;
in the field, custard apples bloom.
Nothing but a minnow is what I am,
while the ebbing tide seals my doom.

Singapore rustles with the soft sound,
of crabs that scuttle across the sand.
My tears well and then stream down,
for the wretched fate of this lonely man.

In Rangkas Betung the oxen low,
each one mooing to summon its mate.
In tears I know there's nowhere to go,
to escape the dark clouds of my fate.

Sailing from Betung Bay and out to sea,
boys from Bogor seek oysters as their prize.
What possibly can I hope my fate will be,
when in a leaking boat doomed to capsize

A pandan mat, consisting of two layers,
is easily folded or rolled by Bangka boys.
Life's regrets cannot be helped by prayers,
nor can my life which fate now destroys.

Samsu soothed Nurbaya with his own verse:

Complain not of the cover protecting your meal,
in Banten food covers are made from bamboo.
Complain not of your turn in Fortune's wheel,
whatever happens will not be determined by you.

A man went to the jungle to hunt a monkey,
and returned with a billy goat, a young one too.
From one's destiny one can never break free,
whatever happens will not be determined by you.

A good plank must be planed, straight and true,
with each of its four corners completely square.
Whatever happens will not be determined by you,
your destiny is something that you must forebear.

Cut a length of rattan, split it in three parts,
the captain of the ship sails near Java's shore.
Follow not the guidance of a broken heart,
lest you wish to destroy yourself, forever more.

Padang Besi is both village and town,
whose inhabitants stand guard there.
Real true love cannot be spent down;
as a reminder leave one strand of hair.

If you should sit in the doorway to sew,
make sure your needle doesn't break.
My love is pure, that you must know,
not the slightest change will I ever make.

The sound of drums, the muezzin's call begun,
the faithful unite and come together in prayer.
As Allah and Mohamad are linked as one,
you and I will always be an inseparable pair.

On Java, the sound of canons fills the air,
there, Dutchmen die on the battleground.
Never shall I love any one other so fair,
never for me, will another ever be found.

Hearing these words, Nurbaya was overcome with emotion and leaned forward, embracing Samsu and kissing his cheek. Samsu repaid her kiss with his own, ardent embrace.

Lost in each other's arms, they suddenly heard behind them the voice of Datuk Meringgih, who called out, "So that's the reason you wanted so badly to go home instead of back to me."

The lovers jumped at the old man's words. Samsu rose swiftly from the bench and stood in front of Nurbaya to protect her.

"It wasn't to take care of your father," the old man continued, "like you said, but to have fun with your lover. So this is what young people do, educated people, people who observe the customs of respect: trick their husbands, so they can flirt with men in dark places, while their own fathers lie gravely ill. It seems this is where the young have it over the old. This is what they study at no small expense and with great effort in elite schools. If that's the case, then we elders are right to think that advancing the young will not raise their standards. It will actually bring them from a noble height to degradation. It means sullying illustrious names and throwing away the high standards and nobility of women, while the old customs and skills, so beneficial to them, are wasted. Women like that must not develop."

His hatred of Datuk Meringgih now too strong—for he suddenly remembered the vow he made in Batavia—Samsu could no longer restrain himself and retorted, "You needn't speak like that! Look at yourself in a mirror! Are you a polite man with an honest and true heart? Do you follow our customs and traditions? If the wickedest of devils walks this earth, then without question, you are that devil."

His face turning dark red as the boy spoke, Datuk Meringgih raised his walking stick high in the air, only to bring it down upon Samsu. But the young man leapt out of the way, pulling Nurbaya with him, so that the Datuk's blow merely struck the bench where the pair had been sitting. Within seconds, Samsu was standing before him, landing blows to his face. With a final kick to the stomach, Datuk Meringgih crashed to the ground, shrieking, "Number Five, help me!"

Just then, from out of the darkness, several men dressed in black came at Samsu, one by one, each with a *kris* unsheathed. Seeing what was about to happen, Nurbaya cried out for help at the top of her lungs, sending the men scattering in confusion and fear.

As the wavy blade of Number Five's *kris* came at him, Samsu ducked to the side and, crouching low, struck the man's hand, sending the weapon flying. Now unable to keep up his attack, and with his men having vanished, Number Five suddenly broke off and ran.

Those who arrived on the scene, including Samsu's father, demanded to know why there had been a cry for help. But they received no reply. And so, Sutan Mahmud asked Datuk Meringgih what had happened.

"Ask your son, sir! After my wife and I were tricked, I was attacked," Datuk Meringgih replied.

Sutan Mahmud knew very well what Datuk Meringgih meant and was ashamed at his son's behavior.

"Trust me, sir, I will investigate this matter carefully and thoroughly," he said. "Whoever is at fault shall not escape punishment, though it be my own son." Then he went home, taking Samsu with him.

After Sutan Mahmud departed, Baginda Sulaiman emerged from his room, having risen from bed in great alarm at the sound of his daughter's cry for help. Though his doctor had forbidden him from going out on account of his weak condition, the old man could not resist, out of fear that something dreadful might have befallen Nurbaya. As he was about to descend from the house into the darkness, Baginda Sulaiman tripped on the stairs and tumbled down. Nurbaya and several others ran over to help him. But when they lifted him, it was all too clear the old man had returned to the mercy of Allah. From Allah we come, and to Allah shall we return!

Nurbaya, shrieking and sobbing, began to beat herself until, oblivious to the efforts made to console her, she collapsed. Baginda Sulaiman's corpse and his daughter's limp body were eventually brought into their house. Once inside, the old man was laid out in the middle room while Nurbaya was carried to her bed. After being splashed with water and made to smell cologne, she regained consciousness, only to continue weeping.

"There's no need to cry," said Datuk Meringgih, "It was your own fault. You killed your own father."

Hearing the old man's humiliating accusation, Nurbaya rose from her bed. Her sorrowful expression vanished, replaced by rage. Her tears dried up and her eyes, already darkened from weeping, grew all the more red, while her lips and entire body trembled. She took on a terrible aspect just then, like a ferocious lion about to leap on its prey.

"What's that you say?" said Nurbaya. "I killed my father, damn you? You're the one who killed him! You think I don't know the despicable things you did to him? It was you who brought him down, you with your treacherous spite and rotten heart! That was all your doing, the burning of my father's shops, the sinking of his ships, and the death of his coconut palms. All his customers unwilling to accept goods from him anymore and defaulting on his loans and everyone running off with his money. When my father fell into poverty, you lent him money, pretending to help, but your real purpose was to cast him down into the deepest pit of all, for your heart, crueler than Satan's, still wasn't satisfied. Even I was dragged into depravity to slake your lusts, lusts lower than any animal's.

"My father is dead, and now you're happy, aren't you? But as of this very second, I am free of your grasp, you villain! Before, I went along with you, because I wanted to defend Father from becoming your prisoner. Now that he is no more, all the bonds that tied me to you are cut. Don't hope for me to come back to you. You are unworthy of me. You look like Death itself. And you could be my grandfather. You behave more vilely than a savage beast. What is there for me to respect in you? The money you obtained by cheating, the blood and sweat of those you oppressed? What good is that money to me? You're so stingy, you won't even use it yourself. Who knows, maybe you came by your goods by theft and highway robbery. I'm filled with a sense of evil just thinking about it. I'd rather have a dog for a husband than you. Get out of here! I'd rather look at filth than place my eye upon you. Divorce me this minute. If not, you're not a man."

"Don't forget, your father still had debts to pay," Datuk Meringgih shot back, his face pale from holding back his anger. "Therefore, *I* now own this house and have rights over it. So it appears you can't drive *me* away, but rather, it's *I* who must drive *you* from here. If you have so much to say, then I will have to turn both you and your father out."

"What are you saying? This house and everything in it are not Father's, but mine, as they're written in my name. No one has any rights over them except me. If you really are a man and have rights over this house, then turn me out of it!" Just then, she took hold of the door's crossbar and said, "The sign of my power over this house is that I'm driving you away like a dog. If you choose to stay, you will find this crossbar taking a bite out of your big, grey, bald head." As Nurbaya squared herself before Datuk Meringgih and pointed the bar at his head, a servant came forward to soothe her with calming words.

Datuk Meringgih descended the stairs and cried out, "Just wait!" before heading off to his own home.

All along the way, he thought of nothing else but destroying Nurbaya.

At the very moment that Datuk Meringgih was being driven away by Nurbaya, Samsu was being driven out of his home by his father.

"You have caused me great shame with your totally inappropriate behavior. Where can I hide my face? How will I wipe off the charcoal you've marked it with? What you did was not something that educated people, people of good breeding do. It's what someone of low birth does, who doesn't know the traditional ways and good behavior. I didn't think you belonged to the second group.

"My good name of long standing, honored and respected by all, my high lineage which has been without blemish, has now been sullied with a stain that can never be erased. Is this how you repay me for the education I have provided for you, which will allow you to go anywhere in the world? Is this the fruit of your studies? I regret all the money I spent to increase your knowledge. Is this what you learned in Batavia? Before you even had the chance to learn anything at all, you go and do this."

Sutan Mahmud paused for a moment, before continuing, "I can't forgive this wrong. It is simply too disgraceful. Get out of here! I have no wish to acknowledge you any longer. The person who did this is no son of mine."

Samsulbahri could think of nothing to say in reply, and simply bowed his head. When his mother heard that her child was being driven from the house by her own husband, she could only weep.

"If you wish to follow your child, go, then, both of you! I don't want to see him ever again," Sutan Mahmud shouted at his wife. Turning, he descended the steps of his home and went off in search of his brother in Alang Lawas.

After Sutan Mahmud left, Samsulbahri's mother tried to soothe her son with sweet words, that he might not take to heart his father's wrath. But Samsu said nothing in return, except to ask permission to go to his room, for he was very tired, he said, and wanted to sleep.

Hearing her son's request, Sitti Maryam's anxieties suddenly vanished, for she now believed Samsu had not been hurt by his father's anger. But the truth was that Samsu was unable to close his eyes and sleep, but wept instead at the thought of his fate and that of his beloved, the unfortunate Nurbaya.

At three o'clock in the morning, he rose very quietly from his bed and got dressed before slipping out through the window of his room. When he reached the gate, he looked back at his parents' house and at that of Nurbaya's. He paused a moment and said softly, "Stay in peace, Mother, and you, too, my beloved! I will go wherever my calamitous fate takes me. If I live long enough, we might meet again in this world. If not, we will await each other in the hereafter. There we can meet again, and be with each other forever, never to be parted again."

Samsu's tears flowed as he uttered these words and he had a foreboding sense he would never again see the two women he loved so much. Gathering himself, he started for the harbor at Teluk Bayur. Though it was very dark and the road deserted, he felt no fear, for his thoughts were still bound up with the evening's events. At around five in the morning he arrived at the harbor and boarded a ship headed for Batavia that very day. So as not to be discovered by anyone who might be following him, he hid away in the cabin of a shipmate he knew.

At seven in the morning, the ship weighed anchor and set sail for the harbor at Batavia.

Later that morning, when she learned her son had left, Samsu's mother caused an uproar sending people in search of him, though none could find him or discover where he had gone off to. And so, three days later, on account of her terrible fear and grief, Sitti Maryam left for her brother's home in Padang Panjang. But once there she could find no consolation or relief. Instead, she grew thinner and thinner, and finally became ill, out of love for her missing son.

10

Memories of Samsulbahri

It is six-thirty, and the afternoon begins its struggle with the setting sun. Daylight will soon be gone. Its duty to bring light and heat to the earth's eastern side accomplished, the sun has been settling beneath the western horizon for the past half hour. Only traces of its passage remain, shooting upwards from its twilight path like a great fan, radiant with a multi-hued beauty. Venus, the morning star, shines like a jewel gleaming in the dark just as the light of other stars begins to shimmer: diamonds set on a spring pin. The birds in the air look for their nests, hoping to rest from the day's work of securing the means of life and storing enough energy for tomorrow. Only the magpies can be heard chittering in the treetops, as if saying "good night" to each other. The cock stands guard outside his coop, peering about and making sure his chicks and hens have gotten safely inside. Their mother has long been in her nest, enclosing her still-tiny chicks in the warm shelter of her feathers. Little bats have left their haunts, flitting here and there on silent wings to hunt flying ants across the sky. Under the trees, large beetles go in search of prey while moths spread their richly patterned wings and soar, lured by the night's offering of sweet flowers. All around, the sound of crickets in the grass is like a prayer house filled with chanting and joyous recitation.

All of a sudden, in the east, from the peak of a tall mountain, softly and imperceptibly, the wondrous daughter of the night rises, like an angel newly descended from heaven. Her arrival is attended by her ladies-in-waiting, the surrounding stars, and the many clouds that guard her borders, the heroes of her army. She comes that her radiant face may shower the earth with light both gentle and fresh.

How happily the creatures of the earth welcome the coming of this lunar princess. Their misery and sorrow at being left by the beloved king of the day are now consoled. Her face, clear, round and very beautiful, is like newly tempered gold, and her pure and silent light washes over the trees and into the crevices of the stones below. Allah's servants, young and old, large and small, who had lain on their mattresses to rest from the daily battle on the field of life, are drawn back outside to taste the pleasure bestowed on them by this princess of the night. Little children who would normally be snoring in their beds now come out to play, chasing after each other, and singing in this silent and lonely place. Families sit in front of their homes, talking with their children and spouses and friends, mulling over the future and what might have been.

Above the seafront in Padang can be seen the silhouette of what appears to be two people sitting side by side, talking softly. Who are they, these two, who purposely sought out such a secluded place, as if afraid of being disturbed by others' company? It is the young couple, the Lover and Beloved, quenching the thirst of their love, their ardent longing for one another. They no longer think of themselves and pay no heed to what goes on around them. It is as if no other creature existed, apart from them and, in that moment, they are truly the happiest and luckiest of all.

Brightened by the beauteous light, serenaded by the waves that break thunderously on the shore, hidden in a quiet and deserted place, free from noise and commotion and prying eyes and ears, they are able to experience the sweetness of love to its fullest.

On the main road, wagons and carts are pulled by great horses walking slowly to their destinations. Along the roadside, Western men walk hand-in-hand with their wives, sheltered by the trees and refreshed by the cool air.

But, when Lover and Beloved are finally parted from each other, sadness and heart-rending grief will replace all this pleasure and happiness and everything that contributed to it—the solitude, the lovely light of the moon, the waves breaking on the beach, the caressing breeze—all becoming an ever-growing and passionate yearning and piercing sorrow.

So it is for the stranger abroad in distant lands as well. All of this frequently brings sorrow and longing beyond measure, from the memory of his own country, his home, the little village in which he lived, his mother and father, relatives and kin, companions and pals, all of whom have long disappeared from sight, but never from his heart. Especially when he realizes that Allah alone knows human destiny, and whether one will be traced back to his dear homeland, or caught fast in the land of strangers, as the *pantun*s say:

If you are sticky with breadfruit sap,
use a coral sponge to clean your hands.
Will I go home? Who knows, perhaps,
or possibly disappear in this alien land.

Where elephants tread, flowers don't grow;
Padang folk swim to the island in the bay.
Villagers greet each other and say hello,
as the stranger counts every passing day.

Over time the night deepens and the moon floats ever higher. The children who had been playing with such cheers and shouts can no longer be heard, as they are now under their bed covers. Those who had been sitting around chatting with each other have gone back inside, no longer to be seen. On the main roads, the buggies grow fewer, for almost no one is traveling now. Soon after, the roadways, which had been so busy earlier, become utterly deserted. Only a group of village guards, dressed all in black, can be seen walking about slowly and silently, that the treacherous might not know of their presence.

The town, once filled before with life, is now completely quiet, like a country emptied of its people. Everyone is asleep. The only sound is the occasional hooting of owls, who sit in the treetops and gaze longingly at the moon, crooning with voices now clear, now fading, as if lamenting and sobbing in broken voices.

Hey, Owl! Why do you yearn like that, never taking your eyes off the moon so high up above? What has made you so sad?

"Oh moon! Oh my soul! My heart of hearts and light of my eyes! When shall you come down to this world and look upon me, filled for so long with this desire for you? When will you fall to the earth, onto my lap, to mend my wounded heart, pierced with the arrows of love, which you shot from your bow into my breast? Have you no pity or feeling in your heart to see me always so sadly perched on this treetop, yearning for you, heedless of fatigue or the elements? Do you really have the heart to see me like someone intoxicated?

"I would fly to you and enslave my lowly self if that would gain your pity. But what strength do I have for all this? These weak wings of mine can't carry me any higher than this tree:

> *White blooms on the thorn apple, a virtual fountain,*
> *thrown up by the waves, oysters perish on the beach.*
> *Though it may be my wish to embrace a mountain,*
> *my arms will forever be lacking in the proper reach.*

"Oh! When will I ever be able to attain my heart's desire? For, when it's daylight again, then your husband, the king Samsu, beams his sharp rays to every corner of this world, and I must hide away in some dark place, lest I go blind from being pierced by his arrows."

Just as the owl cried in melancholy at the top of the tree, yearning for the moon, so, too, sat a young woman, pensive and brooding, by the window of a house in Padang's Kampung Belantung. She appeared to be longing for her beloved as well, so far from view.

She looked to be about seventeen or eighteen years-old, a pretty girl with a slender and graceful body and skin the lovely, tawny color of a plum. Her black, curly hair was gathered in a loose bun with ringlets lining her brow, giving her the look of a young girl recently risen from bed. Her gaze was soft and seemed to brood endlessly on the moon enshrouded by clouds in the distant sky. Profound grief marked her face, and tears fell from her reddened eyes, streaming down her cheeks to the ground like pearls cut loose from their thread. Her ivory-colored wrists were adorned with gold, serpentine bracelets, clearly visible when the sleeves of her Japanese silk blouse slipped back. Her hands were kept tirelessly propped under her chin, which was as lovely as the figurehead on a ship's prow.

Who was this young woman? Why was she in such pain, always gazing at the moon, as if it was the source of her sorrow?

"Oh, my beloved, the all of my love! How did I end up like this? Ever since you left me, I've been here like someone no longer living. I feel the world hemming me into a space no bigger than the one on which you stand, a place where I remain suspended:

> *If a rice plant leans towards the west,*
> *to the west as well its tassel will turn.*
> *If one's soul can never find any rest,*
> *one's body too will soon become infirm.*
>
> *If such is the case, or so it would seem,*
> *a living tree can be consumed by fire.*
> *If this is the way, or such is the scheme,*
> *though alive, I feel as if I will expire.*
>
> *The road to Payakumbuh does not furcate,*
> *and teakwood trees give shade on the way.*
> *Whose heart would not sorely palpitate,*
> *with one's father dead and beloved away?*
>
> *At night an Arab boy with his quill,*
> *composes quatrains until dawn is nigh.*
> *When one is alone, life is ever uphill,*
> *an endless battle with the sky on high.*
>
> *If it is Tanjung Raja that you'd like to know,*
> *in the area of Pulai you should spend the night.*
> *To get to Merangin, it is upstream you must row,*
> *a cud of betel in Supayang and the trip's alright.*
>
> *To know how my fate has been destined,*
> *just look at the petals of the albine flower.*
> *If the flower's stem is broken by the wind*
> *petals are strewn everywhere, with no power.*

"Ah, heart of my heart, light of my eyes! How could you leave me, with such a calamitous fate! During the day, I think of nothing but you and my wretched destiny. I can do nothing else, as my thoughts keep wandering. Though, in body I am here, in spirit I'm never far from you. The image of your face is constantly there before my eyes. Not only can I not work, but I don't want to eat or drink, for rice tastes like dry husks, and water goes down like thorns.

"I do nothing day after day but sit here thinking, chin propped up in my hands, gazing endlessly at things that aren't even there. Look at me! How long I've sat like this, I don't know. I just gaze at the moon in the heavens, for it's through the moon that our gazing can be joined. If you look at it too, I'm sure our eyes will meet there. How wonderful it would be if the moon could join our words and hearts!

"At night, I can't close my eyes for an instant without seeing you there right in front of me. I can hear your voice. I feel your lips on my cheek. Oh! It really does seem like you come to soothe my injured heart with soft and gentle words, to hold and kiss me, to show me your kindness. And then, all the trouble and misery torturing me disappears. But, Allah!, when I come to my senses again and realize it was just my heart playing tricks on me, that I'm still lying in my bed alone, with only my pillows beside me, my sadness only grows and my heart feels crushed. My pillows and mattress are damp from the tears pouring from my eyes, which I can no longer shut in sleep.

"When the cocks begin to crow, it's startling, because it seems like your voice calling me from somewhere far off. The sound of the waves breaking and crashing on the shore reminds me that my beloved is across the deep seas and beyond the tall mountains. Then I feel my breast splitting in two and my heartstrings cut. I lie face down, pressing my breast to my pillow to hold back the pain cleaving my heart, until I almost faint and am no longer aware of the world around me. Twelve hours become like twelve years, waiting for the arrival of day.

"When dawn breaks in the east and birds call out from behind the tree leaves, a sign of the coming day, I awake alone and go out softly, lest I disturb anyone. Although it's still dark and chilly outside, I rinse my face, because I'd be ashamed if people saw my swollen and reddened eyes. But even the cool air and dew cannot refresh me or calm my mind. Instead, they just add to my sadness, for they show with greater clarity how ugly my destiny is, alone and apart from every living being that could heal my sickness.

"There are lots of things I could do during the day, but they're no cure for the wound in my heart. And when night comes, this awful sickness returns to torment me, its ferocity increased.

"Ah! Wretched fate, when will you free me from your shackles and chains?"

Just then, tears began to flow in streams down the woman's freckled cheeks.

"As for you, my love, I'm sure your own troubles aren't as bad, since you're in a big city with lots to console you. But I'm here in Padang, shut up in a little house to hide my unfortunate self, without a mother and father, relatives and friends. Who can comfort me here? No one.

"O, Allah, O God! Why is Thy servant tortured so? What am I guilty of, that I can't receive pardon and forgiveness, so that I might be released from the pain and suffering of this world? I feel incapable of going on. If I'm not released soon, I'm certain my body and soul will escape this transitory world. But if I'm never to be forgiven, it would be best to quickly separate my soul from my body. I can't bear this any longer:

> *Oh Allah, dear Lord God,*
> *Dost Thou not pity Thy lowly servant?*
> *If nothing comes from bearing this torture,*
> *Then it would be best for me to die.*

> *I cannot bear the suffering,*
> *The hurt that comes at any moment,*
> *From disaster I can find no shelter,*
> *No other person's heart is one with mine.*

> *Why is it my fortune to suffer poverty,*
> *As if struck by a giant and forceful wave?*
> *Love and passion remain out of reach,*
> *Where to has my loved one gone?*

What sin did I ever commit,
That I should suffer so?
A living body yet dead inside,
With not one person to show sympathy.

Ever since my father's death,
Torments continually come to me,
There is no respite from anxiety,
All good fortune is now reversed.

Mother left me, then Father, too
My beloved seems to have forgotten me,
After calamity now comes destitution,
A life of woe and utmost grieving.

Why does your servant deserve this fate?
The suffering and torment are unbearable,
If there is no hope of my dreams fulfilled,
I would rather be destroyed and perish.

My dear mother, my beloved father,
Why did you leave your daughter behind?
Have you no pity within your hearts,
To see your orphaned child in sadness?

Why did you leave your child alone,
When always you had watched over me?
The pain I feel seems to have thorns,
Where is the medicine to heal me?

Then, without knowing it, tears again trickled from the woman's eyes and fell in streams around her.

Two hours past midnight, when the crowing of the cocks began, her grief and sorrow reached their peak. She pressed her face against the window sill, sobbing bitterly, thinking again of her unlucky lot, for she was now an orphan with too much suffering to bear.

In the midst of her tears, she felt someone touch her shoulder and heard a soft and gentle voice say, "Nur, are you still awake? It's almost two in the morning."

But Sitti Nurbaya, weeping and seeing in her mind only her destiny, said nothing in reply. She was in the house of her cousin, Sitti Alimah, in Kampung Belantung.

"I thought you had fallen asleep. You went so quickly to your room before. If I had known you were still up, I would have come to keep you company."

Even these words elicited no response from the heavy-hearted Nurbaya, for she could not find her voice.

"Close the window, Nur, so you don't get sick. Just feel that wind coming in here!" Alimah gently placed Nurbaya's hand in her own, and led her to bed.

After setting her dazed cousin on the mattress, Alimah went to close the window where Nurbaya had been seated. At that very moment, fear gripped her heart, for below the window a man dressed all in black appeared to be hiding. She was about to scream, afraid the man might try to force his way through the window. If that happened, what could she do? There were no men in the house to protect them. So she hastily bolted the window and went back over to Nurbaya, who was sitting lost in thought and staring at a photograph of Samsulbahri in her locket. Alimah sat down next to Nurbaya. Taking hold of her cousin's hand and stroking her hair, she said softly, "Nur, don't give in so completely to your sadness. Bear up a bit! Don't you have any pity for yourself? Look here, you're so thin and pale, and your eyes so swollen, all because you've been crying your heart out for days on end. What will become of you if you keep up like this?"

Even as she voiced these words, Alimah's thoughts remain fixed on the man she had just seen below the window. Who he was and why he was there, she could not fathom. She stiffened her courage so that Nurbaya would not see her fear.

"You're right," Nurbaya replied, finally speaking with a sad and halting voice. "I'm so grateful that you're willing to help me through such grief. You're the only one who's still loyal to me and willing to keep me from going astray. You're always a comfort and source of good advice. You're like a mother and father to me."

With these words, Nurbaya's tears once again streamed from her eyes as she said bitterly, "Oh my dear mother and father! How could you have left your child all alone, when my fate is so bad? Why didn't you take your child with you so she could be freed from all this unbearable suffering?"

"Nur, my dear little sister!" said Sitti Alimah, who greatly loved and cared for Nurbaya. "That's not how you show love towards your parents. You know they are traveling, journeying along the very difficult road to find their God. When you call to them and weep, you hold them back. So, no more of that now! Don't call out to those who have gone on before! Calm yourself and pray to God to keep them safe in their graves!"

After a bit, Nurbaya spoke again. "Alimah, I can never repay your kindness, but I do beseech God the Almighty day and night, to shower His mercy and compassion upon you many times over, so that safety and happiness will be yours in the world to come."

"Nur, don't talk like that!" replied Alimah. "You don't have to thank me. I'm not doing it to get something in return, but for no other reason than that I love and care for you. You should know that I'm just like you, all alone with no brothers or sisters. I feel like you're my little sister, who I can depend on to protect me and my fate, which is far from pleasant. I should help you in every way. If not me, then who?" she said, stroking Nurbaya's hair and hand.

"That's why I want to follow your advice and store it away in my heart," Nurbaya replied. "And that's also why I'm always trying not to upset you. But what can I do? Even though I console myself, even though I try to rid myself of these tormenting memories, I just can't do it. The more I try to forget them, the more I remember. The farther I send them away, the closer they come. The more I drive them off, the more they return. I have given up any hope of finding happiness," Nurbaya said in tears, embracing Alimah.

Alimah embraced her cousin and kissed her cheek, saying sweetly, "Even so, don't despair, just be more patient and trust in the Lord of the Entire Universe, for God is all-loving and all-merciful. And doesn't everything happen according to His will? Do you mean to say that He didn't bring you together with your beloved? Wasn't it He who sent you your heart's desire, whom you dream of day and night? Can it be that it always rains, without the sun ever coming out with its warmth? Maybe this time, it's too soon for you to obtain what you desire. So be patient!"

"Of course. That's what I thought, too, at first. I consoled myself with that kind of hope. But, I don't know why, as time went on this hope grew weaker and weaker, until finally it just left me. Every time I think that way now, it's like there's a voice in my head saying it's useless to hope, for God won't send me what I long for in this world and He will not grant my request, even though this desire has sunk deep roots in my heart.

"Oh Alimah! If only you knew how terrible it would be for me to leave this world with such a hope. I'm sure you aren't surprised, seeing my life the way it is now. It's not that I'm afraid to die, and it's not that I love my life, especially since Mother and Father are waiting for me over there. But... what would become of my beloved, once I die?"

"Nur, you're wrong to think that way. It's not possible! I can't approve of this. Surely you don't..." Alimah could not go on, for she was so worried that what Nurbaya suspected was true, especially since the despair which darkened her cousin's face was all too clear. Once again, she tried to drive away her apprehension by soothing her cousin. "If you think that, then surely you're ill and your thoughts unstable. You ought to try your hardest to think good thoughts again. If not, I'm sure your illness will only get worse. And remember, neither your body nor your life is yours alone any more, for there are two others, Samsu and I, who deeply love and care for you. If anything were to happen to you, you don't know the grief and sorrow we would feel. Therefore, if you truly love Samsu and have affection for me, take good care of yourself, so that nothing happens to you. When you neglect and ignore yourself, it's a sign that you don't love Samsu and have no affection for me."

"No affection for you or love for Samsu?" asked Nurbaya, raising her head. "Allah alone knows how I feel about you two. But really, I can't understand why the idea of dying infests my heart and defeats the hope you make me feel.

"Tell me how I can see him. I just want to be with him again. I want to see his face and hear his voice. I want to see it in his eyes, how he feels about me. I want to hear it again, from his lips, just like the last time he said it, before his father drove him away. Maybe he no longer loves me, or is angry with me and regrets what he did," Nurbaya said. With her hands over her eyes to hold back the tears, she buried her face against Alimah.

Alimah gently raised Nurbaya's face and wiped away the tears with her silk handkerchief. "What are you saying, Nur? Earlier you yourself said he loves you very much and that you get a letter from him almost every week, and those letters declare the love and affection for you in his heart. How could you think such thoughts?"

"He could've just made that up. What's written down isn't always true. The tone of a letter isn't always the sound of the words which arise from the heart. If it's true he still loves me, how could he have abandoned me to a fate like this? He went off without saying a word to me. Yes, men's mouths are sweet, but their hearts are seldom sincere," replied Nurbaya.

"Nur, think of what's good for you! Don't be taken in by the snares of the devil! You are ill, very ill. That's why you're not thinking clearly. As far as Samsu is concerned, even though you know him better than I do, I just don't believe it, and I'm even willing to guarantee that he's not a man who would go back on his promise or prove to be false. Instead, he's upright and loyal, and trustworthy, loving, caring and patient. His love for you is no lie, for he has loved and cared for you since he was little. How could your feelings for him have changed?

"It's not that I'm trying to make a winning case for him. He's not part of my family, while you are my dear cousin. Still, I cannot permit these thoughts of yours. What did he do wrong, that you have turned away from him, Nur? How sad he'd be if he knew what you were thinking!"

"Yes," answered Nurbaya, taking her cousin's hand and kissing it, as her tears started to flow again. "You are right. I am sick, and my thoughts are all disordered. And, of course, I shouldn't be thinking like that, for Samsu hasn't done anything wrong. That's clear to me. Yes, it's not right to think like this. Forgive me and pardon the wrongs of your calamitous little sister!"

Opening her locket, she gazed at the picture of Samsu inside. "And to you, Sam, I beg your forgiveness and pardon for my words and suspicions just now," she added, kissing it before placing it against her breast. "I've accused you of something you haven't done. I have judged you, though you were guilty of nothing. But don't be upset. I really am sick and don't know what I'm doing. If this sickness of mine can't be cured, so be it. Just give me some medicine to make me feel better. If you don't treat me soon, I won't be able to live in this world any longer and your efforts to defend me will be in vain.

"Alimah, my second mother and father, show me a way to be free of the hell in this world!"

"Nur, the way to cure your wounded heart is really very simple. Aren't there many ships at sea that can take you to him?"

After reflecting for a moment, Nurbaya said, "You're quite right. But he will certainly not come back to Padang, for his mind may have darkened towards this land."

"If so, then you will just have to go to him," replied Alimah. "Are you afraid of traveling alone to Batavia? Someone could be found to send you there. I've heard that Mr Ali, who loves Samsu very much, has quit being his father's coachman, for he took it hard that the young gentleman was driven away by his father. I'm certain he would be willing to take you to Batavia."

"It's not that I'm afraid," said Nurbaya. "I would cross a sea of fire to be with him. I've thought of this, too. It's the only way. But when I got there, what would I do? He's still a student and has no salary. Even if he were happy to see me, what would we live on?"

"If he truly loves you, he has to have some idea of how you could live together. How could a man as clever and intelligent as Samsu not devise a plan in a town as big as that!"

"Actually, he did send a letter to me earlier, asking me to come to Batavia, for he feels sorry for me and is worried I might kill myself. He intends to leave school and look for work, so the two of us can live together. But is it a good idea to go along with that? Do I have the right to take him away from his studies, which might someday provide a great position and salary?"

"Ah, if only I were rich, I wouldn't think twice about it. I would agree to go right away and wouldn't have him work, so that he'd be more content than a king. But what can I say...?" Nurbaya paused and wiped the tears from her eyes.

"Even though you're not rich, you can still get your wish and I will help you get it. But, as we aren't people of means who own warehouses or ships, you'll just have to be comfortable with that. If, later on, luck is with you, I'm sure you'll find the happiness and wealth you seek."

After thinking for a moment, Nurbaya said with a sigh, "Yes, of course, there's no other way. All right then, I'll go along with your idea and his. But where will I find the money to do so?"

"By pawning what you don't need and from the sale of half my possessions," replied Alimah.

"Oh, you are truly more to me than a real sister," said Nurbaya, kissing Alimah's cheek.

"So, are you really set on leaving? When do you intend on going?"

"This Saturday. But don't tell anybody my secret before I'm safely in Java, so that nothing gets in my way. If your parents knew of my intentions, I'm sure they wouldn't permit me to go by myself."

"Certainly not, unless Mr Ali takes you," answered Alimah. "Are you comfortable with what you're about to do?"

"Yes," replied Nurbaya.

"Will you promise not to brood or be melancholy any more, or weep and sob?"

Her question went unanswered. Instead, Nurbaya embraced and kissed her cousin, "You are truly an angel who always comes to my aid in times of trouble."

"Well then, sleep well, for the clock has struck three-thirty. Let me sleep here with you. If I don't, later on you'll be crying again, for these next few days will be too long for you to wait," Alimah said in jest. Then she lay down on the mattress and bore Nurbaya off to the land of sleep. "Now embrace me and pretend I'm Samsu, and dream of him!"

Nurbaya did not answer the soft and calming words of her cousin, only smiled with still-moist eyes. Kissing Alimah once more, she lay down.

A little while later, Nurbaya was fast asleep in Alimah's embrace. After gazing at her cousin for a few seconds, it was clear to Alimah that grief still marked the young woman's face, but with it, fresh hope.

Just as she was about to close her eyes, Alimah suddenly heard the sound of footsteps moving out from beneath the house. Her heart pounding fiercely, she remembered the shadow she had seen below the window. Then, all at once, everything became completely still and quiet. But she was unable to sleep until the early morning hours, frightened and bewildered as she was at the thought of that man lurking outside.

11

Flight to Batavia

Though it was nearly seven in the morning, sunlight had yet to make its way through every part of the Teluk Bayur harbor, and in the shade of trees, all was darkness still. Several workers made their way to the port on foot, wrapped in sarongs to ward off the cool morning breeze. From the east, monkeys and gibbons could be heard hooting and enjoying themselves immensely, as people sometimes do when greeting the arrival of the sun, which was just now beginning to light up their jungle homes.

A red gleam began to radiate from behind the mountains ringing the harbor, as if intent on piercing the thick clouds. Out at sea, from the thick haze that hung over the water and slowly shifted to the west, several fishing boats emerged, laden with stores of fish hooked the night before. The wind was calm, as was the water, as they headed to shore. To the west, a half-moon shone high in the sky with the gradually faded brightness of unglossed silver.

Though still early, Teluk Bayur was alive with travelers ready to sail out of Padang as well as those who had come to see them off. At eight o'clock that very day, a vessel was leaving for Java and the ship's stevedores were in a tumult loading and unloading freight, as were the ship's hands rushing to prepare the ship. Passengers ran about the pier, boarding and descending from the deck, anxious not to be left behind.

Outside a shop near the port, an old man stood and peered nervously about. After taking a final survey of his surroundings, he went back inside and spoke to a young woman who had hidden herself behind a cabinet.

"It seems no one knows of our journey. I don't see anyone I recognize," he said.

"Lucky for us," the young woman replied. "But it would be wise to check outside one more time. Someone might still be watching our movements."

And so the old fellow went back out and walked about, feigning interest in a few passing things, when really his eyes took to monitoring everything and everyone in view.

With the first peal of the ship's whistle, he and the woman left the shop and walked quickly towards the waiting vessel. Ascending to the deck, they found a place to hide themselves away, and settled in silently. Unbeknownst to them, two men hiding behind a warehouse were watching their every move.

Now certain the recently boarded pair were indeed their intended targets, one of the men said to his companion, "Now you'd better go back, Number Three! Report what you have seen to Datuk Meringgih and tell the boss that I'll follow them on board to Batavia to carry out my orders. I'll find a sorcerer to help and when I'm there I'll scout out some acquaintances and disciples who are willing to join our group."

"All right," answered Number Three, "but do you have spending money?"

"Yes, for now," replied Number Five. "If it runs low, I'll ask for more in Batavia."

With that, the two of them separated, Number Three heading back to Padang while Number Five walked slowly to the dock.

Only after the second whistle, when the gangplank was about to be raised, did the latter leap on board and then hide below deck. Soon afterwards, the anchor was raised and the ship was underway, leaving the harbor behind.

Once the vessel had cleared Teluk Bayur, the young woman who had gone aboard felt brave enough to leave her hiding place and look around for someplace better to spend the voyage. At last, she found one near the captain's cabin. Led there by the woman, the old man accompanying her unrolled his mat and opened up a cloth easy chair he had brought for her to sit on.

"I feel a bit better now, Mr Ali," the woman said after sitting down on the mat. "All in all, though, I'm worried. Disaster seems to be following me. Please walk around and make sure no one has following us, but don't attract attention."

"Very good, Ms Nurbaya! I'll scout around, though to my thinking, no one knows of our journey and no one is following us."

After sitting for a moment, Nurbaya said, "Mr Ali, have you sent the cable to Samsu, telling him to meet us at Tanjung Priok?"

"I did, Miss, yesterday. But even if he's not there, it won't matter. I know Batavia, from my days of escorting prisoners there."

"Right, but it would be best for him to know of our arrival so he can arrange somewhere for us to stay," said Nurbaya.

"That's true," replied Ali, "But are you hungry? Perhaps you had nothing to eat earlier today?"

"Actually, my stomach *is* beginning to growl," Nurbaya said with a smile. She was feeling more elated at having left Padang without detection and from the thought of meeting her beloved Samsulbahri.

"Wait just a moment and I'll ask for eggs and coffee," Ali said, before going off in search of food. Soon after, he came back with several eggs and two cups of coffee. Meanwhile, Nurbaya had taken out a few cubes of pressed rice and other snacks from her bag, and the two of them ate.

About an hour later, a deck officer came up and asked for their sailing papers. Seeing Nurbaya's beauty up close, the man whispered in Dutch to his purser, "What do you think of this woman?"

"Truly a rose of Padang, that one," the purser replied.

"Can you talk her into it? A dozen beers if you do," the officer asked, casting a sidelong glance at Nurbaya.

"It's worth a try, but she looks the proper person. She sure won't be easy to approach. Plus, there's someone watching over her."

"If a dozen's not enough, I'll throw in a half-dozen more," said the deck officer, stealing another glance at Nurbaya from the corner of his eye. "Her freckles and the dimples on her cheeks when she speaks just knock me right over."

"All right, I'll give it a try."

Nurbaya overheard all this and felt great loathing towards the two men. Nevertheless, she restrained her anger, determined not to let them bother her.

Standing in front of Nurbaya with the deck officer beside him, the purser asked, "Going where, then?"

"Batavia," Nurbaya replied tersely.

"Have a ticket?"

"Here," Nurbaya said, handing it over.

After making a tear in the document and returning it, the purser said, "Why stay here? There are better places below. If you'd like, I'll select one for you."

"Thank you, but we'll just stay here, since it's near the captain. If anything happens, we can get to him quickly."

The purser reflected for a moment then said, "If it rains later, or there are waves, it's sure to get wet here."

"No matter. We aren't salt, and water won't ruin us. If there are big waves, we can find our own spot," Nurbaya replied, looking elsewhere.

Taking the young woman's hint, the two crewmen went off to check other tickets.

"What'd I say?" the purser remarked as they walked away. "Even from afar it was obvious to me. Such a woman... a real dove. Seems tame, but hard to catch."

"Never mind that. If kind words don't work, we'll have to think of something else. Let's think! I get weak all over just seeing her eyes and that cool gaze of hers. If you get her, I'll see to it you get a raise."

"Okay, I'll try later, but if I don't succeed, don't get mad at me," the purser replied.

After they left, Nurbaya told Ali about the purser and his friend.

"Don't be afraid," Ali replied. "I'll protect you. If those two try anything, we'll just lodge a complaint with the captain."

As the wind was calm, so too was the sea, its surface like a great sheet of glass, dazzling when struck by the rays of the sun. The ship glided on as if pulled by some wondrous cord, the white wake left behind by the churning propellers the only disturbance on the otherwise placid waters. The sky was clear and all along the horizon, the eye took in a vast plain of blue, broken only by the outline of several small islands to the north and west. Not far from the ship, fish leaped and frolicked in a game of tag, while farther out, some thrashed about as if spooked by the ship's advance. A convoy of porpoises surfaced in the distance, their fins undulating on the water. White-feathered gulls flew back and forth, alighting on the rolling sea, their eyes peeled for an inattentive fish. Others hovered in place, only to plunge suddenly, zooming just above the water like arrows let loose from a bow. In one swoop they would shoot up straight, a fish writhing in their beaks or talons.

As the ship sailed on, the mainland to the east slipped out of view, lost behind the sky's edge, which seemed nearly to meld with the sea in an unbroken expanse of water meeting vaulted blue air. In that moment, Nurbaya felt how truly small she was, for even the large vessel in which she sat seemed but a grain of sand in a vast desert. A sense of the greatness and might of Allah, who brought the universe into being, grew within her as she found herself suddenly frightened by her surroundings. She had nowhere to run if anything happened here at sea, for apart from this little place, death would await her. Her life was held suspended in a very small space, she now understood. On the ship was life; everywhere else was death. "Shall I ever return again to land?" she wondered. "To land, where there's no danger?"

She seemed to have forgotten that people die in greater numbers on land than at sea.

That night, the ship was awash in the brightness of its electric lamps, the wind blowing in from the south, a refreshment for the crew who had labored all day. After dinner, several of the clerks and ship's hands left second class and went up onto the deck, each taking along a musical instrument: a violin, a guitar or mandolin, *keroncong*, flutes, or even a strong voice for those who had them, to sing *keroncong* songs and tunes from the itinerant stage shows. Or the call-and-answer number the group eventually sang:

> *Whence cometh you and where do you go?*
> *From Japan to many a Chinese port.*
> *Do not be angry, I should like to know,*
> *if this flower I see does any man court?*

"Whose is it?" shouted the purser, Ludi, answering the line his friend had just sung. To which someone interjected,

> *Jackfruit and breadfruit tress,*
> *how does one heal a broken heart?*

Back came the reply:

> *Blades of love-grass are bound with a silken band,*
> *no smell is more pungent than that of burning bones.*
> *'Tis easier to view something than to hold it in hand,*
> *as an example, the moon in the sky above your home.*

"That's it!" Ludi shouted again. Cheering and hooting was all he seemed good at. "Keep playing, Yakub! Don't be shy!"

Another pantun followed:

> *Whence comes the lowly leech?*
> *From the padi field to the brook*
> *Whence comes love's speech?*
> *From the eyes falls to heart's nook.*

That one was interrupted by: "Souvenirs of Kota Raja, if you can, bring me one."

"Eh, eh, don't do that!" said Ludi, "Don't steal someone else's line!"

The first composer took his turn again:

> *Quickly, so quickly speeds the boat,*
> *to Surabaya and its port of safety.*
> *Forget your sarong, even your coat,*
> *but dismiss me not from memory.*

"Who's that?" someone asked.

"My little sister," Ludi replied.

In truth, *keroncong* songs and traveling stage tunes like these, if played right, under the full moon, in quiet places such as a boat at that hour, are highly pleasing to the ear, and arouse passion in all who hear them. In particular, such songs always appeal to the young, who like to play music and never tire of singing. Nevertheless, those who sing such songs are rarely nice people, and usually take to reveling in quiet places, deep into the night, often with bad intentions, causing a disturbance and upsetting the respectable. So it was that Nurbaya found their noise and merry-making repellant. She pretended to be asleep and covered her face and ears to drown out their racket.

Later that night, when all was quiet aboard the vessel, the purser Ludi showed up, walking slowly and pretending to check on things. Nearing Nurbaya's spot, he woke her up and said, "Come with me. I'll find you a good place, and if you do what I want, later I'll give you as much money as you want."

Nurbaya stood up and gave the man a shove, saying in Dutch, "If you dare bother me anymore, I will report your unpleasant behavior to the ship's captain. Is it your job to make life difficult for the passengers? Or do you suppose that I am that kind of woman? Open your eyes, and look clearly. Don't confuse the good with the indecent! Now get out of here!"

Awakened by the shouting, Ali rose to protect Nurbaya, but Ludi looked as if he did not wish to press his luck, particularly as he heard Nurbaya speaking Dutch, and so he went away.

Though the purser never came back, Nurbaya and Ali dared not shut their eyes the entire night, not even for a moment, in case he returned to harass them.

That night, the ship entered Ketaun harbor in Bengkulu, but was unable to unload or stow cargo on account of the rough sea, and so waited until the next day. Even though the ship was moored, Nurbaya felt rather queasy, for the vessel took to rolling heavily, a plaything to the waves. Unable to stand, all she could do was sleep on her bench until the ship got underway again to Batavia. Only then did she feel a bit more at ease, eventually rising and walking about. The day turned out to be a fine one and the vessel sailed safely on.

However, that next night at around ten o'clock, the clear sky suddenly turned black as pitch. The glimmering of the stars could no longer be seen, as they were now covered by thick, rain-bearing clouds. All around, the wind was calm, the sea at peace, and the air hot, though it was night.

Just then, lightening flashed in the southern sky, followed by the boom of thunder. Soon afterwards, heavy rain fell, as if poured from the heavens, together with the violent swirl of wind blowing from every direction. Great waves appeared, curling and rolling as high as mountains, only to smash into each other and collapse in the middle of the sea. The great ship was slammed about from all sides, like a useless plank of wood, seawater spraying on the deck and washing away boxes and cargo. All in all, life was made miserable for the passengers aboard, now soaked from head to toe, crying out as they fled this way and that, in search of shelter for themselves and their belongings. But things only got worse, as the relentless pitching of the ship made many sick.

In the midst of the commotion, there suddenly appeared a man dressed completely in black, moving quickly toward Nurbaya who, at that moment, was sitting in a chair, unable to stand from dizziness. Grabbing hold of her, the man lifted Nurbaya and carried her over to the side of the ship, where he intended to throw her into the sea. As she cried out for help with every ounce of strength left in her, Nurbaya recognized the man as Number Five, the man who had tried to stab Samsulbahri.

Ali, startled from his sleep, jumped up and went after the man to save Nurbaya. While the two grappled, trying to hurl each other overboard, Nurbaya was able to wrest herself free of the criminal's grasp. The two men broke and Ali tried to close in again on Number Five, only to be kicked and sent sprawling to the ground. By this time, a crowd had gathered from all the commotion, and Number Five, afraid of being caught, ran off, disappearing into one of the ship's dark corners.

When the captain arrived at the scene, Ali related everything that had happened. The captain, a decent and compassionate man, immediately ordered his crewmen to take Nurbaya to the sick bay, as she had fallen unconscious by the side of the ship, whether from shock or from having been thrown to the deck, no one knew. Though a thorough search of the ship was ordered, the criminal was not to be found.

The next day, a young man who appeared to be waiting for someone paced up and down the pier at Tanjung Priok harbor. After Nurbaya's vessel tied up at the dock, he went aboard, looking this way and that, but was unable to find what he was looking for. He asked several passengers whether or not a young woman named Nurbaya had traveled with them. When he heard everything that had happened to her, he went immediately to the ship's sick bay and there saw Nurbaya lying on a cot. Unable to restrain himself, he ran to her side, embracing and kissing her, and crying out, "Oh, Nurbaya, my beloved, we almost didn't get to see each other."

Just then, Nurbaya awoke and when her eyes met Samsulbahri's, she began to cry and held him even tighter.

"Truly accursed, this fate of mine," she said, "with no end to the perils that beset me. When will all this torment and misery cease? If Mr Ali hadn't been there, I would have found my grave at the bottom of the sea for sure."

"It's all right, there's no need to cry! Perhaps now we'll find happiness, far away from all this evil. Be patient and I'll see to it that we get that happiness. Are you able to walk?"

"I am," replied Nurbaya, "only I'm still worn out and a little dizzy."

"Never mind," answered Ali, who, unseen, had followed Samsu into the sick bay. "I'll help you."

Hearing the old coachman's voice, Samsulbahri turned around and straightway shook hands with Ali, expressing his gratitude for the coachman's loyal assistance.

As they were speaking, the captain entered the cabin, together with the ship's doctor and a police constable, and said, "That's her."

Looking over Nurbaya, the constable was silent for a moment then asked to speak to Samsu alone outside.

"Who are you?" he asked once they were outside.

"I'm a student at the Java Doctors' School. My name is Samsulbahri," replied Samsu.

"What is your relationship to that woman?"

"Although not my real sister, she is more to me than a sister of the same womb."

"What is her name?"

"Sitti Nurbaya."

"And the person with her?"

"Ali, coachman of my father who himself holds the position of District Head in Padang."

"Did the two of them come from Padang?"

"They did. The woman is the daughter of a merchant there."

"If so, then it's true that she is the one," said the constable.

"For what reason are you making such inquiries?" asked Samsu.

"Read this telegram," replied the constable, holding out a cable.

When Samsu finished reading the cable, his face turned pale and his lips quivered. He clenched his fist and ground his teeth. "When will that scoundrel ever be finished tormenting her?" he said.

He then turned to the constable. "This complaint is nothing but lies. His whole purpose is to bully this woman. It's obvious what that man wanted to do to her last night. Datuk Meringgih is her husband, a very brutal man. That's the reason Nurbaya ended up fleeing here. She was to have been thrown into the sea, for sure the work of that villain, too, for the criminal who would have done it was his man." Samsu then told the officer Nurbaya's entire story, from beginning to end.

"I believe you," said the constable, "but I have my orders."

"Of course," replied Samsu.

After reflecting for a moment, he added, "What do you intend to do now, sir?"

"I have to inspect her things," replied the officer.

"All right, I will go get everything she brought with her." Samsu went back into the room, re-emerging soon after with her things. After inspecting the contents, the constable was satisfied nothing was to be found, other than fifty rupiah and some clothing. Ali's box was searched next. Nothing was found there either, aside from a few articles of clothing.

"Whose money is this?" the constable asked.

"Nurbaya's," Ali replied.

"Do you know where she got this money from?"

"I do. It's the money she got from pawning her bracelet, which cost about two hundred rupiah. I myself pawned it for eighty rupiah before we left to come here. Here's the receipt. We used thirty to pay for the voyage, leaving fifty."

"Do you know for sure that the bracelet was her own, and not the property of her husband?"

"Yes, I am sure. That bracelet is an heirloom from her mother, who has since left this world. It was given to Nurbaya before she married Datuk Meringgih."

"Indeed," put in Samsu, "I also know about that."

"All right, then," said the constable, writing down everything they said. "But I have to question the woman."

"That won't be a problem. Only, I would ask that she not be informed right away, for she is still sick and might get worse from receiving such bad news. She has to be taken to the hospital and treated there first," said Samsu.

"Of course," said the ship's doctor. "She is still not well and cannot be taken home yet."

"If you would like to make a written statement about this matter, sir, naturally the questioning can wait until she has recovered," the constable told the doctor.

"I will give you that statement a bit later," the doctor said and then left. Samsu then followed the constable into Nurbaya's room. "This man here wants to examine you in case there are any traces of the mishap last night," he told her. "What happened to you will have to be heard in court," he explained, concealing from Nurbaya the real purpose of the policeman's visit.

After examining Nurbaya, the constable said, "Very well, let's go! I'll show you a hospital where you can be treated."

"Good," replied Samsu.

When all was ready, the three set off for the train station, Nurbaya walking slowly, supported by Samsu. Once on board a train headed to Batavia, Samsu said to Nurbaya, "In Batavia, you have to go immediately to the hospital so you can recover properly. When you've done so, we can put our heads together and figure out what's best."

"Whatever is good for you, I will go along with," replied Nurbaya.

In Batavia, Nurbaya was placed in a hospital and Samsu and Ali came every day to see her. Afterwards, she had time to recover from her illness at the home of a village headman, someone Samsu knew, until the next ship from Padang was due.

"Nurbaya," said Samsu to his beloved when the time came, "there's something important I have to tell you that I've kept secret until now. I was worried your illness might get worse if I told you. But now that you've recovered, I hope you'll stay calm."

"What is it?" asked Nurbaya, startled, as she looked at Samsu.

"Don't worry," he replied when he saw the change in Nurbaya's expression. He tried to smile, in the hopes of dispelling her anxiety. "Remember that constable who came to your ship just after it docked, the one who examined your and Mr Ali's boxes? Remember how you went straight from the ship to the hospital? Perhaps my lack of attention to you may have raised some doubt or suspicion in your mind.

"Even if that's the case, I can't be angry, for it's true, that's the way I acted then. It did seem as if I was ignoring you. But actually only Allah knows how wonderful I felt when I received your news and saw you coming. And God knows how sad I felt at your arrival under such circumstances, because no sooner have we met than we have to part again. Ah..."

"What are you saying?" asked Nurbaya, greatly alarmed, "We have to leave each other again? Why?"

In response, Samsu told Nurbaya about the charges Datuk Meringgih had raised against her: that Nurbaya and Ali had made off with his goods and money, that he had requested that they be detained and returned to Padang as soon as possible.

"He is so cruel. Only my death will satisfy him," Nurbaya said angrily. "Do you believe these accusations?"

"You can't seriously think I would believe you're capable of something like that, Nur!" replied Samsu. "No one who hears this story believes such accusations. But what can we do? We're up against the police now. We have to go along with them. If we have to fight that accursed Datuk, as long as I have life within me, you're not going back to Padang."

Nurbaya made no reply, most likely because she felt her chest tighten.

"What are you thinking, Nur? Why are you so quiet?"

"Because this is very complicated. My heart tells me to do everything possible to avoid going back there. I can't tell you how difficult it was for me to come here and how much I will be reviled by the people back there because I, a married woman, left my husband and run off to another man. If I return to Padang, I'm sure to see all those who mock me and hear their humiliating words. But, yes, what other path can I follow?"

After saying nothing for a moment, Samsu replied softly, "What do you think of the idea of us running away from the police?"

"I suspect it would be useless for us to do that," Nurbaya replied, shaking her head. "In the end we'd surely fall into their hands anyway. Where would we hide? In Java there are police everywhere.

"And if we did do that, it would make me look guilty. Wouldn't it seem that I'm afraid out of guilt and brave because I'm not? Running away would mean fear. As I see it, I couldn't prove my innocence if I didn't fight his accusation. So let me go back first. It won't be difficult to prove that I'm innocent, and the case will be decided quickly. Once it's decided, I'll come back right away.

"I see, but there's no other way to free yourself of that hellish man?" asked Samsu, clenching his fists and pounding the table, to vent his anger. "What I want, now that we're both here, is never to be parted, for we can finally be together. If you return to Padang, we will have to wait to be together again. It isn't a simple night's journey between Padang and Batavia. Wide seas must be crossed first. Within a second, anything could happen, to say nothing of our separation of who knows how long.

"Oh, Sam, you're right, but what can we do except go along with what the police want? This separation won't be hard on just you. It will be especially hard on me. I'm like a bird that's just been freed from prison and has to give itself up again, to go back into its cage and meet its executioner.

"Oh, Allah!" Nurbaya suddenly groaned. "To whom can Your servant turn for help other than to You?"

Samsu was unable to utter a single sound, too full of sorrow at seeing Nurbaya like this.

"I feel crushed by the thought of leaving you again. I can't be happy until this matter is resolved. Let them say that a woman was unfaithful to her husband. That Datuk is not my husband. He's my executioner. He's being protected by the marriage license, but I won't tolerate being called a thief: I am no thief. So I must prove my innocence. But couldn't the case be tried here in Batavia? If it could, how much better that would be!"

"Yes, of course, you're right," Samsu said suddenly, rising to put on his hat.

"Where are you going?" asked Nurbaya, unaware of her beloved's intentions.

"To the office of the Assistant Resident, to ask whether the case can be tried here."

"Yes, good! Do try!" said Nurbaya. "And may Allah bring your purpose to a fitting conclusion."

With that, Samsu left and did not return until two o'clock that afternoon. When he re-entered the room, it became clear to Nurbaya that he had not succeeded. There was too much sorrow in his eyes.

"And so?" she asked, from a distance.

"It's not possible. You have to go back."

"Just as I supposed. What we do?"

"This disaster cannot be averted, so you're going to have to be very careful. Who knows, that executioner of yours may have more schemes in store for you. He seems to be utterly unscrupulous and unafraid to commit all kinds of wickedness. In the meantime, I will look for work here so that we can have a life together when you come back. If I continue my studies, it will be hard for us. As far as I'm concerned, it doesn't matter if I become a doctor, as long as I'm with you."

"You're right, Sam. It's the best path for us. And though I regret that you'll be quitting school, I agree with what you intend to do. I promise, when we're together again some day, I will repay you with the best care and help you've ever had in your life."

"Don't give any thought to my studies. Think of my promise to your father. No matter what, I will defend and protect you," said Samsu. "Besides, I won't be able to continue my studies anyway, since I can't cover the expenses. You know yourself, Father won't assist me anymore."

"When we're together again, I will have my house and lands and all the things still in my possession in Padang sold, so that we can use the money to buy a house here, or whatever else is needed. I will not want to return to Padang. Just let me die in foreign lands. In my homeland there's nothing for me but trouble and torment. Perhaps I really can find happiness away from Padang," said Nurbaya.

"Yes, right. That's right. I agree. What is there pulling me back to Padang? You are here, and I will get my mother to come live with us," replied Sam.

"Ah, how happy I'll be when your mother is with us! I'm sure all my suffering will vanish, and leave us happy. Surely... ah, such dreams seem so fine," Nurbaya said after reflecting for a moment. Her joy soon vanished, replaced by the worry and fear that God would not fulfill their prayers.

"Do you recall those dreams and hopes we shared that night, when you were about to leave to come here, Sam? What has become of them?"

"Don't think like that!" Samsu said. "Don't despair! You're still young and so am I. Who knows, if not now, maybe some day we'll find happiness. How can it just rain from morning till night? After the rain comes the sunshine, refreshing the body and pleasing the heart."

"That's my hope, too! But with all the misfortunes and sorrow I've been through, one after another, I'm just not brave enough to hope again, especially now that I have to return to Padang.

"It's really hard for me to leave you and Batavia. I've felt truly happy here, being in your hands, and because I'm far from that place which has become such a danger to me. It's like something is forbidding me to go back to Padang, as if there were some disaster waiting there for me."

"Get rid of such thoughts! Think of your father's advice to you!" said Samsu gently, trying to soothe his beloved, even as he himself began to worry.

"And all the more so because we have no other choice," he continued. "We have to comply. So, submit and be careful. You'll be there one month at the most, and after that, we will be together again.

"I wish that I could take you back myself, but I can't leave. I have to find work, and if I go off, it will slip through my fingers. What I want more than anything is to have work when you return.

"Plus, you're returning to Padang with Mr Ali, whom I trust. I will tell him to look after you. If you want to come back and don't have anyone to accompany you, just tell me and I will go to Padang to meet you. If I go by ship to Padang via Aceh, I might be able to return that same day and not have to stay the night in Padang. I have to do everything possible not to see my father again. What do you think, Nur? Do you think it's a good idea?"

"Yes, if you're happy doing it that way," she replied, looking straight at Samsu and smiling.

"You sure are good-hearted, going along with everything," said Samsu, kissing her.

"And now change into your clothes, so we can go out for a stroll, and see Batavia. Your ship for Padang leaves tomorrow."

"I have to leave tomorrow and be separated from you again?" Nurbaya asked.

"Yes, for the time being."

After Nurbaya got dressed, the two of them went walking hand in hand and saw Batavia by night. Sam took Nurbaya all around the city, on foot, by buggy, and by carriage. It would be impossible to relate how pleased Nurbaya was to see Batavia's splendor.

"Batavia is so big and so full of hustle and bustle and shops and magnificent homes. It really is the capital of the Indies," she said at one point during their tour.

After they had enough of strolling about, they entered a restaurant, for they were both feeling hungry. They ate a good meal and afterwards Samsu took Nurbaya to a circus that happened to be performing nearby. When the performance ended, it was time to head back and the two of them walked very slowly.

That night Nurbaya forgot all about the suffering she had borne for so long and experienced instead the joy of a free woman whose lover is close by. It was the third time in her life that she felt her fate was a lucky one.

"I don't ask for much or have many wishes," she said as they were walking. "Never mind if I'm not rich or don't have a high position in society, just so long as I can be as happy as I am at this moment. This is heaven on earth. I know that now. Can we be this way forever?"

"Why not? When you come back, what will prevent us from being together?" Samsu replied.

They arrived at the house where Nurbaya was staying and sat down to continue their conversation on the front veranda, filling their hearts to the brim.

"Sam!" said Nurbaya suddenly, "I heard a *pantun*."

> *Your ship arrives from afar,*
> *a flag raised upon its rudder.*
> *Your sister comes from afar,*
> *to see her big-hearted brother.*

"The response goes like this," Samsu replied with a smile:

> In Batak land basil grows on banks;
> a young woman there hurt her knee.
> Unto you I offer my deepest thanks,
> that you should be willing to visit me.

"Another one," said Nurbaya:

> In Sikilang, Sultan Iskandar is protector,
> in Barus, the king there holds his mace.
> Have no regrets when I am no more,
> for everything, there is a time and place.

"Its reply," said Samsu:

> It's hard to count coconuts in a tree,
> sparrows flock together as if on cue.
> I care not what might happen to me,
> as long as I can always be with you.

In this way, the two of them spent the night talking and devising *pantun*, and laughing with each other.

The next day, Nurbaya and the coachman Ali sailed back to Padang escorted by a policeman. With the help of Allah, their voyage was a safe one and they lacked for nothing.

In Padang, the case was examined and it was obvious that Nurbaya was innocent. Behind it all was the treachery of Datuk Meringgih, who had pretended Nurbaya made off with his belongings and money to force her to come back to Padang.

According to him, he did not know at first where Nurbaya had kept his things. As she had fled, he supposed she had taken them with her. But when Nurbaya showed them where the supposedly stolen goods were, it became clear his wife had done nothing wrong.

Even though everyone knew Datuk Meringgih had purposely done this, he was not punished in the least, being as he was a rich merchant in Padang.

After Nurbaya's vessel had departed that day, Samsu stood at the Tanjung Priok harbor, absorbed in thought for some time. Suddenly, he heard a voice within him say that Nurbaya would not be coming back, that this had been their final earthly meeting. Though very worried and confused, he managed to calm himself and asked for help from God, the All-Merciful and All-Compassionate.

12

A Conversation

"Boom, boom!" sounded the great drum. A moment later, the muezzin could be heard calling the faithful for the sunset prayer.

Hearing the call, Ahmad Maulana and his wife made their way to the place of prayer, where they prostrated themselves before God. Their devotion completed, Ahmad did not rise from his prayer mat, but continued praying, right up to the night prayer, and then prayed again.

While he was in the mosque, Alimah and Nurbaya were busy setting out food on a white cloth-lined grass mat spread out in the middle of his house. A little while later, Ahmad came and sat down to eat across from his wife, while Alimah and Nurbaya sat a little way off, listening in case he asked for something.

"It makes me sad to see the fate that Rapiah's been dealt recently. She just turned eighteen and has already departed from this world. Especially when you consider she left behind two small children. The older one, the girl, is just three years-old, and the younger one, the boy, is one and a half," Ahmad said, spooning some vegetables onto his plate.

"Yes, it really is a pity," his wife, Fatima, replied. "Who will take care of those children?"

"That's what makes me even sadder. Nobody in their family has the means to take them in and care for them. The one who died, well, so be it. Let's not worry about her anymore. Maybe she's at peace, for now she's free from all the suffering of this world. But she must be helped with prayer, so that Allah may grant her ease in the coffin. But the children left behind, what will happen to them?"

"Is their father still alive? Surely he's not indifferent to their condition," Fatima asked.

"Their father?" Ahmad snorted, looking at his wife rather sourly. "Hmmph! Why would he want to take on such a burden? Isn't it the custom here that children go back to their mother's brother? Is an aristocrat like Sutan Hamzah going to want to arrange things for his children? He can't even take care of himself! How many of his children here in Padang does he ignore? Least of all now that he's infatuated, it would seem, with his younger wife.

"Even if he were willing to take care of those children, he'd just be adding to their suffering, for they'd be handed over to their stepmother, for sure. You know yourself how a woman behaves towards her stepchildren. Out of a hundred, you rarely find one that is good. Nearly all of them view their stepchild as enemy because it's a child of the other wife. Children who have done nothing wrong and who know nothing of the affairs of their parents are tormented and beaten just to release the heartache their stepmother feels towards her deceased rival, who is often innocent of any wrongdoing and was, in fact, bullied for having snatched her husband from her."

Fatimah could not deny the truth of what her husband was saying and so stayed silent. Instead, she tried to change the conversation by asking, "What did Rapiah die of?"

"I don't know. Some said she was feverish. Someone else said she was coughing up blood. Yet another person said she had some pain inside her. They say that ever since she quarreled angrily with her husband over Sutan Hamzah's new wife, she never got up again, for he kicked her.

"Which story is true, I can't say. But this news is no use to anyone. If the police hear about it, it will end up in court. Not only could we get involved, but if someone like Sutan Hamzah gets punished, there will be hostility between us and Sutan Mahmud, the district head. And then what would become of his young child, with the mother dead and the father away in exile?"

"How could I be so crazy as to reveal such a secret?" Fatimah said.

At that point, Nurbaya rose and went into her room, pretending to look for something, but really to hide the tears she could no longer hold back.

She thought of her own fate, so like that of the woman who had just passed on and the child she had left behind.

After drying her eyes, she came back out and saw that her uncle had finished eating and was now washing his hands.

"Alimah, fetch my cigarettes from my jacket, won't you?" Ahmad said.

Alimah immediately rose to get the cigarettes for her father.

"Now you two eat!" he said, lighting a cigarette.

Alimah and Nurbaya sat down on the mat and began eating with Fatimah.

"To tell you the truth, I completely disagree with the custom of having many wives, for more evil comes of it than good," Ahmad said reflectively as he exhaled a puff of smoke. "I've heard many stories of misfortune and I have seen much suffering with my own eyes."

"Yes, but that is our custom," Fatimah replied. "How can you change it? And even in our religion it's not forbidden for a man to take more than one wife. If we have a son, how ashamed we would be, even without being of high birth, if he had only one wife. It would make him look as if no women sought him."

"So I am not sought after by women, since I only have you as my wife? Aren't you ashamed, Alimah, that your father isn't popular with other women?" Ahmad said to his daughter with a smile.

Alimah said nothing in reply, only bowed her head in embarrassment.

"It seems your aunt here likes men who have many wives, Nurbaya, and so you ought to suggest my name to about a dozen more women. If not, she'll soon be asking for a letter of divorce from me, out of shame at her unpopular husband," he continued.

Nurbaya didn't dare answer either, but only smiled, for she saw that Fatimah was becoming upset with her uncle's banter.

"Another thing that's no good," said Ahmad, the smile disappearing from his lips, "is that marriage is seen as a business. In some countries, women are sold to men, and this means that the men must give money to the women. Here, men are bought by women, because it's the women who give money to the men. With that kind of custom, men and women are only joined together by the tie of money or the desire for good offspring. There's no real binding of love or affection.

"That's why the tie of friendship between husband and wife is easily broken and they divorce so quickly. When they get divorced, the man, of course, marries again, and so does the woman. Thus men have many wives and women have many husbands.

"Among Western people, the husband and wife are not normally brought together by the ties of money or property, but instead by love and affection. And for that reason their relationship is stronger. Because of that love and affection, oftentimes they are unconcerned with property, social standing or rank. And furthermore, they are bound together by a promise of loyalty made to each other. They may not divorce if there is no important reason, and this strengthens the relationship."

"And why should we follow the customs of infidels?" Fatimah interjected while washing her hands.

Alimah and Nurbaya began to clear away the leftovers, directing the servant to wash the plates and bowls, and wipe away the scraps left around the table.

Though engaged in her task, Nurbaya pricked up her ears to hear what her younger uncle had to say, for his thoughts were very much in line with her own.

"They are infidels, we say. But maybe they say *we* are the infidels, because we don't follow their religion. Which one is true, Allah alone knows! It's not something we can decide. All religions come from Him for the salvation of mankind. Of course, each group is going to praise its own religion, just like each person is going to praise himself. But self-praise cannot be a reason to find fault with others, especially if what we know merely concerns ourselves. How can we compare two things if we simply know only one of them?

"With regard to religion, what we know is only our own, and that imperfectly. We don't know anything at all about the others. How can we talk about their good and bad points? How can we compare what is true and what is false between two religions? Just think about it! If I have a stone, and you have one, too, can you say which is the heavier of the two if you don't know the weight of both?"

"But can't this be seen by the eye and estimated by the mind, according to its size?" answered Fatimah.

"Sight and estimation are not always accurate. Tin, which is light, can sometimes be heavier than wood. Nonetheless, you have to see first the size of the two objects in order to be able to estimate their weight.

"Now, what do you know about the religion of our friend, the infidel? Nothing more than its bad points. That's because you hear people's stories and you just go along repeating them like the magpie which copies words it has been taught without knowing in the slightest what they mean.

"It's not good to do that. Don't take something you don't properly know and just start criticizing it. Our religion forbids us from accusing someone of being an infidel or calling someone a Muslim, for all of that is known to God alone. And what's more, because man's heart is not fixed, it's always changing. Virtuous today, perhaps wicked tomorrow. It cannot be fixed, for man is, by nature, weak. Don't scrutinize what is external only, for what is on the inside is the more valuable. And do you know a person's inner self?

"Even if outwardly they are infidels, who knows, in their inner being perhaps they are Muslim. And even though they are infidels, it could be that some day their hearts will turn and they will become Muslim. And furthermore, as I see it, there's nothing wicked about that religion. It's all good, for its intention is only good and its goal is the One God."

Fatimah sat silently, without responding, and so Ahmad continued, after a brief pause, "Though they are infidels, as we say, they do have good customs and ways. Their manners are different and their religion is different. These should not be equated with ours. Our customs and ways are, in truth, mostly good, but there are those that are not right. What's wrong with imitating the good customs of other people and doing away with those of ours that are bad? We won't take those of theirs that are wicked and we'll keep ours that are good, as is proper.

"We imitate many of the ways and customs of foreign nations without reflecting on whether these are good or bad. Jackets and shoes, whose clothes are these? Aren't they the clothes of Westerners? So why wear them? Even Arabs and those who have been on the hajj copy Western clothes. Sitting on chairs, eating at tables, having hanging lamps: these aren't the customs of our ancestors, but we follow these, too. Plates and cups: who made these? But aren't they used as well? Whose customs and ways must be followed by

Muslims? Arab customs? Arabs eat dates and drink the milk of camels. Why not imitate that as well? Which are our original customs and manners?

"Ah, Fatimah, all this is only of this world, not the hereafter. The outer, not the inner sphere. In my view, no matter what you wear or make, so long as your inner purpose is pure and your heart is steadfast, it doesn't make any difference. But even if you properly follow every word which is mentioned in the Book, if your heart is not pure and upright, it will be of no use."

"Yes, that's true," Fatimah now replied, "but our customs are what we inherit from our ancestors. They can't be ignored or changed, just like that. And furthermore, it wouldn't be good for us to toss them out. Both the good and the bad must be followed, for that is the sign that we have customs. If it's a question of adding other rules to them, then good, but use our customs, too."

"Naturally, we shouldn't get rid of what's old merely because we've gotten something new," her husband shot back. "But among those old customs and manners, there are some which were truly good for former times but less—or not at all—useful for today. That's the case with clothes when you first buy them. At that time they're good to wear, but as time goes on, they get old and moldy, and finally all torn and ragged, and can't be used any longer. If we feel bad about throwing out such old clothes because we remember their service to us, all right then, keep them as souvenirs! But we have to buy new clothes, right?

"It's the same way with customs. Change them, according to the times. Even if you don't intentionally change them, they're going to change anyway, for nothing is fixed. 'When the tide surges, the banks will shift,' says the proverb. And that's the way it is."

"All right, now would my elder brother please explain what's so bad about our custom of a man having more than one wife," Fatimah asked.

"Listen. First, the more wives, the more money is needed, for each wife must be provided with a sufficient amount. Otherwise, they're sure to be unhappy. And that's the way quarrels start. And if there are arguments with that many women, then life will certainly be unpleasant."

"It appears that my elder brother has forgotten what he said just now about our native customs, that is, that the man need not give money to support his wife or his children, for these are the responsibility of their mother's brother. The man viewed as a clansman by his marrying into their family is a guest. Even if he has many wives and children, this is no inconvenience to him."

"I haven't forgotten that," Ahmad replied. "That's what concerns me most. The man doesn't have to provide funds or take care of his wife's children, and he even gets his food and clothing from her. If the man is of high birth, when he is to marry he's even paid money and given clothes by her family. So, is that what you would call a man? For, really, it's the man who must make a living and take care of his wife's children, for women are weaker than men.

"If women are compared to men, in terms of the shape of their bodies, their strengths, minds and other things, it's clear that man is the race that protects the wife and children, the kith and kin, the possessions, the home, whether against enemies or for other needs, for the sake of their lives. To the woman is entrusted the children and possessions. But according to that custom you just mentioned, the woman becomes the man, and the man the woman. This does not accord with the natural order of things."

"Perhaps not," replied Fatimah "but it's not the woman herself who feeds her husband, but her parents and relatives."

"Fine, I accept your reply, even though of course there are villages where it's really the woman who earns the livelihood, for she is the one who works, trades and such, while the husband sleeps all day, has a gay old time with cockfighting, contests or gambling. But can you call such a person a man? Can't he be seen just as a stud horse or stud bull, well cared for and fed sufficiently for the sole reason of providing offspring?

"If that man is an aristocrat or a handsome fellow, so be it, for there are things wanted of him, namely his looks or his high standing, so that these will pass down to his children, even if that lineage grows increasingly depreciated in value and public respect. However, if the fellow is not of high birth, is no looker, has a square head, broad ears, eyes which cross, a stub nose, a wide mouth, buck teeth, a hunched back, and is lame on one side to boot, what could you hope for from someone like that? With all those defects you want his children and grandchildren to turn out just as fine as he?"

"How could women want a man who looks like that? The ones who get bought are the high-born good-lookers, clever, position-holders, things like that," answered Fatimah.

"If that's so, it doesn't matter. Things of value are certainly not just for the asking, though a valuable thing like this has little meaning for me. But the custom we were just now discussing, that is, a man who is seen as a guest, can also be found among ordinary folks, and so not just among those who are special.

"What's more, of the qualities you mentioned, only noble birth and good looks can be passed down to descendants. But what's the use of high position and profound knowledge, if these can't help children?"

Fatimah had nothing to say to this, either.

"Second," said Ahmad, after pausing for a bit, "the more wives one has, the more children, and also the more money needed. Just wait a moment," he said, for he saw his wife was about to say something, "I know what you're going to say, that all those children aren't a problem, since they have their uncle to take care of them, isn't that it? But for that very reason there's no relationship of love between a child and their father, just as there is none between husband and wife, as I said earlier. So the man knows nothing of what we call love and affection for his children and wife. All that he knows is a feeling of care and affection for his nephew or niece. But that's not the same as love for his child, his own flesh and blood. And the child won't know love towards its father, only towards its mother, while the love it feels towards its uncle doesn't amount to much. His wife loves her children only because they are her own flesh and blood, but in her heart her husband is someone else. Therefore, it's rare for them to know the happiness of a household, something very valuable to Western people.

"And, just think! Whose fault was it that the child arrived in this world? The child didn't ask to be born. His mother and father did. Once the child is born, it's handed over to someone else, who bears absolutely no blame in this matter. But even the affection and care shown by the uncle himself won't be the same as the affection and care of the child's own father.

"And what is that feeling like? Just give it some real thought! Don't be blind and deaf. Don't just look at custom. Who is closer to the father, his child or his nephew? His child, his own flesh and blood, while the nephew or niece is the child of his sister, even if he and she are themselves of the same blood.

"There are some who believe that a child is actually closer to its mother's brother than to its father, because it was born to the uncle's own blood sister. It's not always known whether a child is the husband's. It could be someone else's, if, for example, the mother was unfaithful to her husband. So the father might be unsure of his child and wife.

"Such a strange thing, in my opinion, originates from the older customs, when a woman could have many husbands or when marriage was not yet as well-ordered as it is today. But those customs are no longer appropriate. Marriage matters have now been well arranged, meaning that each man is sure who his wife is and the woman is sure who her husband is and, when they are married, this is witnessed by the public.

"I don't mean to say that in the case of each and every child, it could never happen that its father wasn't someone else. Of course, it could be that this is the child of some other man. But such things rarely occur, so that in no way should it become an excuse to estrange the child from any of the customs practiced by the people throughout our world, that is, where the ancestral heirlooms are passed down to the child.

"So you see, here is an example which shows that one custom which was once good, perhaps now no longer has any value. Such old customs aren't good. Shouldn't they be stored away in a chest? If need be, they can become mementos of our ancestors from days past."

Fatimah could find no error in her husband's words and so shifted the topic of the conversation a bit by saying, "But isn't having lots of children good, so that our people can increase and multiply?"

"Oh, if that's what you mean, that's very true indeed. Each race should increase in size, as stated in religion. But taking care of the race is an obligation, too. Don't just be good at making people, but unwilling to take care of them. How can such a people grow and progress to perfection if they aren't taken care of properly? We can't do slipshod work!'

"Third, even though it's mentioned in the Book that a man may have up to four wives, that fellow's goods and possessions must first be in surplus after providing perfectly for one wife, and he must also be the fairest of fair in all things to these four wives. Only then is it permissible. Because if not, it becomes a sin, for unfair treatment brings resentment and treachery among the wives. But most husbands are not fair to all their wives. Usually it's the newest that he loves more than the first. He's fonder of the youngest than the oldest, and takes more pleasure in the most beautiful than the ugliest. That's not permissible. All of them must be treated the same: in spending money, clothes, households, love and affection, and other such things.

"Can any of our men do all this? Out of a thousand, you'd rarely find one. Most of them, in such matters, love to excess the wife they prefer. It's impossible to give your love equally to all your wives, for it has been preordained by God that mankind will desire more and love more the dainty over the repulsive. It is behavior such as that which frequently gives rise to jealousy and resentment between the wives to the point where arguments break out between husband and wife and between wife and co-wife. To whichever wife the husband goes, he's greeted with nothing more than a sour look, words unpleasant to the ears, care and attention which is less than perfect, and occasionally abuse and scolding, so that in the end they get to quarreling. Now, would this be a happy existence?

"Furthermore, the wife who has to share her husband with a co-wife won't be straightforward with her husband in any matter whatsoever. There are also wives who become wicked, who do things that are unseemly, because they seek revenge on their husbands for their hurt feelings. Their relationship, which of course is not strong, such as I mentioned just now, becomes weaker and weaker until, finally, all that's left is the marriage license booklet in which both are displayed.

"Even though I'm a man, the way I see it, the husband shouldn't feel put out if his wife, whom he has made into a co-wife, doesn't pay any attention to him, for the husband himself has shown no concern for his wife's feelings. What woman could restrain herself if she saw her husband with another woman? Is there a man who would feel at ease seeing his wife with another man? I don't think there is.

"Fourth, is there a woman who is so patient that she ignores her husband's taking pleasure in having many wives? But frequently such patience is the sign of a diminished love towards her husband. For is it not from a heart which loves that jealousy arises?

"When the wives all love their husband, surely each will think of ways to be more loved by him than by the others. Most of these schemes aren't carried out by improving her behavior or the household or with anything that would win his heart, but through sorcery, love potions, and spells.

"Each wife looks for a sorcerer who is good at medicating that fine fellow, so she might be better loved than her co-wives, and sometimes she spends everything she has to do so. The sorcerer doesn't just use his knowledge, but often potions and medications the husband must take. It's true that good is intended, but those love potions aren't always made of pure ingredients and, eventually, from ingesting too many of them, coming from here and there by different wives, his body just gets wrecked. It's not just one or two fellows who've become victims of a sorcerer this way. And that's too bad!

"An impatient woman, who's sometimes very hurt at being superseded like this, uses poison instead of a love potion, so that he'll return to his home in the hereafter all the more quickly."

"Alimah, bring me a glass of tea, would you? My mouth feels dry from talking so much," Ahmad said to his daughter.

Alimah immediately left the room and came back a short time later with the tea. Re-entering, she noticed that Nurbaya was just sitting there, pretending to sew, but really listening all-ears to her father's words.

"Fifth, when such a woman feels very emotional," Ahmad continued, after drinking the tea, "not only will she give her husband such a concoction, but the co-wife, too, and not out of love for her either, but so that the other woman will be hated by the husband. And there are some who do it so that the rival wife will soon have the earth for her pillow. Who knows, maybe Rapiah was the victim of just such an act. I feel ever so sorry for her!

"Sixth, many women who've been turned into co-wives don't want to re-marry if their husbands divorce them, out of fear of the pain and sadness. If all women were like that, how would it end? How would you increase your race with women who don't want to marry? Maybe at this time such a thing is not too worrisome because most women are still unable to make a living on their own, but if they were as smart as men, they'd want to have their own lives, instead of eating their hearts out from having been made a co-wife by their husbands. Women also marry because they want to find pleasure, not because they want to serve a man."

"That's why it isn't good for a girl to be educated," Fatimah interrupted.

"So that she can stay stupid and forever be the slave of a man, is that it? She can be treated however he wants, just like a buffalo, with a rope through its snout, to be led and ordered about however its herder wishes. If you yourself, as a woman, like your own race to be dealt with in such a way, suit yourself! But if I were a woman, I would never want to accept such a system."

Fatimah fell silent, unable to think of a response to her husband.

"Seventh, the woman who is superseded by another wife won't be straightforward towards her husband in anything, such as I said just now. No need to talk of her looking upon her husband as her beloved, she can't even approve of him as her companion, for in her eyes and heart, the man is a cruel lord and master. How to live in happiness and harmony with a hated enemy?

"Ah, Fatimah, there are many other evils in the custom of taking many wives, and some other time I can tell you more about it. For now, my eyes are heavy. Have Hasan extinguish the lamps and shut the doors!"

A little while later, Ahmad Maulana's home became as dark and quiet as the grave, for the lamps had been extinguished and all the doors and windows shut. Only in the back of the house could the voice of Hasan, Ahmad's houseboy, be heard, humming softly to himself as he lay down to sleep.

In Alimah's room, Nurbaya sat with her cousin and kept sewing. From time to time, she would pause, as if lost in thought.

"Nur, has your illness returned?" Alimah asked.

"No, I'm just thinking about what Uncle said earlier, for his thoughts rang so true in my heart and have made me think about the fate of the female sex," Nurbaya answered.

"Nur, don't disturb your mind with sad thoughts! You still seem ill. And all those sad memories won't leave you. Didn't you promise me that you were resolved not to be tormented anymore?"

"It's not that I'm feeling melancholy, though, of course, this thing has stayed in my mind for a long time. But just think of the destiny of us women! By God, who is by nature compassionate and merciful, we've been diminished compared to men, those friends of ours. I say 'those friends of ours', for in truth that's what they are, even though many of them think they're not our friends, but our lords and masters and we, their slaves. As they see it, they surpass us in strength and wit. It's true that we are weak compared to men and, perhaps, not as clever as them, but the weakness of our bodies and our minds' shortcomings aren't due to a lack of strength or the imperfection of our brains. It's only that our bodies differ greatly from theirs. Bear in mind that we're the race of mothers. We're the ones who carry children inside us, give birth to them, give them milk to suck, take care of and raise them. Men know nothing of such things, only their own pleasures.

"Think of a pregnant woman, vomiting all the time, sick and uncomfortable. Isn't that an illness? Two months after giving birth, our bellies are big again. We feel sick almost constantly. Look at women who give birth almost every year! What's it like for them? Broken in body, old before their time, and dying young. How can we ever be the equals of men in strength, when, it may be said, they are always in good health?

"Moreover, everything a man does increases his strength and the sharpness of his thinking. But women's work, from the house to the kitchen, and from the kitchen back to the house, looking after the children, cooking, washing, and cleaning the household, in no way would add to our strength or our mind.

"Men know this difference and they also know the burden we bear when we're pregnant. But such knowledge doesn't become an insight which might arouse feelings of anxiety and sympathy towards us. No, we are laughed at and teased. There are some who marry again just when their wives are big-bellied or are giving birth. Are we the ones who wish for such an awful fate? Do we seek to be made like this? Since men don't endure our burdens, suffering and pain, they pay no mind to our situation. Rare is the man who thinks that his mother—who has gone through such trouble bearing him, giving birth to him, and caring for him—is also of the race of women, and not of his own, that is, men."

"What you say is true, Nur," Alimah replied, reflecting on her dear cousin's words.

"Let me think about it a bit. First of all, the woman's burden is due to her child, who, correctly speaking, is not just her child, but one shared with her husband. For that reason, the troubles and pleasures that arise because of the child must be divided equally between mother and father. But it's not like that, as I've described just now. And even though it's the woman who endures more difficulties and troubles because of the child, the father receives more happiness from the child than the mother, for later on the child will be better known as the offspring of its father than its mother. For example, if that child becomes a person of high position, who will gain a good name, its father or its mother? When people ask, 'And whose is that fine child?' the father's name will be mentioned, not the mother's. Western women also bear their husband's name. Is this fair to women?

"Ah, justice! Are you in this world or not? If you are, then where are you hidden?" sighed Nurbaya, falling into silent reflection for a moment.

Resuming her train of thought, she said, "When we're two or three months' pregnant, our bodies feel ill and our heads spin, our vision is impeded, our hearing is unclear, our stomachs are always upset, we frequently vomit, and our appetites are uncertain. Food loses its taste and we like what we used to find repulsive. Sometimes we crave what we don't have, or what's difficult to find, or shouldn't be eaten. If we don't get what we want, we feel troubled and sad. Our thoughts are clouded, and frequently we get angry and hateful towards some and affectionate towards others, for no reason. Our behavior also constantly changes.

"When we've been pregnant for six months, our stomach gets bigger and bigger and becomes so heavy it's difficult to walk, stand up, work, stop, sit, and sleep. Things forbidden by custom and tradition increase in number. Certain foods can't be eaten. There's much work that can't be performed, things heard which may not be listened to, and things seen which may not be looked upon.

"When the child is about to be born, we can't do anything, for our stomachs grow bigger and heavier with the passing time, but sitting is no good, either, because it will make giving birth difficult, people say. Going outside the house makes us shy.

"When a man is asked to carry his child astride his waist for just an hour, he says he's tired. But for nine months and sometimes even longer, a woman never ceases carrying the child, day and night, everywhere she goes and, even afterwards, she carries it with her. But women aren't allowed to mention being tired.

"There's no way to express the feelings and pain that must be borne when it comes time to give birth. The world and the universe seem to vanish in that moment. Proper thoughts disappear, replaced by fear and anxiety. The pain is unbearable, and the whole body feels as if it's being broken into pieces. Vision darkens and feelings come and go. If it proves difficult to give birth for some reason, and we can't get help quickly, we are often brought to the edge of the grave. And even if we do get help from a sorcerer or a skilled doctor this is oftentimes too painful, for it can get rough and involve force. Some are operated on, cut open and sewn up, all of which can cause them defects and sickness for the rest of their lives.

"When the child has been brought into this world, for some time to come the woman has to sleep quietly, not being allowed to move or shift about, as well as having to take all kinds of unpleasant medicines, in order to recover quickly. Sometimes the recovery takes a long time, and it's a fact that during this time we have to watch over and breastfeed the child, since it's no good for it to be given cow's milk to drink.

"When we've recovered, we can't take even a little rest, for other responsibilities await us: that is, watching over, caring for and raising the child. Troubles and trials come at any time and we don't know daytime from night because the child's food must be prepared and given, its clothes have to be made and cleaned. If it cries, it has to be cajoled and carried. If it's drowsy, it must be rocked to sleep. If it's sick, it has to be carried and sung to for hours on end. Day and night, you can't sleep or work at anything else, because you're always on watch.

"When the child has grown a bit, toys must be supplied and spending money provided, and it must be taught to perfection, so that later he or she will be a good person.

"No sooner has this work been finished than a new burden arrives, because you're carrying a second child. When these children get big, they must be sent to school and then married off. A girl, even after marriage, still gets help from her mother."

"It really is that way for our women," replied Alimah. "Though I've never given birth, I've often discussed it with other women and helped some who have. So, I know their feelings and their burdens."

"And is it always good how the child repays the mother?" Nurbaya asked.

"A boy, especially, does not know how to repay everything his mother has done for him. Sometimes his mother's milk is repaid with poison. When he takes a wife, he no longer pays attention to his mother. There was once a man who would not even call his own mother, "Mother", because he had become rich or had a high post and was ashamed to have such a common and boorish woman for a mother. And there are even those so hateful they hit and torment their own mothers."

"Of course, boys often behave like that. Girls rarely do," Alimah replied.

"Perhaps out of arrogance, too. Even though they come from their mothers, in their minds, their mothers are lowly, because they are women," said Nurbaya, looking up from her sewing.

After pausing for a moment, she began again, "The second thing that makes us weaker and slower-witted than men is our upbringing, work and responsibilities. In terms of our upbringing, once we get good at walking, and only until the age of six or seven are we even a bit free. We go about here and there, playing outside the house. That's a very glorious time for us, when our hearts feel exalted and we feel free. After that, until we grow old, we have no other life, just going from the house to the kitchen, and from the kitchen back to the house.

"At seven or eight years old, we're put into a cage, like a bird that's forbidden to look at the sky and earth, until we don't know what's happening around us. No one pays any attention to our clothing and food, let alone our wishes and preferences. Meantime, we're made to learn to cook, sew, take care of the household, none of which increases our strength or sharpens our minds.

"Around the same time, boys—besides being sent to school and the prayer house—learn dance, the fighting arts, swimming, horseback riding, and all the rest, to strengthen their bodies and sharpen their minds. Such lessons and effort strengthen men's will, and increases their power and the keenness of their minds, while those for women weaken the body and don't add very much to their intelligence.

"Our work and responsibility to Allah is to bear and nurse children. Our responsibility to the children is to nurture, raise and teach them. To the husband: the housekeeping, fixing the meals, preparing his clothing, and so on. And to the parents and relatives, whatever they might wish for. None of this adds to our strength or wit, either.

"We don't want this nurturing and these responsibilities. They're forced on us. And who benefits from such things? The man and his child. It's the same thing with our womanly attributes. We didn't ask for them. Is it proper that men abase women because we've been given these characteristics? In terms of will and ideas, if women were given education, nurturing, food—in short, everything that men get—we wouldn't come out behind them, and that's for sure."

"That's what I think, too, Nur," replied Alimah. "There is a difference, but only because of the differences in upbringing, education, responsibilities, and all the rest."

"Although that's true, a lot is due to the mistakes women themselves make. What I mean is the mistakes the mother makes. Because she doesn't think enough, many of the things she does aren't good. For example, she forbids her girl to attend school out of fear the child will become bad from being good at reading and writing, and that this will cause shame. Thinking this way is truly wrong, I feel. For something like that depends on the heart, character, behavior and education the child receives. If she is sufficiently clever, if she has seen much and heard much, so that she knows how to differentiate right from wrong, she will be able to weigh the bad and the good in her actions, and thus would not easily fall afoul of men's temptations. And where does all that knowledge come from, if not from school?

"Therefore, women must be educated so that they can be kept from danger and the children of her husband cared for properly. Of course, such cleverness could be used for wicked ends. That's why one needs a good heart and well-formed thoughts. If the woman were not of good character or had been wrongly taught, even if she were not good at schoolwork, she could still do evil. Are there really no wicked women in a race which is still stupid?"

"If you think deeply about it," Alimah said, "it's obvious that we women are like the stepchildren and the men like the real children, because we're treated so differently. And women are given nothing to depend on."

"Of course," replied Nurbaya, "from God we've been given impediments, that is, child-bearing and caring, so that we can't oppose men in anything at all. We're not the equal of men in religion, either, for men are permitted to marry up to four wives, but a woman may not even leave the house. We're denigrated and ignored by our husbands and forced by our parents and relatives to follow everything they say. Our people and our government don't want to help us."

Here, Nurbaya broke off from speaking, lost in thought about the issues and fate facing the race of women.

"Yes, if it were as fair and just as it could be, if men can have numerous wives, a woman would certainly have two or three husbands," said Alimah.

"What? Women have many husbands? Women may not even *look* upon the faces of other men. If we want to leave the house, we have to cover our faces, and the same for the other parts of our body. Even more so, the matter of divorce has been handed over to our good men. Why is that? Why is it only men can divorce and marry women as they please? Can it be that only woman do wrong and receive punishment from men? Are men incapable of committing wrongs against their wives?

"If you speak of tyranny to men, they will just burst out laughing, for as they see it, that is only fair and just. Isn't man the lord and master of woman, and woman the servant of the man? Of course they may do as they please to us. We can be tormented, beaten and flogged, without being given sufficient money for living expenses or a good home. Nor do we have any outlets for our feelings. We aren't allowed to watch games of any kind, as this might bring delight and broaden our outlook. Nor do they let us listen to anything which could dispel our troubled feelings.

"If we make a little mistake—out of ignorance—we aren't given advice or reminders, just scoldings and abuse, sometimes accompanied by kicks and blows. If we're too slow in preparing a meal or their clothing, we'll certainly receive a humiliating reprimand. We can never, ever answer back. We're not allowed to express what we feel in our hearts and must keep it inside. If we make so bold as to oppose them, we'll surely be driven out like a dog. If we are swiftly divorced, no matter, even if we're left with no support, he'll never visit again, so that our every wish becomes blocked."

"Yes, that's true, but such burdens aren't so heavy compared to what must be endured when a new wife arrives," said Alimah. "I would rather be beaten, locked up, or reviled, than made a co-wife."

"Sure," replied Nurbaya, "and that's probably the reason you ended up getting a divorce from your husband."

"Of course."

"Tell me how that came about!"

"It started at the instigation of his mother and uncle. They said I was inciting and egging him on, so that he would hate them, since they never got any money from him the entire time we were married. But I never did anything like that at all. The only thing I did was ask that the daily spending money for the home never go short, because my own parents were not wealthy people. When he heard this, he gave all his income to me. Out of that money, I would give his mother ten rupiah and her brother fifteen each month. I thought that would be sufficient for at least the cost of eating. But it seemed they wanted all of his income, just like before he had married me.

"How could that be, for there were more people involved, and two households now. And didn't they know before we got married that my father had so little money that he couldn't receive my husband in the manner that the children of nobles are received in Padang, with everything prepared and available, and the man just having to come home? Also, my husband was not a man of high lineage. Even so, he wanted to be given a dowry anyway. But when my father said he had none, my husband was willing to go through with it as a commoner, as both sides agreed to this.

"Actually the marriage was undertaken according to the wishes of his parents and sister. When they saw that my husband was giving them less and less, they hated me and tried to coax him into divorcing me.

"After they saw that he wouldn't go along with their provocations, they sought high and low for a sorcerer to make my husband hate and divorce me. I heard they even intended to rough me up so I would go mad or die.

"When that wicked plan didn't work, they married my husband off to a woman with property. When I heard the news, I can't tell you how I felt.

Anger, sadness, and hatred, all mixed together. A shadow passed over my eyes, my head spun, and I couldn't hear or feel anything. My lips and whole body trembled, and my heart beat wildly. I felt split in two and all my limbs went weak, until I fell unconscious onto my bed for some period of time.

"I cried the whole night long, I just couldn't hold back. When my husband and I were together again, it was as if I were looking at an animal. Hatred and anger came to me by turn. I no longer felt the pleasure and love I once had for him. If my mother had not calmed me down, I would have struck him on the head, so inflamed did I feel. I asked for a divorce several times, but he wouldn't grant it. What could I do? The final word on the divorce was up to him. If it were up to me, I wouldn't have waited to see his face again but would've just divorced him.

"From that time on, I didn't pay attention to him, to his meals or his clothing, for my heart had changed. It no longer went straight. Had there been another man to tempt me at that time, I probably would've gone along with it, I felt so sick inside. I wanted to run away, for I was afraid of being left hanging like this forever, neither divorced nor supported.

"One time, when I was walking with my mother's brother—it was nighttime at the Kampung Java market—I saw my husband there, walking around and enjoying himself, buying things with that other wife. The moment I saw them, blackness came over me, and I had no idea what I was doing. My mother says that I immediately chased the woman and grabbed her by the hair and clothes, saying all kind of things to her until we both started fighting in front of everybody there, wrestling about and pulling each other's hair. After people pulled us apart, I embarrassed my husband deeply by speaking vile words, and said he wasn't a man if he wasn't brave enough to divorce me. So he divorced me right there in the market.

"So that was the end of a marriage that had cost so much money and given rise to so many heartaches and difficulties, all caused by his bringing in another wife."

"How long were you with your husband?" Nurbaya asked.

"Not quite a year. Since then, I've vowed that I would never marry again. What's the use of marriage if it just troubles your heart, wrecks your body, and eats up your wealth? My idea of marriage is to obtain happiness and entrust myself to someone. If it can't be that way, it would be better to just remain an unmarried woman, free as a bird, without anyone to prevent me from doing what I want."

"Or to stay a maiden forever," Nurbaya said.

"That won't do, because that's too disgraceful. People would say you're unmarriageble because of some flaw," Alimah replied.

"It's only disgraceful because people say so. If a lot of women refused to get married, it would become normal."

"Maybe," her cousin replied.

After a moment's reflection, Nurbaya said with a sigh, "Of course, that's our lot as women. Will this system ever change for us? Will we ever be held in esteem by men? Even if it's not much, merely for what's needed in our lives would be enough. I'm not asking that women be made the equals of men in every way. No, for I understand that could never be. But what I do ask is that men see women as their younger sisters, if they don't want to glorify and respect them, as do the Europeans. As long as we're not seen as slaves or some kind of lowly creature. Let women seek the sciences useful to them, and allow them to see and hear all that could add to their knowledge. Let them express their deepest feelings and the fruit of their thoughts so they can exchange ideas and sharpen their minds. And give them rights over what should be in their right to do, so they're not just living puppets.

"Matters of the household, in my view, could be compared with those of a state run by two viziers, each of whom possesses nearly the same degree of authority. The one who handles domestic matters is the wife, while the husband is in charge of foreign affairs. All the domestic matters, those of the household, the care of children, cooking, furniture and utensils, and other things, must be under the wife's authority. Therefore the woman must have an understanding of such matters. Foreign issues concern the search for livelihood, work, shelter, and such. These should be under the authority of the man, and the woman shouldn't get involved. In all important matters that affect the responsibilities of both, the two viziers can certainly combine their duties and consult each other to achieve what is best."

"But who would the ruler be?" asked Alimah.

"There wouldn't be a ruler. Everything would be discussed by the two of them for the improvement of the state. If the power of the vizier for foreign affairs has to be made a little greater, so be it. It doesn't matter, because his understanding is more mature, especially in deciding complex issues, just as long as he doesn't forget that his rank is the same as that of the domestic vizier. And never let him suppose that he is a raja, able to whatever he pleases to his mate.

"The two of them are actually one. It only happens that they have two bodies. The domestic vizier needs the help of the foreign affairs vizier. And the foreign affairs vizier must be assisted by the domestic vizier in his work and responsibilities. So they help each other in all their troubles and happiness. As the saying goes, 'What's heavy is shouldered by both, what's light is carried in each of their hands'. And neither should suppose that he or she could live on their own, given the difference in their work and authority.

"Neither should squirrel his or her earnings away. Instead, everything should be gathered together into a single amount. From the total, a portion is given to the woman to cover household expenses, food, and the like. And a portion goes to the man for expenses outside the home. If there is a surplus, it should be kept in both their names or in that of their children. If men don't trust women—men shouldn't think that way, for husband and wife have to trust each other and be equally straightforward—it would be better not to combine money matters. If, for example, the husband suspects the wife isn't very good at managing her spending money, or if the wife feels that the husband is wasteful, they can combine tasks when it comes to matters of money.

"Apart from that, each must find a way to make life pleasant for his or her mate, and always be on guard against hurting the other's feelings. If they become at odds with each other, neither should be obstinate and unyielding towards the other, for if that happens, life becomes complicated and confused. If anger arises, restrain it. They shouldn't say anything or do anything in the heat of the moment, but rather cool their hot blood first, so they don't say or do anything out of anger, for that can cause endless regret later. If their anger won't go away, they should go to sleep, or for a walk. After their anger has played itself out and good thoughts return, they should talk patiently about the quarrel to get at the truth. Only if it can't be resolved in this way should the matter be raised with a parent or teacher, for such people often have many ideas concerning such things. If the couple does this, and the complication still cannot be resolved, it would be better for them to divorce each other. What can you do? Rather than be married in hell, it would be better to live divorced in heaven. But the divorce needs to be done properly. Don't let it become a source of enmity and rancor. When the marriage has been settled properly, the divorce should be settled properly, too. Who knows, maybe their affinity for each other is still there, so it might be easy to get back together. And even if the affinity between them is no more, what good is it if the former husband and wife are enemies? For they lived in intimacy for quite a while and became one. Wouldn't it be better to be considered brother and sister? You can't forget in the blink of an eye those pets you kept, so why should a person, who sometimes has been bound to us with the tie of children, be made into an enemy?

"Quarreling and hurling abuse at one another, even revealing important secrets, shouting and screaming, so that people are shocked, hitting each other until blood flows, or other such things: not only is none of this of any use, but unmasks us as disorderly and impolite and ignorant of the rules and propriety. Moreover, this can bring physical danger upon us. Wouldn't it be better, if we wanted to quarrel, for the both of us to go into a room, close the door, and then discuss the problem or express what we feel in our hearts, gently, so that no one else knows about it? What's the use of our quarrels becoming a public spectacle for those who aren't involved, since we're going to make peace with each other again? My feeling is that matters such as these belong to the secrets of the home. Nothing good will come of them being known by others. It also seems shameful, to act like children, one minute squabbling and the next making up. Just like little kids! They fight, scold and hit each other, as if they wanted to kill one another, but a second later, everything's fine, and they play and run around together, like lovebirds. When such behavior seems strange in children, how much more so among adults?

"Small squabbles sometimes can't be avoided, but they are of no importance. It's just the sign of two people living together in intimacy. People say that even the spoon and the rice pot sometimes fight. Why should it be different with people, whose feelings are never constant? And frequently such squabbling is like the salt that flavors food, because the bigger the quarrel, the better the peace that follows."

While Nurbaya and Alimah were conversing this way, they heard in the distance a cake peddler calling out "Eeee... rice cakes, coconut cakes, peanut cakes, sticky rice and coconut, all so tasty-eeeee! Eeee... rice cakes...!"

"Hah, how many times have I heard that cake peddler calling out like that? It seems there's someone selling cakes even at night here," said Nurbaya, growing tired from all her talking, and beginning to feel the pangs of hunger.

"It might seem that way, but last night was the first time I heard that voice. Usually they don't come around here, since this is a quiet street. Perhaps he's lost his way," Alimah replied.

"Let's call him over, Lim! Maybe his cakes are good," Nurbaya said.

"Oh, why bother? If you want to eat cakes, there's some in the cupboard. I put them there for the next meal. I actually don't like buying cakes on the street, because I don't know who made them, and they're just commodities that have been cooked without proper attention. Sometimes they're dirty."

"Oh, really now, dirty? In Kampung Java Dalam I often bought those cakes with Samsu. We would eat them together in the garden, and I have yet to have one that was dirty. How nice it would be if he were with us now. Let's buy some now, otherwise the vendor will have passed," Nurbaya said, taking her cousin's hand, and asking her to go outside so she could call the peddler over.

"Rice cakes, over here!" Nurbaya called out once they were outside.

After the snack peddler drew near, Alimah asked, "Where are the cakes from?"

"Ma Sati's cakes," the man answered.

"Ma Sati in Kampung Java?" Nurbaya inquired.

"Yes, Ma'am."

"Why haven't I seen you there before?" Nurbaya asked. "The other cake seller often peddles his wares there. I know him well. Amat's his name, right?"

"Yes. He sells in Kampung Java, while I work here."

"But why is it I've only just now heard your voice? Where have you been all this time?" Alimah asked.

"I just returned from Padang Darat," the vendor replied, displaying the cakes inside his box. "I didn't have a good job before, so I became a cake seller for the time being."

"What village are you from?" Nurbaya asked, as she inspected the various snacks.

"Payakumbuh," he answered.

"No new coconut cakes?"

"No, but if you would like some sweet rice cakes, there are some that are still warm," the man told Nurbaya.

"Which ones?"

"These," replied the peddler, opening another of his bins and selecting several warm cakes, which he showed to Nurbaya.

"All right, give me four of those!"

"Why so many, Nur? Eating at this hour isn't such a good idea. We haven't even finished our own rice."

At that moment, the cake peddler shot a look at Alimah from the corner of his eye. If she had been paying attention, she would have seen how angry he became at her efforts to dissuade her cousin. But Alimah was not looking and Nurbaya was too busy picking out her snacks.

After selecting a few more items, Nurbaya paid and the peddler walked quickly out of the yard.

The two young women went and sat on the front veranda, discussing a new topic as Nurbaya unwrapped a cake.

"Why has the peddler stopped calling out?" Alimah asked.

"The people across from us probably waved him over," Nurbaya replied. "Here, have one of these!"

"I just told you, I haven't been eating much these days. Give me one of those coconut cakes. I'll give it a try."

"Don't be like that, Alimah! This may be the last time we eat together. When I go to Batavia, it will be difficult for us to see each other again since Samsu is against returning to Padang. He wants to stay on Java forever. Once I get there, he wants to sell all my possessions here to buy a house there. And once I feel comfortable there, I'll ask you to come. Would you like to come, Lim?" Nurbaya questioned her cousin, eating the cake she had just unwrapped.

"Of course! I'd love to see Java, especially Batavia."

"Why is the sugar in this cake so bitter?" Nurbaya suddenly asked.

"Maybe the sugar went bad or got scorched during the cooking," Alimah replied.

"Maybe this one's good," Nurbaya said, peeling another one. By then she had finished off the first one. "Batavia truly is big, probably ten times bigger than Padang. I couldn't begin to describe its hustle and bustle. Day and night the main streets are filled with people and vehicles and carts, all kinds of things. It's so fine: it's without compare. There are pretty buildings and large shops everywhere. It deserves to be the capital, where the High Government sits. But the real palace is in Bogor, for the air there is cool, while Batavia is very hot. When I return to Batavia, Samsu says we'll definitely take a trip to Bogor.

"Only now do I truly feel at ease, for there's nothing more to stand in my way. When I was in Batavia, it was very obvious that Samsu had not changed in the slightest towards me. Ah, how nice it felt, when I was walking with him, just going around sightseeing, by buggy and cart, seeing the sights of Batavia... I feel dizzy"

"Maybe you didn't get enough sleep last night."

"No. I slept a long time. Oh, everything is spinning."

"Let's go inside. Try to lie down and sleep."

"Yes," Nurbaya answered, as she rose and made to enter the middle room. Suddenly, she fell to the ground. Alimah held her around the waist and brought her inside, laying her on the mattress.

"Please massage my head a bit, Alimah! Maybe I've gotten a chill."

"All right," Alimah said, massaging her cousin's head. A little while later, Nurbaya appeared to be sound asleep.

While she was massaging her cousin, Alimah began to wonder, "Why did Nurbaya suddenly get dizzy? What had she done up until then? It's ten-thirty and she's already fallen asleep. She usually likes to talk until all hours of the night."

Although Nurbaya had drifted off, Alimah kept massaging her head for a while, afraid she might suddenly wake up and because Nurbaya seemed to enjoy being massaged, as she had dozed off so quickly.

A little while later, when Alimah rose to go to bed, she took a close look at her cousin's face. A shock went through her when she saw that Nurbaya was no longer breathing. She shook her cousin, in the hopes of rousing her. But, unfortunately, Nurbaya was no more.

Alimah screamed and wept with such intensity that her mother and father were startled from their sleep and came running. When Fatimah saw Nurbaya stretched out on the bed, no longer moving, she shrieked and wept, stamping her feet and beating her hands together. The entire house became filled with the din of lament. People living on either side of them came rushing in with a great uproar to find out what had happened. But no one could give a clear explanation, other than that Nurbaya had died. That very night Ahmad Maulana went to fetch the doctor, who came two hours later. After examining Nurbaya, it was clear she had indeed passed on. Although he tried everything in his power to save her, it was all in vain.

According to the account given by Alimah, Nurbaya had felt ill after eating the rice cake, prompting the doctor to take the remaining cakes and have them examined. The next day, it became clear that Nurbaya had been poisoned.

Although the matter was placed in the hands of the police, the culprit was never found.

To learn who the wicked man was, we have to go back and follow the cake peddler from the evening before.

After he sold Nurbaya the cakes and left Alimah's house, he arrived at the main road, where a man dressed completely in black suddenly appeared from behind a tree and approached him. Once he was close enough, the man in black asked, "Well, Number Four?"

"She bought some, and I gave her the ones with the palm sugar," the peddler replied.

"Great! Let's get out of here, fast."

"What about this box of cakes?"

"Later. In the safe house there's an empty well. Put the box in there," replied Number Five.

"I'm still worried that someone else took the hit."

"Who else was there?"

"Alimah, but she said she didn't want to eat any cakes because of an upset stomach. That's why she didn't let Nurbaya buy a lot of them. That made me mad. If I wasn't in front of her house, I'd have kicked her so hard she wouldn't have been able to talk anymore," replied Number Four.

"How many did she buy?"

"Four."

"There's no way that Nurbaya could have eaten all four. Just one would be enough to take two or three people to the gate of the grave. Are you sure that all four had the sugar in them?"

"Yes, because those were the ones I set apart."

"If that's the case, we succeeded this time in what we set out to do," said Number Five.

"Follow me!" With that, they both disappeared into the darkness.

The next day, when the news of Nurbaya's death reached Sitti Maryam, herself gravely ill in Kampung Sebelah from the shock of Samsu's departure, she too suddenly returned to her heavenly home, for this most recent news was too much for her to bear.

On that same day, two corpses were carried to the top of Mount Padang, the two women so beloved by Samsu, both buried next to the grave of Baginda Sulaiman, Sitti Nurbaya's father.

13

Samsu's Fate

"Arifin, did I tell you what I saw last night?" Samsulbahri asked his friend the day after Nurbaya had been poisoned. It was around two o'clock in the afternoon, and they had just returned from eating lunch.

"What's that, Sam?" Arifin asked.

"Very strange! I haven't been able to think about anything else. I still don't know what it was or what it was supposed to mean."

"Tell me!"

"As usual," Samsu replied, "I went to bed at ten o'clock. Around midnight, without knowing why, I was up with a start, as if something had woken me up. When I opened my eyes, I saw a kind of white shape standing behind my chair near my desk. I was really scared, because I figured a thief had gotten into my room."

"But if it were a thief, why would he be wearing white?"

"That's why I thought maybe I was dreaming. So I pinched my leg a couple times. But even when it became clear I wasn't asleep, the white shade was still there in full view."

"Maybe you mistook it for something else," said Arifin, refusing to believe his friend's story.

"I rubbed my eyes a few times, but that white whatever-it-was wouldn't disappear."

"Maybe you were afraid, or when you went to sleep, you were thinking a lot about devils or ghosts, so that everything you saw took on a devil's shape."

"You know yourself, Arifin, I'm no coward when it comes to things like that. Plus, I only saw the white shade when I opened my eyes. How could someone who had just woken up be afraid, if he hadn't been having nightmares?"

"What did it look like?" Arifin asked, now starting to believe his friend's story.

"It looked human. It had a head, a body, hands, and feet and was clothed in white silk, coarse stuff."

"Human?" Arifin replied, as he grew frightened, though it was two o'clock in the afternoon and the streets outside were filled with people. "Hiiih! I'm getting goosebumps just listening to this."

"It's true," answered Samsu. "It didn't matter how brave I was, seeing something that strange made my heart start pounding, and for a moment I didn't know what to do. I wanted to cry out, but I was ashamed to. Plus, I couldn't speak, as if someone were choking me. I wanted to get up, but my body and feet felt so heavy. I just lay there, afraid of what might happen to me. Even though I tried to find my courage, my body felt like it was melting, like someone had thrown cold water on my back."

"Then what happened?" Arifin asked, fear gripping him.

"When I looked closely at that white shadowy shape, its face was like Nurbaya's."

"Nurbaya?"

"Yes, exactly, only her face was a little pale. I was scared, but I summoned enough courage to speak, and asked, 'Who's there?'"

"And what did it say?"

"Nothing. It stayed silent and didn't budge."

"Then what happened?"

"Then I leapt up to grab my pistol from the closet, hoping I could get closer to it. But as soon as I moved, the shadow just disappeared, where to, I don't know."

"Boy! You were really brave."

"Just then, I was seized by fear and I kept looking over my shoulder in case it tried to strangle me from behind. But there was nobody there. I lit the lamp and took my pistol from the closet. Only then was I brave enough to check everywhere, under the bed, the table, and behind the wardrobe, but there was nothing. The window and door were still locked."

"If I saw something like that, I'd scream for help, if I still could. If not, I'd be scared stiff."

"After I covered the lamp with paper," Samsu continued, "so its light wouldn't be seen from outside, and put the pistol under my pillow, I lay back down. But I couldn't get back to sleep, because I was afraid it would come again while I was sleeping. I kept thinking how strange it had been. What was it and how should I interpret it? Was it a devil or a ghost?"

"If it were a ghost, why did it look just like Nurbaya? What are ghosts? Aren't they those who have died, like people say?" replied Arifin.

"True, and this was the first time I had ever seen such a shadowy form," replied Samsu, without the slightest idea that Nurbaya had died. "It wasn't a dream. I really saw something."

"And something truly strange, Sam. But I hope I don't ever see something like that. I'd be afraid of that disaster would follow."

"Because I couldn't get back to sleep, I thought of Nurbaya and my mother and our village and a great desire arose within me to return and see them all. And I very much regretted not being able to accompany Nurbaya back to Padang recently. I've never wished to return as strongly as I did last night. All the joys and pains I had experienced since that time we hiked up Mount Padang played out before my eyes. The more I thought of Nurbaya, the more worried I became, and the more I felt how careless and inattentive I had been in letting her go back alone into that tiger's mouth. At times, I was so worried I thought maybe something terrible had happened to Nurbaya."

"Oh, surely not! And she'll be back here soon enough. If not, you should just go and get her. Her case must have been settled by now," Arifin replied.

"That's just what I intend to do. If by next Saturday she hasn't arrived, I'm definitely going to meet her in Padang."

As they continued talking, they arrived at the Java Doctors' School and went to their respective rooms. A moment later, a postman bearing two telegrams for Samsulbahri asked Arifin where he might find the intended recipient, and was then directed to the right room.

Half an hour later, Arifin went to ask Samsu about the telegrams, and saw that the door and the window to his friend's room were shut. He figured Samsu was sleeping away his fatigue from the night before and, not wanting to disturb him, decided to wait until his friend woke up before coming back.

In fact, it had been Samsu's intention, before receiving the two telegrams, to sleep, for which purpose he had even shut his window. After receiving the cables, he closed the door as well, wishing to be alone while he read, particularly as the telegrams worried him a great deal.

"Who sent this cable, and what will it say?" he wondered. "Oh, maybe it's from Nurbaya, telling me she'll be coming soon. But who sent *this* one?"

He opened the first of the telegrams with trembling hands. When he had finished reading both, he fell to the ground, unaware of the world around him, for the cables brought the news of his mother's and Nurbaya's deaths.

Just how long he lay there, he never knew. When he came to again, he was like a man gone mad, unable to think or speak, and incapable of weeping, for his eyes were empty of tears. After absorbing the fact of their deaths for a while, he took paper and pen, and wrote a letter to his father.

In it, he said the following:

Batavia, 13 July, 1897

Dear Father!

Before I tell you what I intend to do and put down on paper everything that is in my heart, I first beg for your forgiveness, a thousand times over, kneeling before you, for the wrong I committed against you that time, and the for the wrongs I am about to commit against you. I still have the courage to call you 'Father,' although you will no longer wish to call me 'Son'.

I am well aware of how difficult it would be for you, a person of good birth and high position, to turn back the flow of words which have already been spoken. But because this request shall be my last, the request of a person who shall not be much longer in this world, a person who shall soon be leaving this transitory existence, and who, at the end of his life, has no other hope than to gain the pardon and forgiveness of his father and mother, relatives and close companions, I feel that I must make a request of you and such is my hope that you will grant this request.

Is it not the case that, for a person who is to be executed, his wishes are granted and his last request fulfilled? This shall be the last time I request anything of you. By the time you read this letter, I will be long gone from this world, and will instead have prostrated myself in the presence of God, to beg forgiveness for all the sins I have committed. It seems that I might not obtain a pardon in this world, even though I have admitted my wrongs and suffered a severe punishment.

Father, why is this the way of the world? Why can I not have justice? Am I not a human being, like others? And is not humanity characterized by forgetfulness, a swayable heart, and uncertain thinking, and is Allah alone not the Eternal and Unchanging? Aren't humans the kind of creatures that may not do simply as they please without the permission of God the Almighty? Is it not impossible to counterfeit the fate of a man, for all of it is recorded on the eternal tablet and promised before his birth? And does not each wrong, no matter how great, also have its pardon? But why does this world not weigh in with justice, hurling instead all kinds of blame at me? Even though I acknowledge those wrongs, I have received neither a pardon nor a light sentence, but what seems instead a redoubling of the tortures meted out to me.

In truth, my wrongdoing was not one which should be treated lightly, but rather one which brings disgrace to you and to mother, our kinsmen, our village, as well as misery to some and despair to others. However, a fair judge must listen to the two sides and not just accuse one of them.

Not just the human heart, which is naturally gentle and easily swayable, but even a hard rock can be penetrated by soft water eternally falling upon it, drop by drop. Isn't iron hard? But then why is it sharpened by stone, which is brittle? And what is harder than a diamond? But this too is ground and polished. How much more so in my case, a young man, who could easily fall into a net like that: how could I hold myself back? In addition, I am soft-hearted, and can't stand to watch others suffering or oppressed, least of all when it is one of my own friends, a playmate from my youngest years, the companion who meant more to me than a brother or a sister of the same womb. How could I allow her to be mistreated?

It is not that I intend to cast all the blame upon Nurbaya, absolutely not. Of course, Nurbaya's heart had long been attached to mine, and it seemed impossible that she would not one day become my wife. I think you also believed this, as did everyone who knew us. Now, should we be offended or angered if a bird, which we have tended to and cared for, even with perfect care, and with a wonderful cage, ample food and drink, flies straight back to its original home, deep in the forest, on the day it is freed? Is it not the case that happiness and tranquility cannot always be brought about by money or property? Doesn't a coolie, from time to time, feel more content and at peace than a king?

How can a person in despair, someone like Nurbaya at the time, be blamed for their actions? She had seen all her wishes and desires, which she had longed for since she was a child, suddenly and forcibly wrested away, so that she had nothing more to hope for.

Someone so struck by disaster that they are forced to endure something more frightening than death, such a person's thoughts are no longer right and they shouldn't be blamed for what they do. Should we be surprised if a person who is exceedingly thirsty no longer thinks rationally and pays no heed to all that he will suffer later because of what he does, but instead quickly drinks water the moment he finds it?

Thus, who was wrong in this matter? Nurbaya? No! Me? No! No one was, for each was only following the fixed road that he or she was to travel. Even Datuk Meringgih may not be blamed, for he was simply doing what is normally done in our land. Though he forced Nurbaya in vile ways and used all kinds of schemes to achieve his vicious ends, even he cannot be condemned, for he *knows nothing of what is good. In his mind, what he did was not evil.*

What is the use of so much money if it will not achieve his goals, no matter how base these may be? What does he care of others' troubles or if his actions crush their hope or cause them to suffer, so long as he can take pleasure and find a release for his lusts? Doesn't everyone act this way? And not just people, but lowly beasts as well. And are not the creatures of this earth constantly engaged in killing each other and bringing ruin upon one another, all to defend themselves? Why shouldn't Datuk Meringgih do the same? Especially towards women who, in the eyes of our people, are not humans but living puppets that must follow their husband's every wish without being allowed to think, to speak, to see, to hear, to smell or taste. Told to work, she simply has to work. Told to be sick, she just has to be sick. And even if told to die, she just has to die. Considered a slave, she may be dealt with as one pleases.

So, what's wrong if a man, whose hair has turned white, who has lost his teeth, and is all hunched over from old age, is brought together in marriage with a maiden who could be his granddaughter? And what is to prevent that same man from having more than one wife? Look at the rooster. It has more than one hen. If an animal can do that, why can't humans, so much more noble, powerful, intelligent and clever? Of course they can, and should do more than that. If ten or twenty mares are given to a stallion, this would still be less, by comparison, if it were permitted to man to have a hundred, or even two hundred wives.

Samsu put his pen down for a moment and tried to calm himself. Frustration welled up in him, for this letter was his only chance to say everything he felt in his heart at that moment, and it was far from perfect. Nevertheless, he tried to continue writing:

So that this letter will not be too long, I should tell you everything that I have had to endure, since the time I lost you as a father.

Punishment and pain, agony and torment are what I have known, but I haven't the words to describe them here. Since I've become fatherless and without kin or village or home or country, I have not known a moment's happiness. All this while my thoughts have been harassed by terrible memories and unending regret. During the day, the shadow of my bad acts is traced before my eyes, as if they had only occurred yesterday. I can still see the look of hatred on your face, can hear the rage in your voice, until my heart seems to die inside me and I am filled with panic, like a man who is to be hanged.

And when this feeling has come and gone, the image of Mother's face floats before my eyes, sorrowful, desperate, like a ship with no captain lost in a storm. I can see just how sad she is to look upon me, her son, the fruit of her heart, her last hope, in such danger that he has vanished from her sight forever. My heart is crushed seeing her sorrow and knowing I cannot comfort her.

After that, our entire family and all our relatives stand before me, muttering and gazing at me with loathing in their eyes, as if they saw a dog that had stolen a bone. It makes me feel such shame that I have to hide myself from view.

At night, these memories and thoughts turn into awful dreams. Everything that has happened to me now crosses my path, as if happening all over again. It's as if Datuk Meringgih came with a sword to cut my head off. I scream in my sleep, only to awaken my friends sleeping nearby. When I dream of Nurbaya, I cry, unable to bear the thought of how sad her fate has made her.

This is what I go through, tormented day and night by evil thoughts and dreams. Do not mention my studies. I can scarcely eat or drink, for rice is like chaff in my mouth, and water like thorns. If you were to see me writing this letter, you would probably not recognize me, so much has my appearance changed.

There are times when the idea of killing myself takes hold of me, but the thought of Mother and Nurbaya stops me, and I fear that doing such a thing would only add to their grief. Nonetheless, though I haven't yet brought a knife to my throat, if *such are the torments and agony that I must endure, I will surely take that road one day. It only increases my misery, knowing that I cannot leave this world, for the sake of Mother and Nurbaya, on whom I have brought such disaster.*

I had to lift them out of the filth into which I had thrown them. That's why I returned to Batavia, with the intention of trying to continue my studies.

But what can I say, Father? It would seem that the punishment and suffering I had borne was not enough to pay my debt. For when I had only just begun to feel a bit free of these torments, having become accustomed to the pain and beginning to hope that I could resist such torture and realize my dream of making Mother and Nurbaya happy before passing on to the next life, just then did my real punishment begin. It was at that moment that the sword fell and severed my head from my body, pierced my flesh, tore my heart, and broke the bones in my body. That was the moment a telegram arrived with the news that Nurbaya and my mother, the two women who still loved me, had been dragged down in the filth and taken from this world.

That was the moment I lost all hope. I could endure the pain no longer and I lost my mind. Now I am an orphan, without mother, father, siblings, kin, village or country. And so, what's the use of living any longer? It would be better to lie with the earth beneath my head than to live on in shame.

At this point in the letter, the pen fell from Samsu's hand, as if he lacked the strength to hold on to the sliver of wood now smearing his letter with ink. So too did his tears pour forth and soak the paper. Overwhelmed with sadness, he could only cup his head in his hands and sob.

"Oh, fate! Don't you pity at all the tribe of Adam? Hadn't he only begun to know happiness, glory, and the heady richness of this world, like a flower about to spread its bloom and waft its fragrance, displaying its charming colors for all the butterflies flying about? Mercilessly and violently you have pulled it from its stem so that it falls severed to the ground, ruined."

Composing himself, Samsu raised his head, wiped away his tears and picked up the pen to continue with the letter:

> *Oh, Father! It seems that the little hope I gained was actually a sign that my end was near. Since you threw me out, curses have rained down on my head again and again, and since that time my fate has never left me, not even for a moment. It hounds my every step, as if it were my shadow, waiting for the right moment to pounce.*
>
> *It toys with me, like a cat toys with a mouse, catching it, only to let it go. It probably smiled to see me gaining some hope. It pulled its long, sharp claws back a bit, thinking, 'I will sink these into your soft flesh and crush you, if you try to get away.'*
>
> *Father, it has at last succeeded in its purpose. I have been seized in its claws and all that is left is utter destruction.*
>
> *As my final act, I beg you, Father, to pardon me in this world and in the next so that I might follow Mother and Nurbaya, who have gone on before me. May all three of us be able to stand together in the presence of God who is just.*
>
> *Finally, I wish to express my gratitude to you, and to all our family and kin, for the difficulties and pain you all were willing to endure to raise me. Allah will repay such goodness, even though I could only repay you with wickedness beyond description, as if milk were repaid with poison. What can I say? All of this is predestined by God anyway.*
>
> *Please accept my final gesture of respect.*
>
> *Stay in peace!*
>
> *Samsulbahri*

Just as he was about to write, "Stay in Peace", Samsu's hands trembled and he was nearly unable to sign his name. His breath became choked and his face pale from holding back the sadness that flooded his chest. He felt dizzy and couldn't see straight, especially since his eyes were filled with tears he had not been able to restrain. And so, resting his elbows on the table, he covered his face and wept from the depths of his heart.

He stayed like this, lost in sadness, for some time and only roused himself when he heard the clock chiming five-thirty. With that, he rose, looked at the letter, placed it in an envelope, and addressed it to his father. Then he washed his face to remove the redness from his eyes and put on his clothes.

He wrote another letter after that, one to his teachers and his classmates. In it, he said the following:

> *To all my teachers and friends:*
> *Please do not be surprised, respected sirs, upon hearing the news that I have felt compelled to take myself to the door of the grave. You are surely aware that life on this earth is different for all human beings. Some have good fortune, others know only misfortune. And yet others have both in turn, happiness and trouble. Although their fates are all different, they do have in common the purpose and hopes held by every living person. Does not every action have a cause and an intended effect? But, when that purpose has gone and that hope has been severed, what use is there in living any longer? Rather than just taking up space in one's village, consuming food, and making life difficult for others, it would be better simply to die.*
>
> *Such a thing has befallen me. Therefore, to my mind there is no use in staying in this world any longer.*
>
> *I hope it will be enough for you, respected sirs, to know the reason for my action. Though I do this, day and night I beg that none of my friends would imitate me in this, and hope they will be spared all the disasters that have beset me.*
>
> *I also beg to offer my gratitude to all my teachers and classmates for the teaching and affection they have showered upon me.*
>
> *Please accept my prostration of respect and this regretful farewell from your unfortunate pupil and friend.*
>
> *Samsulbahri*
>
> *PS: Please divide up all my belongings and effects among my schoolmates as mementos of me.*

After folding the letter, he placed it on the desk and went over to his clothes closet, from which he took a small object. After inspecting it carefully, he put it in his pocket. As he opened the door and was about to leave, he nearly wept again, for he saw Arifin coming down the hall and realized that in a few seconds he would be parting from his dear friend.

He reflected on this for a moment, until he heard Arifin say as he drew near, "You slept such a long time today, Sam! Look at your eyes, they're still red. What's the news just now from Padang? Good, I hope."

"Yes, my mother has recovered," Samsu replied, with great effort.

"Thank God! I'm so happy to hear such good news! But who sent that other cable?"

"From Uncle, reporting the same thing," Samsu answered, turning his face toward the door of his room, so that Arifin would not see his grief.

He examined his room one last time, taking in all the things he had made use of for so long. Then he slammed the door behind him, afraid of gazing too long at everything he would soon be leaving behind.

"Where are you off to now, Sam? Going for a walk?"

"To the post office, to mail a letter to my father."

"To answer that cable just now, of course. Am I right?"

"Yes," came the terse reply.

"Then let me come with you. I was planning on taking a walk anyway."

Samsu was taken aback by his companion's request and did not know what to do. If Arifin came with him, he would not be able to do what he planned. But if he did not grant his friend's request, Arifin would become suspicious, for the two were inseparable and hardly went anywhere without each other.

After a moment's thought, he said, "Fine, but we have to part at the post office, because I have something else I need to do."

Though Arifin was surprised at Samsu's reply—for his friend never did anything without telling him about it—he nonetheless smiled and said, "Sure, I won't stand in your way if you have something else you need to do."

Though smiling, Arifin felt uneasy, not only because of the change in his friend's demeanor but because, upon seeing him up close, it became clear that Samsu had recently been crying. If it were true that Samsu's mother had recovered from her illness, why had the news been cabled twice, as if of the highest urgency? Why not just by ordinary mail?

Thinking it over, Arifin made up his mind to find out what Samsu's secret was. He grew worried that his friend had been crying because he was actually in some sort of trouble. If that were the case, he would certainly try to comfort him.

Along the way to the post office, Arifin kept his eye on Samsu, who seemed so preoccupied with whatever he was thinking about that he offered strange replies when asked a question, and sometimes did not even seem to hear what Arifin was saying. The more they walked, the more worried Arifin became. Why did Samsu look him straight in the face for so long just now, he wondered? And the door to his room shut with such force, as if by someone with something to hide? And why had Samsu stopped so long in front of the school, looking at it as if for the first time?

It did not take long to reach the post office. Once inside, Samsu went straight to the mail-drop and took the letter for his father from his pocket. He looked at it for a long time, focusing his attention on the address, and only then dropped it slowly into the slot, as if sorry he had to send it.

As he stood alongside, pretending to read something on the post office wall, Arifin stealthily watched everything Samsu did. He then looked right at his friend, who turned and said, "Don't be angry, Rif, that I have to part ways. It's not that I don't want to walk with you, it's just that I have an appointment. It wouldn't be nice if I brought you along without first informing the man I am to see. If I go again, I'll definitely ask him if we can go together."

"Oh, okay, no problem. I certainly wouldn't dare go there if I weren't invited. Only, I hope you won't forget to come back later, because we have so much fun together," said Arifin, pretending to smile so as not to arouse suspicion.

"I hope you have a very pleasant time there!" he added as he left the post office. After reaching the main road in front of the building, he looked back and was startled to see Samsu standing alone, watching him as he walked away. In that moment, Arifin could see that Samsu was crying, but his friend didn't seem to notice his own tears.

Suddenly, Samsu got a hold of himself and turned his face away, striding off to the west.

All of this only reinforced Arifin's suspicion that Samsu was planning something, something he didn't want anyone to know about. Perhaps he intended to harm himself. Now convinced Samsu had been lying before,

Arifin was determined to find out what his friend intended to do. If it was something terrible, he would do everything in his power to stop it.

Arifin ducked into a shop, feigning interest in certain items, but actually observing the direction in which Samsu was headed. Once he saw that his friend was going west and not looking back, Arifin left the shop and followed at a distance. From time to time, he hid behind a tree or a carriage, in case Samsu happened to glance back.

After following him for a bit, Arifin saw Samsu disappear into a garden. He quickened his pace, but when he caught up, his friend was nowhere to be seen, lost in the garden's growing dusktime darkness.

Arifin's heart was by now pounding and he grew more and more afraid, aware of some imminent danger that threatened Samsu. He didn't know where to look and so stood poised for a moment, listening for the sound of footsteps. But apart from some noise coming from the main road, he heard nothing at all. Now frantic, he began rushing about, looking everywhere he could.

After searching this way for a while, he saw at a slight distance someone sitting on a bench with his back to him. His hand was raised to his head, as if offering a friendly salute. As Arifin looked more closely, he saw that it was Samsu. He was holding a pistol in his hand.

"Samsu, wait!" Arifin cried out, rushing forward to stop his friend.

But it was too late. At that very moment, he heard the pistol discharge and watched as Samsu collapsed on the bench. He ran over and found his dear companion lying unconscious with his head covered in blood. He didn't know what to do. He struggled to speak, and finally managed to call for help.

A few moments later, as the news that someone had shot himself spread, the garden became filled with onlookers. Eventually, the police arrived to investigate the matter. After Arifin told them what he had witnessed, Samsu's corpse was taken to the hospital.

The next day, the newspapers reported that a young man from Padang, a student at the Java Doctors' School, had shot himself in the Batavia Botanical Gardens. The motive for the suicide was unknown.

14

Ten Years Later

Though time is measured in the fixed units of seconds, weeks, months or centuries, the passage of a single year is experienced by each person differently. For most, it comprises twelve months or fifty-two weeks or three hundred and sixty-five days. But there are those who feel the year draining by, hour by hour, twenty-four each day or, even worse, feel each minute of every long day, all one thousand four hundred and forty of them, every day of the year. There are even those for whom a single year seems to last ten or even a hundred. By contrast, for some, it doesn't last so long, a week in length or a month at most.

The wealthy, who every day know happiness and pleasure, pomp and glory, and who have never experienced or known suffering, or the perils and calamities of this world, will certainly not feel the passage of time. For them, it seems to leap from morning to evening, from month to month, and from year to year. For those who work themselves to the bone trying to make a living, who are absorbed in their careers, there is never enough time. They know its value and frequently complain of its scarcity, saying, "How nice it would be if the daytime lasted more than twelve hours."

But for the individual who bears within him sorrow and suffering or thoughts of revenge or hopes not easily realized, time can taunt and torment without end. For that person, a day feels like a year, and a year like a century.

Though everyone feels time differently, make no mistake about it, time is very valuable if you know how to appreciate it, and very beneficial if you know how to use it properly, particularly as every creature has been given a fixed amount by Allah the Most High for living in this world. When that allotted time has passed, the creature must leave this world and go on to the world everlasting. It's only then that most human beings become aware of themselves and, looking back, see the long road they have traveled.

Those whom fortune has blessed see nothing along that road but shady trees protecting all that passes from the heat of the sun, as well as sheltered resting places, clear springs and cool water where they recovered from their fatigue. Everywhere, delicious fruit flourishes within reach, banishing hunger and thirst, while all manner of brightly colored blossoms and flowers abound, delighting the eye and nose and energizing the body.

However, those whose lives have been marred by ill-fortune and calamity will have nothing on that road save oppressive heat, pouring rain and typhoon winds accompanied by lightning and thunder. Their road twists and curves, frustrating the traveler at every turn and making the ascent and descent a difficult one. Therefore, before we reach its end, we should realize that this road will be traveled some day by our children and grandchildren, our kin, all our good friends and fellow human beings. Is it not our duty, we who have preceded them, to at least do something to benefit them during that later voyage, particularly those whose fate has been one of misfortune?

Plant shade trees and fruit that can be eaten along the side of that still imperfect road. Place benches at the resting spots, dig cool springs, arrange gardens to refresh the eye and delight the mind. And improve the road, so that it becomes level and straight, easy to travel, a road that holds no danger but is safe for whoever shall journey on it. Once its end is reached, regrets and curses will be of no use, for it shall never be traveled again.

One day at five o'clock in the afternoon, ten years after Samsulbahri shot himself in Batavia, two officers walked slowly towards the Cimahi train station, deep in conversation. Though they both spoke eloquently in Dutch and wore the same kind of clothing, even from a distance it was obvious they differed greatly. One was short and round, a sign of his great energy, with blond hair and blue eyes and a nose that was quite pronounced. His face was white and totally devoid of any mustache or beard. He was no child of this land but of a race from "the source of the winds". The man with him was tall and slender, a sign of his agility and suppleness.

His hair and eyes were black, his nose of moderate size, and his mustache, pointed beard, and tawny skin identified him as a child of the Indies. There were other differences between them, these rooted in their demeanor. The face of the Western officer radiated good cheer and humor. His character and expression were in concord, too, for he was always full of delight and laughter, as if he had no concept of a heart filled with sorrow or the troubles of the world. Rather, his thoughts seemed always to dwell in the realm of happiness and joy.

"Why be sad, when you can be happy?" he would say. "What's the use of crying when you can laugh? Doesn't crying depress the spirit and sorrow, ruin the body? Laughter is a tonic for the body's health. Why see something only a hand's span in length measuring two outstretched arms? Why not just roll it up short, and knot it fast?

"Why bother thinking of what tomorrow will bring or the day after, or a month or a year from now? That hasn't happened yet, nor is it sure to. If it does happen, let's just wait until then. 'With age comes counsel.' And what benefit is there in thinking about the past? Isn't it true that what's happened cannot be changed, even were we to pursue it on flying steeds? Wouldn't it be better to think about the present and do our best to transform it into something that affords us happy hearts and tranquil minds?"

Such were the European officer's thoughts. He paid little attention to difficulties and misfortune, while pleasure and amusement were his only loves. And he was quite right to think this way, for he could, inasmuch as all his needs were provided by his work at the time.

In truth, that sort of behavior often pleases the heart, fattens up the body, and makes one appear younger. Not everyone can act that way, though. People who have to work for a spoonful of rice would be hard pressed to imitate the officer. For their lives are not like that of a soldier, whose food, clothing, and housing are all supplied for him. Nonetheless, one needs to think through an issue clearly, for thought is the light of the heart, just so long as thinking is not carried to an extreme. A multitude of thoughts branching off in all directions cannot be healthy for the body.

It was obvious that the other officer, a native of the Indies, was not as high-spirited as his friend, and was even a silent type, someone whose understanding of the world had seasoned with time. Though he smiled whenever his comrade made a joke, something in his demeanor betrayed him as a man who had borne a great deal of pain, pain for which there was no consolation.

The differences between them notwithstanding, the two officers shared many things in common. Apart from their rank, much of their character and behavior was comparable. For example, they both were good-hearted, straightforward, unassuming, and brave, all of which had bound them together in a tie of friendship usually enjoyed by men who have been friends for years, not just six months, as was the case with them.

"What a fine day it is! It feels good to be out and walking about," said the Western officer.

"Quite so," replied his colleague. "It just rained, and not very heavily, so there's no mud, but no dust, either. Where shall we go?"

"Let's go to the train station first, then wander over to the club," Lieutenant Jan van Sta replied.

"Fine," answered the native lieutenant.

"Where did you take your troops this morning, Mas?" asked Van Sta.

"Shooting. At the rifle range."

"And who hit the rose?"

"Several people. Van der Ha, de Kuip, Lewikawang, Mahutu, Suwoto and Prawira."

"Of course, I've heard they're really good."

"They seem to be steady of hand and heart, don't shake, and their eyesight is sharp. Those are especially important qualities for recruits. With men like that, it's easy to take fortresses and defeat strong enemies. I witnessed that myself when I was in Aceh."

"Tell me about Aceh. The more one hears, the more one knows. That's why I'm endlessly shooting the breeze with you."

"All right," Mas replied with a smile. "Later, when we're sitting comfortably at the club or in our own homes. But they're just the usual war stories."

"And so they may be, but there're often a lot of lessons to be learned from them, particularly for someone like me, who's just arrived in the Indies. I don't know the customs and ways of the people here," said Van Sta.

"Say! What do you know, we're at the station!" he continued. "Let's go in for a bit. It just so happens there's a train about to leave for Bandung. Maybe there's a Bandung butterfly who wants to go back to her nest!"

"Even if there were, what would you do about it? She'd be en route. Surely you can't catch a bird on the wing." Mas said.

"Not by hand, of course, for then my hand would have to be dozens of meters long, but with something with a handle, like a gun or a trap, for example. And even if I couldn't catch her, just seeing her would be enough. The eyes want their pleasures, too."

The two of them entered the station, whereupon they did, in fact, see a young woman with a pretty face sitting by herself in first class.

"Well now, what did I tell you!" Van Sta whispered to his colleague. "I was right. Take a look at the angel sitting there in first class. How sweet her glance is. Look! She's glaring at me. Ow! I'm a dead duck!"

Just then, the third bell rang and a few seconds later the train cleared the station, huffing and puffing to the right and the left of the Cimahi Station on its way to Bandung, followed by Lieutenant van Sta's eyes.

"Hey, when are we going to go to Bandung? I haven't done an outing there in some time now," he said suddenly, escorting his companion out of the station now that the object of his ogling was no longer in view.

"Whenever you like, I'm ready to follow!"

"This Saturday night."

"All right. But, Jan, why don't you want to get married? Wouldn't it be nicer to have a wife than to lead this single life of yours?"

"Me, get a wife?" asked Van Sta with a smile, pointing to his cheek. "Ha! My wife has yet to be born."

"How so? You mean to say there's no woman good enough for you?"

"If I were to look for a wife, her beauty wouldn't be the important thing. For me, the main thing would be how she conducts herself and her love for me. I would get married, not because I wanted a woman, but because I wanted a wife. A woman is easy to acquire, but not a wife. The pretty ones are all over the place, but the good ones are hard to find. For me, even if she's ugly, never mind, as long as she's good. Let her be stupid as long as she's clever."

"Hold on a minute! What in the world does that mean?" replied Mas. "You mean to say the ugly ones can be good and the stupid ones can actually be clever? You're always coming up with some saying or another."

"Yes, and why not? Because 'ugly' and 'good' are just words people use. If they say she's ugly, then she becomes ugly. If they say 'good', then she becomes good, too. Take, for example, that young thing just now. If she were to be compared with the stylishly beautiful people in Europe, we would say she was ugly. But compared to a Papuan woman, she'd be very pretty, right? That she would be, but what I meant just now was, let her be not so pretty, as long as her conduct and her feelings were good to me. Never mind if she's not so clever when it comes to other sorts of knowledge, just so long as she's good at taking care of me, my children and my household."

"You're right, Jan. I agree."

"But even if there *were* women like that, I still wouldn't want to get married right now."

"Why not?"

"Marriage is something important, especially for Europeans, for we're bound by several contracts, so it isn't easy to get divorced. If you find a really good wife, all well and fine then. But if not, then what?"

"That's the good thing about being engaged first: one person really gets to know the other. Am I wrong?"

"Yes, even though it's never sufficient, for sometimes in engagements, the behavior and the heart on display aren't the real thing. Instead, each of them puts on a face, so that only after marriage do they find out that they've been tricked. But the biggest obstacle for me is that you get tied down, especially after marriage, and not just for a while, but for your whole life.

"It's true there are good things about having a wife, but there are bad things, too. The good things are: a fixed life; even if the money runs out, you can see where it went; a household that's cared for; and for those who like to have children, these can provide solace. A good wife, of course, is much more of a pleasure than a trouble for her husband. But what I don't like is that we're no longer free. We can't follow the call of our hearts. Occasionally we even have to ask the good lady's permission if we want to do something. And if we wind up with a jealous wife, that's the end of it! The land is in revolt! And we're bound hand and foot."

"But, Jan, isn't jealousy the sign of love? If you didn't love your wife, how could you be jealous? Surely you'd just say, 'Let someone else have her, I don't care. I'll find another one.'"

"True, and you're right! But being too jealous isn't good either. How nice would it be if you couldn't speak to or look at other women? Couldn't go to the club, or anywhere?"

"Ah, in excess, of course, that can be bad. Everything in excess is naturally not good. 'Too full and it overflows. Too good and others take advantage of it,' the Dutch saying goes."

"Right, right, and right again! And that's why I don't want a wife just now. If I had a wife like that, I would be in a hell of a fix. When I'm older and want to be penned in, all right then, but while I'm still young, I love my independence. I don't want to be all tied down by a woman. Let me get tied down when I have had enough of the bachelor's life."

"When you've gotten old, what woman would want you? Even the ones who like you now, they might not be around anymore," Mas said with a laugh. "Plus, when you're old, you're sure not to be tied down, because usually old folks don't tend to run off, for their legs have gotten too weak for getting around. The ones tied down are the youngsters, whose legs are still strong enough for them to run away on."

"Aha, that's what I like," replied Van Sta. "You get more and more cheerful as time goes on. Maybe last night you had nice dreams. That's the best of all! Drive out all the worries and complicated thoughts and trade them for happy ones. Follow the way I see things and be cheerful forever. Long live cheerfulness!"

"Maybe so, but living by oneself, that's not real living," Mas went on, paying no attention to his friend's ebullience. "A woman has to have a husband and a man has to have a wife. Isn't the obligation of every living creature to increase and multiply its race? What would the world come to if everyone wanted to live freely, like you?"

"In Europe many people are beginning to do that."

"Yes, but that way of thinking, never wanting to marry as long as you live... I can't approve of that. If there were some physical defect, like a disease or some kind of flaw, then, all right, it wouldn't matter. But if one remains single just to indulge oneself in pleasure, that's not so good. What would become of the human race?"

"What would happen would be that men and women would be much more independent in matters of marriage than they are nowadays. If you wanted to get hitched or separate from someone, you could at any time, without any obstacles at all, as long as it's with mutual consent."

"That's exactly what I'm talking about! Isn't that called free love? What I mean is, the relationship between a man and a woman unbound by marriage? The woman has no fixed husband and the man has no fixed wife. Each lives with his or her lover. When you've had enough with the one, get rid of him or her, and find someone else. And the children born of it don't know their fathers. Ah! If that's the way it were, in the end we'd be reverting to prehistoric times, when humans went about without clothing, and lived like animals."

At that point, the two lieutenants arrived at the club and sat outside in a quiet spot.

"Note where we are in our debate," said Van Sta, "and tell me what you'd like to drink."

"Whiskey soda," answered Mas.

The waiter came over and Van Sta ordered two whiskey sodas.

While they waited for their drinks to arrive, the native lieutenant took out his cigars and handed one to his friend while smoking one himself. Their whiskeys came and the two men began to drink.

"And another thing I can't countenance is how women think today," Mas continued. "I mean, their wanting to be employed in men's jobs and work like men. If every woman were to do that, what would men do for a living? Would they have to go to the kitchen, manage the house, and look after the children? That would be like rain falling back up into the skies.

"The danger would grow, for most employers like to use women, because they accept low wages and that just increases the number of women who don't want husbands. They think: What's the use of having a husband when I'm already earning enough to live on? But is that way of thinking correct? We live in this world, but not just for our own needs. We have to think of the needs of all. As a man, we're responsible to our wife and children, so we can't just defend ourselves. And the same is true for everybody. We have to be responsible to our fellow man.

"The way I see it, women are wrong to think like that. Why should they be pursuing men's skills and holding men's jobs? Isn't there a purpose to having a job? In that case, the important things are life and happiness. If the husband can't achieve such things, what need is there for the woman to look for them herself? Am I being jealous or spiteful that women will be as smart as men? Absolutely not! The deeper and more extensive knowledge women possess, the better, as long as they don't forget their original responsibility."

"And that is?" asked Van Sta.

"Children, the household, and preparing meals."

"Right, but women see things differently. There is the houseboy for the house, for cooking there is the cook, the seamstress does the sewing, the nanny takes care of the children, for washing the clothes there is the laundryman, and for tending the garden there is the gardener. You can't mean she has to do all that by herself."

"Of course not. But even though there are houseboys, cooks, nannies, and all the rest of it, the woman still has to have an understanding of such things, for all those people I mentioned are just workers who have to work. The one who has to manage them and give orders is, of course, the woman. Would her child get an education if she handed it over to her stupid nanny?

"And as far as having houseboys, cooks, and nannies are concerned, that's only for the well-to-do, even among Europeans. If you can't afford them, then what? Just think, humanity has far more poor people than rich ones. Does our good fellow have to do all the servants' work, even after returning exhausted from slaving away at his job? And what's the wife's job? To be a house flower? Such a division of labor would be truly unjust. Should we be surprised if men, without advancing much, became afraid of having wives and instead thought, 'What's the benefit of getting married if my wife just added to my woes and didn't help me in daily life? It'd be better to stay single, for if it's just a question of women, there are lots along the road.'"

"If it were that way, wouldn't the chasm that separates men from women just get wider?" Van Sta asked.

"If the man were rich, he would have to fulfill all his wife's desires and treat her like a princess. But if he really were unable to supply all her demands, he shouldn't be forced to do so. She should also consider her husband's situation. She can't be deaf and dumb except to her own pleasure!"

"Yes, but a woman has a husband because she wants to have sustenance and happiness as well," the Dutchman replied. "If that's all going to prove difficult, then why have a husband at all? It would be better for her to work and seek her own livelihood."

"That's what I mean. That kind of thinking just won't do, either for the man or for the woman, for it shows they're concerned with their own needs only, and not attending to those they share in common. If a system like that continues, husband and wife will become enemies and end up one day in open warfare. So what I really worry about are the all-around skills being transmitted to women, without any heed to their situation and obligations, because such skills will produce misunderstanding, not correct thinking. For example, she won't be able to live the ordinary life she had previously, but will instead want to live in a grand manner. Mixing with ordinary folk will be something beneath her, too. If she wanted a husband, it would have to be someone rich or with a high position. But as men like that are scare, especially among my people, a woman with such skills would certainly rush off to other peoples, say, to your own or to the Chinese, so that finally her own race would disappear. And if all educated women did that, what would be left of their own people? And, in the end, what would happen to my own? Who would be there to advance it any further?

"To tell you the truth, it's not good for a man or a woman to get it into their heads to live alone, struggling to find work, contending for skills, and becoming enemies in their life together, for men and women are one. They shouldn't separate but should help each other. Men need women and women need men. Don't the Dutch say that 'unanimity brings power, but strife disperses it'? The war of life in this world is certainly not easy. Why make it even less so by discord and strife among women and men?"

"Indeed, indeed," replied Van Sta, as he drank his whiskey soda.

"And there's something else I feel," said Mas, taking a sip of his own.

"And that is?"

"That is, the education of girls of my race. Because women's responsibilities are naturally not the same as men's, I don't think that women need to learn everything a man knows. And a man doesn't need to learn women's skills, like sewing and cooking, for example, if he doesn't have to become a tailor or a cook. What's the use of an engineer's skills, or a judge's, for a woman? Wouldn't it be better to learn skills useful to her?

"I'm telling you all of this, Jan, because I'm truly worried that the women of the Indies are blindly copying the ways and thinking of European women, without considering closely if such ways and thoughts are useful here. As I see it, not everything that's good for European women is good for the women of the Indies. What's good there isn't good here, and vice versa. What is useful here isn't useful there. Take that which is truly good, imitate it, and make use of it."

"All right! I've heard all your thoughts. There's just one thing I want to know. Just now you had me getting a wife and you were hard on my intention of staying single, so why don't *you* want to get married?"

Startled by this question, Lieutenant Mas set back down, untouched, the whiskey he had raised to his lips. Without saying a word, he reflected on the question for a bit, then bowed his head as a single teardrop fell to his lap.

Van Sta was surprised to see his comrade's reaction, and could not understand why Mas had suddenly become so sad. And so he asked, "Why have you gone quiet all of a sudden? Aren't you feeling well?"

"It's not that," his friend replied, lifting his head. "Enough. Don't bring that up again! It doesn't matter."

As it was clear from Mas' gloomy look that he ought not to press the matter further, Van Sta changed the subject.

"Just now you promised to tell me about your experiences in the Aceh war. What about those stories?"

"Oh, yes," the native lieutenant replied, struggling to banish the mournful expression on his face. But he could not, for the thought that had brought on this look had not yet left him. It was as if an ancient wound, nearly healed, had once again broken open. "I almost forgot that promise. Okay, listen up! But first, I should tell you something about me so that the story will be clear. Only I ask that you not get upset when you hear it, for it involves a great deal of sadness."

In speaking this way, Mas' face seemed to grow more and more somber, while his former light-heartedness vanished without a trace.

"It's obvious from my face that I'm no European, but rather a child of the Indies." So began the lieutenant's story.

"For ten years now I've had a career in the army, starting off in the ranks right up until my present position. I entered the military for no other reason than to..." Here the lieutenant broke off, as if unable to utter the words, "... seek death."

"What's that you say?" the Dutchman asked in astonishment.

"'Seek death' is what I said," his friend replied sadly. "But I have yet to achieve that purpose. Apparently, the Malay proverb is true: 'Death is forbidden before one's allotted time.'

"I wanted to die a number of times, but something always got in the way and so I failed. Perhaps I will leave this world without carrying out my promise. I surrendered myself to God's will while waiting for that moment. It was then that I finally realized man may not do simply as he wishes, if there is a sign from God. How many people have there been who don't want to die, either out of fear or because they still need to go on living, but whose lives are taken anyway? But I, who truly longed for death, and who was of no use in this world anymore, was still being protected from death.

"Maybe you don't believe my story and think I'm superstitious. Or you think that when I shot myself in the head I should have died, with no one there to stop me. I tried, but there was always something keeping me out of danger. Take a look, here's the proof I shot myself, right here on my head," Lieutenant Mas said, pointing to a scar on the right side of his head.

"One day I wanted to hang myself. I checked the rope beforehand and the pole I was using for that purpose, for I was afraid I would fail again. The rope and the pole looked sturdy. But for whatever reason, as I was hanging there, the pole broke and went crashing down, along with me, to the ground. So once again I failed to achieve my objective. The third time, I was going to take poison. But when the glass reached my mouth, I heard the sound of the enemy's rifle firing at me. The bullet went through my window and shattered the glass in my hand. The fourth time, I plunged into water in what I thought was a deserted place. But why hadn't I noticed that somebody was there, hidden away fishing in the dark? That fisherman saved me when I should have drowned even though I threw myself like a blind pig into battle. Even in that I couldn't succeed, for as of today I'm still alive, and have even been decorated because of my supposed bravery and courage, and promoted to lieutenant."

"Everybody talks about your bravery and the awards you received."

"It wasn't because of my bravery or courage that I received such awards and the promotion, but because this was my destiny. I, who desired nothing more, was given rank and decoration.

"Others who loved such recognition, to them nothing was given, is that not so?" asked Van Sta.

"Now you know for sure why I don't have a wife. Someone with my despair shouldn't get married. What would happen afterwards to my wife and children if I got what I wanted?"

"But, who knows, perhaps children and a wife might have brought consolation to you."

"I could not, could not have done that! For I had vowed to die as swiftly as possible."

In that moment, the native lieutenant fell to brooding again as the tears welled in his eyes.

"Most amazing, this story of yours!" said Van Sta as he looked sadly at his friend's condition. The truth was, he wanted to find out why the other had lost hope, but was not brave enough to ask, for he felt it must be a significant reason. Perhaps it wounded Mas to speak of it. And so Van Sta turned to another topic.

"But that business of the war, what was that all about?" he asked, to bring his friend back from his crushing memories.

"Ah, yes. I still haven't told you about that. This is what happened.... But before that, there's something I want to ask you before we leave these sad matters behind, and that is, please don't reveal this secret of mine to anyone else. You're the only friend I have who knows about this."

"As if I'd be so crazy as to tell anyone about it, if you didn't want me to," replied Van Sta.

"Now listen," Mas said. "One day, when I was in Aceh, I got the order to check out several villages near Siglie with thirty *Marsosé*, for word came in that a number of enemy troops, led by Teuku Putih, were causing trouble. Apparently our scout didn't really know the roads there and so we got lost. By late evening we still hadn't found our way back.

"At around seven o'clock, we ran into Teuku Putih's army, about 150 men. At first I didn't think there were that many, because it was night and impossible to make a proper estimate. So I concentrated my troops in front to intercept the enemy and we opened fire, and it got pretty hot. After a while I realized we had been surrounded in front and on our right and left flanks. A moment later, we heard rifle shots to our rear.

"When my troops realized we had been cut off on all sides, they panicked and didn't know what to do. Some wanted to flee; others refused to take orders. Only about ten men remained loyal to me. "Be brave!" I told them. "If we're going to die, let's die fighting and not while being tortured in captivity. Sling your rifles, draw your swords, move forward and give your war cries. There's only one way out of this, and that's to fight."

"'Yes, sir!' replied my loyal soldiers and we started shouting and yelling, letting the enemy know we were there, showing them our swords. And luck was with us! All the men who had panicked followed as well so that the enemy gave way and retreated to their right and left.

"When we were about to make a run for it, I heard someone from the enemy's ranks yell, "Mas, the black infidel! Mas, the black infidel!"

"It appeared they knew my name. What's more, in the battle my own men had struck Teuku Putih with their swords. So the enemy retreated step by step, until finally we could no longer hear the sounds of their rifles. After it was all over, I counted my men. There were sixteen left who could still fight. Of the rest, ten were dead and four badly wounded. Several of the loyal soldiers and I were wounded, but not critically. Since I was worried about being attacked again, I wanted to head back, but didn't know the way. As it turned out, there was one Acehnese soldier who hadn't been able to run away on account of his wounded leg. I asked him the way back and promised to reward him if he spoke truthfully and to flog him if he lied. He was willing to grant my request as long as I kept my end of the bargain.

"Only after we checked the remaining fallen soldiers to make sure they were really dead did we head back. As for the four who were wounded, we took turns carrying them on our backs.

"We hadn't been walking long when we reached a familiar road. A little while later, we arrived in town.

"I gave some money to the wounded Acehnese and let him go on the road, as he requested. I also asked him where Teuku Putih was, but he said he didn't know, because he suspected that the Teuku didn't have a fixed location, but kept moving from one place to another.

"Before we reached the town, we stopped for a moment, and I told the soldiers who had wanted to run off that I forgave them this time, but that if they ever tried to desert again I would shoot them or have them court martialed without hesitation. I intended to show them that when hard-pressed or surrounded, it often takes a firm heart and a clear head to get out of a situation. They all begged my pardon and swore they would never run off again. It was at Siglie that my glass was hit by the enemy's rifle fire, as I mentioned before."

"A commander must really stay firm and can't lose his head," said Van Sta.

"Indeed! What would you like to drink now? I'd like a glass of beer!"

"A beer for me, too, then."

And so they each ordered a beer.

"It sounds like the Acehnese knew who you were," said Van Sta.

"Perhaps. I was often lucky during the war, and they believed I possessed some sort of magic and couldn't be defeated."

"Sure, they're very superstitious."

"The second time was at Lhokseumawe," said Lieutenant Mas. As he was about to pick up the thread of his story, a soldier came running over to them. After saluting, he handed the two lieutenants a letter. Mas read it and passed it to his comrade. "Now why is the Captain ordering us over on the double?" he wondered aloud. "Right, let's get moving!"

After signing the chit for the drinks, the two lieutenants walked over to the captain's billet. The moment they arrived, the captain said, "Mas and Van Sta, I have orders for you and your men to proceed immediately to Padang. Tomorrow you'll leave here for Batavia and from there ship out to Padang along with units from several other locations. There's been some unrest over a new tax being imposed. Tell your men to pack up tonight. I expect you'll have good luck there, as always," said the captain to Lieutenant Mas as the two men shook hands. "And you, Van Sta, to return with victory," he said, adding, "Have a safe journey."

"Thank you, Captain," replied the two lieutenants. With that, they left and went to the barracks to give their men the new orders.

All was chaos that night as the soldiers hurriedly geared up for their new mission.

"Now I can go into battle with you and learn from you," Van Sta said, but his comrade heard none of what he said, for he was lost in thought.

That entire night, Mas was unable to sleep. And why was that? Was he afraid of heading into battle at Padang? Impossible! The Lieutenant Mas, famed for his courage, who had been in dozens of frays and always emerged victorious, a lieutenant who feared nothing, who instead sought out death, would never harbor such fears. And yet, his face was pale and his hands would not stop shaking, nor would his sense of foreboding cease.

As he could not sleep, Mas paced back and forth in his billet. Finally, he sat in a chair, only to rise again, imagining he really *was* afraid of going into battle this time.

"Have I not suffered enough pain, after being tortured like this?" he said out loud to himself. "I can't bear my own suffering and now am being ordered to kill my own people. How many have fallen before my weapons, how many have been destroyed at my hands, how many women have lost their sons, how many bereaved of their husbands and children now without fathers? How many people have been separated, exiled, and executed, houses and grain sheds wrecked and burnt, and villages destroyed because of my duties?

"When will I be able to stop this hellish work as an executioner of my own people? Whose lot in life could be worse than mine? And why? What is my sin that I should be tortured this way? Those who know nothing of my fate probably believe I'm fond of what I do. But only God knows how my heart has been shattered, seeing scores of women widowed and children orphaned, so many souls scattered to the winds, the young men crippled by a hacked foot or hand, the homes brought crashing down and burned, the villages and hamlets destroyed in my path, their possessions plundered. But what is there to say? I'm forced to do this to win my death. Why, to this day, have I been unable to achieve my heart's desire? Why hasn't my soul been taken from me? I am even now protected! Has my punishment not come to an end? And, now it's not just my people I'm sent to murder, but my family, relatives, and friends.

"O Allah, O Lord! Has Thy servant not reached the time for his release from this suffering? How much longer must he wait?"

After speaking this way, it was as if Mas heard a voice within him say, "Now is the time when your desire may be achieved. Now you will be released from your torment and joined by those you love!"

Unnerved by the sound of the voice, he felt his heart begin to beat wildly. "Is this voice real or are my thoughts just confused?" he wondered.

He sat back down and brooded over the words that had arisen in him. All his suffering, from the very beginning right through to the present, seemed to float before his eyes. Little by little, without his realizing it, he became exhausted and fell asleep in the chair. A little while later, he woke with a start at the sound of a bugle, for it was now five-thirty in the morning. He stood up and ordered his gear to be taken to the station. He then washed his face and drank a cup of coffee, before setting off for the barracks.

A little while later, Mas and his men got on board a train headed to Batavia.

15

Rebellion

A few days after Lieutenant Mas left for Padang, an old man named Malim Batuah, who was standing in the Bukit Tinggi market, turned to his friend and said, "Has Datuk Malelo heard the bad news?"

"What news is that?" his companion replied.

"It seems the Company will want *belasting* money from us soon."

"*Belasting* money? What kind of money is that?" Datuk Malelo asked with a sour smile. "The Company is never at a loss when it comes to getting money. And who will suffer from such a regulation? The native people, to be sure. Isn't it enough, the money from forced labor and 'guard' contributions, from this and from that? And now they add something else. What is it now?"

"It's a tax on goods or livelihood, collected annually."

"It seems the Dutch are short of funds, so they are thinking of every which way to get their hands on money. But this is intolerable. If we just go along with it, just you wait and see. After this, we'll have to shell out even more. And where are we going to get it all? And why should we pay? We're not slaves or prisoners, or people who pay tribute money to the Company. And furthermore, what is that money to be used for?"

"I don't know, I've only heard what people are saying. Everyone says the sub-district heads will be summoned to the office of the Resident to confer on the matter. We're sure to receive news on how true all this is this from our village heads and leaders."

"Whatever else happens, I don't agree with this ruling," said Datuk Malelo.

All across the country, everywhere the regulation was to be instituted, the native population greeted the news of the new tax the same way.

Word spread quickly, through town and lane, all the way to the villages and tiny hamlets, until old and young, high and humble, men and women, heard about it. They all grumbled for they felt they had been unjustly ordered by the Dutch who, in their view, did whatever they pleased. It seemed to them they were being forced to pay the tax to increase the wealth of the Dutch.

Worried their native subjects would be unwilling to obey the new rule and would oppose it instead, Dutch members of the East Indies civil service held consultations with local government employees to discuss the matter. In Padang Hilir, they met with the district heads, and in Padang Hulu with the sub-district heads, to devise a way to implement the tax peacefully.

All indigenous government employees were ordered to assemble and discuss the issue with village officials and the local population. They had to explain the reasons and need for a tax of this kind, so that there would be no misunderstanding. As a result, the gatherings grew very lively, as the sub- and district heads held meetings with the village heads, and the village heads discussed the matter with their staff who, in turn, brought it to the attention of their clan members.

So that we might obtain an accurate picture of the issue, let us follow these consultations.

One day there gathered at the office of the resident at Bukit Tinggi all the sub-district heads of the Residency of Padang Hulu. The assistant residents were also present, as were the district officers and their staff understudies. After all were accounted for in the council, the head resident stood up and spoke in the local Minangkabau Malay language. "Gentlemen," he began, "before we announce the order we have received, we would like to welcome all who have acceded to our request to gather here, for there is an important order from the Supreme Government about which we must confer.

"As you all know, the lands of the Indies are governed by the Dutch Government. And as you also know, the Indies are not small, but are very large and vast in area. Several islands very great in size, including Sumatra,

Java, Borneo, Celebes, right over to Papua, are among its territories. In addition to these, there are many small islands, like Bali, Lombok, Sumbawa, Flores, Timor, Sumba, Savu, Roti, and others. All of these lands must be supervised and managed by the Dutch Government as well as possible, so that their various inhabitants may live securely and prosperously.

"To achieve these ends, the Government provides its employees with sufficient equipment, housing and offices. Let us name a few of the various types of employees as examples. First, there are those who govern and steer the policies of these lands, that is to say, employees such as all of us here. There are many of them, with many houses and offices. They number in the thousands, from those with the rank of resident right down to the clerks and village heads, and even the governor-general may be included in this group.

"Second, those employees who advance the natives in the areas of knowledge and crafts, that is, the teachers. There are thousands of them with their school houses both large and small, and they have various kinds of equipage, as well.

"Third, the employees who promote plantations and trade, who together with their places and equipment are similarly numerous.

"Fourth, the employees who build the houses, the roads, the canals and drains, the rivers, and so on. Such employees, their offices and equipage are no less numerous.

"Fifth, employees who guard the peace of the land, that is, the army. They account for the largest expenses, but their needs are also very great. And they are not only on land, but at sea as well, to guard trade and the peace of the seas against enemies. These soldiers are equipped with war ships and weapons.

"Employees who manage the Government's funds have been organized as well. Apart from them, there are many more we aren't mentioning here, for to do so would certainly lengthen our discussion. As you can see, gentlemen, everything is managed in the best possible way. Everything that is useful is supplied, and what is unnecessary is discarded. And this, not only in the matter of human beings, but also with respect to animals, plants, land, water, and other things, which are not to be overlooked.

"As you are all surely aware, all of this comes at no little expense, whether the payment of salaries, the building of places and houses, the purchase of equipment, or travel expenses. Think of the cost of just one house or government office, in terms of one month's salary, the cost of furniture etc. Only then will it become clear that these are no few expenses. The Government has to expend tens of millions of rupiah each year to pay for all of this.

"Where is so much money to come from? True, there are agricultural products, coffee, trade, and this and that, but it is obvious that such produce now is insufficient. What is the present thinking on how to obtain additional funds, which are now lacking? When you are at home and wish to use a mat, lamps, chairs and tables, who has to go and buy these items? You yourselves, is this not correct? Surely they couldn't be requested from someone else. Likewise the affairs of our state: we may not ask for assistance from another government. Instead it is we ourselves who must shoulder the burden. Is this not the way it has been since earlier times? Everything that is needed for the state, the state itself supplies, collected from the native peoples of these lands.

"Previously, the income we mentioned just now was indeed sufficient to fund all such requirements, but since those requirements have been growing all the while—because the number of people has been growing all the while too—now all this produce no longer suffices. Perhaps those additional needs are not yet obvious here, but are plain to see in the other lands. Nonetheless, we still have to join together in providing our assistance. We must not allow ourselves to think, what's the use of helping those other lands? For as we mentioned earlier, all the islands that comprise the lands of the Indies are one, whether they are Malay or Javanese, Dayak or Papuan, Dutch or Chinese: all are people of these Indies, and must be united to work together to take our lands forward.

"Never doubt the benefit to all these lands of something done in one of them. Look at the Java Doctors' School. It is only in Java, but it's not just the Javanese who benefit from that school. Minangkabau, Batak, Manadonese, Ambonese and others are able to study there to become doctors. And in the Teachers' Training Academy here, it's not just the Minangkabau people who can study to become teachers, but students from Tapanuli, Aceh,

Palembang, Lampung, Bengkulu, and even from Pontianak and Sambas, as well. And so it is with improvements and advances made in other countries. There is no way these cannot bring good things to us here, too.

"Thus, the Supreme Government has decided that all the inhabitants of these lands of the Indies must join together to assist in dealing with this shortfall. There are fewer poor among you than rich. This assistance in the form of money is called *belasting* and is to be paid each year. Thus it is no different from the annual or Ramadan tithing. It is just that the new tax will be used for our common needs and is not given as a present to the poor for their own.

"The tax is imposed everywhere, both in those lands and countries 'at the source of the winds' and 'those which receive the winds'. In these Indies, almost every place and its various inhabitants have accepted this regulation freely. Only here among the Minangkabau people is this not yet so. You surely know that if the people here are exempted from this new tax, such an action by the Government would certainly be unjust. 'All lend a shoulder for heavy things, and a hand for light ones.'

"Furthermore, if the Minangkabau people here agree to call for this regulation, the Government would be pleased to release them from their coffee contracts, so that they can sell coffee to whomever they want at five or six times the price. And if you really think about it, it is obvious these coffee contracts are no longer fair in this day and age. They are not in line with the times. For just consider who it is that plants coffee and sells it to the Government warehouses. Is it not the people who work in the fields, that is, the poor? Rich people, merchants: do they do this? No. So, who essentially pays the tax? Is it not the poor? Our rich friends have it easy.

"It is for this reason that we requested all of you to gather here, that this order may be conveyed to the local people with an explanation of its rationale and uses. They must clearly understand the matter so they don't end up thinking this money is being asked of them merely to fill the pockets of the Dutch. In no way will the Netherlands derive any benefit from this taxation, only we here will.

"And again, do not misunderstand. All of us Dutch people here are employees of the Government, just as you are, and what the Government is, is not the Dutch race, or the Kingdom of the Netherlands, but none other than the inhabitants of these Indies. The Dutch are here merely to govern, to help and to regulate.

"We feel that this sufficiently explains our purpose. If there are any among you who have any feelings in regard to this matter, speak them now so that we might discuss them together!"

With that, the Resident took his seat and waited to see if there was anyone who wanted to speak. But not a single person wished to express his thinking on the matter.

After a moment's silence, the Resident again asked, "Is there no one who wishes to say anything at all in regard to this matter?"

Just then, a sub-district head stood up, the oldest among all the sub-district heads present. After conveying his salutation to the Resident and all who were present in the council, he said, "Insofar as I see the matter, there is nothing further to say because all of it has been decided by the Supreme Government. Though we may feel something in our hearts and see it with our minds' eye, in my opinion, there would be little to gain in speaking of it anymore, because this would not change the regulation, which has been set. There is nothing more we can do in this regard, except to convey this order to the local people and explain to them the uses and reasons for this new tax. We shall endeavor to our utmost that the local people of this land will follow the regulation. Even so, we are unable to ensure the local people will accept the regulation with a happy mind, for new things are not accepted quickly, especially if what's good about it isn't clear. Moreover, this regulation hurts their wallets. Therefore, let us together make an effort to do this and ask God that this order can be carried out peacefully and safely."

Now let us hear the replies of the civil servants at the village level on this matter. Such meetings, held in homes or village halls, were led by the sub-district heads.

After all the leaders, headmen, the wealthy and their advisors had gathered together with local scholars and other nobles, the sub-district head addressed them, conveying the order he had received from the Resident and explaining the uses and rationale for carrying out the new tax. When he was finished speaking, several present at the assembly gave the following replies.

"With regard to this Government regulation, we don't know the good or the bad of it. But what we initially felt is that the Dutch appear to have forgotten their promise to the Minangkabau people. Was not the 'Long Agreement' set down that we Minangkabau folk do not have to pay duties, taxes and tolls, which resemble this *belasting*? So why are we being ordered to pay these now? Are the Dutch going back on their promise?

"Secondly, the Dutch have also forgotten that we are not their subjects, who have to pay tribute to them. Our lands were never taken by them with the smoke of rifles, but rather by agreement, from comrade to comrade.

"Third, the Resident said the Dutch are here to help govern. But who requested this help? We did not ask to be assisted in governing, but only to defeat the *Paderi* rebels during that period of our history, nothing else. Our thinking about this is, we don't need to be ordered about by foreigners: since the time of our ancestors, we have been ruled by rajas of our own race and felt at ease with that kind of government, nor did we feel it to be any less just. Thus, we have no need to request help from foreigners to govern us.

"Fourth, according to the Resident, the new tax will cover the Government's shortfalls due to the many changes that have been made. What those changes have been, we don't know, for we were not consulted on these matters beforehand. So we don't know if these changes are really beneficial to us or not. We think what we have now is sufficient. There's no need for further changes. Now, as far as these changes are concerned, they're not just for us, but for those in high positions, the rich and those who dwell in cities.

"Fifth, the Resident himself said we may not make requests of other people when meeting our needs. Why doesn't each village supply their own needs? Why must we help the people of the Celebes, Timor and Papua? We haven't even seen what they look like! And who will guarantee that someday those people will help us if we experience trouble or have any needs?

"Sixth, the Resident said that the Government is all of us and not the Dutch race. Why then is everything decided on and done by the Dutch themselves, while the voice of the native people is never in the slightest heard? And the matter of this tax had not been brought to us for consultation earlier on. Once it came into effect, we were ordered to obey, without being allowed to say no. What will people say about us later, that we are people who are governed, or people who governed?

"Seventh, it is said that there are Government employees who build houses, roads and other things. Whose houses are being built? Our homes we build ourselves, and also the roads. What is the benefit to us in supplying employees for that? We don't know anything about the plantation employees here, and we have no need of them. What would they teach us? To plant rice? This was known to our ancestors hundreds of years ago. Husbandry? Our buffalo breed just the same, even though they aren't closely cared for. And those doctors, do they come on medical calls to our village? They stick to the towns, where the rich folk are. We're just village dwellers, poor people, and can't pay their fees.

"As for the army, whose use we are just now seeing, it exists for no other reason than to force us to obey the Company's regulations. And who are those 'enemies from the land and the sea'? If they are our own people, it would be sufficient if we fought them off ourselves, and if they are of a foreign race, what's the point of us resisting them? For aren't the Dutch a foreign race?

"It's the same with the schools. These are restricted to the towns, and solely for the townspeople. If our children want to go to school, they have to walk great distances, for there are only prayer houses in the village."

Such were the replies of the majority of the district heads and village headmen on the question of the new tax.

And now let us listen to what locals in the villages themselves thought.

One night, there gathered in the local mosque all the inhabitants of the Kota Tengah village, near Padang. Following the night prayer, hundreds of villagers from that and other villages came, all of them informed that a big meeting was to be held that evening to discuss the new tax. The leaders in this consultation were those who had made the hajj pilgrimage, religious scholars and teachers, and the elders. Among this latter group appeared Datuk Meringgih, the rich merchant of Padang.

Once they were all present, the Datuk opened the discussion.

"The reason we asked all you clan heads, brothers, friends and relatives to gather here tonight is because we have to discuss a new regulation which the

Company wants to burden us with. That is to say, the payment of *belasting* money. It would appear the Dutch are not satisfied with just sucking our blood, extracting our strength and squeezing our sweat dry. Just think, we have paid the forced labor payments, the guard fees, and other levies, all of which are imposed for our own benefit, they say. In fact, these payments are for them, to fill their stomachs, to slake their thirst, and to enrich their people. What benefit do we native folk derive from all the money we've paid? Are there any among us here tonight who have seen the benefits? Even I, old as I am and living in town, mixing day and night with the Dutch, the Chinese, Indians, Arabs, and others, don't know what the benefit is. Where it goes, and to what use it is put, only the Company knows. They see that we are willing to pay, and so now the Company asks for this tax. If tomorrow we go ahead and pay it, they'll demand even more of us later. Maybe they'll put a levy on our homes, our clothes, our furniture, and our wives and children.

"Don't we have a saying about how greedy and covetous the Dutch are? Don't we say, 'Like a Dutchman seeking land: give him a hand's span and he'll want an arm's length'? A system like this doesn't exist among the colonies of other races, such as those of the English. I have been to Singapore, Penang, Perak and Johor and have never seen anybody there pay a tax like this. Only here does it exist. So this is a fabricated rule on the part of the Dutch to squeeze us as dry as dry can be.

"Naturally, the Dutch want the native population to be impoverished and stupid and thus easily manipulated, and if some day we become completely weakened, for sure we'll be sold off by them as slaves."

Now, why was Datuk Meringgih there, inciting the local people against the Government? Why wasn't he going about the affairs of his business? It was because he knew full well that if this tax was put into effect, he would have to pay a large sum. Furthermore, it looked as if the Government in Padang was keeping an eye on his comings and goings, for people were becoming increasing doubtful about his honesty. Knowing this and being highly incensed against the Dutch Government, Datuk Meringgih wanted to vent his anger and now had a way to do so, by frustrating the aims of the ruling regime. To that end, he had his men go here and there, stirring up the local population against the new tax.

After Datuk Meringgih had finished speaking, a religious leader stood up and said, "In my view, what the Datuk has said is indeed true, for I have been to Mecca, Medina and Jeddah, but even there I didn't come across a regulation like this. It is, of course, difficult to live under the rule of these infidels. We will always be mistreated. In the end they will surely covert us to Christianity, so that we become infidels as well, and accompany them to hell. Their hearts feel no joy at seeing us enter heaven. And so they are looking for companions who will share their fate at the moment of their death."

Listening to the man's words, those gathered in the assembly felt fury stirring in their hearts, while many began to grumble and even call out, "Truly that would not be right!"

Someone else shouted, "Of course, the Dutch are not to be trusted. Their speech is full of double-talk, just like the Indians."

Yet others said, "The Dutch are our enemy, naturally, and will be forever, in matters of religion and other matters as well."

Datuk Meringgih's face lit up at the excitement he saw aroused in the crowd's heart, but rancor soon filled his own when one man was brave enough to say, "From what I hear, the money will really be used for our needs."

"What needs?" Datuk Meringgih retorted immediately.

"Building roads, houses and schools, and offices, for example," the speaker replied.

"For whom will the good roads be, for us or for them? We don't need good roads, but they don't want bad ones. For that reason, we are ordered to build roads for them. And now what other roads will be built with that tax money? And as far as those school houses are concerned, who are they for? Whose children go to school, ours or theirs? How many are there among the gentlemen present here who have gone to a Government school? Do you know what the purpose of those schools is? So that our children will like those people and hate their own.

"Where are the schools in this village? I never went to school, yet became rich just the same. So, what need have we of those schools? What we need are prayer houses and mosques. And do they build these? No! Am I not right? But their churches are enlarged and they make them really fine with our money. And about those offices, there's no need for me to speak of what those are used for. You gentlemen can see this for yourselves every day. Isn't it there that we are judged and penalized, sometimes without us being guilty of anything? If we don't go along with their wishes, we are put in yet another kind of building, a jail, that is."

"What else?" Datuk Meringgih now asked the person who had spoken up before. "Go ahead and speak, so that I can explain the real situation. Don't be happy just listening to what people say. By going along with words without thinking deeply upon them, we become like talking magpies."

The man could say nothing more in reply and so stayed quiet.

After some silence, the voice of Datuk Meringgih was heard again in the hall. "And now I wish to ask all of you present here, must we obey this order and give our noses over to the rope, like buffalo, to be pulled about anywhere they want? We are not animals, but human beings, just like them, with two eyes, a head, feet and hands. Why should we want to be fooled by outsiders? Should we allow them to rule this way?

"In truth, we shouldn't put up with their tyranny," replied an old teacher. "We will end up being driven from our own lands. And where would we go then?"

"So if we don't want to put up with it, then what?" someone asked.

"We resist," shouted several young men in turn.

"To resist is easy so long as we are brave and have weapons," answered the one who had just asked a question. "But isn't there a better way than resisting, seeing that it isn't good to take the work of warfare lightly? It brings no little suffering and calamity. We're not all alone here in this world, but have children and wives, relatives, villages and homes. It's not those going into battle that we're thinking of. Either you're alive, or you're dead, that's what it means to be a man. But those left behind, they're the ones to think of. What will become of them if we lose?"

A reflective mood seemed to settle upon all who heard these words. Datuk Meringgih, grasping the implications of such reflection, immediately replied, "Perhaps, sir, you fear confronting the Dutch. If your heart is divided on this, there's no need for you to join in, for you would surely burden us. We are not women. We are not afraid to die. Those that are left behind we commend to God. He is far better at caring and protecting them than are we."

"It's not that I'm afraid," answered the man. "If need be, I am quite willing to give up my life. What I meant was, is there no other, better way than resisting in order to achieve our ends? If there is, then why not do that?"

"And what sort of way would that be?" asked many who did not appear so keen on war.

"Wouldn't it be better if we went to the High Government together and asked that the rule be cancelled?" the same man replied.

Datuk Meringgih could only laugh. "It would appear that you, sir, do not know the ways of the Dutch, since you have never dealt with them. But I have known them, and not just for a day or two. I have mixed with them for decades and for that reason really know their ways. These Dutch are merciless and show no respect. They don't know how to return a good deed. They only know how to be obstinate and harsh. Whatever they intend to happen, must happen. Don't they say they are the ruling race, that is, the high ones? They look upon us here as slaves, as animals. We may not open our mouths to speak, but must be blind and deaf in following what they want. I would be willing to bet a thousand rupiah to one such a request will never be granted. Moreover, the order comes from Batavia, not the government here. Even if the government here were to approve our request, if the government in Batavia were not happy about it, surely this could never be. In addition, who knows, perhaps that order comes from the land of the Dutch. And who wishes to go there and meet with the Dutch ruler? The way I see it, if we do not want to go along with this order, we should show this by our resistance to it. That's the shortest possible route. If our request is to be granted, they would certainly accede to our wishes all the more quickly. What is wrong with a bit of fighting? That is the game men play. To be profitable, isn't it necessary to lose first?"

Those who had been only somewhat resigned to war were now filled with excitement at the Datuk's words.

"What I'm thinking of is the outcome later," the doubtful man continued. "If we resist, shall victory be ours? For the Dutch have a lot of soldiers and sufficient weapons. If they cannot be overcome, then our efforts will be in vain and in the end we will be utterly destroyed. There's no way of telling. And the new tax will have to be paid anyway."

"Of course, the question of defeat can't be known with any certainty beforehand, for all of this has been predestined by Allah," Datuk Meringgih replied. "If He helps us, even if the enemy's soldiers number in the millions, with boatloads of munitions and weapons, we would surely win in spite of that. And even if we don't win, never mind, for we will have shown them that we aren't women, but men who must be treated with respect. If in times to come they want to make a new ruling, they will think twice about it before doing anything. This is one benefit to be gained from resisting. But if we just stay silent and go along with everything they want, it will be said that we are afraid, and because we are weak they will surely step on us as they would a footbridge, so that we will never be free of their injustices and tyranny, which will just continue to grow. Look at the people of Aceh! What weapons do they have? They are able to resist and still haven't been subdued. The short of it is, as long as we have the hearts of men, things will surely work out."

"What the Datuk says is true," cried out a number of young men who had joined Datuk Meringgih's group. "Those are the words of a real man. Let's cut this short. Anyone who doesn't want to join in resisting may stay at home. Even if they want to take sides with the disbelievers, no one is forbidding them to do so, just so long as they don't stay here any longer, for they will receive no mercy from us, that's for sure."

Such words having been spoken, no one was now brave enough to argue against Datuk Meringgih. All fell quiet for a moment, until an old religious leader spoke up, "There is a means for going to war against the Dutch. If we don't have the munitions, oppose them with something else."

"What is that? Come on, tell us!" shouted several people who were less than brave.

"What the Acehnese used. They opposed the rifles and cannons with verses taken from the Holy Quran, so that the guns did not fire nor did their bullets hit, nor did swords cleave flesh."

"Do you know what kind of magic that was?"

"If I didn't know it, what would be the use of my speaking here? It's not for nothing that my hair has turned all white. I myself have gone to Aceh to seek out that magic."

"Then there's no need to fear. Steady your hearts to resist, and tell them to come here in the thousands," said the brave ones to the weak.

The majority of native peoples saw the new tax this way. They believed the Government had acted haughtily towards them, for which they determined not to pay the new levy. If they were forced to do so, they would resist.

In fact, when a local official in Padang Hulu came to arrest several men suspected of leading the tax rebellion, the local population rose up and killed him. The day after a number of hard-headed elders were jailed in Bukit Tinggi, hundreds of locals converged at the prison and called for their release. Elsewhere, a sub-district head who wanted to impose the tax by force was murdered. He was said to be assisting the Dutch. The same fate was in store for a Dutch district officer who was attacked by locals in his home. After he was killed, his corpse was thrown into the burning house. An assistant resident was even attacked while working in his office. And many Government warehouses filled with coffee were looted and burned, as were the homes and offices of Government officials.

In this way, the whole of Padang Hulu and Padang Hilir was in an uproar. Rioting and violence broke out everywhere, as if the rebels had agreed beforehand to revolt in unison.

What troops were available could not be sent in to crush the resistance, as they were too few in number, and so were ordered to stand guard outside the town. Government employees were told to gather in town where, surrounded by soldiers, they tried to think of some way of protecting themselves if the enemy attacked. As it had been forbidden to congregate in groups, it was difficult for them to discuss the matter collectively.

Going out in the dark without a torch was similarly prohibited, as was dressing in white: this, to avoid looking like the enemy. At night, soldiers patrolled the town while reinforcements were sent to restive areas, assigned to defend outskirts and villages. Others were ordered to guard the houses and belongings of the Government. Even the railroad from the harbor at Teluk Bayur all the way to Padang Hulu was protected against rebel sabotage.

Nevertheless, the native population continued to gather outside of town in secluded locations, discussing the question of resistance. Each made his preparations and readied his weapons for war. Women and children were sent to the mountains. Possessions were buried underground or hidden in secret caches while envoys were dispatched to arrange for a mass attack, including to Aceh, where the people were invited to revolt. As far away as Turkey, the message was sent out concerning the evil of Dutch tyranny.

16

The Battle

After the ship carrying Lieutenant Mas entered the harbor at Teluk Bayur, its fighting force disembarked and marched straight to Padang, their weapons and artillery in tow, to the great excitement of the townspeople, unaccustomed as they were to the sight of soldiers.

"Why have so many troops been brought in?" one onlooker asked another.

"Don't you know? The Dutch colonies will be thrown into chaos, for the locals plan to resist paying the new tax."

In the blink of an eye, news of the army's arrival spread everywhere, both in and out of town, so that even women and children learned of their presence. With that, lively discussions took place about the impending battle. Some could not stomach the thought of it and ran off to hide in the mountains, their families and belongings in tow. The brave stayed in town, though, hoping to witness the spectacle of war. Landowners and Padang's wealthy feared everything they owned would be taken from them. Families blessed with children, kin and friends were horrified at the thought of loved ones trapped by the fighting. The merchants were no less afraid for as they saw it trade would certainly drop on account of the rebellion, while the Government employees contemplated with throbbing hearts the possible defeat of the troops. If that were to happen, the rebels would surely show them no mercy, for they saw all who did not join in the resistance as the enemy. Only the criminals felt a certain joy, for there was the hope of easy pickings and new robbing and looting to pull off. But it was the rebels who were aroused to hot fury at the sight of such a large army sent by the Government, and thought continually of how they might outwit the soldiers.

Once the troops were quartered in the Padang barracks, Lieutenant Mas went to his captain to ask permission for a short leave, for there was something very important he needed to do. He promised to come back right away.

At first the captain didn't want to allow it, but when he saw how emphatically the man made his request, he granted it, but with the provision that he not return any later than six o'clock that evening. Since it was now only four-thirty in the afternoon, Lieutenant Mas thought to himself, "Surely I won't be late in getting back."

Quickly calling for a buggy, he departed for Muara. Once there, he crossed the Arau River by boat and climbed Mount Padang. On the way up, he met a religious mendicant who lived at the top of the mountain and asked him the location of the grave of Baginda Sulaiman, a merchant who had gone to his heavenly home some ten years past. Though the mendicant was quite astonished to hear that name being spoken, and wondered why an army officer would be asking about the grave of "a Malay," he directed him to the spot nonetheless.

Arriving at the cemetery, Mas saw three graves arranged in a fenced-off area near a low wall. Two of them lay very close to each other, while the third was set off a bit from the others. As he approached the site, he could make out the letters on the first two headstones. They were, in fact, the graves he sought. Unable to hold himself back, he ran to them. Falling to his knees between the two adjacent graves he wept inconsolably and embraced the headstones with outstretched arms. "Oh, my beloved Nurbaya and Mother! How could you have gone off and left me alone in this world?" he said between sobs. "You departed without saying a word and without taking anyone with you. Why didn't you ask me to accompany you? Why didn't you wait for me, so that I might accompany you on that distant journey? When I was left behind, why didn't you come back for me? For ten years I was left to wander, searching for the road to follow you. And to this very moment, all my wandering has been in vain.

"When will the time come for us to greet each other again, to gather around and speak, like in the old days? Mother, Nur, please beg God the

Most Holy, the Most High, not to extend my life any longer, but bring us all together again quickly, for living with love like this is unbearable. Ten years are long enough to bear the torment and suffering which no man can bear, and now I deserve to be released from this prison.

"Nur... my dearest! I never believed we would end up like this. Why are other people's hopes and dreams granted, when this happens to our own? What wrong did you commit, what wrong did I commit, what wrong did we commit together, to deserve such a fate? Does it mean that in this world our hopes and prayers which we endlessly send forth, are not granted, but instead brought to pass by Allah in the life to come? Can anyone else have had such misfortunes! For ten years I've endured torment and grief. And for ten years I've borne this longing for you, but still God has not granted my prayer. How much longer do I have to wait?

"But... yes, Nur, I have received a sign from Him that I will soon be with you again, for this is the end of my torment. Let's hope that is His will. Let's both pray together for this.

"Still, there's something I don't know. Will I be able to avenge you? Even if I'm unable to, Allah the All-Powerful will not forget, no wrong will escape His punishment. Let us both someday submit to Him the wrong that man committed against you."

With that, Mas kissed the two headstones and rose slowly. He turned and beckoned to the mendicant, who was standing a little ways off, dumbstruck by the lieutenant's behavior, a Dutchman crying at the grave of a Muslim!

"Sir, recite verses for those people there, for the souls of all those who have departed. Here, take this!" Mas said, taking out ten rupiah in notes and giving it to the man. Overwhelmed with joy, the mendicant, who had never received so great a gift, spent the whole night by the gravesite reciting verses.

While Mas had been making his way to Mount Padang, word arrived from the governor that rebels would enter Padang that very night, intent on wreaking havoc. To avoid bloodshed inside the town, the governor ordered a detachment of soldiers to intercept the enemy before they reached Padang's limits.

And so, around seven o'clock that evening the soldiers, led by Lieutenant Mas and Lieutenant van Sta, left Padang for Kota Tengah. By nine o'clock they had arrived at Tabing and a bit later were very close to their intended destination. From a distance the soldiers could see dozens of men dressed entirely in white and banded together in groups along the road in front of a small store. They were armed with machete-like swords and appeared to be discussing their plan of attack.

When the rebels saw the soldiers coming, they whipped themselves into a fury. They grabbed weapons, unsheathed their daggers, assumed martial stances, and shouted to friends to join them. Some yelled words of abuse, brandishing their weapons and pointing them in the soldiers' direction. When Lieutenant Mas had nearly reached the group of rioters, he ordered his soldiers to halt and form ranks. A district officer accompanying him advanced to the front and ordered the rebels to surrender. But they ignored his command and instead hurled insults at him, remaining fixed in their stances while inviting him forward to duel. Three more times the officer gently urged them to surrender, but to no effect, and so he handed the matter over to Lieutenant Mas, who deployed his troops, ordering them to fire into the air. All together, some thirty rifles sounded. Hearing the rifles and seeing that not a single one among them had been hit, the rioters grew all the more emboldened, for they believed the bullets could no longer harm them, thanks to the talismans and charms they had received from their teachers. Shouting battle cries, they chanted over and over, "*La illaha illallah*"—There Is No God, but Allah—as they advanced. Only when they had gotten very close did the lieutenant give the order to open fire again.

When the rifles sounded for the second time, the front row of rebels collapsed to the ground. There was much shrieking and screaming and many cries for help, though others just kept on chanting. Many among them never again made a sound, for they had been killed instantly. The rioters standing in the rear were momentarily confused, unsure of what to do next. When the rifles fired for the third time, the war was over for them, as many more were killed. Those who survived took off running in all directions, hoping for a place to hide.

At that very moment, several elders and religious leaders came out of a house and began shouting at the deserters to come back. They then drew their own daggers and rushed forward to the scene of battle. Witnessing such courage, the deserters turned back and followed their teachers, shouting war cries and cheering as they attacked the soldiers on two sides. As the enemy had thrown themselves into this new attack with such ferocity, Lieutenant Mas' troops had no time to reload and fire again, and were forced to use their bayonets. Now the battle became hotly fought, with each combatant searching for an opponent. They stabbed and hacked and punched and struck at each other, parrying and receiving each others' blows. Some were captured, others hurled aside. Those that died, fell to the ground. Those who were wounded, bled. Those who were afraid, fled. And those who were brave, pursued. Some went forward while others fell back, and still others leapt about. And all around, above the clamor that rose in a single, indistinguishable roar of rifle and pistol shot, sword meeting sword and knife, were the sounds of the many combatants shouting and grunting. Though the sky was clear in the light of the moon, the area was darkened by gun smoke. And if the two sides' clothing hadn't been so different from each other's—that is, black and white—friend would never have known foe. On each side, Lieutenant Mas and the rebel leaders could be seen rallying their forces, ordering them to move forward while shooting and hacking with their blades.

Though the engagement was brief, many on both sides were killed or wounded as blood flowed on the main road and corpses lay scattered about. The enemy's attacks threatened to overwhelm Lieutenant Mas because of their endless flow of reinforcements from the village and so he ordered his soldiers to slowly retreat. If help had not arrived in the person of Lieutenant van Sta, the fight would have been over. Luckily for Mas, the cheers of van Sta's troops were heard as they reached the battlefield. A little while later, the rebels slowly retreated and when no more reinforcements arrived, they were finally beaten and ran off in disarray, chased by Government forces.

While pursuing the enemy, Lieutenant Mas spotted one of their leaders whose form, movements, and voice were exactly like those of Datuk Meringgih, the man for whom he had been searching for so long. Hands trembling, Mas' heart began to beat faster, his face contorted in a mixture of joy and grief: joy, because he now hoped to avenge the pain he carried within him; and grief, because he thought of all the evil this scoundrel had committed. Seeing that the rebel leader was about to make his escape, he gave chase and soon caught up with him. Now face-to-face with the man, his suspicion was confirmed, for in front of him stood, in flesh and blood, Datuk Meringgih, Nurbaya's executioner.

"Datuk Meringgih, it is really you?" Lieutenant Mas asked.

"Yes, I am Datuk Meringgih, the merchant of Padang," the man replied. "And who are you, that you know me?"

After looking closely at the soldier standing in front of him, the Datuk became so startled he fell back a few steps, crying out, "Samsulbahri! You're not dead? Or is this a devil?"

And with that he leapt forward to hack at Mas with his blade. The lieutenant jumped to one side, calling out, "Wait, Datuk Meringgih! I've much to say before I kill you."

The Datuk straightened himself, for he was curious to hear what his enemy had to say.

"Datuk Meringgih, I am Samsulbahri, who died ten years ago, and was sent back from the grave to punish you for your vile crimes. I shot myself in Batavia, because I preferred to die rather than live burdened by the suffering you caused, but God did not grant me that wish. I must first avenge myself of all your wrongs. That was why the bullet I aimed at my head did not pierce my brain, for my friend Arifin's shout made me jump. My hand wavered, and the round merely broke my skull. When I came to again, I begged the doctor and all those who knew about it not to spread the news that I had survived. I knew it would be better for people to think me dead. I sought death several times, but did not find it, for God extended my years, so that I might punish you for all your sins.

"For ten years now, I have borne unendurable suffering and grief, and for ten years I have borne vengeance against you in my heart. Only now has God given me this opportunity. And only now can I avenge the people you harmed, you, the greatest of all villains! Your wealth made you arrogant in the face of God, who gave you such riches. You thought that being so rich meant you could do whatever you wanted. Those who occupied high positions, you brought down. Those who were exalted, you humiliated. And those who had wealth, you impoverished. You have no sense of mutual regard, nor concern or pity whatsoever for anyone, and only wanted to satisfy your wicked and base lusts.

"So, you treacherous man! Your wealth brought no good to your colleagues or companions, your fellow man, or even to you yourself. Instead it brought all manner of danger, suffering, and sorrow to the entire village. It was not right that you should be blessed by God with a weapon that strong.

"With your wealth, you severed child from father, younger sister from older brother, lover from beloved, and comrade from his friend. With your wealth, you brought down Baginda Sulaiman, so that from grief he returned to the mercy of Allah. With your wealth, you forced his child to accede to your base desires, and with your wealth you separated that woman from me, her beloved, and bullied her until she nearly died at sea. Then you accused her of stealing your goods, the blood and sweat of others, which you had obtained through treachery. When you were no longer strong enough to force Nurbaya, who was innocent of that deed, you murdered her with poison.

"With your wealth, you separated me from my parents and my family, and ended all my hopes of becoming a proper person, so that my mother passed out of this world from all the sorrow she felt. All that isn't even a hundredth of the sins you must account for.

"Datuk Meringgih! Don't you feel the wrongs you've committed? Don't you fear God, who gave you all that power? Aren't you ashamed before your fellow man, whom you cheated? And don't you take pity on those who have become your victims?"

He broke off speaking, for he was so filled with rage he could hardly breathe, and needed to restrain himself.

The Datuk did not say a word, for he saw the truth in what Samsulbahri said. And only then and there did it become clear to him that he had never done any good with all his possessions. If he died in this fight, his goods would surely be divided among those who remained, and what would he take to the grave? Nothing more than an evil name, and the oaths, curses, and revilement of all those whom he had mistreated. And they would surely bear down on him in the grave. If he had done good deeds, perhaps there would also be those who would pray for his soul.

Only then and there, when he was almost at the door of the grave, did he see clearly that the goods of this world were of little value in life in the eternal lands. Regret arose in his heart over what he had done in the past.

But what could he say? Now that he felt regret, there was nothing he could do to correct his misdeeds.

After a moment's silence, Samsulbahri spoke again, wiping away the tears that flowed in spite of his effort to control himself. "Datuk Meringgih! I'm going to show you that there is something more powerful than you and your wealth. Even if you were a hundred times as rich, I wouldn't hesitate to repay your wickedness, and your wealth will not free you from my hands. Receive your punishment!" With that, Samsu raised his pistol, took aim, and fired at his enemy.

But the Datuk leapt forward at the very same moment to hack at Samsulbahri with his sword, crying out, "Taste my hand, Dutch dog!"

The two men crashed to the ground. Datuk Meringgih had been pierced through the heart by a bullet, but not before landing a blow to Samsu's head with his sword.

Later, when Lieutenant Mas was taken from the battlefield, the soldiers found among the rebels' corpses two who were dressed entirely in black. One's neck had been almost completely severed by a broad sword. The other's chest had been pierced by a bayonet. These were the corpses of Number Five and Number Four, punished by the Almighty for their wickedness.

Two days after the battle, an officer lay sleeping under white sheets at the hospital in Padang. He looked very pale and ill, and nearly his entire head was wrapped in white bandages, with only his face visible. Near his bed, arranging vials of medicine, an attendant stood ready in case the patient suddenly awoke. Just then a Dutch doctor came in to check on the wounded man's condition.

Hearing the doctor's footsteps, the patient stirred from his slumber and gazed at the doctor with lusterless eyes. The doctor greeted him and asked, "How are you?"

"A bit better, even if the pain in my head hasn't quite gone away," the man answered softly.

"The headache will persist for two or three more days," the doctor replied while examining the patient's scalp and the veins of his upper arm. "What was his temperature this morning?" he asked the attendant.

"I wrote it down, sir," the attendant answered, showing him a checklist. After examining it, the doctor fell silent for a moment.

"Doctor," the patient said suddenly, "even though I said I felt more at ease, it's not, in my view, because I will get better. Don't be angry if I say I won't live much longer in this world. It's what I feel. And please don't hide your opinion from me, out of concern, perhaps, that I'm afraid to die. That is absolutely not the case. I've sought death for a long time, everywhere and only now have I found it. I am grateful for that!

"Last night I was visited by my beloved and my mother, both of whom have long since departed this world. They promised they would return for me today so that all of us could go to their resting place together."

The patient had to stop speaking as the effort of doing so greatly weakened him. Once again, he held his head in pain.

"If you're tired, you ought not to speak for a while," said the doctor.

After a moment's silence, the patient summoned the strength to continue. "It's all right, Doctor. Don't worry! The pain in my head has returned a little. Before I depart from this world I have a request to make of you."

"What is it? Tell me! It will certainly be granted."

"I very much wish to meet with Sutan Mahmud, a district head here in Padang. Could that be arranged?" the patient said in a halting voice.

"Of course," the doctor replied, though he did not understand why an army officer wished to meet with a Malay from Padang. "He will be sent for right away. Is there anything else I can do for you, sir?"

"No. Just that. Thank you!"

"All right," said the doctor. He then went to have Sutan Mahmud summoned.

After that, the patient went back to sleep, exhausted from the exertion of speaking.

Two hours later, Sutan Mahmud came to the hospital and was brought by the attendant to the wounded officer's room.

Seeing the patient's face, Sutan Mahmud was startled, for the patient looked exactly like his son, Samsulbahri, who had died in Batavia ten years before.

Tears filled his eyes as he recalled the fate of his hapless son, who had killed himself out of despair, a fate he never would have supposed was in store for his beloved boy.

In truth, he had never ceased regretting the way he had driven Samsulbahri away: an impulsive sense of shame and affront to his own social standing and position. And so his wife died of sorrow and his only son killed himself out of grief. After Samsu died, he thought more clearly about the matter and realized his son's misdeed had not been so offensive after all.

Sutan Mahmud could not blame Samsulbahri for loving Nurbaya, for ever since Samsu was a small boy he had been with Baginda Sulaiman's child, as if they were children of the same womb. He had believed, even hoped, that Nurbaya would one day become his son's wife. It didn't matter that Nurbaya was not well-born. Her beauty, intelligence and comportment were enough to compensate for a diminution in Padang's aristocracy. His own wife, Samsu's mother, had not been a person of high birth either, but this had not been an obstacle in their life as husband and wife. It would have been a natural right for Samsu to sit in state with his bride, the lovely and quick-witted Nurbaya. Such were Sutan Mahmud's memories as he stood looking down at the wounded soldier's face.

Just then, in his mind's eye he saw his son and Nurbaya living happily together, just like a married couple: Samsu a doctor, and Nurbaya cradling in her lap a baby boy: his own grandson.

"Ah, if only it hadn't been for that damned scoundrel Datuk Meringgih, surely I wouldn't have dreams for memories, but things would have actually turned out that way. And if it weren't for my birth and high position, perhaps I wouldn't have driven my dear son away.

"Now what can be said? For they are no longer in this world. May all their dreams and desires, those they never achieved here, be obtained in the life hereafter."

Sutan Mahmud did not even notice the tears that fell from his eyes to the floor.

So, Sutan Mahmud, this is the truth of the matter: 'Regret in advance and there's a gain. Regret afterwards and it's no use.' So says the proverb. You can shout even to the heavens, but your

> *mistakes can never be repaired. If you hadn't been so quick to pass judgment on your son that time, perhaps this suffering and sadness would not have occurred and all your dreams would have come to pass. But because you were still so bound up in the grandeur of your position and your good birth, such was the outcome.*
>
> *You blurted out a sentence on your son, and the suffering and death of several people are what you got in return. Your guilt in this misdeed is undeniable, for you were the head of a village, a parent, someone to whom all your 'children' could turn for requests and explanations, a place of shade in the heat, a place of shelter in the rain. It is you who must undo what is knotted, clarify the muddy, and fix that which is broken.*
>
> *If you passed such a heavy sentence on your own son, thinking you had to do it for the sake of your social standing and high position, how would you have justly and properly carried out your responsibilities towards other people?*
>
> *Each misdeed is punished and this indeed is God's punishment for you. Would that you pluck from it the moral lesson.*

While Sutan Mahmud waited for the patient to wake up, brooding on the fate of his unfortunate son, for whom he now longed, the doctor stepped back into the room. A few moments later, the patient came to and opened his eyes, glancing about. When he saw Sutan Mahmud, he stared at him for a moment. Then, closing his eyes again, he motioned for the man to come closer. The doctor and the attendant stood off to one side, to give the two men privacy.

When the district head had drawn near, the patient said slowly, in a broken voice, "Sir! I requested that you come, for there is a secret I wish to reveal before going home. It is at the request of your own son, Samsulbahri."

"My son, Samsulbahri, who died in Batavia?" asked Sutan Mahmud, greatly shocked.

"Yes, that Samsu, who lives," the patient replied.

"Samsu did not die? My son did not die?" Sutan Mahmud asked in astonishment.

"Yes, it's true."

"Where is he now?... But how do you know all this?"

"Because I was in the hospital where he was being treated," Mas replied. He then went on to describe how Samsu shot himself in Batavia and the reason he was said to have died. He then entered the army, the patient explained, to seek death, but never found it. Finally, he was ordered to Padang to put down the riots over the *belasting* tax.

"If that's the case, then he's in Padang right now," said Sutan Mahmud, his face shining with joy.

"It's true. He and I came here together and fought side by side. He was a lieutenant and his name is Mas. That's his real name, "Sam", spelled backwards."

It appeared as if the patient grew increasingly exhausted from speaking until, finally, he could barely utter a single word. His face grew more and more pale and he frequently held his head in pain.

After remaining silent for a moment, he spoke again, lifting his head slightly, as if worried Sutan Mahmud could not hear him.

"This was his message for you: When... he... dies... please... bury... him... between... his mother... and... Nurbaya... *Allahu Akbar*!"

When his words had ended, so too did the patient's breath as he fell back on the bed and calmly passed on to his heavenly home.

His death seemed very peaceful and gentle, for his face did not alter, but rather looked like that of someone sleeping, while his mouth still formed the trace of a smile, as if happy to be leaving this transitory world. Still, it was quite a shock for Sutan Mahmud to see this man die so suddenly. After briefly moving his lips in the recitation of prayers, he went over to the doctor and asked, "Do you know a Lieutenant Mas who came from Batavia, together with that man who died just now? Where is he now?"

"Lieutenant Mas?" asked the doctor, surprised.

"Yes, Lieutenant Mas, who came to Padang to fight the rebels," Sutan Mahmud replied.

"There's no other, just him there, the one who just died," the doctor said.

When Sutan Mahmud heard these words, he let out a shriek and ran over to the body lying on the bed. Sobbing uncontrollably, he embraced his son and kissed him repeatedly, for he now knew the patient who had just died was none other than Samsulbahri, for whom he had longed these ten years past. He had died before his father's own eyes, without Sutan even knowing it.

"Ah, my dear son!! Why didn't you say so earlier: I didn't realize you were my very own child. But gazing on your face before, I had my suspicions. Only I wasn't brave enough to confirm them, for it seemed impossible. Ah, my son, why wouldn't you just come out and say it, rather than concealing yourself until you were no more? Perhaps you were still angry with your father, and so wouldn't say "Father" to him anymore?

"I have long realized my mistake in passing that severe punishment on you without first examining the matter as thoroughly as possible, and have been tormented by regrets ever since. I beg your forgiveness: in this world and the next.

"Oh, my son! For the last ten years of your life, why didn't you come back to me instead of just now, at the end, when I no longer recognized you?

"The wrong you suffered at my hands was truly great, but you should also know the shortcomings of those who are old, like your father, who are bound by the customs and ways of their village. And now what's the use of my living any longer? I'm all alone in this world, for you, my son, are no more, while your mother has long since left me behind. Take me with you, so that we can all be together again, as we were before. Don't leave me all alone in this world!

"Oh Allah! Oh God! Take my life quickly so that I may see my son and wife again!"

And just then, Samsulbahri's father fell unconscious to the floor.

The following day, a corpse was borne out of Sutan Mahmud's house, shouldered by four village chiefs. As was the custom in Padang, the body was covered with a white cloth and sprinkled with flowers of every sort while the front, back and sides were canopied by yellow parasols, a sign that someone of the aristocracy had died. Ahead of the corpse walked two young men who burned aloe wood and incense carried on a small, round silver tray. Another man carried flowers and sandalwood water. To the left and right of the corpse walked several high-born youths bearing lances and round shields, swords and pennons, along with the usual accoutrements carried in burial ceremonies for the children of royalty. But the stretched drums were not heard, for they had been forbidden by the religious scholars.

Behind the corpse could be seen religious pilgrims and scholars, all of whom chanted praise to Allah while reciting prayers continuously. Behind them walked dignitaries, state employees, headmen, elders, intellectuals, aristocrats, and the ordinary townspeople of Padang, followed by uniformed soldiers who brought up the rear.

Initially, there was to have been music and a rifle volley salute, according to military custom, but the religious scholars would not allow it. When the ceremony was over, vehicles lined the street, standing at the ready for all the dignitaries from the various races of Padang.

And whose corpse was being borne to its grave? None other than Samsulbahri's, the son of Sutan Mahmud, the well-known district head of Padang, who was honored and esteemed by all as a person of high aristocratic birth. To his close companions, Samsulbahri was a good-natured person, kindly, warm and affectionate, someone who always helped others without consideration of appearance or race. To his family, he was a beloved child. In the army he was Lieutenant Mas, famous for his gallantry and bravery, who had assisted the Government in many a wartime pinch. For that reason, while he lived his chest had been pinned with various decorations and medals.

Among the many who accompanied his mortal remains was an old, hunched over man with white hair who walked slowly alongside, from time to time asking to join in shouldering the body. With tears welling in his eyes, he said to himself, "Yes, this is the burden borne by a man blessed by God with a long life. All who were young and preceded him, he has had to send off alone to the grave, until his turn came to be sent there by others.

"How heavy it is for those who have to watch their dear ones born and taken back by the Almighty. I saw his mother born, and ten years ago I accompanied her to her burial place. This child of hers I also saw born. And now I have to accompany him to his grave as well. What about me, when will it be my turn? And who will take me to my grave?" Such were the thoughts of the coachman Ali, whose heart was tightly bound to Samsulbahri and his mother.

Among the women who joined in the cortege was Sitti Alimah and her parents, for she came to remember Sitti Nurbaya, the beloved of the one who had died.

After Samsulbahri's body was taken to the mosque and prayed over, it was brought to Mount Padang, the burial ground the deceased had requested. Once there, Samsulbahri's corpse was lowered into the ground between his mother's grave and that of his beloved, Sitti Nurbaya, as had been his wish in the last moments of his life. Then the daily summons to prayer was whispered to the corpse, the grave covered over, and the final prayers and confession of faith recited.

Dutch dignitaries and those of other races joined together in covering the grave with handfuls of dirt, followed by sandalwood water and flowers. Finally, a high-ranking officer delivered a speech, reminding all of the departed's courage and loyalty to the Government. He had been the first native person to attain the position of lieutenant in the army. The speaker then wished peace and happiness for the soul of the departed in the world of the everlasting.

Next, Sutan Mahmud expressed his thanks to the dignitaries and to all who, with inconvenience to themselves, had come to mourn and join in the blessing ceremony for his son. He begged forgiveness for any of his son's sins and mistakes that might weigh on him in the grave, and asked everyone to pray for his son's salvation. After that, the mourners returned to their homes. Only Sutan Mahmud, along with several who had completed the pilgrimage to Mecca, remained behind to pray. At a certain point, even the pilgrims left, leaving Sutan Mahmud and the coachman Ali lost in thought as they sat together on a large rock. Samsulbahri's father was grief-stricken by the death of his son and full of regret for what he had done in the past.

When day turned to night, the two of them finally left, leaving the dark silence behind to cover the grave. Only Samsulbahri remained, alone, in his first and final place.

Beware, O man, of your condition, for that too will be you in the end!

One day, two months later, two young men rode in a buggy in the direction of Muara. Though they were dressed like Europeans, their black hats identified them as natives.

One was a doctor and the other an inspector. Each held flowers in his hand. When they reached Muara, they crossed the Arau River and climbed Mount Padang. Arriving at their destination, they saw a line of five graves, of the same size and shape, lying close to one another, each with a marble headstone inlaid with gold lettering. On the first grave was written, "This is the grave of Baginda Sulaiman. Died 5 Ramadan, 1315."

On the second was written, "This is the grave of Sitti Nurbaya, the daughter of Baginda Sulaiman. Died 5 Zulhidjdjah, 1315."

On the third was written, "This is the grave of Samsulbahri, child of Sutan Mahmud, Penghulu of Padang. Died 5 Syafar, 1326."

On the fourth was written, "This is the grave of Sitti Maryam, wife of Sutan Mahmud, Penghulu of Padang. Died 5 Zulhijah, 1315."

And on the fifth was written, "This is the grave of Sutan Mahmud, District Head of Padang. Died 8 Rabiulawal, 1326."

The two young men approached the graves and sprinkled the flowers they carried over them, particularly on the second and third ones, as tears welled in their eyes.

"Bakhtiar!" exclaimed the doctor. "Did you ever think when we walked up here with Samsu and Nurbaya, some eleven years ago, that we would now be visiting their graves? Do you ever think of that time, three months before we left for Batavia?"

"To tell you the truth, Arifin," replied the inspector, "I never at all imagined... but what can I say? For man is unable to do as he wishes, but must keep the promises he has made. Even so, the five of them are clearly in their designated places, each next to the other. But we here... it's not yet clear, where we'll be, or with whom."

"But why did the Lord Sutan Mahmud pass on so suddenly? What did he die of?" asked Arifin.

"Longing for his wife and son. Sorry for what he had done."

"It's very sad," Arifin replied.

After telling several religious mendicants to pray at the graves, the two men went back down the mountain and home. Only they who were buried there stayed on, forever and ever.

Glossary

cempadak	A large, rind-covered tropical fruit (*Artocarpus integer*), related to, but much more delicious and digestible than, jackfruit
Company	Throughout the colonial period, the Netherlands East Indies government was casually referred to as "the Company", a reference to the long-gone United Dutch East Indies Company
datuk	The common honorific for an elder or non-royal personage of status within a group in many areas of Sumatra
duit	A coin of very small worth during the colonial era
dukun	Traditional herbalists and healers, usually male, of the Malay and Indonesian world. Dukun are still in demand for a range of physical and spiritual practices, all requiring specialized *ilmu*, from midwifery to counseling to sorcery and spell casting
hajj	Pilgrimage to Meccah to be performed by every Muslim if they have the means
hulubalang	Here, a kind of village police official
ilmu	From Arabic, "science, learning, advanced knowledge" but also, particularly in Indonesian usage, knowledge of the realms of the supernatural, esoteric and occult. Also

	in this text, apparently underworld argot for stolen or smuggled goods
kafir	Arabic for "the one who rejects", that is, who does not accept the teachings of Islam, "a disbeliever"
kelewang	Broad-bladed chopping swords, somewhat like bolos and machetes. Mentioned elsewhere in the story are *parang*s, another kind of sword
keeling	A traditional and rather derogatory term for South Indians
keroncong	A small instrument resembling the ukulele. *Keroncong* also refers to a sweet-sounding and highly syncopated type of string-band music that seems to have originated in eastern Indonesia from old Portuguese tunes and further developed in Batavia's *creole* society from the 18th century onwards
ketuk-ketuk	A wooden or bamboo cylinder with holes rapped with a stick to summon villagers to prayer or in an emergency
kris	The famed traditional knife-like stabbing weapon throughout the Malay world. While some *kris*es had a straight blade, more typically (and famously) the blade was wavy. The forging of fine blades was the work of master craftsmen who were believed to invest this weapon with magical powers and properties. The ownership of a *kris* was an indispensable accoutrement of an aristocrat, and at least one was worn daily. It was treasured as a family heirloom and passed down through the generations
lemang	A cake of sticky rice and coconut milk, cooked in a length of bamboo lined with banana leaves
lokan	an edible bi-valve (*Polymesoda sp.*) found in muddy estuaries and mangrove swamps
mamak	In the matrilineal, matrilocal society of the Minangkabau people of West Sumatra, the offspring of a married couple

	are primarily the responsibility of the older brother of the wife, the *mamak* of her offspring
Marah	A traditional title in the Minangkabau area of West Sumatra, designating the offspring of the marriage between a person of *sutan* status and a commoner
Marsosé	The feared constabulary force formed by the Netherlands Indies government to suppress local rebellions and, typical of the Dutch divide-and-conquer tactics, made up in great number by Ambonese Christians from the eastern part of the archipelago
Mas	A respectful general term of address or reference for mostly but not exclusively Javanese males of approximately the same age as the speaker, somewhat like "Mister"
ontgroening	From Dutch, and literally meaning "taking out the greenness"
Pak	The normal, polite form of address for any older or mature man
pantun	Four-line Malay verse form dating back at least to the 15th century. Structurally, *pantun* are usually in an "ABAB" rhyming pattern and consist of two equal parts which are often related in a highly allusive and metaphorical way
pendekar	The expert practitioner of the Malay martial art of *silat*. Traditionally believed to have attained the highest level of fighting skill by extraordinary inner discipline and excellence of character
Putri	From Sanskrit, here an honorific like "Sitti", meaning "lady", "esteemed woman" etc
penghulu	The name of a senior grade or ranking in Padang, West Sumatra, a kind of District Head
proposal money	Among the Minangkabau of West Sumatra it was then customary to give money to a prospective son-in-law as part of a marriage proposal

ringgit	One ringgit was then worth 2.5 gm of pure gold
salak	The fruit of the thorny palm (*Zalacca edulis*), famed for its hard "snake-skin" outer peel and surprisingly astringent taste
Samsu	The name Samsu is a variation of the Arabic word "syamsi", meaning "the sun"
Sitti	From the Arabic, a lady or girl of good family; also an honorific, as in Sitti Hawa (Eve) and Sitti Maryam (Mary, the mother of Jesus)
srikaya	A delicious jam-like condiment made from eggs, sugar and coconut milk, often spread on toast or bread at breakfast
sutan	A hereditary aristocratic title passed down from father to son in the Minangkabau society of West Sumatra
syeikh	Designation for an Arab, especially as a descendant of the Prophet Muhammad, or else a native of the Hadramaut region of the Arabian Peninsula, or simply a religious scholar
tuan	"Mister". Invariably used in addressing or referring to Westerners and other foreign Asians of stature or prestige. Also, "Boss", "Big Boss" etc. The District Officer referred to here appears to be Sutan Mahmud's Dutch counterpart (and thus to whom Sutan Mahmud must defer in key issues)
tuanku	An honorific, primarily for royalty, but also for religious scholars, in West Sumatra etc
wajik	A cake of sticky rice grains, coconut milk, and palm sugar, often diamond or rhomboid shaped

Acknowledgements

I began my study of the Malay and Chinese languages at Nanyang University ("Nantah") in Singapore in 1970. This is my first, and, *insya'allah*, not my last, gesture of tribute to all there who launched me on this lifelong voyage. More recently, I am very grateful for the encouragement I received in my efforts to do justice to this magnificent novel from a number of people, prominently my dear wife, Scholastica Auyong, daughter of old Malaya; my sister, Amanda Stimson, who gave me a gentle push into translating, and Caroline Herrick, editor of the erstwhile *Persimmon* magazine of Asian arts and literature and my oldest friend. All of these read and commented critically on this translation as it evolved. Without the patient tutelage of Muhammad Gunawan Yasni (who gave me marching orders to undertake this translation first in preference to any other) and Sjamsir Sjarif, anthropologist extraordinaire, both Minangkabau sons of West Sumatra, on so many vital linguistic, cultural and historical matters, this book would have far less than it is. To these names I would add the truly invaluable assistance of members of Teraju and Bahtera, internet list-services of worldwide Malay and Indonesian translators and interpreters. Of course, I reserve the right to claim first and foremost responsibility for the numerous shortcomings in this endeavor.

However, the person I most wish to remember in completing this translation is Anderson G. Bartlett III, who some three decades ago big-heartedly gave a very green young man first one writing job in Indonesia and then a second one there. Had he not done this, ultimately *Sitti Nurbaya: A Love Unrealized* would be translated by someone, but not by me. In recognition of that generosity I would like to cite a *pantun*, one I am sure Samsu and Nurbaya would have known:

With golden bananas sail away,	*Pisang emas bawa belayar,*
ripen one upon a crate.	*Masak sebiji di atas peti,*
A debt of money you may repay,	*Hutang emas dapat dibayar,*
but the one of kindness outlives your fate.	*Hutang budi dibawa mati.*

About the Author

Marah Rusli was born in Padang, West Sumatra, on August 7, 1889. The only child of a civil service district head in West Sumatra, he was educated at a Dutch-medium school in Padang and thereafter at the influential Raja's School in Bukittinggi. Upon graduation in 1910, he entered the government-run Veterinary School and, after graduation, commenced his lifelong career in veterinary service. During his time of  services as a government veterinarian, he had postings in Sumbawa and throughout Java.

In 1911, Marah Rusli married a woman from Bogor, West Java, Nyai Raden Ratna Kecana Wati. Although this marriage was against his parents' wishes, it proved to be a happy and lasting one that produced three children.

In his role as a writer, in 1926 Marah Rusli co-authored the first report on *Lepora bubalorum*, a form of leprosy in water buffalo found only in Indonesia but it is for his fictional work that he is well known. In addition to *Sitti Nurbaya*, he also wrote two other works of fiction, but neither of these is generally considered an equal to *Sitti Nurbaya: A Love Unrealized*. First published in 1928, Sitti Nurabaya is still in print today and has been translated into several foreign languages.

In the history of Indonesian literature, H.B. Jassin, the preeminent Indonesian literary critic, named Marah Rusli the first modern Indonensian novelist.

Marah Rusli died in Bandung in 1968. In 1969 he was posthumously named as recipient of a special literary award by the government of Indonesia.

CPSIA information can be obtained at www.ICGtesting.com
233879LV00001B/79/P